P9-CBU-922

THE PATIENTS WERE DYING.
BUT NOT FAST ENOUGH.

THE PHYSICIAN WAS SICK.
AND DEATH WAS THE CURE.

Why would someone put to hideous death
six patients who were already terminally ill?

Why would someone kill a doctor who was already
lying in bed hopelessly paralyzed?

The questions were brain-teasing—and the answers,
as they rose from the darkest human depths,
twisted the nerves to the breaking point. But for
Dr. Paul Richardson, nothing, not even hazards
to his life, could make him turn away from the
final ghastly discovery and ultimate diagnosis of
monstrous medical evil. . . .

SINS OF COMMISSION

"A compelling story . . . written by a physician
. . . it gives the layman a chance to watch the
medical profession at work within its own private
domain."—*Houston Post*

SIGNET
NIGHTMARES COME TRUE ...

SINS OF COMMISSION

A NOVEL BY
HAROLD L. KLAWANS

A SIGNET BOOK

NEW AMERICAN LIBRARY

NAL BOOKS ARE AVAILABLE AT QUANTITY DISCOUNTS
WHEN USED TO PROMOTE PRODUCTS OR SERVICES.
FOR INFORMATION PLEASE WRITE TO PREMIUM MARKETING DIVISION,
NEW AMERICAN LIBRARY, 1633 BROADWAY,
NEW YORK, NEW YORK 10019.

Copyright © 1982 by Harold L. Klawans, M.D.

SIGNET TRADEMARK REG. U.S. PAT. OFF. AND FOREIGN COUNTRIES
REGISTERED TRADEMARK—MARCA REGISTRADA
HECHO EN CHICAGO, U.S.A.

SIGNET, SIGNET CLASSIC, MENTOR, ONYX, PLUME, MERIDIAN
and NAL BOOKS are published by New American Library,
1633 Broadway, New York, New York 10019

First Signet Printing, February, 1987

1 2 3 4 5 6 7 8 9

PRINTED IN THE UNITED STATES OF AMERICA

To Dr. John H. Watson, whose modesty has prevented several generations from appreciating what he taught Sherlock Holmes about the nature of diagnosis.

AUTHOR'S NOTE

As a neurologist, I have worked and taught at two major medical centers in Chicago. Like these, the Austin Flint Medical Center—and, in fact, all large American teaching hospitals—attempts to integrate the delivery of quality health care, research, academic excellence, and teaching, a juggling act which even the late P. T. Barnum would have admired. The atmosphere described in this book is obviously colored by my experience in the hospitals where I have practiced medicine, but any other similarity between Austin Flint Medical Center and any particular existing medical institution is entirely coincidental.

In the same way, the diseases depicted here all exist. I have taken care of patients with these disorders and, I hope, have diagnosed and treated them correctly. The patients in this book, however, are entirely fictitious. Their only similarity to any patients living or dead is that they share the same disease. The physicians and students portrayed are also entirely fictitious.

In medicine, sins of commission are mortal, sins of omission venial.

—Theodore Tronchin
1709–1781

PROLOGUE

It is not unusual for patients to die in hospitals. Most often their deaths are neither unexpected nor dramatic. Mrs. Schiff's death was both. At 8:00 on Saturday night her beloved husband, Morrie, went home. Mrs. Schiff had been resting quietly, having undergone a minor surgical procedure earlier in the day. She had been a bit tired but otherwise felt fairly good. Rabbi Schiff kissed her and left. He would never see her alive again.

At 8:30 she no longer was well. Her face felt stiff and frozen. She tried to call out but couldn't—she couldn't make a sound. Her arms and legs were suddenly thrown into a massive, convulsive spasm. She looked around in terror. She tried to scream but no sounds came out. She couldn't stop the agonizing contractions.

A nurse on duty heard the noise of the bed as it shook below Mrs. Schiff. There was nothing the nurse could do by herself so she immediately paged the doctors. They arrived in a matter of minutes but failed to stop the seizures. By 8:41 the spasm had spread and become more intense and more prolonged. Mrs. Schiff could no longer breathe. The look of panic and agony disappeared from her face, and by 8:47 she was dead. The exact cause of death was unknown. No one who saw her convulsion had ever seen one like it before, and they all hoped never to see one like it again.

CHAPTER 1

W HO the heck was the shortstop for the '27 Yanks? What kind of a question was that for a forty-four-year-old neurologist to worry about? Paul Richardson knew that he ought to be thinking about more serious matters: the research lab, the paper he had to present in New York in less than a week. The forty minutes or so he spent each morning driving from Highland Park to the hospital were too important to waste.

It was Gehrig at first; Lazzeri at second; Jumping Joe Dugan at third; Irish Bob Meusel, Earl Combs, and the Babe in the outfield; with Pat Collins, Johnny Grabowski, and Benny Bengough behind the plate. So many people got that wrong and said Bill Dickey, but Dickey didn't get to the majors until '28 and didn't become their regular catcher until '29.

Ninety-six percent of all hospital beds in the city of Chicago are located on the routes followed by the horse-drawn streetcars of the 1880s. This fact should not surprise anyone. Hospitals have always depended upon easy public access. Over the years, of course, the modes of such access have changed, although the locations of the hospitals have not. Horse-drawn streetcars are no longer seen on the streets of Chicago. Even the horse-drawn milk wagons, which long outlasted them, have been gone since 1951. The roads that once carried the streetcars have adapted fairly well. Being wider than their contemporaries and longer and straighter, most of them have become major thoroughfares of one sort or another.

Austin Flint Medical Center had originally been located at the crossing of two major streetcar lines. The streets that carried these lines were now expressways, expressways that make it easy to reach the medical center from all parts of the city and all of Chicago's suburbs to the north, south, and west.

But who the hell played shortstop? It was the right question to ponder today. The first day of a new rotation at the medical school. By tomorrow he'd be so involved with patients he wouldn't be able to devote sufficient time to issues like this, issues upon which no one's life depended. The horn from the car behind him notified Richardson that the light had changed and he could turn onto the Edens Expressway and start south.

Durocher?

No, he didn't start until '28.

Everett Scott? Maybe he'd be so busy in the next few weeks he'd remember not to eat lunch. It would be good to lose 15 or 20 pounds. He was big-boned and at almost six feet could carry 190 but 210 was too heavy.

Scott? No. They traded him in either '25 or '26. God, I must be getting senile to forget such things. I should be able to remember that entire lineup. Maybe I need to be worked up for my memory loss. Maybe I should be the one to see a good neurologist. The paper will be okay. It still needs some work but it'll be okay. I should have spent more time in the lab. Then I'd be sure we were right. Maybe it was "the Lip." No, it couldn't have been Durocher.

The opening trumpet fanfare from Mahler's Fifth blared forth from the FM radio and changed the subject of his musings just in time for him to get into the express lanes.

Was that Herseth playing the trumpet and Solti conducting? Remember that old Scherchen version on Westminster?

Not everyone who was heading for the neurology office that morning had to come as far as Paul Richardson. Herb Westphal, the senior neurology resident, was washing up in one of the on-call rooms. For Herb, it had been a bad weekend. It wasn't so much that two deaths in a weekend were unusual. After all, hospitals can be very unhealthy places. Lots of people die in them. Two deaths weren't that strange. But two from seizures, seizures like he'd never seen before. And he was certain that they had been absolutely identical. He had only seen the tail end of the first—Mrs. Schiff with her eyes still open and looking around as if she could still control them; her body arched off the bed; her legs extended with every muscle frozen; unable to breathe. The 20 milligrams of Valium he'd given never even touched her.

Then there was Mitchell. Herb had been there as soon as anyone. Mitchell had been their patient for years. It had been like an instant replay—all of the patient's muscles seemed to go into spasm at once. Except his eyes. They had remained open, looking at Herb Westphal, asking him to do something to stop the spasms. Herb had tried everything he knew. Dilantin. Valium. Nothing had helped. It had all happened so fast. The spasms became stronger, lasted longer. Mitchell could no longer breathe. Then his eyes closed and it was all over. He'd ask Dr. Richardson if there was anything more he should have done. Maybe the chief had seen such seizures before, the kind in which you are awake until the very end.

As he edged his car into expressway traffic west of Chicago, Al Schilder began his trip from one hospital to another, from one life to another. From twenty-four hours of moonlighting as an emergency room physician to a full day as a neurology resident. He hated it, but his family liked to eat. Although his training would be over in twenty-seven months, it seemed as if he'd already spent a lifetime learning medicine. He had done an internal medicine residency and had been in the service for two years before he met Richardson and decided to change fields, beginning a residency in neurology under him. His wife had not been thrilled by the prospect of three more years of struggling to survive on a resident's stipend. Neither of them was sure whether it was worse to be completely broke or to have Al moonlight on his nights off so that they had even less time together. On top of that, once every year or two the hospital would fire a resident for moonlighting. But with four small children she couldn't work and they needed the money. Al would be almost thirty-three before he could make a decent living. At least Dr. Richardson ignored the moonlighting. Richardson liked Al and enjoyed having him around. They were both old southsiders and Sox fans, and Al was well read. Anyone who combined such features should be an outstanding resident. But Al was not a stellar resident. He was a good doctor, but Richardson knew that he lacked that something extra.

While Richardson was maneuvering his car out of the express lanes and into the Loop, John Adson and Renee Weber were stumbling out of bed, having almost recovered from their jet lag. John and Renee shared his small apartment in the Rohe students' and nurses' residence, an old building built in 1906 which was tucked in between the hospital itself and the lecture halls and laboratories of the medical school. Their window looked out on the medical school; they could even see into the anatomy lab. When Richardson's father had gone to the University of Chicago, medical students had gathered in the anatomy lab to watch the Maroon football team play in Stagg Field. To watch Amos Alonzo Stagg, the grand old man himself lead them on the same field that would later give birth to the Manhattan Project. But from this anatomy lab, the view was less intriguing—John Adson's apartment on the fourth floor of Rohe and other buildings that were even less interesting architecturally.

Renee brushed her teeth and then made the bed while John used the small bathroom. A quick shower, a shampoo, and a shave. John preferred taking baths but the tub was even too short for his five-foot-nine-inch frame. Finally, he used Renee's blow dryer to arrange his light brown hair into what the preceding generation would have recognized as a Prince Valiant cut. This done, he dressed very carefully, putting on a new tie over a white shirt, the collar of which was too worn to ever again look fresh.

Vacation was over for both of them. It was time for John to start a two-month rotation on neurology and he was excited to get started. He felt lucky that Dr. Richardson would be his teacher for at least the first month, since all the students raved about his teaching.

Renee was less excited about seeing the head of neurology. She just wasn't comfortable with the new experiments yet. And Dr. Richardson really depended upon her. Sometimes too much.

Renee was a small woman in all dimensions from her short sandy hair to her size four feet. With a robust voice usually characteristic of a much larger person, she called John for breakfast. When she talked, her big voice often sparkled and animated her otherwise ordinary features. She had been a bright undergraduate but one without direction. Then, one summer she had worked in Richardson's lab. She then considered going to medical school but found she hadn't taken the right prerequisites. So she went to work for Richardson full time and had now been with him for two years. From time to time she talked about going to graduate school but neither she nor Richardson took this talk seriously.

Richardson, for his part, loved her independent spirit. The way she pursued each problem to its conclusion saved him a lot of time and effort. In the two years she had worked for him he had given her more and more responsibility and he had spent less and less time in the laboratory. As long as he reviewed things every couple of weeks just to make sure she was on the right track, everything went well. Sometimes she felt that Richardson forgot that she didn't have a Ph.D. or even a Master's degree and expected too much from her. But then again, no other chief would have given her such freedom and responsibility. She hoped she would get to go over the project with Richardson again this morning. Maybe then she would understand it better. After all, he was a good teacher.

When she had started working for him they had been studying Parkinson's disease. She had known almost nothing when she had started in the lab and it had taken her a couple of months to fully understand what Parkinson's disease was. And now Richardson was shifting the emphasis somewhat and looking into the possibility of developing some animal models of human muscle diseases, especially myasthenia gravis. Maybe Dr. Richardson would get enough free time so they could go over the experiments again and maybe she could take some time off from the lab and make rounds with John and the entire neurology service. She would enjoy that.

* * *

While Richardson inched his way through the Loop and listened to WFMT play three different recordings of the concluding section of Beethoven's Ninth, Renee and John kissed each other goodbye and headed off in separate directions. Renee went to the neurology labs on the sixth floor of the Kamm Research Building. John joined several other students heading for various locations in the hospital complex.

Chief Resident Herb Westphal was already in the hospital starting his morning rounds, checking on each of the patients Neurology was following. As always, his wide shoulders were bent forward so that he appeared shorter than six-feet-two and heavier than his one hundred and eighty-odd pounds. His slouch had developed when he was the first of his friends to start growing and he had just never seemed to know what to do with all of himself while waiting for them to catch up.

Herb couldn't put the old saw out of his mind. He'd learned it the first week he was on medicine as a junior medical student. Bad things always come in threes. Strange diseases, cardiac arrests, emergency admissions. Always in threes. And it had already happened twice. Two down. One to go?

Mrs. Roberta Todd really didn't expect anything to happen. She was still half asleep when someone in a long white coat entered her room. She didn't recognize the doctor, but there were so many, and, like the others, this one checked her intravenous and then left without saying anything. They often came in to give her injections through that plastic tube. Injections that were supposed to prolong her life. Not save it—that was out of the question—but prolong it. Suddenly she felt more alert, more awake than she had felt in a long time. It felt strange and good, as if there might be some real hope.

Sue Evans left her room on the fourth floor of Rohe a few minutes after John and Renee, about the same time Walt Simpson left his room on the sixth floor. She went to the hospital to check a patient. As she walked past the nursing station she saw Herb Westphal.

Mrs. Todd's strange feeling of euphoria was being replaced by an even more peculiar sensation, closer to terror than fear. Not to mention the pain. Her arms and legs were in spasm and it was getting difficult to breathe. If only someone would come in now to check the intravenous. Couldn't they hear her bed banging against the wall? To her it seemed as loud as thunder.

Herb sat at the nursing station looking at the vial of Valium, which he rotated between his fingers. He was finally in his last year of his neurology residency, having spent nearly eight years at the medical center: four years as a medical student, one year as an intern, and, at last, three years as a neurology resident. As chief resident, he had spent his final year juggling his time among working in the research laboratory, keeping his teaching service organized, and, of course, moonlighting in outlying emergency rooms. The extra $1,200 Herb received as chief resident was helpful, but it wasn't enough. The payments on his Datsun 280ZX were more than he had anticipated. Herb planned to become a member of the Neurology Department on July 1 when his residency would be completed. Then there would be no need to moonlight in some emergency room for an extra $150 a night. All he had to do over the next few months was to get some of his research projects completed and get his academic career launched. He hoped that the rule of three was just a superstition. Perhaps some things come in pairs.

As the Reiner version of the "Ode to Joy" faded from his memory, Paul Richardson's car finally approached the medical center. He enjoyed the view of the complex from the expressway. The collection of buildings spread out before him reminded him of the disjointed skeleton he had studied during his first year in medical school. The scattered structures of the Austin Flint Medical Center had more in common with that box of bones than they did with a real patient. Even an etherized patient. Despite being laid out on an operating room table, the anesthetized body remains a single unit whose parts still have a recognizable connection with each other. That was not true of the hospital complex. It was as hard for a patient to find his way from X-ray to Cardiology as it would be for him to figure out how to fit the tibia to the femur. But at least there was some logic behind the box of bones. The various parts obviously fitted together in some way, but their exact relationship was learned only through long experience. In contrast to the ontogeny of the skeletal system, the Austin Flint complex just grew. It began as a hospital, added a medical school in the early part of the century, and had been adding buildings of various sizes, shapes, and styles whenever the need arose or the money was available.

There were the Walshe and Altrock wings of the original hospital, which still housed most of the patients. They dwarfed the smaller structure, which had begun as the Isbell clinic and now was the home of Neurology and several other clinical departments. Not far away were the Kamin research laboratories, and behind the Rohe student residence were the various buildings of the medical school, each carrying the name of some half-forgotten benefactor: White, Donahue, Sullivan, Schalk.

Sue Evans heard the banging of the railings and looked into Mrs. Todd's room. It looked like the patient wanted to scream and Sue felt like she wanted to scream as well. Terror filled the room but Sue got hold of herself and remembered what to do. She pushed the emergency button, picked up the phone, and told the operator to put in a triple page for the neurology resident on call. Then she remembered seeing Herb Westphal earlier and stuck her head out of the room to call him and the floor nurses.

He was in the room in less than twenty seconds and by the time he got to the bedside he was already drawing up something in a syringe—something he had in his pocket. He injected the substance but nothing happened. Mrs. Todd's entire body was in spasm. Her back was arched off the bed. Her face was contorted, but her eyes were still wide open, staring first at Sue, then at Herb, and then back at Sue. Westphal refilled his syringe and injected it into the IV again and repeated the procedure once more. A total of 10 ccs more of Valium. The spasms continued, growing stronger by the second. All of her muscles seemed to contract at once. Her face was twisted into something grotesque—half smile and half grimace. Not a grimace of pain. More one of rage. A rage against dying, against the dying of the light. Her chest wall stopped moving and her diaphragm froze solid. She no longer moved air in or out. Westphal gave up on Valium and tried Dilantin. Mrs. Todd's eyes finally closed. Despite her rage and their efforts, the light was going out. The doctors tried to compress her chest and force some air out but couldn't. After several minutes of unsuccessful attempts at resuscitation, Mrs. Todd was pronounced dead. The group of doctors who had gathered so quickly dispersed slowly, one by one, to return to their respective routines. The fact that most of them had never even met Mrs. Todd before they had started pounding on her chest or breathing into her mouth did not in any way decrease their personal sense of defeat. It was one hell of a way to start a week.

At the same time Herb had given up trying to save Mrs. Todd, Paul Richardson drove into a small lot behind the oldest part of the hospital complex and took the elevator to the fourth floor of Isbell. The offices of the Neurology Department were located at the south end of the fourth floor. He unlocked the door, turned on the light, and took off his jacket. He usually got to the office before anyone else. He had formed this habit when he was a resident and continued the tradition when he became a staff member. Now that he was chairman of the department he felt he was probably too old to change his ways. He was only forty-four, but somehow working continuously with an endless stream of kids in their early twenties made him feel old. Each year the medical students trooped in and out. Their names and faces changed but their ages remained constant. His didn't.

He started the coffee as he did whenever he got to the office first. At home he never made the coffee in the morning. Bobbie always did that. She always got up first and started the coffee, even on mornings when she could sleep late. At times she complained, but Paul thought that she would have felt hurt if he made the coffee. Anyway, he always toasted his own English muffin while reading the sports section.

As the coffee began to brew, Richardson scanned the bulletin board. Chris often left important messages pinned up there. He was more likely to notice them here than in his office. As far as he could tell, there were no messages, just an old list of patients on the service and a memo from the Office of Student Affairs listing the students assigned to neurology for the spring quarter. As he started to read the latter, Richardson smiled to himself. He still looked forward to each new quarter, although the increasing age gap between him and the students bothered him even more than his receding hairline. The excitement of teaching, of converting students into doctors, of enticing them into neurology was what he enjoyed most about his job. That and the few really challenging diagnostic problems. These came all too infrequently to satisfy Richardson. But he knew that common diseases happened commonly and that patients were better off that way. There were four names on the list:

1. John W. Adson   4th year
2. Susan Deborah Evans   3rd year
3. Linda Rebecca Sharp   4th year
4. Walter Elliott Simpson   4th year

His eyes lit up immediately. Two of the names were quite familiar: Sue Evans and Walt Simpson. They were both bright and hardworking. He had met John Adson a couple of times and liked him. At least there was only one junior student. It was almost the end of the year, so one junior might not work out too badly. Adson, Evans, Sharp. Was Sharp really Shapiro?

It was 8:25 when the coffee was done and he gazed out the window as he sipped his first cup. It was beginning to snow. It shouldn't be snowing on the first day of the spring quarter. The Sox would be starting their season in just one week or so. Richardson hoped the neurology team would have a better year than the Sox. He looked up as the outer door opened. It was Chris Gowers. Richardson smiled a good morning greeting to her as he watched her take off her coat. Her round, straightforward face, full breasts, and wide hips made up a classic peasant figure. Had Renoir known her he would have thought her beautiful and painted her. If he had, the world would have concurred with his judgment. Unfortunately for Chris, Renoir died long before he could have painted her and today, women with the kind of figure he loved are more in style on the walls of the Art Institute than walking on Michigan Avenue.

"Did you start the coffee?"

"Don't I always?" he replied.

It had almost become a ritual that Chris would ask this question each morning as she arrived. Chris had been Richardson's secretary for more than four years. Only Richardson himself had been a member of the department any longer.

Four years ago. To Richardson it seemed more like a generation ago. He was just recovering from his affair with Carol Voss then, and Chris seemed to sense that it was necessary to be close but always maintain her distance both physically and emotionally—to keep her personal life separate from his. She was obviously too bright to be a secretary and too well educated. And she worked too hard. Richardson never knew why she hadn't finished college and wouldn't go back, any more than he understood why she wasn't married. Their relationship did not allow such questions. With the students it was different. They were there for such a short time. Short but intense. There were no built-in ground rules, and sometimes the intensity caused trouble. By now, Chris had become indispensable. She knew more about the administration of the department than Richardson did. And besides, Richardson liked having someone else who was over thirty around the office.

Herb Westphal was the next to arrive. He started to ask the chief a question about the three patients and then decided not to. He'd ask later when he'd had more time to think about it. The better he understood what had happened the more he could learn from his questions.

"Herb, when will we get started today?"

"The students are in orientation until 9:00, but I told them to show up here as soon as they could."

"Good. I'll give them a brief pep talk and then you can get

them started. We ought to be able to spend most of the afternoon making rounds. How many new consults are there?''

Herb looked at his note cards and answered, ''Four.''

''How many other patients are on the service?''

After another look at his cards, Herb replied, ''A total of eighteen.''

''Who else is on service this quarter?''

''Al Schilder and Donna Batten.'' Richardson nodded at the first name and smiled briefly at the second. Paul Richardson considered Donna Batten a gem. She had been the most beautiful medical student Richardson had ever taught. Her long blond hair trailing behind her continued to intrigue him. He always smiled when he thought of his success in seducing her into neurology. Most of the doctors in the medical school just wanted to seduce her. Yet her mind was more interesting than her body. She could see the forest while looking at each tree. So many students got lost learning individual facts and never grasped the patterns. Hell, the facts changed every ten years. There were new blood tests, new medications, even new diseases. But the observations remained. The clinical patterns survived.

Donna had gotten married before medical school and remained so. In fact, she was happily married and, despite her alluring appearance, was quite straight and a good doctor. Better than most of her fellow workers and instructors would admit. But since they all had fantasies about her, it was hard for them to recognize her as their professional equal, let alone as a better doctor. Richardson interrupted his reverie long enough to ask Herb another question.

''What's Adam Stokes doing this quarter?''

''He's still in the EMG Lab.''

''How long is it going to take him to learn how to jab needles into people?''

''He's only been there three months, and he likes it, boss.''

Richardson shrugged his shoulders. He found it hard to believe that anyone could like doing EMGs. Spending all day sticking fine needles into patients' muscles and recording the activity. The EMG was an important test, but to actually enjoy doing it, that he couldn't understand.

"De gustibus. Let's see, there will be a total of seven on the service, counting you."

Herb didn't like walking into patients' rooms with an entourage. But he knew Richardson performed better with an audience and would be unhappy if someone suggested that a smaller group might be better. He'd organize it as well as he could. "The way things have been jumping around here we should have more than enough work for that many people. We've got patients coming out of the walls. I think I'll assign two students each to Schilder and Batten. They'll go over the students' workups before the patients are presented to you. It'll be easier for you if they check the workups first. And if you don't mind, I'll stay in the lab as much as possible after things get organized."

Richardson nodded his assent and went back into his office to get some administrative work done. Herb sat down to help Chris with some insurance forms. Then he remembered that he wanted to ask Dr. Richardson about those peculiar seizures. He'd get to that later, after rounds. There was no real hurry.

At a few minutes after 9:00 the medical students began to arrive. The first to appear was Walt Simpson, who had worked on research with Richardson off and on since he had been a first-year student. As always, Walt's wing-tipped shoes were freshly shined as if to complement his high, polished forehead. His hair was light brown and sparse—a characteristic that he shared with Paul and which endeared him to Richardson's heart despite Simpson's neatly knotted maroon tie. Within a few minutes all four of the students had assembled and, appropriately enough, Walt assumed the role of leader and introduced the other students.

"Dr. Richardson, this is Susan Evans."

"Yes, I know. I've known her almost as long as I've known you, Walt. How have you been, Susan?"

"Fine, Dr. Richardson."

"This is Linda Sharp," Walt continued. A few deep lines crossed Walt's forehead in stark contrast with his otherwise smooth, fine features. Richardson waited just long enough to observe this effect before he turned to the young woman.

Richardson did not know Linda Sharp so he gazed at her

as if he could learn all about her through one brief intense stare. Linda had shoulder length straight black hair which she brushed back from a not quite center part. She had fine black eyebrows and dark eyes which were so black he couldn't tell the pupils from the irises. Together they emphasized the pale whiteness of her high cheekbones and long neck. She had long eyelashes, a large but almost sculpted nose, and full lips. Each feature taken alone was almost ordinary but taken together their effect was dramatic. It was Richardson who ended his own brief survey.

"When did your father change his name from Shapiro to Sharp?" Dr. Richardson asked. Another opening, another show.

Linda looked a bit flustered but managed to get a response out. "When he finished college and went to work in a bank. But how did you know?"

"I've never met a Sharp who wasn't once a Shapiro. Your mother, of course, is Russian Orthodox?"

"Yes," she confirmed as she bit her lower lip out of both bewilderment and embarrassment.

"You are John Adson," Richardson continued.

"Yes, sir," John answered.

"How did you like London?"

"I loved it, but how did you—"

"Wasn't it bleak and windy? It usually is in March, or at least it used to be."

Schilder and Batten arrived in time to break up Richardson's act. When the introductions were completed, Richardson sat back at his desk and began his pep talk.

"You all look as perplexed as you would be if I had just surmised—or, to be more correct, perceived—that you had been in Afghanistan."

The students looked at each other with puzzled frowns. Richardson shook his head slowly. He could never accept the students' failure to recognize the "sacred writings" of Conan Doyle. It was all right not to know T. S. Eliot or Ring Lardner, but this was something else. What better way to learn the art of observation than to read Sherlock Holmes? The residents had all heard this routine before, but they enjoyed it, especially Herb.

"Sherlock Holmes, the greatest of all consulting detectives," Richardson continued, "as you all know, was based upon a physician, Dr. Joseph Bell of Edinburgh. Conan Doyle had been a medical student in Edinburgh and had worked for Dr. Bell as his clerk. His role in Dr. Bell's outpatient clinic was apparently something like your role here, though more superficial. Conan Doyle would interview the patients first and then bring them in to see Dr. Bell. Dr. Bell would look briefly at the patients and then make observations that amazed both the patients and his student clerk. Dr. Bell wrote some excellent advice for medical students: 'You must learn the features of each disease as well as you know the features of your best friends. It is a simple thing to recognize your friend even in a crowd of medical students dressed alike in their whites. Superficially the students might all look alike, differing only in certain characteristics. But if you know these characteristics you can recognize your friend.' Your job as medical students is to learn these characteristics of the major diseases. My job is to teach you this art of observation and deduction. I expect you all to learn to observe the small details and hope that some of you will learn to understand their importance.

"Linda certainly looks as if she could be Jewish. Yet she is wearing a Russian Orthodox cross. My conclusion: her father is Jewish and changed his name from Shapiro to Sharp and her mother is Russian Orthodox.

"John's recent trip to London is revealed by his new reflex hammer. It is a type of hammer that is available only in London in a shop near the National Neurologic Hospital on Queen Square. The hammer looks unused and he didn't have it when I last saw him around the hospital four weeks ago. So I surmised that he had recently been to London.

"You four will be assigned the new patients in rotation and will be responsible for taking a complete history and examination. You will then review it with one of the residents and after that you will present the patients to me. You will have much more responsibility than Conan Doyle had. You will be expected to see each patient every day, to keep track of their clinical course and all laboratory studies. You will go over the clinical and laboratory findings with the residents and then present the follow-up to me each day. We give you a great deal of responsibility. I hope you can live up to it. One more thing. Don't get embarrassed if you can't answer my questions. If I asked questions you already knew the answers to, you wouldn't learn very much and my job is to teach you more than you already know. I'll do the same thing to the residents and with them I'll start with even harder questions.

"Dr. Westphal will assign the new patients and also divide up the eighteen patients already on our service for whom you will be responsible. Herb?"

"We have four new consults to see today, so I can give one to each of you. John, you see Mr. Romberg on 7 East. He's supposed to have Parkinson's disease. Linda, you take Mr. Moon in the Intensive Care Unit. I saw him last night when he was unconscious, so we'll go over him together. Walt, you get Miss Wolman on 6 West, and Sue, you see Dr. Sanders on 6 West.

"I think," Westphal continued, "it would be best if we went over the details of a comprehensive neurologic examination now, so let's go over to 6 West. Everybody should pick up a patient list from Chris on the way out and we'll divide up the patients on the way."

As they filed out, Susan Evans stayed behind. "Can I talk to you for a minute, Dr. Richardson?"

"Sure. What can I do for you?"

"I'd rather not work up Dr. Sanders."

"Some student has to do it, Sue."

"I guess so, but why me?" she asked.

"I know it's difficult to be a doctor to one of your professors, but you're almost a doctor now and I'm sure you can do it."

"I'd rather not."

"Give it a try."

She nodded her head without enthusiasm and hurried to join the rest of the team.

After they had all left, Richardson went back to the outer office to get some more coffee and see what he was scheduled to do for the rest of the morning. Renee Weber was coming down to go over some results, but otherwise his morning looked good. In theory, Dr. Richardson spent one third of his time seeing patients, one third teaching, and one third doing research. In reality he never got into the lab anymore, though he still went over everything with Renee at least once every week or two.

It was sort of fun being a one-man department again, even if it was only for two weeks while Russell Levi and Arnold "Bud" Chiari were away. Usually they arranged it so that only one out of the three of them would be away at a time, but Russell had planned his vacation six months ago and Arnold was right to stay at the NIH the three extra weeks. He had gone there on a three-month leave to learn some research techniques and as always it was taking longer than expected. Richardson had been a one-man department before. In some ways he liked it better that way, juggling the patients, teaching, and doing research all at once. It kept him out of mischief.

Chris looked up from her typing and remarked, "You cheated."

"What do you mean, I cheated?" Dr. Richardson complained.

"You knew John was in London. He has been living with Renee for over a year and you reviewed this year's theater season with her so they would see only the best shows while they were in London."

"But I don't really know that they went together, at least not officially. Anyway, it helped me make a point, and a teacher is allowed to stretch the truth in order to make a point. And nobody else guessed."

"Renee will figure it out when John tells her."

"Certainly," Richardson smiled. "That's why I like her."

Chris shook her head. "Herb said he wants to talk to you sometime before rounds."

"About anything special?"

"Something about some patients who had seizures and died. He wanted to see if he handled them right. He seemed very disturbed."

"Okay. Page him after I see Renee."

He spent the next hour polishing up the manuscript of the paper he was to present in New York the following weekend. No matter how hard he tried to shape each sentence, no matter how carefully he selected each phrase, this stuff was not literature. The real question was whether it was science. His ability to write a simple declarative sentence while describing an experiment wouldn't be enough. If the data wasn't there it just wouldn't hold up, no matter how many times he reread Hemingway to improve his style. But the data was there and it looked good. His job was to make sure it sounded good, too.

At 10:30, Renee Weber came in to go over the research.

"What's the latest gossip?" Richardson asked her.

"I've only been back for a day and a half."

"So? There must be something new."

"You know Dr. Sanders?"

Richardson nodded.

"He's supposed to be interested in Donna."

She could tell that her words had affected him by the tone of his slow response, "Donna who?"

"Donna Batten, your resident."

"That jackass. She wouldn't give him the time of day."

Chris buzzed the intercom to tell Richardson that Mrs. Hammond was on the phone and just had to ask him a question. Richardson picked up the phone and half listened to her litany of complaints. He absentmindedly rummaged through his desk, found a small metal box of Dutch cigars, fingered one, put it in his mouth, located a match, and lit it. All the time he never missed a word. Renee sat back and waited. She had no other new gossip to tell Dr. Richardson. After all, she couldn't tell him her suspicion that he was having an affair with Chris. That wasn't new anyway. She'd wondered about that for two years. She knew most of the female med students and residents and knew that many of them were interested in him. She was sure it was his intensity—that and his concern for them all as individuals—that made him so attractive. But as far as she knew, nothing ever developed. Perhaps he was already involved. That being the case, Chris was the obvious choice. But of course it was possible that he just wasn't interested in such things.

Finally, Richardson was able to get in a few words. He advised Mrs. Hammond to change the schedule of her medicines and to call him back in a week.

As soon as Richardson hung up, he and Renee got to work going over last week's results. The experiments just hadn't worked as they'd hoped.

"Can't we just go back to Parkinson's disease?" Renee pleaded.

"Why, Renee? Don't get discouraged just because one or two sets of experiments didn't work. You know it took us almost six months to set up our original Parkinson disease models. When you started working here we'd already been working with those models for years. You've never tried to set up a new model. It's never easy."

"It's just that I'm not quite sure why we got into this bungarotoxin bit in the first place. I just don't have a feel for it yet."

"Look Renee, alpha-bungarotoxin is nowhere near as exotic as its name. As you well know, it is one of the active ingredients in the venom of the cobra. It's what makes the cobra one of the deadliest snakes in India. You understand what happens when a cobra bites someone."

"Sure," Renee nodded. "The person becomes paralyzed."

"How soon?"

"Almost immediately."

"Okay. And what causes the paralysis?"

"A number of components of the venom," she responded, "including alpha- and beta-bungarotoxin but especially alpha-bungarotoxin."

"Right. What is the mechanism of action of bungarotoxin?"

Renee thought for a minute. "It prevents the muscles from responding to the nerves."

Richardson smiled. "You know, for somebody with a background in science you do damn well." Now they both were smiling. "The mechanism of bungarotoxin is just like myasthenia. Your problem is one of impatience, Renee. Don't worry. I don't expect miracles.

"Now," he continued, "our problem is to give just the right amount of bungarotoxin to make the guinea pigs weak, but not to kill them. Then we have to be able to reverse the weakness with Tensilon. If we do that, we have our model of myasthenia."

"It's easier said than done, Dr. Richardson," Renee complained. "I've done it three times now and the Tensilon hasn't worked even once."

"Rome wasn't built in a day. I'm sure this will work. It's worked in other labs. It'll work in ours. It's just a matter of time. Let's figure out a new dosage schedule."

Over the next half hour they outlined a new series of experiments using a slightly lower dose of bungarotoxin. Richardson hoped this would produce only a moderate degree of weakness, which they could then reverse. As she left, Renee remembered to have him sign a requisition form for more bungarotoxin. They had to send to Maryland for it and it always took at least three weeks to get it. They were using more bungarotoxin than they had anticipated. By bitter experience Renee had learned to order more drugs than they needed just to be sure they didn't run out.

Chris brought in the morning mail and started back to her desk. Then she stopped. "You ought to know that Al is worried."

"Al? About what?" Richardson asked.

"Sanders and his house staff committee are making noises about too much moonlighting going on around here."

Richardson sighed. "When he and I were residents here, he held down at least two different jobs. He never felt it interfered with his work here. It did, but he never thought it did. I guess there's nothing worse than a reformed alcoholic."

The mail included some reprint requests, a letter notifying him that a paper on his and Herb's laboratory research had been accepted for publication, a bill for a book that he couldn't remember ordering and was sure he had never read, and a notice from Dr. Sanders's secretary informing him that, because of Dr. Sanders's illness, official notification of next year's research fellowships would be delayed. Among his other administrative duties, Sanders was in charge of the fellowship grants. Richardson had requested a two-year postdoctoral fellowship for Herb Westphal. It was a foregone conclusion that Herb would receive one, since it was neurology's turn to get a fellowship and everyone knew how good Herb was. He'd done some research with Sanders in the past. Still, it would be nice to get the official notification so that some of Westphal's salary in the next year's budget could be used for something else. It shouldn't be too long. Sanders was only in the hospital for pneumonia and soon would be back to work. He wondered why he was supposed to see Sanders in consultation. Pneumonia was not a neurologic disorder. Sanders probably had migraine headaches. He deserved them.

Chris buzzed the intercom. "You've got a long-distance call from Dr. Voss."

"I just talked to her last week."

"Should I tell her you're busy?"

"No, I'll talk to her."

"You know it'll just upset your whole morning. It always does."

"I'll talk to her. She's a friend of mine."

"Some friend!"

"Chris, stop it."

"All right. I'll tell her you're in."

Richardson picked up the phone and began with an unnecessarily ebullient "Hi, Carol!"

"Hi, Paul."

"What can I do for you today?"

"I need some help on the project we're starting. We're having a problem figuring out what dose of cocaine to give the monkeys."

"Why don't you ask Dan?" The minute he said it he knew he wished he hadn't. He shouldn't still be bitter.

"You know more about cocaine than he does."

"That must be why he keeps using my slides."

"Paul, don't."

"I'm sorry."

"Will you help or won't you?"

"Don't I always? Send me a copy of the protocol and after I look it over I'll give you a call. Fair enough?"

"Talk to you soon. You're a love."

"A love" was one thing he knew he wasn't. Why did he let things linger on? Once you pronounced someone dead you should bury the body. Perform an autopsy if necessary. Bury them. Mourn them. But don't keep them on a respirator. And their affair was dead. But Carol was also a scientific protégée.

Carol Voss, the scientist: that he was willing to take credit for. Carol, the person: that was a different issue.

Just before afternoon rounds Herb Westphal came up to the office. He was in that awkward stage between being a resident who had to call Dr. Richardson by his full name and being an associate who would call him by his first name. Herb solved this in his own way. "Chief, in the last two days we've had three patients die of seizures."

"Patients do die from seizures, Herb. Even in the best of hospitals," Richardson answered him, half concentrating on a paper he was reading.

"Yes, but I've never seen patients die like this. After twenty-four hours of recurrent seizures, yes, but this was different, Chief. I've never seen anything quite like these seizures."

Paul Richardson put down the paper and looked up at Herb. "In what way were they different?"

"The seizures didn't last too long at first. The patients had some sort of generalized spasm, which kept getting stronger and lasting longer. But they seemed to be awake. Finally, the spasms kept them from breathing and it was all over." Herb kept shaking his head, looking down at his hands and the empty vial of Valium he was still fingering. "I'm not sure what happened to them, or if they were treated right, or maybe even overtreated."

"What did they get?"

"Dilantin, phenobarbital, Valium, or combinations of them."

"What kind of doses did you use?"

Herb thought before he replied. "Usual doses, or maybe even less than that."

"Did you give enough to cause a respiratory arrest?"

"Hell, they died before I had a chance to give them too much."

"So we didn't kill them by overtreating them," Richardson commented.

"You're right, Chief. I'm sure we didn't do that."

"Did you see all the patients?"

"Yes."

"Herb, take your time and describe everything you saw."

Richardson sat back and began to search for another Dutch cigar.

Herb thought for a minute. "They were all identical. I'm sure of that. They were all the same and different from anything else I've ever seen."

"Different?"

"Yes, instead of having just plain generalized seizures with their arms and legs jerking back and forth, the arms and legs were continuously extended."

"A tetanic seizure?"

"No. It was like tetanus in one way. They were awake most of the time. But it was too fast and the spasms didn't start in the jaws," Herb replied.

"How do you know they were awake?" Richardson asked between puffs.

"By their eyes. They kept looking at me."

"Was the spinal musculature involved first?"

"Yes."

"What did the posture look like?"

"In the patients who were still awake it was strange. The entire body, except the head and the heels, was arched off the bed. Damnedest thing I ever saw."

Paul sat quietly for a few minutes. He crushed out his cigar, relocated the box, picked out another one. Schimmelpennincks from the tax-free shop at Schiphol Airport in Amsterdam. He looked out the window. The day was still bleak and dreary. Neither doctor said much, and finally a passing elevated train seemed to jolt Richardson out of his meditation.

"Do you know much about India?"

Herb was used to his boss's quirks, his free association from patients to baseball to obscure composers to characters out of ancient-Roman history, but he was still a bit surprised.

"Indian native medicine has contributed a number of things to medicine."

"Sure, reserpine—we both know that those patients didn't die of reserpine-induced parkinsonism, for Christ's sake," Richardson flashed. Then he asked another question. "Did you manage to get autopsies?"

"Only on the last one."

"One out of three. For a batting average that's not bad. But we ought to do better than that."

"I'm as disappointed as you are. I tried as hard as I could to get autopsies. In fact," Herb added, "I had to lie to get that one."

"Huh?"

"The first patient was the wife of an orthodox rabbi who wouldn't even think of consenting to such a thing. The second had no relatives we could locate to give us consent, and the last patient had told her family that if she died she didn't want to be cut up."

"Christ, it's as if somebody didn't want you to get an autopsy. What happened?"

"The family felt she had suffered enough before she died."

"So how did you get the permit?"

"I used the old tuberculosis ploy," Herb explained.

"What?"

"Come on, Boss. You know the tuberculosis ploy. You must have used it yourself. We told the family that we were afraid that the patient might have had TB and that it would be very important for the family to know."

"Did it work?"

"Only when we told them how important it would be for the grandchildren's future health."

"You know, over the years I've heard doctors use routines like that at least two dozen times, and how many times do you think anybody ever told the family the results of the autopsy?"

"I don't know," Herb answered.

"None."

"Figures."

"What did they find on the autopsy?"

"Grossly the brain looked normal. We won't get to cut the brain for two weeks."

"Herb, are you sure it was completely normal?"

The chief resident nodded his head.

"No sign of infection?" Dr. Richardson continued.

"No."

"No evidence of bleeding?"

"No."

The older physician went on, as much to himself as to Dr. Westphal. "The only things I know that can do that are bleeding, infection, and toxins," mused Richardson.

"We'll find out in two weeks when we cut the brain," Herb reminded him.

"Unless the brain is normal. And since we can't glue her back together at that point, we'll have to worry about something other than an infection or a hemorrhage."

They didn't have to wait two weeks to worry.

CHAPTER 2

Rounds started in the conference room on 7 East. The four students and the two residents were waiting when Richardson and Westphal arrived. John Adson had seen Mr. Romberg in the morning. John had taken his history and examined him. He had then reviewed Mr. Romberg's entire record and Dr. Batten had gone over everything with him. Richardson sat at the head of the conference table while Westphal sat on one side between Donna Batten and Al Schilder, facing the four students. Richardson hoped this formal division into classes would disappear as they got into the quarter. He sat back and took out a small cigar as John began to tell Mr. Romberg's story. One thing about fourth year students was that they had done this often enough to know the ritual—the codified formula: age, race, sex, complaint.

"Mr. Perry Romberg is a forty-seven-year-old white male who was in good health until five years ago when he first noticed a tremor of his right hand." As John went on giving a detailed synopsis of the history, Richardson listened with only one ear. What Richardson like best about these standard formal presentations was that he could follow the logic and still think about other things. He was sure he had met John before. That was it. Last year's departmental party. John had come with Renee. Richardson had been favorably impressed by him. They'd talked about the variety of career opportunities medicine offered. John wasn't interested in specializing.

27

Like many of his contemporaries, John was really going to go out and deliver medical care. All but a handful of Richardson's medical school classmates had shunned general practice in favor of specialty training. Maybe John's class would do more good than his had. John was sure he just wanted to go into family practice—out west somewhere—and "do his own thing." Richardson wasn't sure he knew what John's "thing" was, but maybe John didn't know yet either. Who did at age twenty-six?

Despite his musing Richardson still managed to catch the salient points. Mr. Romberg apparently had had parkinsonism for five years and had been on L-dopa for four years. He must be wrong about the seizures. There must be some other explanation. Things like that didn't happen. Nobody in his right mind would kill people in that way. There must be some other explanation. Some sort of encephalitis. The only unusual feature was that Mr. Romberg had never improved as a result of getting L-dopa. In fact, despite rather high doses of L-dopa, his parkinsonism had continued to progress so that now he was almost bedridden. There were many reasons why a patient might not improve on L-dopa. Richardson wondered if John or Donna had asked Mr. Romberg about all of them.

When John finished his presentation, Richardson suggested that before they discuss the problem of L-dopa resistant parkinsonism, they should examine Mr. Romberg. After all, if he didn't have parkinsonism the failure of L-dopa required no explanation. They all followed John and Richardson into Mr. Romberg's room and John introduced Dr. Richardson. Like many patients, Mr. Romberg was both embarrassed by the large crowd and at the same time flattered by all the attention he was receiving. At times, Richardson felt a bit guilty about his entourage. However, he obtained some consolation in his belief that the patients also profited by this system. The students and residents had more time to be completely thorough, and often, in going over the same story again and again, patients would recall important details they had forgotten. Of course, no system was perfect and it didn't always work out that way. Richardson began with his usual opening. "Dr. Adson and Dr. Batten and I have been going over your history, so you won't have to go over everything again, but I will have to ask you some questions and hear your answers myself.''

Over the next five minutes he carefully dissected the history and was able to confirm the story he had already heard. Mr. Romberg had had Parkinson's disease for five years. He had been on L-dopa for four years. He took his medicine regularly and was still taking it. He was on a high dose and yet felt that it had never helped. He denied taking other medications. Next, Richardson examined him and demonstrated the key physical findings to the group. Mr. Romberg had a mild tremor of the fingers as his hands rested in his lap. The tremor had all the characteristics of a parkinsonian pill-rolling tremor. Stiffness was present in Mr. Romberg's arms and legs. His face was frozen and almost expressionless. When Richardson finished the examination he told the patient that he agreed with the diagnosis of Parkinson's disease. He then said he would confer with Mr. Romberg's doctor and order some tests to see how they might help him get better.

As they walked back to the conference room, Richardson shook his head and remarked to Donna, "If Romberg's history is true, then he is virtually unique in my experience."

When they got back to the conference room, the students and residents sat around the table while Richardson stood at the blackboard. He turned to Sue and asked, "What's the diagnosis?"

"Parkinson's.''

"Why?''

"He looks like he has Parkinson's disease," Sue answered.

"In what way? Try to be more specific.''

"The tremor and stiffness are the most obvious features," she replied.

"Anything else?''

"His face.''

"Anything else?''

When none of the students answered, Dr. Richardson moved up the ladder. "Donna?''

"His voice.''

"What about it?'' Richardson was warming up to his subject.

"It was soft and monotonous.''

"Right. Now you students should all see him every day and talk to him and memorize that voice, its slow . . . halting . . . na . . . ture . . . with . . . un . . . natural . . . stops . . . and . . . spaces . . . mixed with sudden rushes. Combine this loss of control with a monotonous pitch and you have parkinsonism. When you see him, study his face. He can move it but still it is frozen without the moment-to-moment play of emotions you usually see. And his eyes never seem to blink. He stares like a reptile. Learn that voice and that physiognomy so that you will recognize parkinsonism in the future. Walt, what goes wrong in the brain in Parkinson's disease?"

"There is no dopamine."

"Why, Al?"

"The cells that make dopamine are not working right, so they don't make enough dopamine."

"'Good. Now if the problem is lack of dopamine, why don't we just give the patients dopamine, Linda?"

"I'm not sure."

"Guess."

"I don't think dopamine can get into the brain."

"True, dopamine cannot cross the blood–brain barrier, so we give L-dopa which can cross into the brain. The brain makes dopamine out of the L-dopa and the patient gets better. Right, John?"

"Right."

"Wrong. Mr. Romberg didn't get better. Why? Let's think about it for a while. What are the reasons for failure of L-dopa? Start very basic, Donna."

"Wrong diagnosis."

"Correct. If a patient doesn't have Parkinson's, L-dopa won't help. But Mr. Romberg has Parkinson's. Another reason, Al?"

"Noncompliance."

"Meaning?"

"Maybe he just doesn't take his medicine."

"He seems like a reliable guy, but you're right. You never know. Patients often don't take their medicine and then lie about it." Richardson wrote on the board:

1. NONCOMPLIANCE

"How can we prove whether he has been taking his medication? Sue?"

Silence. It was time to move up to the residents.

"Donna?"

"Do a spinal tap and see if there is evidence that he is taking L-dopa and if it is getting into his brain."

"Does everybody understand that?"

Several of the students shook their heads.

"Donna, would you explain that?"

"If Mr. Romberg takes his L-dopa and it gets into his brain, then traces of the L-dopa will be present in the spinal fluid that bathes his brain. If we do a spinal tap and take a sample of this fluid and send it to the neurology lab, they can see if there are any traces of L-dopa in the fluid."

"What other causes for failure are there, John?"

"Taking certain vitamins that block the effect of L-dopa."

"Do you know which vitamins?"

"Vitamin B_6," John answered.

"Does Mr. Romberg take vitamins?" As he asked this, Richardson wrote:

2. VITAMIN B_6

"No."

"Are we sure?"

"I asked him. Dr. Batten asked him. His doctor warned him not to take vitamins."

"Okay, any other causes? Anyone?"

"Sure, boss," said Herb Westphal. "Taking medicines that block the action of dopamine such as phenothiazines, like Thorazine."

3. PHENOTHIAZINES

"Anything else, Donna?"

"Thyroid disease."

"Mr. Romberg seems to be a good candidate for this."

4. THYROID DISEASE

"You didn't mention his thyroid surgery."

"How did you . . ." Donna stopped. "You saw the scar, of course."

"Of course."

"He is on thyroid replacement," said John.

"Is his replacement adequate?"

"I think so."

"And he denied taking Vitamin B_6 or phenothiazines. This is getting more interesting. If we can prove he is telling the truth, then the chase will be on." Richardson looked at the list on the board and wrote the appropriate test opposite each entry.

1. NONCOMPLIANCE—do lumbar puncture
2. VITAMIN B_6—do lumbar puncture
3. PHENOTHIAZINES—do phenothiazine levels
4. THYROID DISEASE—do thyroid evaluation

"Donna, make sure the appropriate tests get ordered."

They walked down one flight and across the building to 6 West. Walt Simpson got Miss Wolman's chart and started his presentation. As usual he was too serious. Richardson had known Walt for three years and wondered if he ever just relaxed and enjoyed himself. The story was short and simple. Age, race, sex, complaint. In some ways Walt reminded Richardson of himself when he was a medical student. He'd had the same need to do more than just become another doctor. The same arrogance. Was it really arrogance or just a mistaken feeling of self-importance, that what he was going to do with his life was more important than just being a doctor? Had he really felt that way? Sometimes it was hard to remember your own feelings. He didn't want to believe that he was driven by a need to do great things. It was more a need not to be bored. Richardson had enough friends who thought they were going to win Nobel prizes. They weren't all lean and hungry, but in many ways they were just as dangerous. Of course, a trip to Stockholm would be nice.

From the history it seemed clear that Miss Wolman's left-sided paralysis and double vision were psychiatric in origin and not neurological. Richardson's examination confirmed this impression that there was no evidence at all of neurologic disease. As he was writing out his consult and recommending that she be seen by a psychiatrist, he heard an emergency page for the neurology resident on call. Both Schilder and Westphal got up to answer the page.

"If it's another seizure, don't give the patient anything."

"You mean just watch the patient die?" asked Herb. "That's hard to do."

"I know it is." Richardson paused. "I guess it won't make much difference. Do whatever you think is best."

Dr. Sanders was on the same floor. Sue went out to the nursing station, got the chart, returned to the conference room, gave the chart to Dr. Richardson, and started her presentation.

Sue seemed a bit nervous as she began. A bit tentative. Was she always so unsure of herself? She shouldn't be. But she had been through plenty. The wrong diagnosis can do a lot of harm.

"Dr. Sanders is a forty-six-year-old white male . . ."

He is two years older than I am, Richardson thought to himself. He'd never realized that before.

". . . who was in his usual state of health until two days prior to admission."

"When was that?"

"A little over a week ago. At that time," she continued, "he began running a temperature and coughing."

"Did he take chicken soup?"

"No, he just went home and went to bed."

"With anyone we know?"

"I didn't ask," she responded angrily.

"Sorry, I didn't mean to embarrass you. Go ahead and I'll keep my mouth shut." He had only been trying to relax the atmosphere a bit, get her to loosen up a little. He tried hard never to embarrass a student. He always remembered to call them doctors in front of their patients. He'd have to be more careful in the future.

As Sue told the story it seemed to be a straightforward case of acute bacterial pneumonia. Sanders had been admitted one week ago and had been placed on intravenous antibiotics. Although he was fairly sick for a couple of days, he had improved remarkably toward the end of last week. Over the last two days, when his doctors were about to stop the intravenous antibiotics, Sanders had complained of slurred speech and trouble swallowing. Sanders felt that his swallowing was worse today. Sue had been on Infectious Disease last week when Sanders had been admitted, and she said that they all felt it was a simple pneumonia and were surprised by his swallowing difficulty.

The crew gathered around Sanders's bed while Richardson examined him. He carefully tested Sanders's swallowing and concluded that there was a definite weakness of the tongue and throat muscles. There appeared to be some weakness of Sanders's arms and legs as well, but this was minimal.

"Did they do a myasthenia gravis test?"

"Yes," Sanders replied. Then, looking straight at Sue Evans, he continued, "In fact, this beautiful young thing did it all herself. Unfortunately, we were not alone."

"You sound like you're feeling pretty much back to normal."

"If it weren't for this swallowing I'd be okay. What do you think it is, Paul?"

"I'm not sure, but we're going to start with a spinal tap to make sure you haven't got low-grade meningitis."

"If that's what you have to do, do it." As Richardson turned to leave, Sanders tapped him on the arm and said, "Give my love to Bobbie."

That was one message Richardson would not relay. They went back to the conference room and Richardson began to write the differential diagnosis on the blackboard.

1. MYASTHENIA GRAVIS

"What's against this diagnosis, Sue?"

"The negative Tensilon test."

"You're right. The weakness of the myasthenia is virtually always overcome by Tensilon for a minute or two. If the patient has trouble with his eyes or with swallowing, within two or three minutes after Tensilon the improvement is obvious. Tensilon tests are not always positive, but almost always."

2. MENINGITIS

"How do we prove whether or not he has meningitis?"

"Do a spinal tap," said John.

"That's what we'll start with. But if it's meningitis, he shouldn't have weakness of his arms and legs."

"Could that weakness be the result of being sick and in bed for a week?"

Richardson shook his head, but his reply was interrupted by the return of Herb Westphal, followed by Al Schilder.

"It happened again, Chief."

"What?"

"Another of those damn fits."

Schilder shook his head back and forth. "I've never seen anything like it before. I thought the patient was awake and then he was dead. Jesus Christ!"

Westphal also seemed perplexed. "The goddamned Valium didn't touch him."

Schilder continued to shake his head. "His face looked . . ."

"Hold it. One at a time. Let's start at the beginning, go through the middle, and get to the end. Herb, tell me what you saw."

"We got to him not long after it started. He was just down the corridor, and when we got there he was lying in bed and his face was stiff and contorted. But he was awake and looking around."

"Are you sure he was awake? Those weren't just roving eye movements?"

"No, he would look at you. He couldn't move his face or turn his neck. But he could move his eyes, and he looked right at me. He couldn't change his expression, but damn it, you could see that he was frightened."

"Then what happened?"

"Someone slammed the door and he had a fit. His neck and legs stiffened and went back, the rest of his body was just lifted off the bed, and he stopped breathing. Al got there then with the Valium. I don't know how he got it so fast. He must have an in with the nurses. We gave him 10 milligrams intravenously and nothing happened, so we gave him 10 milligrams more."

"Wait a minute. Did he stop breathing before you gave him the Valium?"

"Yes, I'm sure. It wasn't the Valium."

Schilder confirmed the chief resident's version. "No question about it. It wasn't a real respiratory arrest. It was as if his diaphragm and all the rest of his respiratory muscles were in a spasm. And, damn it, he was still looking at us."

"We gave him 10 milligrams more and then he quit looking at us."

Then Schilder added, "His face didn't change. It didn't relax, but he looked different. The fear was gone."

"Didn't you try to resuscitate him, Al?"

"We couldn't do mouth-to-mouth because of the spasms."

"He had terminal cancer, so no one wanted to get too vigorous," Adams added.

"A most peculiar story."

"It's just like the other three, Boss."

"That is what makes it peculiar."

The conference room was crowded. Not only the neurology service had gathered around to hear the story, but also the nursing staff and the rest of the house staff on the floor. Richardson looked at everyone. He tried to reassure them that what had happened was not anyone's fault. He had to be absolutely sure before he made any public accusations. They reviewed the appropriate management of acute seizures and then Richardson called a halt to the session.

"Herb, come back to the office with me. The rest of you can see your other patients."

When they got back to the office, he told Chris to call Dean Willis and say that he had to see him that afternoon.

"What should I say when his secretary asks what you want to see him about?"

"That it's a matter of life and death."

"That won't work. Everything is a crisis around here."

"Tell her someone is running around the hospital killing patients."

"You're kidding."

"I wish I were."

The two physicians went into Richardson's office. Herb closed the door and saw that Richardson was looking through the pharmacology books in his bookcase. Herb never knew how Richardson found anything in that office except for the various-sized metal boxes of Dutch cigars, all with green price tags in guilders. Herb found the box he was looking for before Richardson found the book he wanted. Herb took a cigar, a Panatela, and sat down to light it. Richardson was looking through a large German text on pharmacology and translated aloud to himself as much as to Herb.

"*Nux vomica*, the seeds of a tree native to India, the *strychnos nux vomica*. The principal active ingredient is strychnine. The term *nux vomica* has nothing to do with vomiting. *Vomica* refers to the cavity that is a feature of the seed. The cavity is attributed to the imprint of the finger of the Creator. We always seem to blame everything on God. Strychnine produces excitement of all portions of the central nervous system, including the brain and the spinal cord. It is a powerful convulsant and—here's what I'm looking for—the convulsions have a characteristic motor pattern. The movements of the seizure consist of symmetrical thrusts, which may be brought about by any sudden stimulus."

"Even noise?"

Paul continued, "including sounds, touch, light. It doesn't mention the sudden slamming of a door, but I'm sure that would be more than sufficient. The patients finally develop full-blown convulsions in which the body is arched in severe hyperextension so that only the top of the head and heels of the patient are touching the bed. At this time there is no respiration because of the severe spasm of the respiratory muscles. Death results from failure of lower brain centers due to the impaired respiration."

"Sounds like our patients."

"The bastard. Listen. The muscle spasms are excruciatingly painful, but the sufferer is awake until the very end. He is usually extremely apprehensive—what an understatement! —and fearful of impending death as he awaits each successive seizure."

"There are a lot of nicer ways to die," Herb commented.

"And to kill people."

Richardson rummaged around his desk, found a box of miniature cigars, and lit one. He looked at the ashtray and pondered a bit. He wondered to himself whether Sherlock Holmes could have determined the shape and size of different cigars made with the same tobacco just by looking at the ashes. "Herb, tell me everything you can about the cases."

"The first one I know about was the night before last around 8:30 or so, just after visiting hours were over. The patient was a Mrs. Schiff, the wife of Rabbi Morris Schiff, an orthodox rabbi. As far as I can tell, she wasn't doing too well. She came in for evaluation for weight loss and loss of energy. The workup had shown metastatic disease with cancer involving the lungs, liver, and hip."

"Any neurologic problem?"

"The initial examination was described as WNL."

This was the usual shorthand for "within normal limits." But no one really did a complete neurologic examination on a patient without neurologic complaints, so Richardson usually interpreted it as "we never looked." Richardson thought for a minute and then asked Herb, "Did she have any neurologic problems?"

"No."

"Are you sure?"

"Pretty sure. No neurologic complaints were recorded in the chart."

"Metastases to the brain could have caused her seizures."

"Yeah. I talked to the rabbi at great length. I'm sure there was no reason to suspect brain metastases."

"They could still have been there."

"The CT scan was normal."

Richardson shook his head. Sometimes he still could not get used to the progress. She'd even had a CT scan—computerized tomography. Such a simple procedure and one of the truly great advancements in medicine. All the patient did was rest with his head in a rotating machine, receive the same amount of radiation as he would for a series of skull X-rays and you get a picture of the brain. An outline of the brain and its cavities which showed most tumors, most blood clots, most strokes. No more pneumoencephalograms. Mrs. Schiff had been lucky. She got a CT scan to make sure there was no cancer in her brain. A few years earlier she would have gotten a pneumoencephalogram. First, they would have done a spinal tap, taken out 10 ccs of spinal fluid and put in 10 ccs of air, then 10 more, then another, to up to 50 or 60 ccs. Thank God they didn't have to do pneumos anymore. Everybody got sick from them. Fever. Headache. Those guys who invented the CT scan certainly deserved their Nobel Prize. Just ask anybody who had ever had a pneumo.

"That helps. So what happened?" Richardson asked.

"The rabbi went home, and about half an hour later the nurse heard a noise and went into the room."

"Did the roommate notice anything?"

"She was in a single room. They were thinking about getting a private duty nurse but decided she didn't need one. They had just done a simple node biopsy earlier in the day for tissue diagnosis, and she was feeling okay. I talked to the nurse. You know her, Melkerson."

"She's good."

"She got there and the patient was being lifted off her bed by a severe seizure. She called the intern and they paged me. They didn't have any Valium on the floor so they gave her IV phenobarb. When I got there, they had given her 240 milligrams and she was still in a severe spasm with her face frozen and contorted, but she wasn't awake or breathing. And she died."

"Did they try to resuscitate her?"

"No, she had terminal disease. There didn't seem to be any reason. Why resuscitate someone with metastatic disease who's going to die soon anyway?" Herb asked.

Why *kill* someone with metastatic disease who was going to die soon anyway? Paul wondered. He didn't ask Herb, but he doubted if Herb had an answer either. The second death had occurred on Sunday morning at about 10:30. The patient's name had been Mitchell, a black man in his sixties who had a known brain tumor that had been operated on a year or so earlier, and he was not doing well. "What do you mean, 'not doing well'?" Richardson asked.

"He was going down the tubes."

"Any previous seizures?"

"No."

Again Herb had gotten there shortly after the nurse had discovered the seizure. The seizure sounded just like Mrs. Schiff's. They had given him Valium, but Mitchell had gone into a spasm, quit breathing, and died, and there was no reason at all even to attempt to resuscitate this old man—an old man without relatives, without hope. No reason to try to extend his life and suffering. But was there any reason to shorten it? Every once in a while a hospital would have an epidemic of sudden deaths in terminal patients. A plague of mercy killings? Could that be happening here? Right under their noses?

"Was he awake when you got there?"

"Yes, and it was just like the others."

Richardson didn't even pay much attention to the rest of Herb's narrative. It was the same thing over and over again. There must be some reasonable explanation. Herb again told him about Roberta Todd, who had just died that morning. She'd been fifty-four years old and had had a metastatic tumor. No known brain involvement. She had just been given some pain medication and was sleeping. Her roommate had a visitor, and they went into the lounge to leave Mrs. Todd undisturbed. When they came back the patient was having seizures. From there on it was just like the others. Frozen face, tetanic seizure, respiratory spasm, death. Why kill people who were already dying? Most mercy killers picked patients who were dying more slowly or suffering more.

Today's patient, named Henry Erb, was another patient with known carcinoma—a seventy-year-old male with bladder cancer who had just returned to his room from recovery and was sleeping quietly. The nurse was checking him every fifteen minutes. When she went back in he was seizing.

"Will we get an autopsy?"

"Unlikely."

"Go down and draw some blood on him."

"What?"

"Just do what I asked. Get me 20 ccs and freeze it in the lab, and don't let anyone know what you're doing."

"That's not legal."

"What?"

"It's not legal to draw blood from a dead patient without a permit."

"It's not legal to kill people either. Just get that damn blood and take it to the lab. Spin it down and freeze it. Get going. You're not exactly stealing his precious bodily fluids."

As Herb was about to leave, he suddenly turned to Richardson and said, "It couldn't be strychnine."

"Why not?"

"I've used that in the lab. We all have, and we've used Valium and phenobarb or even Dilantin to stop the convulsions. But none of them worked in these cases. They didn't make any difference at all."

"They only help if you give the animals small doses of strychnine," Richardson explained. "In the lab you're trying to produce seizures you can treat and study. You're not trying to kill the guinea pigs. You use about one tenth of the average lethal dose or even less. But if you give enough strychnine, nothing helps. The dose used here was much greater than the lethal dose, so the other drugs wouldn't do a damn thing. Now get out of here and get that blood."

He buzzed Chris on the intercom. Dean Willis would be able to see him now for a few minutes. He told her to call and tell Willis that he was on his way. He crossed the street to the new medical school building and took the elevator to the tenth floor. For once he didn't have to wait for half an hour. The meeting with Dean Willis was like all of Richardson's previous meetings with him: cordial, short, and nonproductive. The two of them rarely saw things in the same light. As important as Richardson might be in the medical center, he would never be a member of the dean's inner circle of advisors who really ran things.

When Paul entered the office Dean Willis was looking at the one sheet of typed paper which rested on his desk directly in front of him. He motioned Richardson to sit down and continued reading. As he read there was a slight smile on his face. Or was it a frown? Richardson couldn't be sure. But it probably didn't matter. The dean's smiles were as studied as his frowns, and as calculated. The only spontaneous act Richardson had ever observed in him had been a sneeze. Finally Willis finished reading, looked up, and immediately took charge. "I hope you're here about something worthwhile. I've a very busy schedule today. I just finished with the Student Grievance Committee and in twenty minutes I have to meet with some people who are interested in helping our building program."

"Since we're supposed to preserve lives, I think this is worthwhile."

"Well, what is it this time?"

"There have been four deaths in the hospital over the last three days," Richardson began.

"Actually, there were eight deaths over the weekend. That's about average for a weekend. Nothing unusual. People die in hospitals."

"Die, yes. Get murdered, no."

"Murdered?"

"Yes, murdered."

"You must be wrong. Nobody murders patients."

"I wish I were. But I'm pretty sure I know what happened. Four patients had peculiar seizures that killed them, and I'm sure the seizures were due to strychnine."

"Strychnine?" The smile or frown which had been frozen on the dean's face was now entirely gone.

"That's right. Somebody gave strychnine to four patients, and they all died."

The dean's attitude changed. He shook his head in disbelief. "Are you sure, Paul?"

"Ninety-nine percent." Richardson told him everything he had learned from Westphal. As the story dragged on, Dean Willis got a bit fidgety. He looked at his watch. It was time for his meeting.

"Can you prove these four patients were actually murdered?"

"Prove?"

"Yes, prove. In a court of law you need proof, not conjecture. After all, maybe we're experiencing some sort of epidemic of a weird form of encephalitis or something. We all know you're fond of brilliant, obscure diagnoses. Sometimes you've been wrong, and you might be wrong now. After all, you are fond of zebras."

"Zebras?" Paul responded.

"Yes, zebras. If you were in a room with ten other physicians and you all heard hoofbeats, ten doctors would identify those hoofbeats as belonging to a horse and you'd wonder why it couldn't have been a zebra."

"Okay, I like exotic diagnoses," Richardson admitted. "But there's a lot at stake here."

"There sure is. We've got 940 patients in the hospital who would be panic-stricken by this story of yours, not to mention more than 4,000 employees and over 800 physicians. Hell, there are three physicians who are also patients right now. We can't make wild accusations. Too many people could be hurt. There's too much at stake. I'll need some proof before I do anything."

"Proof? It may be too late by the time we can be 100 percent sure. We need the police in on this. Let them collect the proof. That's what their job is. Call them. The least they can do is make it harder for the murderer to kill someone else."

"Someone else?"

"Sure, how do we know he'll stop with four?"

"You're getting carried away, Paul. We're not even positive that there have been any murders."

Paul Richardson stopped for a minute. Was he absolutely sure? Could it be something else? A viral infection of some sort? Maybe. He'd be more sure after they studied the blood Herb had gotten from the last patient. His voice became calmer, less demanding, almost pleading. "We can't just do nothing."

"I am not going to call in the police until I have some more evidence."

"More—"

"It wouldn't be good for our patients or for us, and we can't afford that kind of publicity right now. We're in the middle of a big fund-raising campaign."

Now he was pleading. "We have to do something."

"We will. Prepare a confidential memo with all the details. Then give me a copy and give one to Collier."

"Collier?"

"Yes. As head of pathology this comes under his jurisdiction, and they are doing an autopsy on one of the patients."

"Then what?"

"I'll go over it with him, and if he agrees, I'll call in the police."

"That may take days."

"That's what we're going to do. Don't talk about this to anyone, and make sure Ms. Gowers doesn't either."

"Ms. Gowers?" Richardson frowned. "Oh, Chris."

Richardson walked back to his office slowly. Some day he hoped he would have a meeting with Willis that wouldn't leave him with a bad taste in his mouth.

As far as Richardson was concerned, the career of Thomas Willis verified the Peter Principle. If Willis lived long enough he could end up a President of the United States.

Willis was originally brought to Austin Flint to be head of the Renal Division when Richardson was an intern. The house staff had hated him. In their view, he nearly destroyed Renal singlehandedly. The teaching went to hell. Patient care became more mechanical, less personal. The night call schedule increased. But somehow, and Richardson never really understood this, the number of patients increased. The interns and residents weren't concerned with the percentage of hospital beds filled each day—the administration was.

Willis prospered, and of course so did the Renal Division, especially when Willis's skills as a fund raiser improved. A few years later when the Department of Medicine needed a new chairman, he was the only one who could do the job. And Willis did the job well. The average daily census of bed occupancy went up. Income increased and donations grew. The research endowment tripled in less than two years. Teaching? Who cared? No one—until it got harder to recruit new interns. The solution? Put Willis in the dean's office where he could raise money and play politics to his heart's content. As luck would have it, the only open position was Dean of Student Affairs, a traditionally quiet job. Willis would have plenty of time to do what he did best. But times had changed. Being Dean of Student Affairs in the early seventies was not a vacation. It was probably the most sensitive job in the whole medical center. There were five exciting years filled with student strikes, boycotts, and faculty unrest, all, it seemed to Paul, aggravated by Willis's failure to deal honestly with the students. But he eventually solved those problems by his clever machinations and was named Dean of the Medical School.

Through it all the medical school survived and in some ways even prospered. The endowment had grown. That meant more support for research and even for teaching. If only the means to that end had been more palatable.

Maybe Willis was right. Maybe it could be something else. Some oddball infection. After all, new bugs and new diseases did crop up every once in a while. Look at Legionnaire's disease. One day it didn't exist, the next day it was an epidemic.

When he got back to his office, Richardson called Renee Weber in the lab and told her to get twelve guinea pigs. He'd be over in twenty minutes to supervise an experiment. They'd use the serum that Herb had brought over and left for him.

By the time he arrived at the laboratory, Renee had put two guinea pigs in each of six cages. Each guinea pig weighed about half a pound. They were between eight and twelve weeks old. Pure white, an inbred albino strain. Being albinos, their eyes reflected light as bright red dots, just like the pictures from Kodak Instamatics before they put on the flash extenders. Bright red dots in the middle of each eye. They gave half a milliliter of the serum to each animal in the first cage. Almost immediately each animal threw its head back, extended all four legs in a severe tetanic convulsion, and expired.

"Wow, that was impressive!" Renee exclaimed.

"Page Herb and have him bring some Valium and phenobarbital up here." To Richardson it was more than impressive. No simple infection could do that. It had to be a poison. Not a new form of Legionnaire's disease.

While they waited, Richardson calculated the highest dose of Valium and phenobarbital they could give the guinea pigs without killing them. "How much serum do we have left?"

"Eighteen ccs."

"How many guinea pigs?"

"Ten."

"Is the camera around?"

"Yes."

"Set it up to take pictures of the animals. We may have to show them to Willis."

"Why Willis?" Renee asked.

Richardson didn't answer that question. He was about to make up a reply when the phone rang. It was Dr. Westphal.

Renee told him that Dr. Richardson wanted him to come up to the laboratory and to bring some Valium and phenobarbital. "He said he'd be up here in ten minutes," she repeated to Richardson.

Richardson didn't reply. He got up and walked to the window. The lab was on the sixth floor. Aside from the few people walking to and fro between the hospital and the parking garage, the streets were almost empty. No one used the streets anymore. No one just went for a walk. No more street vendors. Today most of the people who seemed to use the city streets were prostitutes and drug pushers. The "L" trains seemed very far away. In the depths of the Depression, his father had had an office overlooking the "L" tracks. Now Paul had an office overlooking the "L" and his office was in an even worse neighborhood. That's what was called upward mobility?

He looked at his watch. Herb would be there soon. Herb had seen all four patients die. Maybe it could be something else. What if this new virus or bacteria made a toxin which built up inside the body like tetanus or diphtheria? That seemed more farfetched than a zebra. But it was possible. Maybe it wasn't murder. Maybe Willis was right. He'd have to be absolutely sure before he made this diagnosis. After all, why murder people who were already dying? It just didn't make any sense. And why use strychnine? Sure, there was plenty of it around the medical center. In his lab. In Physiology. In the Pharmacology labs. He looked through the cabinet where they kept the medicines and couldn't find any strychnine. "Renee, where is the strychnine?"

"In the cabinet, I suppose."

"It's not here. When did you last see it?"

"We haven't used it in months. I don't remember when I saw it last."

This is crazy, Richardson thought to himself. Nobody in my department would steal strychnine to kill people. We've got better poisons than that. We've got tetrodotoxin, cyanide. Anybody who really knew neurology wouldn't use strychnine. He gazed out the window, but his mood was interrupted by the arrival of Herb Westphal. Richardson told Herb how much medication to give the guinea pigs.

"That's enough to kill them."

"Not quite, but almost."

They gave nothing to the animals in the first cage, Valium to those in the second, phenobarbital to those in the third, and both Valium and phenobarbital to those in the fourth cage. They then gave half a cc of serum to each guinea pig. Within seconds each and every guinea pig had a tetanic convulsion and died. They pretreated the last two animals with phenobarbital one half hour before they injected the serum to see if giving the guinea pigs time to build up their brain levels of phenobarbital would help. It didn't.

Herb shook his head. "Just like the patients."

"It answers your question."

"What question?"

"Why didn't the Valium or anything else help? The dose was just too damn high. Now that I've answered your question, you can answer mine."

"What's that, Chief?"

"Why kill these particular patients?"

"Who knows?"

"Renee, how long will it take to get the film developed?"

"Two weeks."

"Shit! Can't we get it done faster than that?"

"If I slip the guy in photography five bucks, we can get it in two days."

"Get it there first thing in the morning. Give him ten bucks and tell him we need it in twenty-four hours."

"Do I take the ten bucks off the grant?"

Richardson reached into his pocket, pulled out his wallet, and gave Renee $10. "No, I'll pay for it, but do it first thing in the morning."

"Okay."

"Then I want you to nose around Physiology and Pharmacology and see if they have any strychnine. Tell them you want to borrow some. We need it for an experiment and ours ran out."

"Sure."

"And more important, find out whether any might be missing from their labs. And, Herb . . ."

"Yeah."

"Call the pharmacy and see who else might have strychnine, let Renee know, and then she'll borrow some from anybody else who has it."

"Okay, Chief."

"Do it first thing in the morning. If we're lucky, by the time we have the movies back we'll know some more." Richardson paused and then in a quiet, determined manner went on. "I may not be absolutely sure. But I'm pretty damn close to that. Herb, I'm going to write up everything you told me about the patients as well as the results of these experiments. It ought to make one heck of a memo. That plus our movies ought to be enough to convince Dean Willis that something has got to be done."

Dean Willis didn't have to wait to see the movies. He called the police late that same night, shortly after Dr. Collier, who was in the hospital for elective surgery, died after a brief series of seizures. The chase was on.

CHAPTER 3

EVEN to the most casual outside observer, it would have been obvious that Tuesday started off much differently from most days for Paul Richardson. As always, the coffee and newspaper were waiting for him when he came downstairs. Today, however, he only glanced at the sports section. That was most uncharacteristic, especially since the Sox had won the day before.

Bobbie never really understood why it took him less time to read about a loss than it did to read about a victory. She had read the headline, "Sox Rookie Blanks Pirates" and was sure that a game like that was worth at least five minutes. But Paul just scanned the headline and then studied the news section, page by page. But, of course, there was no mention of the murders. It was almost as if they had not really happened. He wondered if Rabbi Schiff felt the same way. Would there be any more to come?

"Paul, your coffee is getting cold."

"What's that, dear?"

"I said, your coffee is getting cold."

He took a sip. "It is. I'll get myself some fresh." He poured more coffee into his cup and started his English muffin. As he looked out the window, he told Bobbie about the four murders and his talk with Willis.

Bobbie listened carefully. "So that's why you didn't sleep well."

"That and the fact that we couldn't find our strychnine."

"Why is that so important?"

"I think those four people were killed with strychnine."

"Are you sure?"

"That it was strychnine? For all practical purposes I'm pretty sure. Herb's story of what he saw was a perfect description of a strychnine seizure. Like he was reading it out of a textbook. That it was my strychnine, I'm not as sure. But it probably was. It's missing. I know that much for sure."

"Even if it is, it's not your fault," she reminded her husband.

"Maybe not, but we should have kept the strychnine locked up better."

"How many years have you had it in the lab?"

"At least eight."

"Nobody ever stole it before?"

"No," he answered.

"So many people go in and out of your lab. Don't blame yourself. If whoever took it couldn't have gotten it from your lab, he would have gotten it somewhere else."

Bobbie's comments must have helped because Paul sat back and read the sports section. It was worth eight minutes. As a rule Richardson tried not to talk to Bobbie about patients he was taking care of, but he did mention that Sanders was in the house with pneumonia. Bobbie appeared uninterested, which seemed like a healthy response. At one time her lack of interest in his patients and his work had been unhealthy. God, it was hard to remember how far they had drifted apart four years ago through apathy and their absorption in their own problems. That's when Carol Voss came along. She was so interested in him, in all that he did. What a mistake he had made. And Sanders. Did Bobbie believe that had been a mistake, too? That was one thing they had never discussed. His affair with Carol—they had gone over that backwards and forwards. But hers with Sanders—never. However, they had survived and their marriage was stronger than ever. The two kids were doing well in school and in between volunteer work and housework, shopping and car pools—especially between her car pools—Bobbie managed to take one or two graduate school courses each quarter. She was majoring in Tuesday and Thursday mornings. That fit her schedule best, so whatever was offered she took. English lit, history, political science, philosophy. At first it seemed strange to Richardson that she was taking such a variety of courses, but he knew she enjoyed them all and whenever he could, he did some of the reading so that they could share more of their lives. He especially liked reading ancient history and philosophy.

The drive to the hospital took fifty minutes. Both Richardson and Chris arrived at the office at the same time, so he let her start the coffee. He went into his office and dictated a brief memo describing the four seizure-related deaths and his belief that they were caused by strychnine, as well as the results of yesterday's experiments with the guinea pigs. The memo resembled many of his scientific papers. First the clinical data, then the laboratory data that supported the clinical observations, and finally the conclusions. He gave the dictated tape to Chris and told her to type it up as soon as she could. While he was at Chris's desk he looked at his appointment book, and frowned. Had he known about Collier's death and what that would do to his afternoon, he would have been more unhappy. But Willis had been very successful in keeping things quiet. The hospital staff didn't know about the murders, and, of course, the public knew nothing.

Richardson was to see two patients between 9:00 and 10:00, make rounds at 10:00, meet with Renee Weber and Herb Westphal for lunch to go over their research, and spend the afternoon juggling time between an office full of patients and some more inpatient rounds. By that time the movies would be back, and they'd know if anyone else was missing any strychnine. Then maybe he could talk to Willis and Collier.

Chris brought him his coffee, with cream and saccharin, in his Wedgwood mug. He continued to use saccharin even though he never lost any weight. Maybe it helped him avoid gaining more. He was still thirty pounds lighter than when he had graduated from high school twenty years earlier, and few, if any, men he knew could say that. However, even fewer had weighed 220 when they had graduated, but he tried to suppress that memory. Chris also brought in the charts for his first two patients.

"Were you serious yesterday?" Chris asked.

"I'm always serious—at least most of the time."

Chris frowned. "Were you serious about somebody running around the place killing people?"

"I was, but I was told officially such a thing could not happen. It would make the hospital look bad. Especially when we are starting a new forty-million-dollar fund-raising campaign."

"Is that what Willis said to you?"

"Not entirely," Richardson answered. "So I said what I could. I reassured him that as far as I knew only poor patients had been killed, so that it shouldn't hurt our image with the rich."

"Dr. Richardson!"

"Actually it might be better if a few rich people did die—after leaving us everything in their wills. That's a great idea. Send a memo to Dean Willis saying that he is right. I was too blind to see it. The problem is not to prevent further deaths but to make sure we profit from them."

"How should I sign that?" she asked with more than a touch of sarcasm.

"An anonymous donor," he responded quickly.

"What did he really say?"

"He was concerned about causing any unnecessary panic among the patients and the staff. And, as much as I hate to admit it, he's right about that. He said he would discuss it with Jim Collier and ask him to look into it."

"Why Dr. Collier?"

"As the head of Pathology, I guess he's also in charge of forensic medicine. He's a good man and as honest as can be. The memo I just dictated was about the murders. Transcribe it while I'm seeing patients this morning, so we can get it to Willis and Collier. Then I'll stop by and talk to Jim later today."

"You can do it while you're on rounds."

"Huh?"

"He's in the house."

"Nothing serious?"

"No, he's on the OR schedule this morning for a hernia repair."

"What time?"

"Let me check. The schedule's on my desk somewhere." She came back a minute later. "Eight o'clock."

"It's probably done by now. I'll see him this afternoon. Don't frown like that—I'll find the time."

She shook her head and went back to the office to work on the manuscript for the upcoming meeting in New York. Richardson sat down and turned on the FM. He recognized the last movement of the Sibelius fiddle concerto, paused and listened intently, until he was sure that Heifetz was the fiddler with the Chicago Symphony Orchestra with Hendl conducting.

Then he settled back to review the patients' charts. Sometimes it bothered him that he could remember that Joe DeMaestri hit .203 for the 1951 White Sox and that his major contribution that season was a triple against the Boston Red Sox. A Boston Red Sox team with Ted Williams. The splendid splinter. Big Ted missed the next year, making the world safe for South Koreans. Richardson could give you the lineups of every game he'd ever seen and even the few that did not involve the White Sox. But even with his superior memory he still felt the need to review patients' charts to keep them all straight. Of course, in a single week he might see fifty or more different patients, and even in the Frank Lane era, the Sox rarely used that many players in an entire season. But still, his ability to recall obscure ball players both fascinated and aggravated him. Who else remembered Gus Keriazakos, Al Kozar, Joe Kirrene, Rocky Krsnich? Thank God, this fixation ended in 1955 when he went to college. Only to be replaced by culturally more worthwhile memory games. Obscure American playwrights, twentieth-century composers, ancient history.

He picked up the chart and read the name "Sue Evans." That was one patient he could recall quite clearly. She had been admitted to the hospital during her first year in medical school. That was over two years ago. She was twenty-two years old at that time and had been quite healthy except for migraine headaches. She was originally seen by Dr. Kappers. Aaron was head of the department at that time, a good neurologist. Aaron had now moved on to bigger and better things in Boston. Richardson scanned Kappers's detailed notes:

Age, twenty-three. Race, white. Sex, female. Height, 5'5." Weight, 121 lbs. Such a short succinct description of a bright, worried medical student. There was nothing exceptional recorded about her on the chart. Maybe Kappers had been right not to have ever noted anything else. Hair, neither blond nor dark, neither short nor long, neither brushed back nor freely flowing, just always in front of her face. Eyes, neither blue nor gray but somewhere in between. Nose, small. Mouth, soft. Chin, strong. Complexion, fresh, if she ever kept her hair away long enough so you could see it. Nothing exceptional. The kind of woman anyone would be proud to take home to his mother, if only she weren't so damned unsure of herself. Chief complaint: trouble speaking, poor coordination. History of illness: first noted slurred speech two weeks ago—progressive since onset. Now obvious. Not on drugs. Noted difficulty walking one week ago. Getting slowly worse. No other complaints.

Kappers's initial impression was probable multiple sclerosis, and he admitted her to the hospital. After she was in the hospital, they had done various studies, and Dr. Kappers told her that she had MS. Her slurred speech and walking difficulty cleared quite well and she went home.

Richardson saw her first two weeks later. He inherited her because Kappers's schedule was too full. Sue was quite depressed when Richardson first saw her, though neurologically she was back to normal. Richardson attributed her depression to her inability to deal with the diagnosis of MS. When he had first reviewed her record, Richardson had found no real support for the diagnosis of MS. In fact, there were several inconsistencies: there were too many cells in her spinal fluid and the spinal fluid protein was too high. Richardson became convinced that Sue didn't have MS. He was not sure what she had had, probably some form of encephalitis, but it was unlikely that she had multiple sclerosis. When he told her that he was pretty sure she didn't have MS, it seemed to snap her out of her depression. But the improvement had been short-lived. Over the next few months he had seen her through a rather severe period of agitation and depression. Then she seemed to "put her act together." Over the next two and a half years she had done quite well, was an honor student in medical school, and in fact, yesterday afternoon was the first time he had seen her that distressed in over a year.

If only she were more sure of herself. Was she that way because she was afraid she had MS, that she couldn't rely on her body, on her future? She knew just enough about neurology to know that you couldn't prove that a patient didn't have MS. MS was a tough diagnosis to live with. The attacks are so unpredictably scattered. First one attack, then maybe one, two, or three more years without any, then another one, and then . . . ? There was no way to know. Was she still worried about the diagnosis? Or was it something else? Had her small-town background not prepared her for the real world? She often seemed a bit naive to Richardson. He shouldn't have made that crack about Sanders yesterday.

Chris buzzed the intercom and told him that Dr. Evans was waiting. Chris always got that right. Before, it was Sue, but now that she was on the service, it was Dr. Evans.

"What brings you in today, Susan?"

"I want my favorite doctor to tell me again that I'm okay, that I don't have MS."

"You're okay. You don't have MS. Anything else I can do for you?"

"Thank God I'm not paying for this."

"People who don't pay for medical care always get their money's worth."

"Dr. Richardson, I'm worried." Her facial expression as much as her words ended the interplay.

"What's wrong?"

Her migraine headaches had gotten worse. This had happened before when she took birth control pills, but she denied being on the pills now. Her left hand was also bothering her. It seemed a bit numb from time to time.

"Step into the next room and undress, and I'll examine you."

She didn't play her usual word games with that gambit, so Richardson knew she was distressed. He examined her thoroughly. Her reflexes were all normal. Because of her complaints of numbness, he paid special attention to the sensory examination. But he could find nothing. Her ability to feel a light touch of cotton, a pinprick, and even a vibratory sensation from a tuning fork was normal.

When they got back to the office Richardson turned to her.

"Are you having trouble with a man?"

"How did you know?"

"You're obviously anxious and depressed. From the story of your headaches, it's been going on for four months. You aren't four months pregnant, and it isn't school. You'd tell me if it were your family. It doesn't take Sherlock Holmes or even Ellery Queen to know it must be a man."

"Yes, it's the *same* man."

"What *same* man?"

Richardson sat back and lit up a cigar. Sue took out a Marlboro. "It all started when I was a first year medical student, before I got sick. I met this guy and I fell in love."

"Nothing wrong with that."

"He was older than I."

"Was he married?"

"No."

"Was he in love with you?"

"He said he was, but when I got MS—I mean, when they said I had MS—he just split."

"The 'So long, it's been good to know you' bit."

"Yes. I needed help then and he just dumped me."

"It's probably a good thing you found out."

"That's bullshit, Dr. Richardson." She paused and then continued, "I'm sorry. I shouldn't have said that."

"No offense taken."

"But I really loved him and needed him more than ever before."

"I know."

"Then I met you and you told me that I didn't have MS."

"Did you believe me?"

"I wanted to."

"Did you?"

"I guess so. He found out."

"How?"

"He's at the medical center. I told my friends, and he found out and called me. He wanted us to get back together."

"Nothing like a fair weather lover."

"And I loved him, so I went back to him. I almost moved in with him, but I got to his apartment early one afternoon and found him in bed with a girl."

"Well, at least it wasn't a guy he was in bed with."

"It could have been," she said with obvious disgust.

"You're kidding."

"No, I'm not. He's capable of anything."

"Sue, I'm not sure I understand."

"Why?"

"That was all two years ago."

"I know, but I never got over him, and I've been seeing him again. He keeps calling me. I just can't say no. I have to get away from him."

He reassured her that he could find nothing wrong and told her to see her patients and be back in half an hour for rounds. If she wanted to talk some more, they could go out for a drink after work.

He wrote a note in her chart:

NEUROLOGICAL EXAM: Normal
IMPRESSION: Increase in headaches clearly related to emotional distress.

Numbness in left hand could be emotional, could be real.

Was my diagnosis wrong? Maybe Kappers made the right diagnosis after all.

The second patient was Mrs. Duane Turk. She was fifty-one years old and had been referred by her internist because of headaches. Many patients and almost as many doctors had difficulty reconciling two facts: patients with brain tumors frequently have headaches, but patients with headaches rarely have brain tumors. Mrs. Turk's headaches were definitely not due to a brain tumor. They were just tension headaches and her neurological examination was normal. Richardson gave her as much reassurance as he could and dictated a note to Dr. Mallory, who had referred her to Richardson.

After Mrs. Turk left, Chris brought in the memo he had given her, and Richardson reviewed it. He instructed Chris to make three copies and deliver one to Willis's office and one to Pathology. He would take one with him, and if Collier looked well enough, he'd give him one when he made rounds.

The entire team gathered in Richardson's office to start rounds. This was the ritual they would go through each morning for the rest of the quarter. The students and Schilder and Batten arrived at the hospital at about eight o'clock. They then saw all of the patients on the neurology service with each student seeing just those patients he or she was following with one of the residents. Each patient was seen and examined every day. This ensured that the patients had enough opportunities to tell them about any new complaints or ask questions or express their fears. It was up to the students and residents to relay what they learned to Richardson. They also reviewed the charts each morning, checked the laboratory results, went over the X-rays with the radiologists, and reviewed the brain wave tests. Then, at 10:00 they all would gather in the neurology office and present the details to Dr. Richardson.

It took about forty minutes to go over everything. There were two new patients to be seen. Mr. Moon in the Intensive Care Unit and Mr. Harold Wallenberg on 7 East. Only two of the patients being followed had to be seen that day—Mr. Romberg and Dr. Sanders.

Chris buzzed him on the intercom as they were about to leave to tell him that Mrs. Hammond was on the phone.

"Not that woman again?" Richardson moaned.

"You'll have to talk to her."

"What's the problem?"

"She's constipated," Chris replied.

"Again?"

"Still."

Richardson picked up the phone and listened to Mrs. Hammond for a few minutes, or more accurately, half listened. An old woman with mild parkinsonism. Trying to live by herself. She had to share her complaints with someone. It might as well be he. Mrs. Hammond must be nearly eighty. As old as the Villon prints on his office wall. What was that story Dick Florsheim told about the dying Jacques Villon? Being taken to the print shop in his wheelchair just to smell the printer's ink again. Jacques Villon. One of the few artists

who really did his own etchings and lithographs. Not like
Dali or Chagall. He did his own. A man with uncompromis-
ing standards. Like Villon, Mrs. Hammond did things for
herself at an age when most people give up. She had her
standards, too. It was time to give her some advice and then
to tell her to call back in one, no, two weeks. Make it three
weeks.

As he led the team into Mr. Romberg's room, Richardson's quick gaze took in the entire room. Why do all the
rooms in a hospital have to look the same? Smell the same?
Have the same paint, the same pictures? Richardson remembered that at one time he could tell which floor in the hospital
the elevator was opening onto by the picture he could see.
Renoir on 2. Picasso on 3. Not anymore. Monet on all floors.
The same Monet wheat field on each stop. And not even
different versions at different times of the day so you could
associate evening with the second floor, or morning with the
fourth floor. The same identical picture on each floor, as if
some psychologist had shown them that this added touch of
depersonalization would help patients conform better to the
hospital routine. Or maybe an economist. Then he saw something which brought individuality back to the patient. He
walked past Mr. Romberg and stopped at the bed of the other
patient, a tall seventy-year-old man with a Lincolnesque appearance who was reading *A Study in Scarlet.*

"Mr. Marfan."

"Yes, doctor."

"I know your name because it is on the door and here at
the foot of the bed, but we have never met, have we?"

"Not that I know of."

"I can assure you that we haven't. But," Dr. Richardson
continued with a twinkle in his eye, "you have a grandchild
who lives in Highland Park."

"Yes, I have three grandchildren who live in Highland
Park."

"One is nine years old."

"Yes, but—"

"A girl."

"Yes."

"Your daughter's child?"

"Yes, but—"

"She goes to the Green Bay Road School?"

"Yes."

"And she is, of course, in the fourth grade."

"That's right, but how did you know?"

"And she misses her grandfather very much and wants you to get well soon."

Mr. Marfan smiled. His smile only partially masked his amazement. But he was no more astounded than the students. Herb just stood back and enjoyed the show. Richardson certainly knew how to teach the importance of observation and deduction. He wondered if Richardson would ever explain this sequence. Sometimes he preferred to keep everyone in suspense all day, and sometimes he never gave any explanation at all. Mr. Marfan was about to ask Richardson again how he knew these things, but rather than answer that question, Richardson just told him that he hoped he'd be seeing his grandchildren soon.

Dr. Richardson asked Mr. Romberg how he was doing. The patient said that he felt about the same. Richardson asked him again about taking vitamins and other medications that would interfere with L-dopa. Again, Mr. Romberg denied taking anything except L-dopa and his thyroid medication. Richardson asked him if the spinal tap had bothered him at all, but it hadn't.

They went back to the conference room and Richardson walked up to the blackboard. His notes from yesterday were still there as if they were some sort of permanent witness to yesterday's teaching rounds.

1. NONCOMPLIANCE
2. VITAMIN B_6
3. PHENOTHIAZINES
4. THYROID DISEASE

"Where do we stand, John?"

"There are no phenothiazines in his urine."

"Does that help us?"

"That means he's not taking phenothiazines, so we can eliminate number 3."

"Anything else completed?"

"We did the LP. That will give us information on numbers 1 and 2."

"Okay. How about the endocrine evaluation?"

Donna spoke up. "That may take a bit longer than usual, with Sanders in the hospital."

"Can you call Dr. Hunt today and make sure he gets seen?"

As they walked over to 6 West, Richardson asked Herb to make sure that his lab got the spinal fluid results as soon as they could.

The test was a research procedure and Richardson's lab was one of only two in the country that could do it. But it was important to get it done. If Mr. Romberg was taking his L-dopa and not taking Vitamin B_6, and his thyroid function was normal, the pursuit would really be on.

They gathered in the conference room on 6 West and were joined by the two interns assigned to 6 West. Linda Sharp went through a long detailed presentation. The same formula— age, sex, etc. Richardson settled back to listen and watch Linda. The patient named Wallenberg was sixty-two years old. He had had high blood pressure for eight to ten years and had been on medication for the last six years. There was no history of diabetes or heart disease. Linda really ought to try to keep her hair out of her face.

Medical students didn't look like that when Richardson was in school. Certainly not the women in his class. If they had, they certainly would have been married. Now so many of the girls were single. Why was that? Were more of the guys single, too? Was it just that it was easier to live together?

Mr. Wallenberg had been admitted to the hospital because of three brief episodes of dizziness, each lasting less than an hour. During the first one he saw double, but during the second and third ones his left arm and left leg were weak. Linda felt that his neurological examination was entirely within normal limits. Hopefully her WNL really meant that and not "we never looked." He would have to check her examination closely, so he'd know how much he could rely on her.

"What's your diagnosis, Linda?"

"Transient ischemic attack, or TIA."

"What's that mean in English?"

"Well, for some reason, for a few seconds, he wasn't getting enough blood up to his brain. Not bad enough to cause a stroke, but bad enough so his brain didn't work right for a while."

"Good. Now what was the reason for his TIA?"

"I'm not sure, Dr. Richardson."

"Dr. Sharp, did you personally check his blood pressure?"

"Yes, sir."

"What was it?"

"145 over 95."

"In which arm?"

She thought for a moment. "Right arm."

"What was his blood pressure in his other arm?"

"I don't know."

"Would it be important to know his blood pressure in both arms?"

"I guess so," she said without much conviction.

"Did you ever hear of Bernouli's principle?"

The students looked a bit bewildered until Walt Simpson spoke up. "What does first year college physics have to do with neurology?"

"Usually very little. John, what is Bernouli's principle?"

"That was three, no four years ago. Let me think a minute. It has something to do with pressure and speed. As the speed goes up, the pressure . . . ," John hesitated, and then added with a bit of uncertainty, "goes down."

Richardson rapidly shifted gears. "What do you know about the blood supply to the back of the brain, Sue?"

"There are two vertebral arteries. One comes up each side of the neck and then they combine."

"Right. The blood comes up each side from the two vertebral arteries. Walt, what is the source of the vertebral arteries?"

"The subclavian arteries—just before they go into the arms."

"Good. Now what happens to the blood flow to the arm when you exercise?"

Richardson looked at Walt so Walt again answered. "It increases."

"Correct. What if you exercise the arm, and the subclavian artery is partially blocked? In that case the blood supply still increases by increasing in velocity. And what does that do to the pressure in the subclavian artery, John?"

"According to Bernouli's principle, the pressure should go down as the velocity goes up."

"And since blood flows from high pressure to low pressure, what will happen in the vertebral arteries?" Richardson answered his own question. "The blood will go up one artery and then down the other into the subclavian where the pressure is low, which is why it's called a subclavian steal. The subclavian artery steals the blood from the brain and the patient has a TIA."

The students nodded their heads, and Richardson asked, "What single TIA—subclavian steal—was observed by more people than any other in the history of the world? Perhaps ten million and more, and no one knew what it was?"

As they all looked at Dr. Richardson with expressions that varied from blank to openly puzzled, he was smiling to himself. It was time to make his point, even if it involved a little stretching of the truth. "Any takers? Think for a while. In what occupation would subclavian steals be an occupational hazard?" There was no reply. "Anything in which the patient suddenly uses his arms vigorously and repetitively?"

"Carpentry," John ventured.

"No, I've never heard of ten million people observing a carpenter at the same time. Something that's very vigorous, involves the arm and you only do part of the time?"

"Painting an apartment," guessed Sue.

"No," said Richardson with a chuckle. "I'll give you a hint. It has to do with music."

"Playing a violin?" Walt guessed.

"Close, but no cigar."

"Conducting!" exclaimed Linda.

"Right. Now who was the most famous conductor of the first half of the twentieth century?"

Silence.

"You kids are getting too young. Think. Before 1950 and not Xavier Cugat."

"Toscanini, Arturo Toscanini," answered Linda.

"Correct, and he was a very vigorous conductor. Not exactly a Bernstein, but far from Fritz Reiner, and do you know what happened during his last broadcast with the NBC Symphony Orchestra? I remember I was in high school at that time. He was conducting Wagner and I was listening on the radio. All of a sudden it was obvious that something was wrong. He had lost control of the orchestra very briefly. There were twenty or thirty seconds of silence, and then they cut in with a recording of Brahm's First Symphony. The irony of it—to juxtapose Brahms and Toscanini's Wagner. And with Walter conducting. In about two minutes Toscanini was back conducting. Later, the papers said that 'the Maestro' had stumbled and dropped his baton and then recovered. Linda, I know you were only three years old in 1954, but what do you think happened to 'the Maestro'?"

"From your description, it sounds like he had a TIA."

"Why did he have it?"

"I suppose the vigorous movement of his arms caused a subclavian steal, and then he recovered."

"That's my guess. But 1954 was almost a decade before the subclavian steal syndrome had been described. No one had ever heard of it in 1954, so of course no one diagnosed it in Toscanini."

They went in to see Mr. Wallenberg, but Richardson could learn nothing more than he already knew, except that Mr. Wallenberg didn't feel right for a few seconds before each spell. He did learn that Mr. Wallenberg's blood pressure was the same in both arms. Richardson had never seriously thought that Mr. Wallenberg had a subclavian steal, but that fact had little to do with teaching. After hearing this Toscanini story none of the students would ever forget to measure blood pressure in both arms, and that was what counted.

In the hall outside Wallenberg's room they discussed the workup for the cause of Mr. Wallenberg's attacks. If they were going to prevent him from getting a stroke, they'd have to find out what was causing his TIAs and then do something about it.

Sanders's room was just across the hall. The entire team went into his single room. Sanders's voice was a bit softer and more slurred.

"How was breakfast?" Richardson asked him.

"We ate better as interns."

"I'm not really interested in a critical evaluation of the culinary abilities of the dietary department. I want to know how your swallowing was."

"Not much different."

"Your voice seems a bit more slurred."

"I didn't sleep well."

"Why?"

"Just lonely, I guess." Even Richardson noted that Sanders was looking directly at Sue when he made his last remark. Sanders continued, "What did my spinal tap show?"

"Sue?"

"It was entirely normal."

"No cells?" Richardson asked her.

"None."

"Normal sugar?"

"Yes."

"All right, Professor, so I don't have meningitis." Sanders looked straight at Richardson. "Do you have any other ideas?"

"We're going to repeat your Tensilon test."

"You don't really think I have myasthenia, do you?"

"No, but I want to be sure."

Schilder went out to the nursing station to get the Tensilon. Richardson watched Sanders swallow and asked him to count from one to twenty. They gave Sanders the Tensilon and two minutes later watched him swallow again and count from one to twenty. There was no real difference.

"Well, Professor?"

"Your voice got a bit stronger, but that's not specific. I'd have to call that test negative."

"At least I haven't got myasthenia, but what have I got?"

"I'm not sure."

"Where do we go from here?"

"I'm not sure," Richardson paused. "I think we'll start with skull X-rays, including views of the base of the skull, and let's make sure we get an EMG."

Next they headed for the Intensive Care Unit to see Mr. Moon. Westphal turned to Richardson and asked, "Boss, what was the bit with Mr. Marfan?"

"Oh, that."

"Yeah, that."

"Nothing could be simpler. My daughter is in the fourth grade at Green Bay Road School."

"So?"

"This week they did an art project in which they made masks out of vegetable trays from the supermarket. Mr. Marfan had one on his bedside table. Ergo, he has a grandchild in the fourth grade at the Green Bay Road School. Since the initials on the mask were R.K., it had to be his daughter's child."

"But how did you know it was a girl?" Linda asked.

"Aesthetic sensitivity," Richardson replied.

As they got to the Intensive Care Unit, Richardson thought that it looked like they might go through the morning without another murder. Unfortunately, a triple page for Dr. Westphal brought his optimism to an abrupt end. "Herb?"

"Yes, sir?"

"If it's another one, don't do anything. Just watch the patient."

"That's hard to do, but okay."

"Al?"

"Yes, sir?"

"You go with Herb. We'll finish up here."

Linda presented Mr. Moon's brief but unfortunate story. Lawrence B. Moon. Age 68. Normally in good health until the morning of admission. Then he had had a massive stroke, a hemorrhage in the brain, and wasn't breathing when he was brought into the emergency room. He was now on a respirator. Richardson examined him and found no evidence of brain function. He turned to the Intensive Care Unit resident. "Mr. Moon is dead."

"His heart is still going strong."

"But his brain is dead, and death is a neurologic diagnosis. There is no purpose being served by keeping his heart going. He is dead."

This was always a difficult decision but a necessary one, and after a brief discussion they decided that any further support was useless.

Westphal and Schilder came back. Schilder looked tired and dejected.

"Another one?"

"Yes."

"Same?"

Schilder just nodded.

Richardson grabbed a phone and called Dean Willis's office. The secretary answered, "Dean Willis's office."

"This is Richardson. I want to talk to Willis," Richardson demanded.

"The dean is busy."

"Cut that crap. I want to talk to Willis *now*."

"One moment please."

Dean Willis got on the line. "Paul, what do you want?"

"Listen, we've had another one. That's five."

"Not five, six," the dean corrected him.

"Six? Who the hell makes it six?"

"Dr. Collier."

"Christ! Not Jim!" Paul hesitated for a moment. Then he added, "I hope that's enough for you to call the—"

"I've already called them. They're here now. Don't tell anyone about Collier or anyone else," Willis warned Richardson. "The police will be by to talk to you later today."

"All right."

"And remember, keep quiet."

"Damn it!" Richardson slammed down the phone.

"What's up, Boss?"

"Nothing, I . . ." Richardson looked at the clock. It was noon. "Herb, let's go back to the office. Break for lunch, everybody."

CHAPTER 4

As soon as they got back to the office Paul Richardson and Herb Westphal each took a cigar. Herb located a pack of matches in the pocket of his white coat, lit his, and offered a light to his chief. Richardson held the small cigar between his thumb and forefinger and rolled it back and forth. For what seemed like a long time Richardson said nothing; then he looked at his senior resident. "Describe everything you saw."

"When we got there the patient was in the middle of a seizure. He was awake and looking around the room, but his face was frozen. It was the same kind of seizure as the others—a series of uncontrolled spasms of the entire body. His arms and legs were extended; his back was arched."

"Had they given him anything?"

"No."

"What did you do?"

"Nothing."

"The best thing. What happened next?"

"I almost broke my neck."

"How?"

"I slipped. There was water or something on the floor next to his bed," Herb explained.

"What happened to the patient?"

"He continued to convulse and then stopped breathing and—"

"Don't tell me. Since he had terminal cancer, nobody tried to do anything dramatic."

"Not quite, but almost," Herb answered. "He had terminal Hodgkin's."

"Big difference! What else do you know about him?"

Herb took a small pack of three-by-five cards from his pocket. In a few seconds he had found the one he wanted.

"His name was Willie Prader. Early forties. Originally diagnosed as having Hodgkin's disease three or four years ago."

"What stage?"

"Stage four."

"That's not too good."

"He didn't do well either," Herb continued. "He was expected to die during this hospitalization. There wasn't much more anyone could do for him."

"Except kill him."

"These weren't mercy killings, were they?"

Richardson shrugged. "I don't know."

They sat quietly. Herb offered Paul another light and Richardson nodded. Richardson didn't say anything about Collier. He couldn't understand how Jim Collier fit in. How long had he known Jim? It must be at least eight or ten years. A good pathologist. A good teacher. He didn't have terminal cancer; he was in the hospital just to have a routine hernia repair. A mercy killer wouldn't be interested in him.

Chris brought them both some coffee and cake. "It's like the proverbial smoke-filled room in here."

"So turn on the air conditioner. Oh, and Chris, there's something I want you to do for me as soon as you can."

"What's that?"

"See if you can locate a copy of Dr. Collier's curriculum vitae and bibliography. There might be one with that grant application we sent in last December."

"I'll check."

"If it's not there, get one from his office."

Neither Herb Westphal nor his chief had anything more to say. They both sat back silently. Richardson leaned over and flicked on the radio.

WFMT was playing a Bruckner symphony—the fifth. Forgetting his perennial diet, Richardson began eating a slice of cake. How could some people recognize different conductors? Recognizing fiddle players was possible. That he could understand. They each had their own tone, their own style. But conductors? Especially today, when they moved from orchestra to orchestra. And in Bruckner, where each good idea was slowly repeated over and over again! It wasn't slow enough to be Knappertsbusch. Renee's arrival broke the mood.

"Is this a private wake or can anyone come in?"

"Come on in, Renee."

"Hi, Herb."

"Hi, Renee."

"You guys have a gas mask you can lend me?" she asked.

"I guess it is a bit thick in here, but the air conditioner is on now. That should help. Now, let's see . . . I thought we'd get together today to go over Herb's role in the alpha-bungarotoxin project."

The three of them discussed the difficulties they were having producing an animal model of myasthenia. It was decided that Herb would do muscle biopsies on all the animals and see what they showed. After that Herb left to get some lunch.

Renee asked, "Is Walt Simpson going to work in the lab again this summer?"

"Yes, why?"

"To be honest, he's not my favorite medical student."

"I know that," Richardson conceded. "But Walt's a bright guy and he certainly is interested in the work."

"Yes, but he's such a drag. He's so uptight. It's hard to work with him."

Richardson thought for a minute. Any bright, aggressive student who wanted to take charge in the lab was a threat to Renee's domain. How could he tell her that she had to put up with them without insulting her? And Walt was certainly bright and aggressive. And a staunch seeker of truth. Maybe his idea of research was a bit too idealistic for Paul Richardson. He was always sure there was a right answer, an absolute truth, a single final diagnosis, and he wanted to spend his life looking for it. A sort of twentieth-century Ponce de León. "Try to see if you can get along with him. He may just become a great researcher."

"Or kill us all in the effort. He expects us to work twenty hours a day like he does."

"He'll have his own independent project this summer, so your contact with him shouldn't be that great."

"Thank God, and if he learns to clean up after himself . . ."

"Everyone is supposed to do that."

"Not Simpson. His time is too valuable for that."

"I'll talk to him."

"There's one more thing."

"What?"

"I won't be able to start the new animals for a few days. We're out of bungarotoxin," she explained.

"When did you place the last order?"

"I ordered some just before I went to London and some more yesterday but they're very irregular in filling orders. I called them this morning, and they said we should get some by the end of the week."

"Good. You can start the new experiment next week. That will give Herb enough time to set up the biopsy procedures, and you have more than enough other work to keep you busy."

"Dr. Richardson?"

"Yes?"

"Uh . . . how is Dr. Sanders?" she asked hesitantly.

Richardson was a bit surprised that she asked but responded, "About the same."

"Thanks. See you tomorrow."

In the forty minutes before the clinic, Richardson went over his mail, reviewed the part of the manuscript Chris had typed, and wondered about Jim Collier and how he didn't fit in. Could Walt really become a great research worker? A great scientist? Could anybody he trained become a great researcher? An All Star? Or was that just a fantasy of his? Carol Voss was doing pretty well. She wasn't a star yet, but at least she had made it into the Big Leagues. He turned off the radio too early to learn that Bernard Haitink had been the conductor of the Amsterdam Concertgebouw in that performance of Bruckner's Fifth Symphony.

At one o'clock Chris buzzed him on the intercom. "There's standing room only out here."

"The Sox should only draw so well when the season opens."

"That's not all," she continued. "There are two men waiting to see you on important business."

"If they're drug salesmen, I won't see them."

"They're policemen."

"Tell them I'm busy."

"I did, and they're still waiting."

"Hell! How are we going to see all the patients?" he wondered out loud.

"Dr. Adson and Dr. Sharp are here, and if it's all right with you, they would like to see some of the patients first."

Richardson chuckled. "How long did it take you to talk them into that?"

"Not too long. Especially Dr. Sharp. She is really enthusiastic."

The two men in the office were police detectives and had just come from Dean Willis's office. Richardson immediately recognized the elder of the two policemen, Detective Thomas Ward. Richardson had helped Ward in another case in which narcotics and amphetamines were disappearing from the hospital pharmacy.

The detective spoke first. "Hi, Doc."

"Tom," the doctor replied with a nod of recognition.

"It looks like I need your help again, Doc."

"Can I ask you a question first?"

"Sure."

"When you were around here years ago for that narcotics case I assumed you were a narcotics detective. This is a homicide. Are you a homicide detective too?"

Detective Ward smiled. "I'm neither. I'm like you. I sort of specialize in peculiar cases. Ones that need special handling. So does my partner. I almost forgot. Dr. Paul Richardson, this is Detective Robert Locke."

Detective Locke and Dr. Richardson shook hands as Tom Ward explained how the system worked. Anytime a homicide detail or a narcotics detail went out on a case the reporters found out and publicity followed, often too quickly. So, for sensitive situations the city had a special detail that kept a very low profile.

"And of course you two are that detail?"

"Part of it, Doc," Ward nodded.

"Doc."

"Yes, Tom."

"We need your help. There have been six murders here, as far as we can tell. We've only been called in officially about the sixth one."

"Mr. Prader?"

"That's the one. We're supposed to investigate it as quietly as possible. Look into it as a death under mysterious circumstances. But be very diplomatic and avoid any and all publicity."

The detective worded his first question very carefully. "Doc, how sure are you that these were murders?"

"As sure as Ivory soap is pure."

"But not 100%"

"No, just ninety-nine and forty-four one-hundredths percent."

"That's what we figured. But the dean said you were't absolutely certain as to the cause of death. It might be something else. So it's not homicide and we investigate as best we can and keep our eyes and ears open and try to make sure that there are no more mysterious deaths."

"I guess that's the best approach," Richardson admitted without much enthusiasm. "If there's a minimal amount of publicity there won't be any panic. And it's better that way. But can you keep it quiet and still do something?"

"We're going to have to try. We did it last time. Hell, your pharmacy was supplying one heck of a lot of street drugs and we cleaned it up and even got some convictions and the hospital's name never even came up. This place still has powerful friends. The word is out. *No* publicity and *no* more deaths."

"What about the murderer? Aren't you guys going to try to find out who did it?"

"Our orders are to make sure there is *no* publicity and *no* more murders."

"And if you happen to catch the murderer, too . . ."

Bob Locke, who had been letting his senior partner do all the talking, broke in, "Doc, I'm not sure you understand. The lid is on. The mayor doesn't want this place to get any bad press. Hell, we're not even homicide detectives. But they think we can keep our mouths shut, and maybe, with luck, we'll find the killer. But our first job is to make sure no one else gets killed.''

Richardson shook his head. Tom Ward continued, ''It's not as bad as it sounds. Last time the same approach worked. We cut off the supply of drugs first and then got the dope peddlers. It's the same this time. We have to report our progress directly to Dean Willis, and he's got a direct line to City Hall.''

''That's a hell of a way to run a railroad.''

''That's why we need your help,'' Tom emphasized.

''Why me?''

''Two reasons. First, you and I know and trust each other. We've worked together before. You know things about this hospital we'll never know. Second, you knew they were murders before anyone else. How come?''

''What else could it have been? Four identical deaths in patients with very different medical problems.''

''Now there have been six,'' the senior detective corrected him.

''I know, and I just don't understand how Dr. Collier fits in.''

''No one fits in,'' Tom Ward responded. ''Some lunatic is probably running around the hospital killing people, and Dr. Collier just happened to have a single room.''

''So you think these are just random victims?''

''What else, Doc?'' answered Bob Locke.

''I'm not sure. But I doubt if they really are random. Look, Tom, do you really think there is a lunatic running around killing people just because they're there?''

''That's the party line. If anything gets out, that's what we're investigating.''

''But why?''

''If that gets out, it won't really be the hospital's fault.''

''Christ! What do you really believe, Tom?''

''I don't know.''

''Bob?''

''Just some crazy jackass,'' the younger detective guessed.

It was obvious to Paul Richardson that Willis was still hoping that there was no problem, that there had been no murders. But if the patients had been killed, the murders must have been done by a maniac who was killing people at random. And of course the hope was that the killer was not someone who was part of the hospital staff. It could be anybody who could get a white coat or a janitor's outfit and move around freely. But not a doctor or a nurse, just a lunatic. A raving lunatic was probably easier for the hospital to survive than the scare of a mercy killer. Mercy killers were usually nurses or other hospital employees familiar with hospitals, diseases, patients and their prognoses. But it could be a mercy killer who just made a mistake with Jim Collier. After all, if the murderer were a mercy killer he was right five times out of six. An .833 batting average wasn't that bad.

Richardson was sure they were wrong on virtually all counts, but something was missing. He tried to explain it to the two detectives. As far as he was concerned, the murderer had to be someone with a great deal of medical knowledge— enough to understand the medical histories of all the patients. The choice of victims was not random. There had to be something tying them together. There was some motive, but still he couldn't see where the Chairman of the Pathology Department fit into the pattern.

Richardson went over the cases in great detail with the two detectives and explained why he knew they were all killed with the same poison.

"What poison do you think he used?"

"Strychnine."

"Do you think somebody could get strychnine around here?"

"There is a lot around the hospital."

"Is there any missing?"

"It's hard to be sure. Strychnine is not a drug, a controlled substance, like morphine. It's made by chemical supply companies and you order it just like any other chemical. And you store it like any other chemical."

"You mean it's not kept under lock and key?" The detective looked at Richardson in disbelief.

"Of course not."

"But it can kill people!"

"Only if injected in large amounts. Hell, half the chemicals in my lab are that dangerous. You just can't keep everything locked up."

"Does every lab in this place have strychnine?"

"We're already trying to find out who has it and if any is missing."

"That's the kind of help we need. Keep us informed."

"Does everything I find out go back to Willis?"

Detective Ward thought for a minute and said nothing. Bob Locke spoke up. "Tom, you know we have to report anything we find out directly to Willis."

Richardson exclaimed, "Then I'm not sure how much I can do."

"Do what you can, Doc. And Doc . . ."

"Yes?"

"Whoever is doing this is not just crazy. He's dangerous. So take care of yourself."

"Why should I worry?"

"You blew the whistle on him."

When the detectives left, Richardson buzzed Chris. "How many patients are out there?"

"Dr. Sharp is seeing Mr. Stilling and John is seeing Mrs. Caffey. Mr. Danlos is waiting."

"That's not so bad. Call Dean Willis for me, and sometime this afternoon I want to talk to Dr. Hunt. He may know something about the fellowship applications."

A few moments later Dean Willis was on the line. "Did you meet with the police?"

"Yes, but . . ."

"I hope you told them everything they wanted to know."

"Sure, but I wish we could do more."

"Like what?"

"I don't know. Have more police here to make sure . . ."

The dean interrupted him. "We're not going to have policemen on every floor stopping everyone. You can't run a hospital that way."

"I guess not."

"And maybe your diagnosis is wrong. Maybe it's some damn infection and maybe we'll have to quarantine the place. But right now that's all we can do and that's all we are going to do. We may well have a murderer on our hands, but this is all we can do now."

"There must be . . ."

Again Richardson could not finish his sentence.

"And Professor Richardson," Willis always used titles when he was pulling rank. Richardson was thankful Willis couldn't see his grimace. ". . . stay out of it. Let the police worry about it. You have other things to worry about."

Richardson slammed the phone down. "I suppose I should just stay in the lab and play with the guinea pigs."

Linda came into the office as Richardson hung up his phone. She had finished seeing Mr. Stilling and was ready to present him.

As she went through the standard presentation, Richardson's thoughts wandered even more than usual. Hell, he must have seen Ben Stilling forty times and knew his history backwards and forwards. He looked at Linda, admired her figure, and noted that she wore no rings on her fingers. She's probably twenty-six years old. He liked the way she used her hands as she talked. It was almost as if she were trying to mold each word as she described the patient. Was that her artistic nature expressing itself or her heritage? Mr. Stilling was seventy-one years old, had had Parkinson's disease for eight years, and had been on L-dopa for four years with a good response. How did she know Toscanini? Maybe he'd underestimated her and the other students. Finally, she finished her presentation and they went to the examining room to see the patient. On the way, Richardson told her that when he had first seen Mr. Stilling in 1969 he had looked about like Mr. Romberg looked today.

Linda had a hard time believing that. Except for a little slowness and stiffness, Mr. Stilling was doing quite well and appeared to her to be almost normal. The contrast between the healthy outpatient and Mr. Romberg was striking.

"Do all your patients do this well?" she asked.

"Maybe not quite this well, but the majority of them improve a great deal with proper medication. Most parkinsonian patients take L-dopa and get better. The biggest problem is side effects."

As they entered the small examining room, Dr. Richardson and Mr. Stilling greeted each other warmly. Richardson turned to his student. "Did you ask Mr. Stilling about side effects from L-dopa?"

"He's not on L-dopa anymore," Linda corrected him.

"That's right," Richardson nodded. "Five years ago he was losing weight so we switched him to Sinemet. Do you know what Sinemet is?"

"Sure, you gave us a lecture on it."

"I know I did, but you had six lectures a day and an incredible amount to learn and remember."

"I remember Sinemet. It's part L-dopa and part carbidopa. The carbidopa makes it less likely for the L-dopa to cause nausea and vomiting."

"Excellent. Now, what did he say about side effects?"

"He reported that he gets sick to his stomach almost every morning."

"You didn't tell me that before," Dr. Richardson said.

"I suppose I didn't, Dr. Richardson. But you always seem so busy. Dr., uh . . ." Mr. Stilling stopped, a bit embarrassed. "I'm afraid I've forgotten your name."

"Sharp."

"Thank you. Dr. Sharp spent over half an hour with me, and you don't have thirty minutes to talk to me every time."

"That's true, I don't." This was one of the advantages of having the students see the patients first. And it really worked if the students were bright and interested and cared, like Linda. And she knew Toscanini. "Do you feel sick every morning?"

"Every morning, Dr. Richardson," the patient replied.

"After breakfast?"

"Yes, after breakfast."

"That could be due to the caffeine in your coffee. How many cups do you drink each morning?"

"Three or four."

"That's enough to do it."

"Would coffee without caffeine make me feel better?"

"In all probability."

"If I could get relief from that sick feeling each morning, I'd gladly give up coffee for Sanka."

"You try that, Mr. Stilling, and let me know what happens." Richardson then gave him a prescription, wrote a short note in his chart, and told him to make a follow-up appointment in three months.

Back in the hall they were joined by John and Donna. John had seen Mrs. Caffey, who was being followed by Dr. Richardson for some neurological problems related to her pernicious anemia.

"John, did you notice her earlobes?"

"Her earlobes?" John just shook his head. There seemed to be no end to the number of things he was supposed to notice and remember.

"Certainly. Patients with pernicious anemia tend to have abnormally long earlobes. You must learn to observe even the smallest details. There is a paper in the *Anthropological Journal* called 'The Surface Anatomy of the Ear.' I highly recommend it. There's a copy in the cardboard box on my desk."

Donna frowned. "Looking for an article on your desk usually takes longer than reading it."

"Dr. Batten," Richardson responded, "are you criticizing my filing system?"

"No. I'm just learning from previous observations. The last time, I was looking for a study on manganese poisoning, and I found it between a translation of Rokitansky's autopsy report on Beethoven and an article on the diagnosis of multiple sclerosis. Some filing system."

Richardson tried to ignore her remarks and asked John to present the next case. John began the standard presentation. Sixty-eight, white, female. No complaints. Short, sweet, and concise. No frills but no major omissions. Richardson liked the way John handled himself. John would never make the world forget Sir William Osler, the greatest clinician in the history of American medicine. Hell, it already had. But he'd be a good solid doctor. He began to feel a bit sorry he'd said that about the earlobes, but he knew he had to emphasize and perhaps even overemphasize observation. If you don't look, you step in it. It's as true in medicine as it is in the streets of New York.

Mrs. Caffey was doing fine. Richardson renewed her prescription for Vitamin B_{12} injections and sent her on her way.

As they were seeing Mr. Danlos for evaluation of his parkinsonism, Chris interrupted him to say that Dr. Hunt was on the phone.

"Ramsey, can you do two things for me?"

"If it doesn't involve too much work."

"Do you know anything about next year's research fellowship applications?"

"Not much. Why?"

"I wondered about Herb Westphal's application."

"They have all been decided, but the official letters won't be sent out until Sanders signs them."

"Can you send me a copy of Herb's?"

"Either that or I'll call you. What was the other thing?"

"I'm waiting for your consultation on a patient of mine."

"Who's that?"

"Mr. Romberg."

"The residents are going to present him to me tomorrow."

"Okay."

Like the patient they had just seen, but again unlike Mr. Romberg, Mr. Danlos had done quite well on L-dopa. Richardson once more stressed the difference between Mr. Romberg's failure to improve and the marked improvement shown by both Ben Stilling and Peter Danlos. The four of them then went to see Mr. Danlos. They carefully questioned him about possible side effects and decided to continue him on the same dose.

"Dr. Richardson, you forgot to ask him about one side effect."

"Which one, John?"

"Increased sexual activity."

"When that side effect was first reported, we had the largest series of parkinsonian patients on L-dopa in the country. The drug companies called and asked if any of my patients had complained of that problem. I told them that some of my patients had noted it but none of them complained."

The students both smiled. Linda perhaps a bit shyly. But only perhaps.

"Seriously, though, fewer patients returned to significantly increased sex lives than went back to work, but which one made headlines?"

"The sexual activity," John immediately responded.

"You're right. Which just goes to show what the country is really interested in."

The four of them worked their way through the afternoon. The discussion of each patient was spiced with anecdotes that Richardson hoped would stimulate the interest of the students, such as the stories of the great actress with familial tremor and George Gershwin's brain tumor.

Linda saw the last patient, a Mr. Cohn, a twenty-seven-year-old man who had increasing difficulty walking for the last three months. She presented the history and physical quite succinctly. Succinctly enough to hold Dr. Richardson's attention completely, or almost completely. The expressive movement of her thin strong hands was stiff competition.

When she finished, Richardson was pleased that she had put things together as well as she had. Especially since she was just starting on the service.

"What's your diagnosis, Dr. Sharp?"

"Spastic paraplegia."

"That's not a diagnosis. That's just a description of your physical findings. It just means his legs are weak—due to what?"

"Something wrong with his spinal cord."

"Good, but what?"

"I don't know."

"What could it be?"

"A tumor or MS."

"What should we do to find out?"

"A myelogram."

"What will that do for us?"

"Well, it will show us the spinal cord, and if he had a tumor, we should see it."

With each correct answer Richardson asked a tougher question. "How soon should we do it?"

"I don't know."

"If it were your spinal cord?"

"Right now."

"Your spinal cord is no more valuable to you than Mr. Cohn's is to him. Let's see him."

Richardson's examination confirmed Dr. Sharp's findings. He was always pleased when he could find something on a patient that other doctors missed. He was even more pleased when he could find no more than his students found. Especially if the students interpreted the findings correctly. Linda Sharp had done this.

They all agreed that Mr. Cohn should have an emergency myelogram. Richardson asked Donna if she knew who was on call that night.

"I am."

"Good."

"What's so good? I was hoping for a quiet night so I could go home and have dinner with Chet."

"He should understand."

"He should, but . . . skip it."

"Call neuroradiology and set up a myelogram, and you can do it as soon as it's set up. Then call Hugh Jackson and tell him we might have some business for him tonight. Linda and I will discuss the procedure with Mr. Cohn."

They carefully explained the problem to Mr. Cohn. He had trouble walking because his spinal cord wasn't working right. They weren't sure why it wasn't working, but there could be something pressing on it. If there was, it was important to find it and do something about it, or it could get worse. They explained the myelogram, which involved doing a spinal tap and putting some dye into his back and then taking some X-rays. They also discussed the possibility of having to do some surgery. As they finished, the neurosurgeon, Hugh Jackson, joined them. Richardson reviewed the history and findings with Jackson. The neurosurgeon agreed with the need to do the myelogram, and together they reviewed the X-ray procedure and possible surgery with Mr. Cohn. By the time Donna got back with the news that the myelogram was scheduled for 6:00 P.M., Mr. Cohn had signed a consent form for the procedure.

Donna and John took Mr. Cohn to the admission office while Jackson went back to finish some work. He would meet Donna in radiology at 6:00 to do the myelogram.

Richardson, still feeling gratified, turned to Linda. "If we save this kid's cord, you ought to go out for a drink to celebrate."

"I usually don't drink alone."

"We'll all go out."

That may not have been exactly what Linda had in mind, but Richardson didn't seem to notice.

Chris left at five as Richardson sat down to dictate some notes to referring physicians. Cohn, it turned out, had been referred from an outside emergency room by a Dr. Al Schilder. Richardson hoped Schilder had had sense enough to tell Cohn not to mention this fact to anybody else. He called Bobbie to tell her they were doing an emergency myelogram, so he'd be home late. They'd eat together later without the kids.

He hated missing dinner with the kids. He often left in the morning before they got up for the day. That wasn't too bad as long as he got home early enough to spend some time with them in the evening. They were growing up so fast. Joshua was already fourteen and an avid Sox fan. Carolyn was nine and almost as pretty as her mother. With his and Bobbie's schedules, they didn't eat together when he got home, but he usually did something with the kids. A game of chess with Joshua or one of Clue with all four of them.

He finally got a chance to look through the mail. There was a large envelope from Carol Voss in Washington. It had been mailed last Friday. She knew Paul wouldn't say no to her request. Richardson slowly shook his head and began to read her description of the new experiment. Carol Voss as a medical researcher. It was a good experiment and it was all hers. It was hard for him to remember her as she was when they first met. A third year medical student who didn't know what to do with her life. She was about to quit medical school and just, as she put it, "split." She thought she might like to try to work in his lab instead of seeing patients. Slowly over the next two years she seemed to find herself. She worked hard and learned how to handle herself in the laboratory. Why had she ever wanted him to be her lover? Wasn't it enough to be her teacher, her mentor, her confessor? That damned intensity of his. He was totally committed to anything he did and she misinterpreted it. He and Bobbie had just let their life slide by and Carol was so vital. Carol was sure no one would invest so much time and interest in her and not want to make love to her. She was right. How long had it lasted? Six, no eight weeks. Then the intensity was gone. It dragged on only until she and Walker . . . why the hell had she done it that way?

There was a knock on his door and Sue came in. "I hope you didn't forget we have a date?"

"How could I forget about you?" Richardson asked.

"It's not that hard for some people."

That was no way to build up her self-confidence. How had she let herself get so taken by some jerk?

They got into his car and drove to the Holiday Inn not too far away. Richardson told her that that was where he always took good-looking young women. She ordered a vodka gimlet, and he a bourbon and ginger ale. She seemed a bit more relaxed as they talked about possible internships. Richardson wasn't quite sure he should be there with her. He just wanted to give her a little supportive psychotherapy. They'd better talk about something safe. If she had anything she wanted to talk about, she'd get around to it. A safe topic wasn't hard to find, since Sue was just finishing her third year in medical school, and she was facing major career decisions about where to intern and what field of medicine to go into. She had decided to go into internal medicine and then someday to go out into practice and take care of sick people. She had pretty much decided to intern at a hospital where she would take calls only every fourth or fifth night and have plenty of time to read.

"That may be a mistake."

"How can you say that?"

"An internship has nothing to do with reading articles."

"But you're always telling us to read papers on the latest advances in Parkinson's disease or God knows what."

He chuckled. "I do suggest some crazy things. Today I told John to read something on the shape of the ear."

"You were kidding."

"No, I think I was serious."

"Then how can you say that it's a mistake to go someplace where we'll have plenty of time to read? That doesn't seem logical."

"You're not an intern now. You're a student. Medical school is a time for reading. An internship is not for reading. You can do that later. An internship is for one thing and one thing only, and that is learning how to think on your feet about sick people. It's about being with a sick patient, with a whole floor of sick patients at two o'clock in the morning, and one of them is vomiting blood and one can't breathe, and it's all up to you. There is nobody else there but you. That's what it's all about. The facts you learn as an intern are meaningless."

"What do you mean?"

"What pediatrics book did you read?"

"Nelson's."

"The standard textbook. One thousand four hundred thirteen pages of facts. In five more years two-thirds of the facts will have changed. You know what I like about Nelson's text?"

"No."

"It's the only honest textbook in all of medicine."

"What do you mean?"

"Look at the index."

"The index?"

"There's a single entry that summarizes so much about the futility of learning the 'facts.' "

"What's that?"

" 'Birds, for the, pages 1 through 1,413.' "

"I'm not sure I understand."

"In the long run the facts will be all wrong. They're for the birds. It's learning how to handle sick people, how to make decisions, how to understand patients and diseases that counts. If you go to someplace where you have all that time to read and contemplate, you'll have time yet for a hundred indecisions. Don't do that to yourself or your patients."

"But every third night, with so many patients."

"It's tough but it's worth it."

"I know, but it's a bit scary having all that responsibility. And sometimes I get so involved with sick patients."

"That's a mistake, Sue."

"Why, you care about your patients."

"Of course I care, but I don't get involved. The secret to survival is not getting involved. Patients don't always understand it. Nor do many doctors. Patients aren't our parents. They aren't our children. We can't be expected to love them. In fact, we shouldn't love them, or even like them as close friends. If you like someone, it might blur your judgment and you can't afford that. Obviously, I often care too much. But I try to keep my distance. A distant closeness. It's safer that way. For both the patients and me."

"Dr. Richardson." Her tone was more formal.

"Yes?"

"Can you do me a favor?"

"What?"

"Assign another student to Dr. Sanders."

"Why?"

"I still can't get over him."

"You mean that story you told me today was about . . ."

"Yes," she answered quietly. "I don't know whether I hate him or love him or both, but I do know that it's destructive and I can't deal with seeing him each day. The SOB won't leave me alone and just be a patient."

"Okay, I'll have John—"

"No, not John. Let Walt do it. He was on infectious disease with me when I was following Dr. Sanders for his pneumonia. We've already gone over the case together. He knows as much as I do about it."

"All right. Walt it is."

When Richardson got back to the hospital the myelogram had been completed. Mr. Cohn was doing fine. Jackson and Richardson went over the films with Donna and Linda. There was obviously something pushing on the spinal cord. They'd have to do surgery that night. They all discussed the surgery with the patient. Linda decided to stay and scrub in with Jackson and the neurosurgery resident. Donna went home. She hoped Chet hadn't eaten yet. Richardson headed north to the suburbs and dinner with Bobbie. The kids would still be up. They'd play a game of Clue. On second thought, maybe they'd play something else for a change.

CHAPTER 5

WEDNESDAY morning was bright and clear. Spring was almost in the air. Almost but not quite. On a day like this you could believe the baseball season would start next week. If yesterday's game was representative, the Sox were already in midseason form; they had lost 8–3. It didn't even seem worthwhile to read the box scores. For once, the news section was of greater interest. There had actually been a time when Paul read both the sports section and the news section every morning. But that was before the long night of Viet Nam. For those six years the front page closely resembled the back. Each morning the headlines would give a score much like a sports page. One might think that that would make the war at least palatable to sports fans. For Richardson, however, there were two major problems. The first was his observation that the score on the sports page at least reflected the season. If the score was over 80 it was the basketball season; below 10 made it the baseball season; in between was the football season. Body counts followed no such reliable pattern. You couldn't tell the season by the reported number of dead. Besides, the sports scores really happened. They were valid. They reflected reality. The same was not true of the Viet Nam body counts.

Bobbie had finished packing the children's lunches and sat down with her third cup of coffee and the editorial page. She saw that Paul was reading the news section. "There is only one curious thing about the hospital murder story, if that's what you're looking for.''

"I am. What was so curious about it?"

"I read through the news section twice while you were shaving and couldn't even find a story." Paul blanched at that bit of information. Bobbie continued, "That's what's curious. There is no story."

"I guess Willis got his way."

"You told me how he wanted to keep it quiet, but how did he manage it?" she asked her husband.

"He has connections in City Hall and I guess they're pretty good ones. After all, he was born and bred in 'de heart of de great sout side.' ''

Bobbie frowned. She never liked his imitation of "hizzoner de mayor." "So what? So were you."

"You grew up in Minneapolis. Growing up in Chicago was different. It's hard to appreciate that difference without having lived in it. Sure, I was brought up on the South Side, but you can't consider a Jewish neighborhood in South Shore to be 'de heart' of this city. South Shore was worlds away from Bridgeport. We had nicer homes, maybe, but they controlled the city. Hell, we even had a Republican alderman for a while."

"Paul, why do you let Willis bug you so?"

"I just can't get used to the way he does things and the reasons why he does them. He's such a fake. Do you know why he became a Sox fan in the first place?"

"No. I can't say I've investigated that major issue."

"Because Mayor Daley was. Everyone in Bridgeport was then. It was a way of life there. In South Shore we had more Cub fans than Sox fans. In Bridgeport everyone who counted rooted for the Sox, so our dean became one of the faithful."

"Is that really so bad? Becoming a White Sox fan for reasons other than true faith is not blasphemy, Paul. If Willis isn't a true sufferer like you are, what difference does it make to you? Even you admit that his clout has often helped the hospital."

"I guess so. In fact, sometimes it has helped us a lot. I never really appreciated how much influence he has. Six people get killed and he has enough clout to keep it out of the papers.''

"And off TV."

"I wish I was sure that was the best approach. We've got to find out who is doing it and why, so we can prevent more killings."

"The police are setting up security measures, aren't they?"

"That won't work. This lunatic or jackass or whatever else you want to call him has the strychnine and obviously can get around the hospital as he pleases. Of course, that's not much of a trick."

"What do you mean?"

"You've never worked in a hospital. You have no real idea how chaotic things are. Doctors going one way, transporters another way—with or without patients—students, interns, residents, janitors, visitors. We probably get more visitors a year than most major art museums. An organized form of chaos. I'm sure if you put on a white coat, you could walk into the newborn nursery and take a baby without any trouble."

"Oh, come on now. You must be exaggerating."

"It's been done, believe me. Security won't help. We're supposed to save lives. How can we do that if we don't find the killer?" They both sat silently. Paul began studying the box score of the Sox game.

After a while Bobbie began again. "It's more than just the murders, isn't it? Something else is bothering you. You tossed and turned all night."

A deep breath later, Paul answered, "I think the strychnine came from my lab."

"Are you sure?"

"Pretty much so."

"What does that mean?"

"I don't know. We don't keep it locked up, but . . ." Paul paused and stared at his empty coffee cup again.

"But you're afraid it's somebody—somebody you know."

"That's right. Maybe it's one of my kids. Somebody who goes in and out of that lab all the time. Somebody who works for me."

"None of them could do anything like that, could they?"

"I don't think so. I don't think any of them could murder

anybody, but I'm not much of a judge of character, as you well know.''

"I'm not so sure of that."

"I am."

They were interrupted by the phone. It was Paul's mother. She would be able to take care of the kids over the weekend. That meant that Bobbie could go with Paul to New York for the weekend. They'd fly out Friday evening as early as possible. Maybe have dinner at Oscar's. On Saturday Paul would give his paper in the morning and then they could go to the museums and see a show. Bobbie would see if they could get tickets for *Candide*. Even if they changed most of the numbers and left out some of the best ones and ruined the orchestration, the score was indestructible. But, Richardson wondered, did they have to leave Lillian Hellman's name off altogether?

Traffic was worse than usual. The fact that the sky was clear enough to see the Sears Tower from Lake County, thirty miles north, was no consolation. It might have encouraged medieval travelers to see the spires of Amiens from afar, but Sears Tower did little to uplift Richardson's spirits.

If the Neurology Department was typical, the fact that there had been six murders, not just one murder, was known throughout the hospital. Furthermore, the murders were the main, if not the only, topic of conversation. As Richardson listened to the various conversations that morning, he became more amazed that Willis had kept it out of the news. Twenty-one hours had gone by since the last murder, or at least it appeared that way. Maybe the increase in security was helping. Everyone had his or her own theory. Most seemed to support the police version, even though they didn't know the "official police version." It was just as easy to believe in the crazy lunatic hypothesis. The problem was that it was just a hypothesis, and in science a hypothesis has only one purpose—to be proven wrong.

Donna and Chris seemed to think it might be an epidemic of mercy killings, but almost everyone else seemed to subscribe to the theory of the random selection of victims. Except Herb, who just nodded and kept his mouth shut, and

Adam Stokes—as always, he had his own theory. This one involved a fiendishly clever but diabolical scheme that was not only logical, but, unlike all the other theories, accounted for all the victims, including Collier. Stokes conjured up a notion that the tumors in five of the six victims had been caused by some government experiment that had gone wrong, like all those sheep out west, and the CIA was getting rid of the patients to hide the evidence. This would explain the lack of news coverage and the lack of autopsies. After all, the CIA is both powerful and ubiquitous. This would not account for Dr. Collier who had no tumor. But Stokes even knew how Collier fit in. Collier was an international expert on cancer. He was the hospital's leading expert on tumor pathology. Obviously, since one of the patients managed to get away from them and have an autopsy, the CIA had to get Collier out of the way. They had to kill him before he had time to study the slides. How they got all those patients here at the exact time that Collier was going in for elective surgery, Stokes didn't know, but he figured the police could work that out. That's what they got paid for.

Richardson smiled. He hoped no one would repeat Stokes's fantasy to the police. Stokes's theories were usually best left unrepeated. The Rube Goldberg of the neurology service. But even Richardson had to admit it was the most complete theory yet proposed, because it accounted for Collier's death. He himself had no ready explanation for all six deaths.

Maybe the good were being called early to heaven and the wicked were being visited by destruction. By some modern-day Brother Juniper. Even then, Collier just didn't fit in. Unless his death hid something about the other patients.

Finally things settled down. Chris went back to the outer office and Richardson and his group began card rounds. Chris interrupted them to tell Dr. Richardson that the Committee on Human Investigation would not meet today since the only thing on the agenda was a report by Dr. Collier. Also, there would be a brief memorial service for Collier at 11:30 in the chapel.

Herb started rounds. Richardson knew Herb was disturbed; otherwise he would neve preempt the students' role. "I think we ought to do something about Mr. Moon."

"What can we do? He died."

"He's still in the ICU. They're supporting his pressure with dopamine and he's on a respirator."

"Christ. I suppose they even have his electrolytes in good order?"

"Yes."

"Those jackasses. Any change in his brain function?"

"No, of course not."

He buzzed Chris. "Get me the ICU resident who's handling Moon." About two minutes later Dr. Biedl was on the phone. "Dr. Biedl, this is Dr. Richardson."

"Yes, sir."

"About Mr. Moon . . ."

"Yes."

"He's dead, for God's sake. Pull the damned plug."

"I'm not going to play God."

Richardson sighed. "'The horror, the horror.' Confirming the fact of death isn't playing God. Keeping his body alive when his brain is dead is playing God."

"We're not hurting anybody."

"Not hurting anybody? The family is probably going through hell and that damned expensive care unit must be costing seven hundred bucks a day."

"He's got Blue Cross and Blue Shield."

"I don't care if he's got a Blue Carbuncle. He better not be on that goddamned respirator when I make rounds." Richardson slammed down the phone. "I don't really understand it. Dead is dead. And there's no way to change that fact. Can't we just let people die when they're dead? With at least a little dignity?" No one said anything until several moments later when Richardson spoke again. "Let's get started."

According to Walt Simpson, Sanders was having more trouble swallowing and his speech was now definitely slurred. Herb had gone over the skull films with the neuroradiologist, but they were absolutely normal. They debated doing an angiogram but finally decided to get a CT scan and a repeat spinal tap.

"I'm not sure why you want another spinal tap, Dr. Richardson," Sue Evans pondered aloud.

"Why not, Sue?"

"Well, the first one was normal."

"Yes, but in some types of nerve inflammation, the first spinal tap is normal and only a later spinal tap shows any changes. So we may have to do one or even two more. Walt, how is he doing otherwise?"

"His pneumonia is clearing beautifully."

Since both Tensilon tests had been negative and the muscle enzyme studies were normal, Richardson didn't even care about the EMG.

John brought them up to date on Mr. Romberg. The spinal fluid studies were back. They showed that he was taking his medicine and that it was getting into his brain, even if it didn't help him.

"Where does that leave us, John?"

"Well, we've ruled out the first three things."

"What's that?"

"Not taking his medicine, taking Vitamin B_6, and taking phenothiazines."

"So what's left?"

"A thyroid problem."

"Right. I talked to Hunt; he'll see him today."

Linda began to tell everyone about last night's surgery on Mr. Cohn when Dr. Richardson interrupted and asked her to give them a full presentation since everyone had not been around the previous afternoon.

"A complete presentation, Dr. Richardson?"

"Yes."

"Okay. Mr. Robert Cohn is a—"

"Is his first name Robert?" Richardson asked.

"Yes—"

"Is he related to the real Robert Cohn?"

"I'm not sure I know who you mean."

"Doesn't anybody know who the real Robert Cohn was?"

Only Herb and Donna knew immediately and they both just nodded almost imperceptibly.

"He was once the middleweight boxing champion of Princeton. You may not be impressed by that fact. Jake Barnes certainly wasn't." Linda's look of mild bewilderment was replaced by a smile. "And Lady Brett probably wasn't." By now a glint of recognition shone on everyone's face. "But

I was. A Jewish kid who could box. More than that, he actually hit people. Maybe he hit the wrong people, for the wrong reasons, but when he got mad he really hit somebody. He was probably the first Jew in Western literature who actually went out and hit somebody.

"Robert Cohn also wrote a novel and I have always believed that it was a better novel than Jake Barnes said it was. Just as Robert Cohn was a better fighter than Jake Barnes or Hemingway would admit."

For a few moments no one said anything. Then Walt Simpson spoke up. "You talk as if Robert Cohn was a real person."

"So?"

"But he never existed."

"What do you mean? He still exists."

"There was no Robert Cohn. Hemingway invented him."

Richardson looked at Walt and then looked out the window. He spoke softly and slowly as if he was speaking only to the window. "If you read Hemingway's *The Sun Also Rises* and Robert Cohn doesn't exist and Jake Barnes doesn't exist, then you haven't really read it." Then he turned to Walt and continued, "He must have existed. He had an affair with Ava Gardner, and if that's not existing, I don't know what is."

Linda went on with her presentation. Richardson half listened since he had heard it all before. Did people actually doubt the reality of Robert Cohn's existence? That's almost as bad as saying that Sherlock Holmes hadn't existed. Or Dr. Watson. He looked up as she began to describe the surgery.

The exploration was negative. They didn't find any tumor. They didn't find anything. The spinal cord seemed to be flattened a bit, as if something had been pressing on it. Dr. Jackson thought there might have been a fluid-filled cyst pressing on the cord, which they cut open during the operation without ever really seeing. In any case, the patient was stronger this morning.

Linda also gave a follow-up on Wallenberg. So far the workup was negative. There was a bit of additional history from his wife. From what she said, Mr. Wallenberg looked pale for a brief time before each of his attacks. It certainly sounded like the episodes could represent periods of irregular heartbeats. A monitor that would record and analyze his heartbeats for twenty-four hours was going to be used.

There were two new patients to be seen on 6 West. They would begin their rounds there. As they started to get up, Richardson turned to John Adson. "John, when you were in London did you visit St. Bartholomew's Hospital?"

"No, why? Is there anything special there?"

"Anything special! It all started right there. On New Year's Day, 1881. They have a special plaque now to commemorate it. It's in the curator's room next to the pathology lab where young Stamford introduced Watson to Holmes and Holmes said those deathless words."

John's eyes sparkled. "You have been in Afghanistan, I perceive."

"And you have been studying more than neurology, I perceive."

"I didn't know they actually put up a plaque."

"Not many people do. As far as I know it's not listed in any guidebook."

When they got to 6 West they went in to see Dr. Sanders first. His voice was weaker and more slurred. He was breathing fairly well, but he was weaker. It was obvious that nobody knew exactly what to do next. Richardson told him that they were going to do another spinal tap to see if there was any increase in protein. If the protein was up, it would suggest he had nerve inflammation, the Guillain-Barrè syndrome. As they left, Richardson's distress was apparent. "We will have to watch him closely. He may not be able to breathe on his own much longer. We may have to use a respirator."

Fortunately, he didn't hear Schilder's remark, "It couldn't happen to a nicer guy."

They gathered in the conference room and Sue Evans presented the first case. The patient was a twenty-three-year-old woman named Gail Vinson. She had been in excellent health until three months ago when she had a spell at a party. She just suddenly stopped what she was doing, stared out into space, smacked her lips several times, and then passed out.

"Did she have any warning?"

"I don't think so."

"Are you sure? Did she notice anything before the attack?"

"Yes, she did—a bad taste in her mouth."

"What's that called, Sue?"

"An aura."

"Right. Walt, what's an aura?"

"It's a warning of a seizure."

"Actually, it's the first part of the seizure and serves as a warning for the rest of the seizure. What kinds of auras are there, John?"

"There are a lot of different kinds."

"Why?"

This was the kind of dialogue Richardson loved. Asking the right questions and leading the students to the right answer. Making them show what they really understood. When the kids were good it worked, and these kids were good. "Why, John?"

"Well, the kind of aura depends on what part of the brain is involved."

"Such as?"

"Well, if the part of the brain that is related to sight is involved, the patient might see lights, and if the part related to taste is involved, the patient often has a bad taste in his mouth."

"That's right, and historically that was one of the first things that proved that different parts of the brain did different things. Irritation of one area causes sounds, so that area must have to do with hearing; irritation of another area causes visual phenomena, and another causes movements, and so forth. What was Dostoevski's aura?" Silence. "Dostoevski had seizures of an unusual nature. He described them in his letters and his novels. Many characters in his books had seizures that were really his seizures.

"There's a good article about that by Alajounine. It's in *Brain,* around 1962 or 1963, I think. Anyway, Dostoevski's aura was a very religious feeling of immense joy and eternal harmony. So intense that he could bear it only for a few seconds, but so important that he would have sacrificed ten years of his life rather than give it up.

"Dostoevski was sure that Muhammad, who had seizures,

had the same experience, that Muhammad's experience in paradise had been an attack of epilepsy. Unfortunately, our patient is more prosaic. But just think: if Dostoevski was right and Muhammad's trip to paradise was a seizure, the right doctor with a little bit of phenobarbitol could have changed the course of history. We might have control of the oil instead of the Arabs. I never had a patient with the kind of aura Dostoevski had, but I did see one woman whose entire seizure consisted of the feeling that she had just had an orgasm. Let's go on. What did the examination show, Sue?''

"Nothing. It was normal. But she is very disturbed. Somebody told her that seizures starting at this age could be due to a tumor and she's frightened."

"There could be a tumor, but that's unlikely. Let's go see her."

As they entered the room, Richardson was struck by two things. First of all, Sue hadn't mentioned how good-looking Miss Vinson was, and second, Miss Vinson was reading a book about the Hittites. She looked up from her book, and Richardson introduced himself with his usual spiel and shook hands with the patient. He suddenly stopped, looked at her other hand, glanced at the shoes resting by the bed, picked up the book and gazed briefly through it, smiled, and said, "I guess there are only a few things I'd like to know and then we can clear up everything. Am I correct in my assumption that you haven't had any more grass since that first spell?"

"I didn't tell anyone that I'd smoked that night."

"But you haven't smoked any more?"

"No."

"Don't. You are left-handed?"

"Yes."

"And no one else in your family is left-handed?"

"No one."

"Are you sure?"

"Yes, but how did you know?"

"Put your hands together. Palms together. Your right hand is smaller. The fingers are shorter and the nails are longer. Your glove size, I would guess, is seven."

"That's right."

"But a seven fits your left hand snugly and, at the same

time, is loose on your right hand despite its much longer nails. Am I correct?''

''Yes.''

''Tell me honestly now. Don't you have to buy two different shoe sizes, 8 for the left and 7 on the right, maybe even 6½?''

''I don't believe it. How could you know that?''

''Look closely. Not only is your right hand shorter than your left hand, but the nails are not as wide. There is only one explanation. Early brain injury, before the age of four. Probably at birth. If it happened then, your parents might not have known about it. That's why you are left-handed. The part of your brain controlling your right hand didn't work right, so you became left-handed, and since you are at the University of Michigan, it didn't bother your IQ, so it must have happened very early in life. Frequently such things lead to seizures beginning at about the age of twenty, and at times marijuana can bring out such seizures. So we don't have to worry about your having a brain tumor. It's just the same old injury you've had all your life.''

There was a knock at the door.

''Hi, mom.''

''Oh, I don't want to interrupt. I'll come back later.''

''No, Mrs. Vinson, come right in. We need your help. It is my feeling—no, my belief—that your daughter is left-handed because of a brain injury she sustained early in life, and that that injury is also the cause of her seizures.''

''You mean . . .''

''Yes, she doesn't have a brain tumor.''

''Are you sure? We were so worried. The other doctors said . . .''

''Yes, I'm sure. Can you answer a few questions for me?''

''If I can.''

''Tell me about her birth.''

''Labor was terrible, almost thirty hours, and she didn't breathe at first.''

''How long was she in an incubator?''

''Twelve days; then we went home.''

''Tell me about the special shoes.''

''She dragged her right leg when she was learning to walk.

We went to an orthopedic surgeon, who gave her a brace and special shoes, and it got better.''

Richardson smiled, gave each Ms. Vinson more reassurance, and then led the team into the hall. John looked a bit puzzled. ''Couldn't manual labor make one hand a little longer than the other?''

''It can't change the width of the nails. While it is true that manual labor will make one hand up to one size larger, only the muscles get bigger. There's no change in the length of the fingers. I refer you to the article 'Upon the Influence of a Trade upon the Form of the Hand.' If you are interested, it is also in the cardboard box on my desk.''

''Dr. Richardson.''

''Yes, Sue.''

''I'm sorry I didn't recognize the hemiatrophy, but I just didn't see anything.''

''On the contrary, Sue, I'm sure you saw as much as I did, but you failed to notice the correct detail, to observe the important fact. Without that you cannot draw the correct inferences and make the correct diagnosis. But that's why you're the student and I'm the professor. Don't feel bad. Hemiatrophy is one of the things even trained neurologists miss at times.''

''I can understand that about the hemiatrophy, but how did you know about the pot?'' Donna asked.

''A good guess. She was at a party. It happened early in the evening as Sue said. There probably had not been enough time for any alcohol to have an effect. You must always look for precipitating factors. So I guessed.''

''How did you know she went to the University of Michigan?'' asked Herb.

''Another time, Herb. Right now we have work to do.'' He wasn't about to tell them about the book slip for Bob Marshall's bookstore, or that she was reading the text from a course he'd taken fifteen years ago. That made it seem too elementary. No one else had seen her shoes either. They were at the side of her bed, and the right one was one size smaller.

As they stood in the hall talking, Richardson saw Renee coming out of Sanders's room. What the hell was she doing in there? John saw her too, and his response was anger—not surprise.

It was time for the memorial service for Collier, so they would have to finish rounds in the afternoon. Herb Westphal decided to skip the service and check Sanders again. The students were not expected to go, and John especially seemed anxious not to go. Neither Schilder nor Donna was interested, so Richardson ended up going by himself. Richardson would have preferred not to go. But perhaps Michael "Hinky Dink" Kenna, the most crooked of all the aldermen ever to serve on the Chicago city council, had said it best: 'If you don't go to other people's funerals they won't go to yours.' In the chapel he located an empty seat next to Carl Weigert. Dr. Weigert had been Collier's associate for at least ten years. They had worked together quite closely over most of that time, and Weigert had worked on most of Collier's research, including the studies of muscle pathology they did for Richardson. As they left the service, Richardson turned to Weigert and said, "I suppose you will be taking care of most of Jim's administrative duties?"

"Willis asked me to."

"When you get around to it, we need that report he was doing for the Committee on Human Investigation. We need to comply with federal regulations or I wouldn't press you."

"Did he complete his report?"

"Yes, he told me last week it was being typed, so if you can find a copy, send it to me."

Weigert nodded and they started off in separate directions. Linda was waiting for Richardson outside the chapel and walked him back to the neurology office. "Mr. Cohn is better."

"Thanks to you."

"I didn't do anything."

"Sure, we would have made the diagnosis without you, but you made it, and you knew what to do."

"I did, didn't I?"

They stopped at the entrance to the department. Was there something else she wanted to say? "Is there something else you wanted?"

"We saved his spinal cord, so you owe me a drink."

"We'll all go out when things get quieter."

Detectives Ward and Locke were waiting for Richardson in the office.

"Say, Tom, I think you've put on some weight over the last few years."

"Not much."

"About seven pounds, I'd guess."

"Only six."

"I would have thought seven. What brings you back so soon?"

They were there to explain the new set of complicated security measures designed so that the police would know who went where in the hospital and when they went there. Everyone was being monitored: doctors, nurses, students, visitors, janitors—even the hospital administrators. Access to each floor would be checked, and access to the building itself tightly controlled. This was designed to prevent further murders. Since it had already been more than twenty-four hours since the last murder, they felt the new measures had obviously been successful.

"And here I was hoping we'd break Dale Long's record."

"What?"

"For most consecutive days that patients were murdered in one hospital."

"What are you talking about?"

"Getting into the record books. Right there with Dale Long's record of hitting home runs in eight straight games. We could have set a new record for killing patients on consecutive days."

"You're out of your mind."

"Of course, we'd have to limit that to consecutive days on which patients were killed intentionally. The record for unintentional murders boggles the mind."

"Cut it out."

"Oh, well, you can't cry over missed opportunities. But just think, after Dale Long's records, we could have tried for DiMaggio's 56-game streak and then Lou Gehrig's consecutive game record of 2,041."

"Look, Doc, be serious.."

"I am serious."

"We may have stopped him."

"Unless," Richardson pondered, "the murderer has already done what he wanted to do and is through."

"Lunatics are never through. They're never satisfied. They're just crazy. Usually their success leads to more and more murders unless something gets in the way. We're here to get in the way," Locke explained.

"What if it is a mercy killer?" Richardson countered.

"Just the same," Locke responded. "Even if it is a mercy killer who carefully selects his victims. They keep carefully selecting them and killing them until they get caught or someone stops them."

The senior detective terminated the younger partner's explanation. "Dr. Richardson?"

"Yes, Tom."

"Did you find out about the strychnine?"

"Not yet. But I should know by late this afternoon or tomorrow morning. Stop by then. I may have a movie for you to see."

"A movie?"

"Yes, of strychnine poisoning. Not in a patient. In guinea pigs. Then you'll know what we're dealing with. And one more thing, Tom."

"Yeah?"

"I've been wondering why strychnine. Why is the killer using strychnine?"

"It's a poison."

"Sure, but we've got better ones around the place. Narcotics which cause you to stop breathing in seconds. Curare-like drugs which paralyze your muscles in less than a minute. Potassium. Inject it through an IV and it stops your heart in a few seconds. That's what George C. Scott was going to use to kill himself in *Hospital*. So, why strychnine?" Richardson asked the detective.

"Not everybody knows about all of the other things but everybody knows about strychnine."

Dr. Richardson nodded his agreement. "I guess so." The physician did not seem convinced. "Maybe I was wrong. Maybe whoever did this is not very sophisticated medically."

"Maybe he just wanted to see the seizures. Like an arsonist likes to watch fires," Bob Locke suggested.

"I doubt that," Richardson responded. "Nobody really saw all the seizures." Except Herb, he thought to himself. "And, as far as I know, nobody watched them start." Richardson looked at his watch. "Look, I'm already late for lunch. I can tell you one more thing, the fact that things have stopped around here rules out an epidemic. You guys may get in the way of lunatics but you won't have much effect on bacteria."

"That's the way we figured it," Ward concurred. "We're after a killer and as you point out, most likely someone who's not too smart about medicine and drugs."

Richardson nodded his head slowly in agreement. Or, he thought to himself, somebody who wants us to think the killer doesn't know much about medicine.

CHAPTER 6

ALTHOUGH you couldn't tell by looking at him, Richardson rarely ate lunch. Usually coffee and a couple of cookies carried him through the day. Once in a while Chris would pick up a sandwich from the cafeteria for him. But at least once every two weeks he and Donna Batten went out for lunch together. As he was planning to leave the office, Chris motioned to him and placed the phone on hold. "It's Dr. Voss on long distance."

"Not again. Did she say what she wanted?"

"No. She called to talk to you, not to me."

"Tell her I'll return her call later."

That was all he needed today. He waited for a few minutes in the first floor lobby and then walked out to the parking lot. It was still bright and clear. You could see downtown without any difficulty. He reached into his pocket, found a small cigar and some matches, and began to smoke. It was better to think about something other than Dr. Voss. Something other than the six murders. Something. Anything. Donna. As always, that made him smile a bit to himself. The image of that day in his office over two years ago was as clear as if it were just yesterday. But too many of his memories were that clear. She had been a senior student then and had spent two months on Neurology, and then another two months. During the last two months she was the only student on the service and they had worked quite closely together. The last two weeks had been during the annual meeting of the American Academy of

Neurology, and it had been just the two of them against the world. It started late one day after making rounds together all day—a day during which she broke Carol Voss's record for most passes received during a single day (twenty-two—thirteen from interns, six from residents, one from a student, and two from patients). Unlike Carol, she was bothered by the constant sexual interest that she provoked. Not enough to change her behavior, to become less provocative, but nonetheless bothered.

Richardson remembered the time when Donna had stood half in his office, half in the doorway. She was as far away as she could be from his desk and yet still be in the office.

"Dr. Richardson, can I ask you a question?"

"Sure."

"It's sort of personal."

"Go ahead."

"Why do so many women come here to work with you?"

"I'm not sure."

"You must have some idea."

"It can't be my resemblance to Paul Newman."

"You don't look like Paul Newman."

"That's why it can't be."

"There have been rumors in the past as to . . . some things between you and . . ." Donna paused.

"That's not why you came and why you stayed."

"No, it isn't. Not at all."

"Why did you stay an extra two months?"

"Because you're the first man in the medical school here who took an interest in me who didn't try to go to bed with me."

"That's the reason." He paused and then added, "I'm safe."

"It's not just that. You care about the people who work for you. You get involved in our lives. You help us."

"And I'm safe."

She was right in a way. He wasn't trying to have an affair with her. That didn't mean he didn't want to. He just wasn't trying. Robert Morley doesn't try to have an affair with Dianna Rigg. So he was safe for her. It was also safe for him. And they both benefited from it.

Donna tapped him on the shoulder. "I'm here."

"Gorgeous as ever," he commented. She smiled. To him it was a Pepsodent smile and always would be. "Where shall we go?"

"I don't care."

"Let's head for Greek town."

He let her in the car and walked around to the driver's seat. He knew that there were rumors around the medical center about Donna Batten and him, but as long as Bobbie didn't hear them or didn't believe them, that was no problem. In fact, the very existence of the rumors boosted his ego. The last time there had been rumors, Bobbie had heard them from Sanders. From Sanders, of all people.

They went to the Greek Islands and ordered Greek salads, saganaki, and gyros. The afternoon's patients would have to put up with the onions. As they drank their first glass of retsina Richardson drew a deep breath and started, "Carol called today."

"What did she want?"

"She sent me a new research protocol she needed some help on."

"And, of course, you're going to help her."

"I guess so."

"Why?"

"She's a friend of mine."

"Some friend—she leaves you high and dry and goes off with a friend of yours."

"You know the part that bothers me most? Aside from my total lack of judgment?"

"No."

"It's not that she ran off with Dan Walker, Professor Dan D. Walker. What the hell—she's single and he always acted as if he were single. I couldn't blame her even if she did leave the project in the middle. That's not what bothers me." He hesitated.

"Are you sure?"

"Yes. Things between us were all over by then. I'd told Bobbie, and she and I were working things out. Thank God we did. Carol was aggravated and unhappy. So she split."

"Then what does bother you? That she went with a friend

of yours? Did he know that you were depending on her to finish that work before she left?''

"Dan? Sure he knew that. But, hell, he has no scruples. That's not it. It's one thing to dump me and my laboratory, such as it is. That's not the problem. You know the research that Carol was working on for me?''

"Yes."

"She gave all the original slides and even the lab notebooks to Dan. I had to make copies of the slides from their articles after they were published." He hesitated, then continued, "Twice, at international meetings, Dan has spoken before me and shown my slides.''

"What did you do?"

"Nothing.''

"Didn't you say anything?"

"No, how could I? What else could I do?''

"Didn't you say anything to Dan?''

"No.''

"Why?''

"He's a friend of mine. I'm sure he thinks I gave her the slides to give to him.''

"Why does that hurt so much?''

"As Mark Twain said, 'A woman is only a woman, but a good slide is two years' work.' ''

"Paul, come on.''

"I thought I knew her and could rely on her. After all I'd done for her. So our affair didn't work out. It was a mistake. I still looked on her as my prize student. I didn't expect her to work here forever. I'd encouraged her to take her residency outside of Chicago. I didn't expect a life commitment from her. Just a little loyalty—if not to me, to my ideas, my work.''

"Paul, you're so naive sometimes.''

"Bobbie says that, too.''

"Once you and Carol were lovers, there was no going back. You should have known that.''

Richardson decided to change the subject. "There are rumors about you and Sanders.''

"I know.''

"Are . . . ahem . . . I shouldn't ask.''

"You want to know if they're true?"

"I don't have any right to ask."

"You do in a way. We've always been completely honest with each other."

"Yes, that's true. You probably know more about me than anyone except Bobbie. But that doesn't mean you have to tell me everything."

"There's nothing to tell. Sanders has been persistent and a bit pushy. But I can handle him. It's the rumors I can't handle."

"How so?"

"Chet has learned to accept you."

"He probably can't conceive of your going to bed with me."

"But Sanders would be another story."

"He's a lot closer to Paul Newman, with a bit too much grease on his hair. Has Chet heard the rumors?"

"I think so. Things have been a bit strained at home."

"So that's why you didn't want to stay and do that myelogram. Who started the rumor?"

"Probably Sanders himself. He's good at that."

"How well do I know. If it hadn't been for him, Bobbie would never have . . . oh, well."

They were both quiet for a while. There were always so many rumors around the hospital. They were halfway through the gyros when Richardson again changed the subject. "What do you know about Jim Collier?"

"He wasn't very nice."

"What do you mean?"

"He was head of the promotion committee and never gave anybody a break. Ask Linda. She took endocrine as an elective and couldn't get along with Sanders."

"I won't ask why."

"I don't really know what happened. But in the end she didn't get credit for it and had to give up her summer vacation and take an extra clerkship. She had to borrow another $2,000, and they still put it on her record as an incomplete and Collier told her that it would affect her letters of recommendation for internships."

"I always knew he was a bit pompous. I figured that was

standard for a pathologist. They all think they know more than anybody else. It's easy to know what's wrong with a dead body. It's not so easy when the body is still alive. Did anyone else have trouble with him?''

''Probably half the students in the place.''

''Anybody else from Neurology?''

''Herb.''

''What kind?''

''You'd better ask Herb.''

''I may just do that.''

It was getting late, so they skipped coffee and headed back for the medical center.

On the way back to the office he stopped at the lab. Renee wasn't there, so he left her a note reminding her to get the movies and bring them to his office by 4:00. When he got back to the office Chris told him that everyone was waiting for him on 6 West. He put on his white coat and headed upstairs.

Walt presented the new patient, Mrs. John Robin. Mrs. Robin was only thirty-one years old, but she had been sick for many years. At age twenty-six she was discovered to have kidney failure, and two years later she received a kidney transplant.

''From whom, Walt?''

''What do you mean?''

''Did she get it from a twin?''

''No, not from a relative. The kidney was from a patient who died; his relatives donated the kidney.''

''A cadaver kidney. So she must have been on lots of drugs so she wouldn't reject the kidney.''

''Right. She's been on steroids and Cytoxan for three years.''

''Go on.''

''The present problem is that for the last two weeks she's had progressive weakness of her right leg.''

''That poor lady.''

Richardson's examination of Mrs. Robin confirmed the right-sided weakness. He learned nothing more from talking to her. In the conference room they discussed the possible diagnoses. Richardson stood at the blackboard and turned to Sue. "You watched me examine Mrs. Robin."

Sue nodded.

"What did I find?"

"Weakness of her right side," she answered.

"Involving what?"

"Her arm and leg."

"Was that all?"

"No, also her face, I think."

"Walt, what does that mean?"

"Whatever is going on must be above her spinal cord."

"Why is that, Linda? You're our expert on spinal cord tumors."

Linda flushed a bit. "The nerves to the face are above the spinal cord."

"Right. So, whatever is going on involves the brain itself. Where in the brain, John?"

"The left side."

"Right. The left half of the brain controls the right side of the body. If the lesion is on the left side of the brain, what else might be affected?" Richardson looked around. "Sue?"

"I'm not sure."

"John?"

"Her speech."

"That's right. The left half of the brain almost always controls speech. But she has no speech difficulty. Why not? Donna?"

"The lesion must be small and selective."

"Or?"

"It's too early. Her weakness is just mild. As things progress it might become involved."

"So what's going on, Walt?"

"A stroke."

"You don't think Mrs. Robin had a stroke, do you?"

"No, I guess not."

"Why not?"

"Strokes usually happen very quickly and she's getting slowly worse," Walt answered.

"What gets slowly worse, Linda?"

"Tumors."

Richardson wrote on the board.

1. BRAIN TUMOR

"What else, Al?"

"A hematoma."

"A blood clot. Where, Al?"

"Outside the brain. Pressing on the brain."

2. SUBDURAL HEMATOMA

"Anything else, Sue?"

"A brain abscess."

3. INFECTION—BRAIN ABSCESS

"Any other suggestions? John?"

"Why not MS?"

"She's got enough other problems without giving her MS, but you're right; she could have MS."

4. MS

Richardson stood back and looked at the list.

1. BRAIN TUMOR
2. SUBDURAL HEMATOMA
3. INFECTION—BRAIN ABSCESS
4.MS

"I guess that covers the potentially treatable problems. How should we start, Walt?"

"Get a CT scan and maybe even an angiogram and look right at the brain."

"Let's start at the beginning, not at the end. We'll get a brain wave test and some X-rays of her skull, and then we'll see what else we have to do."

"Boss," Herb asked as they left the conference room, "why did you say 'poor lady'?"

''We're not going to be able to help her. We'll try, but I don't think we'll help her.''

''Why?''

''She had a wart on her lip.''

''A wart?''

''Yes, a wart.''

''I'm not sure I know what you're getting at.''

''I'll bet she has progressive multifocal leukoencephalopathy.''

''I hope you're wrong.''

''So do I, Herb.''

When he got back to the office, Chris was out looking up some articles in the library, but there were two things waiting for him on his desk. A copy of Collier's curriculum vitae and a note that Renee would be up with the movie. That gave him forty minutes. He sat down, rummaged around for a big cigar, lit it, and began to read. The curriculum vitae was not up to date. Some vital statistics were missing.

Birth Date: September 1, 1925

Place of Birth: Cleveland, Ohio

Education: Western Reserve University, Western Reserve Medical School

Residency: Massachusetts General Hospital

There was no space for date of death and none for cause of death. What the hell was the cause of death? A psychopath? A mercy killer who made a mistake? The CIA? A crazy son of a bitch? Richardson had always been bothered by filling in death certificates. Cause of death. Do we ever really know The Cause? No, probably not. Why not just say ''cause of death—the brain stopped,'' and list other things under contributing causes?

What he really wanted to review was the rest of Collier's CV, not the bare essentials. Christ, Collier must have been a member of every national and international cancer society there was. He'd been on the editorial board of *Cancer*. The list of publications was impressive. He scanned it once and then looked carefully. He found an article on Hodgkin's disease. That's what Mr. Prader had had. And breast cancer, that's what Mrs. Schiff had had, as well as carcinoma of the bladder. What did Erb have? Cancer of the colon? That's right. Collier had studied that and even the type of brain tumor Mitchell had. He'd written so many articles—was that just a coincidence? Five coincidences? Or the CIA? Stokes couldn't be right, could he? There was a knock on the door, and Herb Westphal let himself in.

"Did you find out if anybody else has strychnine?"

"Nobody except us, Physiology, and Pharmacology."

"Did Renee find out anything?"

"Both Physiology and Pharmacology have all their strychnine. Physiology keeps it under lock and key, and the Pharm department has only one unopened bottle, which is at least seven years old and probably isn't any good anymore."

"And ours is gone. Shit. Tell me, Herb, who has access to our lab?"

"The residents, the students."

'Other than the people in the department."

"Everybody."

"What do you mean?"

"Renee loves visitors. You know that. She gossips all day long, off and on. People are always walking in and out. And last quarter, when Donna was doing some work in the lab, it was like State and Madison."

Richardson frowned.

"You ought to get into the lab once in a while, Boss," Herb admonished him. "You have no idea how busy a place it is."

"Thank God it's that busy."

"Why?"

"If that many people go in and out, anybody could have taken the strychnine."

"Would just anybody know how large a dose to give?"

"Maybe, maybe not. But it couldn't be somebody from Neurology. It just couldn't."

Paul picked up the phone and called Chris, who had just returned from the library. He asked her to call the lab and ask Renee to come down and bring the film with her. He also asked Chris to see if she could locate Ward and Locke and ask them to stop by around 4:30 or 5:00. While they waited for Renee, Herb and Paul talked a bit about the murders, but they got nowhere. Collier just didn't fit into any logical scheme. Renee got there a bit out of breath. Richardson asked her about people coming and going in the lab. She confirmed the popularity of the lab and the fact that lots of people file in and out, from Dean Willis on down.

"Dean Willis?" Richardson seemed genuinely surprised.

"Yes. He likes to show off the guinea pigs to important visitors."

"Why?"

"Jumping guinea pigs are easier to look at than ones with cancer."

Richardson chuckled. "Say, maybe that's why he's trying to keep things hushed up."

"Dr. Richardson, you don't think . . ."

"No, I was just hoping. Let's see how the movies came out."

Herb put the film in the projector. The three of them sat and watched in silence as the guinea pigs twitched, then convulsed, then flipped over and died. One after another, despite Valium and phenobarbital. They died one after another, twelve in all. They had killed twelve guinea pigs. The killer had six to go to catch up.

As the film ended, Chris buzzed Richardson to tell him that Ward and Locke would be up in fifteen minutes. Richardson asked Renee to leave but asked Herb to stay. While waiting there didn't seem to be much to say. Herb rewound the film and then looked up progressive multifocal leukoencephalopathy in Vinken and Bruyn's *Handbook of Clinical Neurology*. He couldn't find anything at all about warts. As soon as the two detectives arrived, Herb started the projector.

"Pretend this is a person. Not a guinea pig, but a real live person. The first thing that happens is he begins to twitch. His face becomes frozen. But he's awake. He's alert. He can see and hear. He knows what's happening. He can't control his muscles. Now his arms and legs extend painfully. He can't breathe . . . and, so it goes." Six times they watched this. Then Richardson stopped the camera and turned on the lights.

"Is that what happened?" Tom asked, while Locke kept repeating, "Crazy asshole, crazy bastard."

"That's what happened."

Tom Ward was astounded by what he'd just witnessed. "I've never seen anything like that."

"That's why we have to catch the bastard."

"We're trying. With our new security arrangements in place, it looks like things have quieted down. We may have stopped him. Now we can put more effort into catching him."

Locke was not sure they should talk in front of Herb Westphal, and only after hesitating, he asked Richardson, "Did you find out anything about the strychnine?"

Herb Westphal started to answer but Paul Richardson cut him off. "No, not yet, but we're working on it. So far nobody is missing any strychnine."

Locke nodded.

"If I'm going to try to give you an insider's view of this," Richardson continued, "I'm going to need help. I'm going to work with my two residents, Herb here and Adam Stokes."

"If they're okay with you, they're okay with me. How about you, Bob?"

"I guess so."

"The first thing we're going to do is review all the charts of the dead patients and maybe even talk to their relatives."

"That may be tricky, Doc."

"A resident can probably do it on the basis that he needs more history for some research or something."

"But how will that help?" Locke asked.

"Maybe they're tied together in some way."

"Like what?"

"I don't know. 'The good called early to heaven.' 'The wicked visited by destruction.' Who knows? But we'll find out what we can. And at the same time we'll try to find out who could have gotten hold of strychnine and given it to the patients."

The four of them said good night. It was 5:30 and Chris had already left. Ward and Locke left, but Herb stayed behind. "Why did you lie to them about the strychnine?"

"I don't want them bothering us. If they knew it came from our lab, and told Willis, we'd have nothing but aggravation."

"Then why the movies?"

"It obviously impressed them."

"Yes."

"Hopefully enough to get them to bug the higher-ups to do more to solve this goddamned business. We're here to save lives, but not by helping them to investigate crimes. That's their business."

"That's crazy, Boss. You want the cops to do more, but you're lying to them. Either shit or get off the pot."

"I'll tell them about the strychnine tomorrow, but first you find out where everybody from this department was when these people got it."

"You don't really think . . ."

"No, but I want to be able to know, not just think. So ask around."

"I feel like Archie Goodwin."

"And I look like Nero Wolfe—get out of here."

Before he left, Richardson called Bobbie to say he was on his way home. She had gotten tickets to *Candide*. Nuts, he hadn't even looked at the manuscript of the paper he was going to present on Saturday.

CHAPTER 7

RICHARDSON stood by the toaster, looking into the back-yard. The fog was so dense that he couldn't even make out the swing set. Even worse, the fog was gray and not yellow. The fog should be yellow. Watson wrote about the fog being yellow. It was yellow in Prufrock, too, and in Gary. But Gary was getting cleaner. You could see it now. You could actually see the buildings. Not just a dirty orange cloud. Of course, considering the architecture, maybe the orange cloud wasn't so bad after all.

"You won't have to read the front section."

"What's that, dear? I wasn't listening."

"I know. I said you won't have to read the front section of the paper."

"Why not?"

"There's no mention of the murders. The only mention of the hospital is the spring fashion show."

"Groan."

Bobbie smiled. Paul's muffin was done. As he got it out of the toaster oven and began to butter it, Bobbie asked, "Do you think they'll be able to keep the newspapers out of it completely?"

"Probably; especially if there are no more murders. Nothing is deader than yesterday's corpse."

Bobbie poured more coffee for both of them, ignoring the last remark, while Paul read the sports section. The Sox had won handily four to zip. Maybe things were looking up. Maybe he'd go to the opening game.

"I made our plane reservations."

"What flight?"

"The 5:00 on United."

"I'll meet you at the airport."

"Please get there this time."

"I will. That only happened once."

"Once is enough."

The sun was just beginning to burn off the nonyellow fog when Richardson arrived at the hospital an hour later. Chris was not around yet, so he started the coffee, got the page operator on the phone, and had her page Dr. Stokes to come to the office as soon as he got in. As the coffee brewed he went back into his office.

As always, Richardson's office was balanced between chaos and order. It was located at the very end of the oldest building of the hospital. The elevated train tracks were just below his window. The trains themselves were too high up to be seen, but they could be heard and at times felt, despite the brick masonry and the many layers of paint. He really didn't mind the rumble of the "L" as the train flashed by; it often triggered his memory. Going to Sox games. Going downtown. The Loop. The old building had some advantages, too. Richardson liked the fourteen-foot ceilings. He could have his office lined with bookcases and still have room for his pictures. There were books everywhere, but with no real order. The *History of Medieval Cities* by Pireene was lodged between two volumes of neuropathology. Ring Lardner, well worn, was among a group of almost unread neuroradiology books. Bertolt Brecht and T. S. Eliot were there. Both seemed out of place among the treatises like *Therapeutics in Neurology*, *Animal Models of Human Neurologic Diseases*, and *Genetic Disorders Among the Jewish People*. Hopkins's *The Discovery of Dura-Europos* separated volumes 3 and 4 of *Clinical Pharmacology*. What really contributed to the chaos were the piles of papers, reprints in covers sent by authors, pages torn from journals and paper-clipped together, photocopies—especially photocopies. The articles seemed to appear by spontaneous regeneration. Chris doubted if he ever read them all. They collected everywhere. They formed piles on every available surface and stacks in corners. Each had a number on it referring to where it should go in his files if he or Chris ever got around to filing them. On his credenza was a large wooden card file, a present from Bobbie, intended to get him to organize his files and move them from the living room to his office. She had been partly successful. At least the reprints were all at the office now. The card file was planned to contain a cross-reference file of all the reprints and papers filed by author and subject. Someday he was going to hire someone just to put the files in order. But first he wanted to be sure that everything was numbered correctly and that he had the file system he really wanted. At the moment it contained some slides, an extra hammer, three chess pieces, and several tin cigar boxes, all empty. Other tin boxes and chess pieces were scattered throughout the room, crowning many stacks of papers.

Five years earlier he had bought the entire chess set at the British Museum. The pieces were copies of a set dating back to the twelfth century and found on the Isle of Lewis. He had carefully set up the chess board and pieces in one corner of his office and started a chess game by mail with Dr. George Bruyn from Amsterdam. As pieces were removed from the board they were put to use holding down piles of papers. The game itself had long been forgotten. George was sure Richardson would have had to resign in six more moves anyway. The board was lost under a pile of reprints.

His desk was in one corner. Behind and to the side of it was a large bulletin board. It was divided into three parts: Answer Immediately; Answer Soon; Answer Someday.

Letters, memos, telephone messages, and scribbled notations were stuck on by tacks, pins—everything but a jackknife. Chris was tempted each week to move the "Answer Immediately" letters to "Answer Someday" and see if Richardson would notice. Richardson always wanted to add a section entitled "Ignore as Soon as Possible." This would be reserved for such things as official memos on the propriety of wearing ties while seeing patients and "Helpful Hints on How to Teach Medical Students."

If the desk and bookcases were chaotic, the walls were an interior decorator's nightmare. There were original prints everywhere. Across from him were two Jacques Villon etchings with a small envelope stuck in the corner of one. If Chris wanted Paul Richardson to see a message and do something about it, she put it there. By now she had done that so often that Richardson no longer paid any attention to such things. The letter had been there for months. Other etchings and lithographs were grouped throughout the room: a Toulouse-Lautrec of Yvette Giubert; a colored Vlaminck, catching the loneliness of a storm in northern France; three Hiroshige woodblocks; a pale Giacometti of the artist's studio; several small etchings by Johnny Friedlaender; a Léger serigraph; a small Camille Pissarro; a Ben Shahn; and a Richard Florsheim lithograph of oil derricks.

He was smoking his second small Schimmelpenninck when Adam Stokes came by. "You paged?"

"Yes. How busy are you on EMG?"

"Not busy at all. I'm catching up on my reading."

"Good. I want you to do something for me this morning."

"What?"

"Get the charts of the five patients who were killed."

"Just the five patients?"

"Huh?"

"Not Dr. Collier?"

Richardson thought for a moment. Maybe all six were tied together. "No, get all six and go over them with a fine-toothed comb. See if anything relates those people to each other."

"Any special thing I should look for?"

"If I knew what we were looking for, we wouldn't have to look. All I want is something to go on. An idea, an indication. No more. But something, anything. You may have to get in touch with the families. But not yet. Just get the charts. Not only of this admission, but all the records."

"Where do I get them?"

"Detective Ward has them. He knows you're going to review them with me. When Chris gets here she'll get them for you. And two more things."

"Yes?"

"Do it today. We'll go over the charts later this afternoon. And—this is most important—do it by yourself. Don't tell anyone else what you're doing."

"Nobody else?"

"Nobody."

"Not even—"

"Not even!"

Chris came in complete with a fresh coffee cake. She cut a piece for Stokes and a small slice for Richardson, and then she and Stokes went to the outer office to get in touch with Ward.

One small cigar later, Richardson was shuffling through the cardboard box on the corner of his desk, looking for his copy of an article from *The Journal of the American Medical Association* on "Transient Global Amnesia." It should have been there. But all he could find were three copies of "On the Polyphonic Motets of Lassus." He couldn't even remember why he had had Chris make the copies for him. It had seemed like a good idea at the time. As he continued to look, Renee came in. He greeted her with his usual, "What's new?"

"Not much."

"Anything wrong in the lab?"

"No, we're getting started. No real problems."

"Well, what brings you by this morning?"

"I, uh, need a favor."

"Anything special?"

"No, I, uh, just want to, uh, take tomorrow off."

"That's not an overwhelming request. If there's no work that has to be done, I don't see any reason why not."

"There's nothing in the lab I have to do tomorrow. We're going to start most of the big experiments next week."

"So take off."

"Thanks." She seemed quite relieved.

"Can I ask why it's so important to you?"

"How did you know it was so—"

"You rarely hem and haw. In fact, sometimes you've just told me that you were taking off. But usually with more notice."

"John is going to Los Angeles."

"Why?"

"He's going to intern there, and he's going out for the weekend and I, uh, I . . . we're going to look for an apartment."

Richardson smiled. "It looks like I'm going to have to find a new technician in a few months."

"I hope so."

Richardson was tempted to ask why she went to see Sanders, but it didn't seem to be the right time. "What do you know about Dr. Collier?" he asked her.

"He was a bastard!"

"Ms. Weber!"

"I can't help it. He was. He never gave anybody a break. The students all hated him. Ask Linda, or Herb—or John. Ask anybody. He was a real SOB."

"I thought Sanders had a copyright on being a bastard."

"They're both the same."

"Not exactly. Collier was never the playboy of the Western world. Or was he?"

"No. Not that I've heard."

"If you haven't heard any gossip, then there isn't any. Well, back to work. You're not being paid to gossip."

The students began to file in. Sue was the first to arrive, and she turned on the ventilator to get rid of some of the smoke. Richardson buzzed Chris and asked her if she had gotten a copy of Dr. Collier's report.

"No, how could he send it out?"

"I asked Dr. Weigert to send it to me."

"Are you sure the report was completed?"

"Pretty sure. We'll need it by next week."

"I'll call."

"No. Things are probably all screwed up there. Let's do it the right way. Send them a memo."

"A memo?"

"Sure, it's official business. Send a memo from the Committee on Human Investigation requesting the report. Send it straight to the secretary, so we won't have to bother Dr. Weigert. He's got more than enough to do catching up on Collier's other administrative work."

"Okay."

"If I see Weigert before we get it, I'll ask him again."

Sitting at his desk, he found a letter from Cleveland dated February 13. He'd never seen it. It was still unopened. He found his letter opener and slit it open. It was a letter of inquiry asking him if he would be interested in the position of head of the department in Cleveland. Only if they moved the university to Chicago. But he'd have to be a bit more polite in his response. He tacked the letter on the board. It ended up in the "Answer Soon" section.

Everyone had collected. It was time to start card rounds. Over coffee and coffee cake they brought Richardson up to date on all the patients.

Linda had gone over Mr. Cohn in great detail and felt that he was definitely getting stronger. The surgery was a success. They didn't know what his disease was, but he was getting better. You can't argue with success.

Mr. Romberg was no better. They knew what was wrong with him. He had Parkinson's and yet they couldn't help him. Or did they really know? Did he really have Parkinson's disease?

"Has Ramsey Hunt seen him yet, John?"

"Yes. Dr. Hunt thinks that Mr. Romberg is taking enough thyroid. But to be sure, he ordered some thyroid tests. They're being done."

Richardson listened to the "L" and then asked, "Did we get his electrolytes?"

"Yes."

"And . . ."

"They're all normal."

"Including the calcium?"

"The calcium was low normal, sort of borderline."

"Repeat the calcium."

"Okay."

"And get a skull X-ray."

"A skull X-ray?"

"Yes."

"Can I ask why?"

"To keep me happy."

"I thought skull X-rays were always normal in Parkinson's disease."

"They are."

"Then why get skull X-rays?"

"To see if they're normal."

John was a bit puzzled. Even Herb had a hard time following the logic.

"Walt, how's Sanders?"

"A bit weaker—especially his swallowing. He's on a diet of liquids only."

"If it gets worse," Herb interrupted, "we may have to take him off all liquids, too. His swallowing is terrible."

"How's his breathing?"

"Not bad. Not good, but not too bad. He certainly doesn't need a respirator."

"Yet," murmured Richardson. "Are his arms and legs weak, Walt?"

"Definitely."

"His eyes?"

"No."

"Good."

"Good?"

"Yes, good. Myasthenia would involve the eyes. Since his eyes aren't affected, it's not myasthenia. We don't have to worry that we blew the diagnosis. What's back on his workup?"

"The brain scan was normal. So was the lumbar puncture."

"Normal protein?"

"Yes."

"Shit! What the hell is wrong with him? Everything is normal and he's going to hell right before our eyes. We may have to repeat the LP."

Mr. Wallenberg was doing well. He had had no new episodes. He was on his monitor.

Mrs. Robin was not doing well. She was weaker. The brain scan was to be done today. Her skull X-rays were normal.

The Moon family had been spared the expense of another day in the ICU.

Ms. Vinson was going home.

"Did we ever get skull X-rays?"

"Yes."

"And?"

"Radiology said they were normal."

"Did you look at them, Herb?"

"Yes. You were right. They show the atrophy of the left half of the brain. Just like you predicted."

"Is she on her anticonvulsants?" the chief asked.

"Yes. She'll be in to see you in six weeks when her semester is over."

There was one new patient to be seen on 6 West. She had been worked up last night by Al Schilder. There was another consult, but the patient hadn't been seen yet and would have to be seen in the afternoon. Once they got back into the routine of teaching and taking care of patients it was easy for Richardson to forget about the six murders, to ignore those six deaths and deal with live patients.

As he led them out past the EMG lab, Paul Richardson noticed a small boy, perhaps three or four years old, waddling in the hall, holding his mother's hand. Richardson stopped and signaled to the group to stop and watch. At the other end of the hall the boy dressed in a hospital gown and his mother paced very slowly back and forth.

"What do you see, Walt? Describe everything as well as you can."

"He's walking funny. Kind of waddling."

"Very good. What else?"

"He's kind of short."

"What do you mean?"

"Well, I'd expect him to be taller."

"Taller?"

"Uh, he's so chunky."

"His arms aren't."

"I guess not. But his legs are."

"Excellent. He has very thick legs and he waddles. Are his thick legs strong or weak?"

"I'd guess they're weak."

"Why?"

"Because of the way he walks."

"Okay. Anything else?"

"His posture is funny."

"Funny? That is not an acceptable descriptive term. Try again."

"His back goes in and his stomach is pushed out too far."

"Very good—lumbar lordosis is the phrase you were looking for. Let me summarize the major diagnostic features for you," Richardson continued. "A young boy with weak thick legs and lumbar lordosis. Linda, give me the diagnosis."

"Muscular dystrophy."

"Right. What type?" A resident-type question. "Al?"

"Pseudohypertrophic."

"Not pseudohypertrophic. Never use that term. Use the real name. Duchenne's. Duchenne's Muscular Dystrophy."

"Why not pseudohypertrophic, Boss? That's the usually accepted name for it."

"How is it that one fine morning Duchenne discovered a disease that probably existed in the time of Hippocrates?"

When no one answered, Dr. Richardson continued, "Charcot asked that question more than a hundred years ago. Charcot, who did as much as anyone to found modern neurology, wondered about this. Why is it that we perceive this so poorly, so slowly? Why is it that we have to see the same signs and symptoms over and over again before we recognize that we've seen it before, that it represents a specific disease? Duchenne couldn't have been the first one to see muscular dystrophy, but he was the first one to recognize it as a specific disease.

"You students wonder why I like to keep the eponyms, to attach the name of some dead Frenchman to a disease. It's because men like Duchenne should be honored. Too few physicians have ever been able to abstract their observations and invent a 'new disease.' They should never be forgotten. You all did quite well on that. You're learning the truth of Yogi Berra's law. To wit: you can observe a lot just by watching."

As he finished his tale the paging system announced an emergency—a triple page on 5 West. Richardson wondered if it could be number seven. Another triple page for Cardiology, then for Anesthesia on call. None for Neurology. It was a cardiac arrest. An emergency. Not a complete catastrophe.

Once they got to 6 West the story Al Schilder told was a common one. Unfortunately, too common. The patient named Marcel Dax had been brought into the hospital by his son late last night. He had been well yesterday—his son talked to him in the afternoon and made arrangements to pick him up so that he could have dinner with them. When the son got to his father's apartment, the door was open, and his father was sitting at the table. The son called him, but his father wouldn't or couldn't talk. Mr. Dax seemed to understand, but he was mute.

"Oh, Christ. How long did he have high blood pressure?"

"At least twelve years."

"Marcel Dax. That's not a common name. A French name. Was he born in France?"

"Yes."

"When did he come here?"

"Late '30s."

"How old was he?"

"Middle twenties. Twenty-seven or twenty-eight."

"Was he married?"

"No, he met his wife here."

"They speak English at home?"

"Sure."

"Did you try to speak French to him?"

"Are you serious?"

"Yes."

"What difference would that make?"

Richardson ignored that question and turned to Linda. "What's the diagnosis?"

"Aphasia due to a stroke."

"What's aphasia, John?"

"The inability to speak."

"Not quite. If your tongue is paralyzed, you can't speak, and that's not aphasia. Try again."

John answered more slowly. "It's not that the patient can't move his tongue. It's that the brain can't put the words together or make the tongue and vocal cords work right."

"Pretty good. Aphasia is the inability of the brain to understand or use language."

Step by step Dr. Richardson led them through the neurology of speech so that they understood that aphasia was due to an injury to certain centers in the left side of the brain. He then explained that when a bilingual patient such as Mr. Dax had a stroke with aphasia, the original language was often spared. Then, to nail it all down, Richardson got up and went to the blackboard. "I want to tell you the story of a patient of mine. A German Jew. Born and bred in the fatherland as a reform, integrated, assimilated Jew. That's important to understand. What do you know about assimilated German Jews in 1900, Al?"

"They were pretty well assimilated as far as I know."

"Right. They spoke only German. No Hebrew. No Yiddish. Only German." He wrote on the blackboard:

1. GERMAN

"He married in the twenties, had two children, was active in the Communist Party. His wife, who wasn't Jewish, was more active. Come 1933 he got out. His wife didn't. His kids didn't. He got into France. He lived in hiding throughout the entire war with a French family and their daughter. When he learned that his wife and children were dead he married the French girl. They had a child. They spoke only French. They had the one child, a girl, the delight of his life."

2. FRENCH

"His French wife died in 1949 and he moved here. There were some cousins living here. He learned English."

3. ENGLISH

"Went into business as a toy manufacturer. He was free and accepted for the first time in his life and after a few years became successful and rich. When he was sixty he retired and traveled extensively. He took a trip to Israel and for the first time really became a Jew. At age sixty-two he learned Hebrew."

4. HEBREW

"For the next four years he spent six months in Jerusalem and six months here with his daughter. He went to synagogue each day. Then at age sixty-six he had a stroke, and it involved his speech. Now what language was he left with? Let's look at the possibilities."

1. GERMAN
2. FRENCH
3. ENGLISH
4. HEBREW

"German?" He pointed to the board. "The language he was born with and raised with. His only language until he was thirty years of age. The language he'd married in and had two children in.

"French? The language of safety. The language of his second marriage. The language of his daughter. They always spoke French.

"English? The language of freedom and of success of the last fifteen or so years before his stroke.

"Hebrew? A latecomer. Learned only at age sixty-six.

"Which one?"

No one was sure. Most held out for German. Sue went for French, Donna for Hebrew.

"That's right, Hebrew. Not German. Not French. Not English. Hebrew. Hebrew—but why? I'm not sure I know, but I think it has to do with the meaning of the language. The emotional meaning to the patient. That language which has the greatest meaning—emotional meaning—has the widest representation in the brain and is most likely to be spared. Hebrew meant the most, was the most important language, so it was the one that was least affected. Today he lives in Jerusalem and each day walks to the Wall." He paused and reflected that no matter what language you could speak, that would be a good life. There was little else to add to the story.

They went to see Mr. Dax and found he could speak neither English nor French, nor Hebrew, nor Yiddish. Nor anything. Unfortunately, his stroke had not spared any language.

Herb went back to the office with Richardson. They each took a cigar and Chris got them some coffee.

"How many pots of coffee do you make each day?" Herb asked Chris.

"Don't ask. I can hardly keep up. Sometimes I think I measure out my life in coffee pots."

"Coffee spoons," Richardson corrected her. "Did you get the charts for Stokes?"

"Yes. Ward said they'd like to see you this afternoon."

"Before rounds—say 2:00 if it's okay with them."

"I'll call."

After Chris left, Richardson turned on the FM and listened to a few bars of Prokofiev's Romeo and Juliet. The smoke gathered from both cigars as the two doctors sat in silence. One at the height of his career, the other just beginning his. Twenty-eight and just getting ready to start his life. How old was Mike Gram when he finished? Aside from Herb, Mike Gram had been Richardson's favorite senior resident.

The contrast between Herb and Mike was astounding. Big Mike. A real American success story. Poor family. Went to college on an athletic scholarship. Baseball. Two-time All-American second baseman. Bonus offers in six figures. He turned them all down to go to medical school. Richardson tried to remember the years involved in Big Mike's training. Medical school—four years. No, he took off one year to do research. Internship—one year. Residency in internal medicine—three years. Army—drafted at age thirty-two because of Viet Nam, for two years. Residency in neurology—three years. Total—fourteen years. If he'd been as good at hitting a baseball as he was at tapping reflexes after those fourteen years, he'd be ready to retire. Instead he was thirty-six and getting ready to go out and make a living for the first time. At least Herb was only twenty-eight.

It was time to get down to business. Richardson ground out his cigar and turned to Herb Westphal. "Did you find out anything else?"

"I'm sure nobody else lost any strychnine."

"How's that?"

"I took some from Pharm and some from Physiology and gave it to a few guinea pigs. Somebody could have replaced it with something else."

"And?"

"They looked like Mr. Prader and the other patients."

"Christ! But it does prove that the missing strychnine is ours, all ours. How much did we have?"

"Renee isn't sure. But apparently we had a heck of a lot."

"Yeah, we had enough for students to do experiments in the days before students quit doing experiments. There was probably enough to kill a score of people. Did you find out where people were—"

"Everybody is accounted for during at least one, if not more, of the murders. Al has the best alibi."

"How so?"

"He was moonlighting during the first three and Dr. Collier's death."

"Some alibi. With Sanders around, he might be better off admitting to murder."

"And as for Mrs. Todd's murder, Donna, Al, and I were with you when she got it."

"Is that a sure alibi?"

"Of course. Strychnine works almost immediately in such large doses."

"Unless it was put in the intravenous and went in slowly and just built up. Then whoever did it could have put it in half an hour or more before the patient died. That would explain why you slipped on something when you went to see Prader. The murderer could have put the strychnine into the IV bottle. But in order to keep it concentrated enough, he might have had to spill out some of the fluid. But that would take a lot more strychnine. Did we have that much strychnine in the lab?"

"Yes, Renee said we had at least three bottles."

"Then we're all in trouble. Except Al. The rest of us were around the hospital or could have been at the times of all the murders. How about Renee?"

"John was on call and they were both around the hospital."

"How about any other students?"

"Do you really think a student—"

"Why not a student?"

"What do you have against students?"

"Nothing, but there is nothing to rule out a student. After all, as head of the Promotion Committee Jim Collier certainly had lots of enemies."

"You don't kill someone over a single course or two."

"You might if it made a difference of graduating or not."

"I don't know chief."

"It might be easier to kill Collier than flunk out."

"All right, maybe if it made a difference of flunking out or not."

"Or whether you might get the residency you wanted—if you're sick enough and whoever did this must be either very sick or very desperate or both." Richardson paused. He really did like the Stokowski arrangement better. Then he looked directly at Herb. "I've heard that some of my best friends had problems with him."

"Is that an accusation, Boss? I'm having enough trouble with the cops."

"Huh? I thought we were working with them."

"Since I got to more of the patients than anyone else, they keep checking and rechecking my alibis, and now you want to supply them with a motive."

"I . . ."

"Well, there was no love lost between Collier and me. In medical school, he didn't want to give me credit for some of my research time, since I quit in the middle. I would have graduated six months later, but we worked it out in the end."

"I never did understand why you quit."

"I just lost interest."

"All of a sudden?" Richardson asked.

"Yes. If you want a motive for killing Collier, a motive that involves a physician, you won't have to go very far."

"Why?"

"He was going to support a move to fire every resident who was moonlighting. He and Sanders."

"They'd have to fire everybody. They couldn't do that."

"But they'd get some people canned and—"

"So we'd only have 147 residents with motives and opportunity and enough knowledge, not counting the staff. But if someone killed Collier for that reason, why not Sanders, too?"

"Maybe he will," the Chief Resident replied.

"It could be a *she*."

"If it were a she, Sanders would have gotten it first."

Richardson nodded his agreement. "I'll talk to Ward and Locke about their investigation. They'd better have a good reason."

"Do me one other favor, Chief."

"What's that?"

"My office is beginning to look like yours."

"Is that a complaint?"

"Yes."

"What's the problem?"

"It's those damn charts that you and Simpson are reviewing. There must be hundreds of them. They're piled up all over the place. What are you two doing?"

"It was Walt's idea. I guess he'd seen some patients with bad meningitis and discovered that there isn't much information on what happens to people who develop meningitis in the hospital, so we're studying every case of meningitis in the hospital since the advent of penicillin. We're looking at both hospital-acquired infections and ones acquired outside the hospital in the same years, and we're going to compare the two groups. It's a worthwhile project. I'll get Walt to get to work and clean things up. In fact, ask Chris to have him come by this afternoon."

CHAPTER 8

R_{ICHARDSON} turned off the FM. He often did this when he really wanted to concentrate. In his office the FM and cigars were for pondering, not for concentrating. He sat down with the draft of the paper for Saturday. If he could get through it now, Chris could type it this afternoon and he could check it over again in the morning. If he could only get Bernstein's songs out of his head and get to work in this best of all possible worlds. The paper was a continuation of the first project on which Carol Voss had worked. That time seemed so long ago. An antediluvian age. It had started as a simple attempt to produce a new animal model. It seemed to work, and they published it under the simple title, "An Animal Model of Myoclonus."

Carol had been so pleased to see her name in print. She should have been. Publishing an article while still in medical school was something Paul hadn't even contemplated while he was a medical student. Learning all he thought he was supposed to learn had kept him busy enough. She was even happier that their names were linked together publicly: "By P. Richardson, M.D., and C. Voss, B.S." It all seemed so simple and straightforward. Simple, straightforward. Things were never that simple. Or that straightforward. For three years it had just seemed to be a nice little model but not now. The original idea was still accepted but not his newer work. No one else seemed to be able to reproduce it. That would all be a thing of the past now. The paper he was working on proved their argument quite well. Renee and Herb had worked on it extensively, and the pathology of the animals' brains done by Weigert was beautiful. It was hard to believe that Weigert had only published two papers in the last three years. God, he ought to get back into his lab and do less administration. The work was magnificent. A few more like this and Weigert would be able to apply for a promotion to full professor, not just associate professor. Crazy system. Publish or perish. If you published enough papers in the right places you became a professor. Without the papers, no professorship. Teaching? Irrelevant. After all, this was a medical school. In fact, the pathology was probably the best part of the paper. He wondered if he should include Collier as coauthor. After all, Jim had done some of the early work, set up the original protocol. But, then he had turned it all over to Weigert. Collier never had had much faith in the project. The authors would be Richardson, Westphal, and Weigert. The brains showed just what they had wanted them to show. "The Pathology of Myoclonus." A great title. Not exactly "They're Playing Our Song" but not bad. What would Collier's brain show? "The Pathology of Strychnine Poisoning." It would be normal. It would look normal. Strychnine doesn't alter the structure of a brain. Only its function. And only enough to kill you. If you survived, there was no damage. Jim's brain would be normal. Somebody else could go to that brain cutting.

He made a few corrections in grammar, a few in punctuation, one in syntax, caught a major error in one of the tables, added one paragraph and two references, sat back, lit a cigar, and then began to sing the opening song of *Candide,* taking all the parts himself. He didn't hear the Haydn concerto that served as counterpoint.

At 2:00, Chris buzzed him and told him that Detective Ward was waiting for him and Mrs. Hammond was on the line. "Is she still constipated?" he asked.

"She didn't mention that. She said that she had a new problem."

A new problem? Her feet. What was wrong with her feet? They ached. Was it getting worse? No, but the foot doctor said it might and that worried her. When had she seen the foot doctor? Six months ago. "Well, Mrs. Hammond, it sounds to me as if your feet are doing pretty well so why don't you just continue your medicine and call me in three weeks. Okay, two weeks." He held the phone for a few seconds and then softly put the receiver down. He went to the door, gave Chris the manuscript along with some typing instructions, and asked Ward to come into his office.

"One more thing, Chris. Did you get hold of Walt?"

"He'll be here by 2:30. Al said rounds will start at 3:00."

"Fine." Richardson closed the door and walked slowly to his desk.

"Did you learn anything, Doc?"

"Yes."

"What?"

"That you're investigating my chief resident, Herb Westphal."

"How did—?"

"That's not the question. Are you investigating Herb Westphal?"

The detective shrugged. "Yes."

"Why, for God's sake?"

"He was always nearby. He saw all the patients."

"Except Jim Collier."

"He was in the hospital that night, too."

"I didn't know that." Richardson seemed surprised.

"He was, and he hated Collier."

"How do you know?"

"That's not the question, Doc. I'm supposed to find out such things. They're called motives."

Richardson pursued his point. "How?"

"Willis told us."

"He didn't do it."

"How do you know that?"

"You saw the movies."

He couldn't tell if Ward nodded or shuddered. "Yeah, I saw them. What a hellish way to go." Ward looked at Richardson with a puzzled expression. He wasn't sure he understood. "What's the movies got to do with whether or not Herb Westphal is a killer? I don't see it."

"Remember how quickly the animals died?"

"Yes."

"Strychnine in those doses works in nothing flat."

"So?"

"So Herb was with me seeing a patient when Mrs. Todd got it and when Prader did, too. He couldn't have done it. Lay off." This last was much more a demand than a request.

"Paul." The change from Doc to Paul was not lost on Richardson. "We've worked together before, and I respect you and trust you. You've always been straight with me in the past. If you say Herb Westphal is out, he's out."

Richardson's response was much quieter and softer than his demand had been. "He's out. He didn't kill those six people."

Richardson acknowledged to himself that he could not be that positive on the basis of the evidence itself. But he knew Herb as well as he knew his own son. In some ways, better. Over the years they had spent so much time together. He knew Herb could not have killed those five patients. Could he have killed Collier for some deep, dark, personal reason? Maybe. But even that seemed unlikely. The other five? Never. Maigret was right. If you knew the psychology of the suspect, you knew his guilt or innocence. Herb was out. Should he tell Ward that maybe the deaths weren't that acute? It was possible that the strychnine had been given slowly in the IV bottle—not acutely. So, on the face of it, Herb could be guilty. Herb or any of the kids. He just couldn't believe it might be Herb or any of his kids. None of them could be involved. It was bad enough that it was his strychnine. Did that make him an accomplice? What was the legal term? An accessory before the fact. It was time to let it out. His strychnine. In Dr. Collier's brain, and Roberta Todd's and Willie Prader's and the others.

"I did find out where the strychnine came from."

Ward looked up. "Where?"

"My lab," he almost whispered.

"Are you sure?"

Richardson assured Ward that he was and told him why he was so sure. Herb had been so damned thorough. He had located every milligram of strychnine in the whole medical center. He'd made sure that no one thought any was missing and then he'd tested what was in the various bottles and ampules to make sure no one had pulled a switch.

Ward interrupted Richardson's explanation. "Who could get it out of your lab?"

"Anyone. We never kept the lab locked up, and that place is like State and Madison. Everybody comes and goes."

"Everybody?"

"Almost. Even Willis."

"Dean Willis?"

"Yes. He liked to show it off. Jim Collier used to come by when he worked with us, and Carl Weigert and almost anybody else in the whole damn center."

"But mostly the people from Neurology."

"Look, Herb was with me during two of the murders and so were Al Schilder and Donna Batten."

"That leaves your secretary, Dr. Stokes, and Renee Weber."

"You are efficient."

"Your secretary's out because she was at home during most of the killings."

"And Stokes?"

"We're not sure."

"And Renee?"

"Same. She wanders around this place fairly freely."

"Look. She wouldn't do this. She couldn't."

"How do you know who would or could do this?"

"I guess I don't," Richardson conceded.

"We don't think anybody here is involved. It's probably some lunatic or a mercy killer, if there's any difference between the two. Like you said, anybody in Neurology could get hold of better poisons and ones that would not point back at them. We had to check up on everybody. No hard feelings?"

"No. No hard feelings."

"Good. I still expect you to try to help us."

"I will."

With that, Ward left. Once he was alone, Richardson was no longer as sure he had done the right thing. If only he had thought of it sooner, they could have tested the IV fluid. Then they would have known whether the murderer injected it directly through the line or put it in the bottle, and whether the murderer was with each patient five minutes before the spasms started or half an hour or even an hour before. But he had to lie. It would give him a freer hand. After all, if he were wrong . . . he'd rather find out himself than have the police tell him.

Richardson walked across the hall to Herb's office. God. Herb was right. There were charts everywhere. There must have been six hundred of them. He looked around until he found what he wanted—the protocol—and went back to his office. In a few minutes, Walt would be there. He told Chris to send him in as soon as he got there.

Then Richardson settled down, found a cigar, turned up the FM, and started reading: "Protocol for Institutional Review of Meningitis. Purpose of the study project: To explore the impact of antibiotics on meningitis developing in hospitalized adults." That was medicalese for two real questions as far as Richardson was concerned. Were the same bugs still causing meningitis? And were fewer people dying because of antibiotics? Or had the use of antibiotics over the years changed this so that more and more cases of meningitis were being caused by bugs that weren't killed by antibiotics? Every year there were new antibiotics. He could hardly keep up with them, but it also seemed that every year there were new bacteria. The bugs seemed to have less trouble keeping up. Especially the bugs which managed to survive and then flourish within the hospital. The infections they caused were often resistant to antibiotics. That was infectious disease for you. You could explain the whole field while standing on one foot: You can kill all the bugs some of the time and some of the bugs all of the time. The game is always the same. Each year the players change and you can't tell the players without a scorecard. As Hillel said, "All the rest is mere commentary."

"Method." This section went on for four pages. But all it meant was review the charts and find out which bug the patient had, which antibiotics were used, and who won. The data collection form looked simple enough. He'd go over the whole thing with Walt and make sure he got started.

He settled down to read Sharf and Harel's classic study, "Pancreatic Encephalopathy," but within five minutes Walt Simpson arrived.

"Chris said you wanted to see me."

"I want to go over the meningitis study again. I want to make sure we know where we are going. And I want to make sure we get started."

"I, uh, already did get started. Three or four weeks ago."

"How are you doing it?"

"Chronologically, like you asked. I'm going through the charts year by year. Medical Records arranged them all alphabetically, and I had to go through and divide them year by year."

"There must be 600 of them."

"Closer to 650."

"So those piles aren't random."

"No, sir. They're year by year."

"How far have you gotten?"

"1963."

"That's not bad. When are you going to get to the rest?"

"One of these days."

"Better sooner than later."

For the next ten minutes they reviewed the protocol. As they worked Richardson was again impressed by Walt. The kid was bright. His mind was like a sponge. But so stiff, so rigid. They'd have to work on that. Things weren't all so black and white. You had to see the gray to really understand, to really plan research.

By the time they finished, everyone else had arrived for rounds. Everyone except Herb, who was taking off to work in the lab.

The patient they had planned on seeing was spending the afternoon in X-ray, but there was an emergency consultation in the Intensive Care Unit, so they started there.

Donna had seen the patient during lunchtime. Richardson preferred to have residents see the emergency consults until the students had more experience.

"Nobody really knows what happened to this patient. She was brought into the emergency room unconscious by her husband. He found her unconscious when he got home at 10:00 P.M. Monday."

"When had he seen her last?" Richardson began.

"Friday."

"Where was he over the weekend?" he continued.

"That's part of the problem."

Richardson frowned.

"He's a heavy drinker and was out drinking all weekend. Mrs. Turner had been under psychiatric care for years."

"For what?"

"For depression."

"Any suicide attempts?"

"Not that we know of, but Mr. Turner isn't much help. When she came in he was half stoned and didn't tell them anything. The ER staff thought she'd had a stroke and admitted her to the ICU, and her doctor here thought she'd had a stroke, was in coma, and would die. Like Moon. But she didn't die, so today they asked me for a curbstone consult."

"And?"

"She's much different than Mr. Moon was."

"In what way?"

"Oh, she's in a coma, all right," Dr. Batten conceded. "She doesn't breathe on her own and she won't respond to pain, but her eyes respond to light. If I put cold water in her ears, her eyes move, so her brain stem is intact, and she has sudden jerks of her body."

Richardson's eyes lit up. "Jerks?"

"Brief spasms in which her arms and legs jerk all at once."

"Both sides at the same time?"

"Yes."

"What did you do?" Only one out of ten first year residents would have done it. Did Donna? Richardson hoped so.

"I chased down Mr. Turner."

"Good girl."

Donna smiled. "I found out about the psychiatric history and one more thing."

"Yes?" hopefully.

"She was on antidepressants, and the bottles are empty. Her last refill was for 200—three weeks ago. That leaves 100 unaccounted for."

They went in to see Mrs. Turner. The exam was as Dr. Batten had reported except the patient had a temperature of 103 due to a pneumonia that had started on Wednesday.

Richardson turned to the group. "She clearly has an antidepressant overdose. Nothing else would cause the clinical picture. Part of her brain is depressed and not working. She can't breathe. She doesn't respond to pain. And part of the brain is excited and overworking and causing these spasms. They're the key. This mixed picture can't be a stroke. It must be an OD. But what kind of OD? Antidepressants. They are one of the only things that cause coma with myoclonic spasms. You should read the article by Burks in the *Journal of the American Medical Association*. Sometime in 1974. It gives a good clinical description, while the one we published in *Neurology* later that year explains the basis of the muscle spasms. So now we will save her life, I hope. How should we do that?" He looked first at Walt Simpson, but Walt made no reply. He then looked questioningly at each of the other students, but none of them was sure what to do. He proudly turned to his first year resident. "Donna, what should we do?"

"Give her eserine."

"Why?"

"The antidepressants block acetylcholine in the brain. Eserine increases acetylcholine in the brain and will overcome the block."

"Right. Do we have any?"

"Right here," said Donna, pointing to her jacket pocket. "I stopped at the pharmacy and got it."

Richardson beamed. This is what made everything worthwhile. The long hours. The missed meals. Not having enough money for a new car. Bobbie was right. They needed a new car. If he'd gone into private practice, they'd have the money. Hell, this was better.

Donna got a syringe. "How much should we give?"

"Two ccs."

Sue interrupted their dialogue. "How long will it take to work?"

"Five to ten minutes."

Dr. Batten gave the injection and they waited. Five minutes. Nothing happened. Ten minutes. Nothing happened. Fifteen minutes. Nothing. Twenty minutes. Still no response.

"Give her 4 ccs this time; we didn't give her enough before," Richardson instructed.

Dr. Batten gave the injection and again they waited. Five minutes. Nothing happened. Ten minutes. Nothing. Fifteen minutes. Twenty minutes. Still there was no change at all.

"I guess we were wrong," Donna said softly.

"You weren't wrong. I know that. Al, go across the hall and get the portable EEG machine in here." She couldn't have been wrong. It was his kind of diagnosis. What he'd taught her. She couldn't have been wrong. What was taking Al so damn long? Maybe he should have gone into private practice.

Al was back in five minutes with the machine and a technician and in another ten minutes the machine was hooked up and they all gathered around Dr. Richardson and listened. "The brain activity is very slow. Much slower than normal. Two to three waves per second. It ought to be eight to thirteen. We're going to keep the machine going and give her another 4 ccs."

Dr. Batten drew up another 4ccs and gave it to Mrs. Turner. They all waited. Five minutes. Nothing happened. Ten minutes. Nothing. Fifteen minutes. Neither Mrs. Turner nor her EEG changed at all.

"How much eserine do you have left?" the Chief asked.

"Ten ccs."

"Give her 6 more."

Dr. Batten drew up 6 ccs and again gave the injection through Mrs. Turner's IV. They waited five minutes. Nothing happened. Ten minutes. Nothing. No, something was happening!

"Look," Richardson exclaimed. "It's getting faster. It's up to five waves per second. Now it's up to six or seven. It will work!" Triumph.

"Dr. Richardson?" It was John Adson who had deserted the machine and was at the patient's bedside. He shouted, "She's moving her arm!"

They all felt like cheering.

"Why did it take so much eserine?" Sue asked.

"It's a matter of how much drug she took. If she only took a few antidepressants, then a small amount could overcome them. She must have taken a carload, so we had to use a lot."

"She's still moving," Al reported.

"Who's on call tonight?"

"I am," Al responded.

"Stay with her. The eserine only lasts half an hour or so. Find out how much she needs and keep giving it to her." Richardson looked at the clock. "It's almost 5:00 and I'm tired. Let's call it a day. Check the sick patients to make sure everybody's holding their own and then go home. We'll start bright and early tomorrow."

Had he been observing his own gait as he walked back toward his office, Richardson would have noticed how jauntily he was walking. It had been close, but he'd known that Turner was no Moon—and Donna had known it, too. That's what was important.

When he got back, Chris had left for the day and Adam Stokes was waiting for him with an armful of charts.

There was still some coffee, so they each took a cup and settled down to work. Richardson scanned the pictures. There were no new messages. Just the old envelope.

"Let's do them in order."

"In order?"

"In the order of their deaths."

"That makes Mrs. Schiff first." Adam handed the slim chart to Richardson. He looked at the face sheet. "Name, Schiff, Deborah; age, seventy-two; profession, housewife. That's not true—she was a rabbi's wife—a rebbitzen. That's a harder job than being rabbi sometimes. Place of birth, Cleveland, Ohio; religious preference, Jewish." The next sheet was the death certificate. It added little. Under "Cause of death," two simple words, "Metastatic carcinoma." Just two words. Richardson exploded.

"Hell! She didn't die of cancer. She was murdered."

"What do you want them to put down? She was dying of cancer. She would have been dead in a couple of weeks."

Richardson knew that was true. But it seemed wrong. A blatant half-truth. No one knew why she'd had a seizure. Maybe it was just a peculiar terminal event of her cancer. But still it seemed wrong.

"We're all dying of something, at some rate. She was

killed. Adam, you went through the whole chart. What did you find out?''

''Not much that you don't already know. She hadn't been sick before. This was her first admission here and the only other times she'd been in a hospital were to have kids.''

''In Cleveland?''

''Yes.''

''How long had they lived here?''

''Since 1948.''

''What was the final diagnosis?''

''Cancer of the breast with widespread metastases.''

Richardson looked up for a minute, trying to remember something, shuffled through some papers, and located Collier's curriculum vitae. ''He wrote four papers on breast cancer.''

''Who?''

''Jim Collier.'' He paused, then asked, ''Did she have an IV going when she died?''

''Yes.''

''Let's go on to number two.'' Stokes gave him Mitchell's chart. It was much thicker than Mrs. Schiff's chart had been. This had not been his first admission to the Austin Flint Medical Center. Richardson began to read the face sheet.

''Mitchell, Silas W. Hospital number 312 416. Admission Number 3. Date of last admission August 23, 1979.'' Less than a year ago. He'd been on Neurology then, Richardson recalled. For vomiting. They were all worried that it might be due to pressure from his brain tumor. But it had only been the summer flu. ''Age sixty.'' Richardson interrupted himself. ''He looked a lot older than sixty. How long had he had that brain tumor, Adam?''

''Five years.''

''That's long enough to make him very old.'' Richardson continued reading. ''Profession, vendor.'' Richardson remembered. Mitchell sold beer at the ball parks. At Sox Park in the summer. The stadium in the winter. He'd moved here from Cleveland. With Veeck gone, there had been no reason to stay in Cleveland.

''Cleveland again.''

Stokes said nothing.

"Cause of death, brain tumor." There was nothing more to say about that. "Next of kin, none. Adam, you went through this whole chart." Adam nodded. "Did you learn anything at all?"

"That you made the diagnosis one Sunday at the ball park."

"We lost that day, three to one, on errors in the eleventh inning. No shortstop."

Stokes ignored him and continued. "You admitted him here. Jackson operated and then he got radiation. He did okay until this year and then things went to hell."

"What was the final tissue diagnosis?"

"Cerebellar astrocytoma. I even went up to Pathology today and went over the slides with Dr. Paget. There was no question about it. A typical cerebellar astrocytoma."

Richardson reached for the curriculum vitae again. Collier had written only one paper on brain tumors. A five-year study of cerebellar astrocytomas. Published two years ago. Mitchell had been part of that study.

"Did he have an IV in when he died?"

"Yes. He'd been pretty dehydrated when he came in, so we were giving him plenty of fluid."

They went on to Todd, Erb, and Prader. All three had cancer of some sort. Cancer of the bowel, cancer of the bladder, Hodgkin's disease. They all were on IVs. They'd all lived in Cleveland at one time. Richardson had never liked Cleveland. But that was no reason for this. And Collier had written at least one paper on each of these types of cancer.

Then he looked at Collier's record. "Cause of death, respiratory arrest." Well, that was one step closer to reality. Collier had died as a result of respiratory arrest. He couldn't breathe. So he died. But that wasn't the cause. It was the means of death, the mechanism, but not the cause.

"He just doesn't fit, Adam."

"What do you mean, 'doesn't fit'?"

"Except for Cleveland, Ohio, and the IV he had in him when he died, he didn't have anything in common with the other patients. You wouldn't kill someone over Cleveland, Ohio. Philadelphia, maybe, and only if they were going to send you there. But not Cleveland."

He went up to the blackboard, which was hung at the back of his office door, and wrote:

PROPERTIES SHARED BY VICTIMS:
1. CLEVELAND

"This is probably just coincidental, but we'll have the police look into it."

2. TERMINAL

"All except Collier."

3. CANCER

"All except Collier."

4. IV

"That's important. That's how the strychnine was given."

5. LOW RISK OF AUTOPSY

"Why was that important? Sooner or later we'd figure out the strychnine. With or without autopsies. Autopsies often show more than biopsies. Maybe somebody had something to hide. A doctor? They all had different doctors. The only one who saw them all was Herb, and that was after the fact, and he didn't see Collier. Was there something to avoid? Some reason for no autopsies? And if that failed and we got an autopsy? We did get one. The next best thing to no autopsy would be no pathologist."

Stokes interrupted. "We still have lots of pathologists. Weigert and Paget and . . ."

"Yes, but no one with Collier's expert knowledge of tumors. I just don't know." Richardson went back to the blackboard.

5. LOW RISK OF AUTOPSY

"Again, Collier doesn't fit. He died right after surgery. We had to do an autopsy."

For several minutes neither of them said anything.

"Adam, all things considered, your theory is probably best."

"What? Oh, you mean that the CIA killed them because something the government did caused the cancers?"

"Yes. And if it's true, we'll never solve it. I hate to admit it, but you could be on the right track."

"It does explain a lot. Including the news blackout."

"Say it ain't so, Adam! I just don't want to believe it."

As Stokes began packing up his attaché case, there was a knock on Richardson's door. It was Linda.

"I hate to bother you."

"What's up?"

"It's Mr. Cohn. His legs are much weaker."

"We'll have to go see him."

"Let's zip."

Zip. As he got up to go with her, he wondered if *zip* was the complete opposite of Erica Jong's *zipless*. Zipless—an affair without involvement. An impossible fantasy for Richardson. He'd learned that the hard way.

"Come on, let's zip."

"Please don't use that word," he requested.

"What word?"

"Zip."

"Why not?"

"It sets too many associations into motion."

"Like what?" He was sure she knew. Hell, she'd been an undergraduate when *Fear of Flying* was all the rage. She must have read it. She was just setting him up.

"I'd hate to tell you what," he admitted.

"Tell me."

Richardson hesitated and then sang, "Zip, Walter Lippman wasn't brilliant today."

Linda looked at him with a puzzled expression. That wasn't what *zip* had reminded her of.

"It's a song from *Pal Joey* by Rodgers and Hart. You're too young to remember Rodgers and Hart. 'On Your Toes,' 'The Boys from Syracuse,' and 'Pal Joey.' The girl sings

about all the celebrities she's interviewed. The most interesting interview she'd ever done was with a stripper from
Minsky's.''

''Oh. I thought you meant something else.''

He sang on. ''Zip, Walter Lippman wasn't brilliant today.
Zip, will Saroyan ever write a great play? Zip, I was reading
Schopenhauer last night. Zip, and I think that Schopenhauer
was right.'' Whew, discretion was the better part . . . But
was *zip* the opposite of *zipless* for Linda, too?

There was no question about it. Mr. Cohn's legs were
weaker. The question was, would he need more surgery?
Should they do another myelogram? At least Donna wouldn't
have to come in. It was probably just some swelling. Richardson decided to hold off on the myelogram and put him on
steroids to reduce the swelling.

What a day it had been! It was after 7:00 and he still had
work to do.

''You look a bit frazzled, Dr. Richardson.''

''I am, I guess.''

''You need to relax a bit.''

''So?''

''You owe me a drink. You can take me out now and kill
two birds with one stone.''

''Why not? Sounds like a good idea. I don't feel up to that
long drive right now.''

Richardson didn't get home until after 9:00. He really
hadn't relaxed very much. He and Linda had gone to the
Holiday Inn for a couple of drinks. Mostly they talked about
her. He'd finally gotten the story of her problem with Collier
firsthand. She had worked on a project with both Collier and
Weigert for two quarters. During the second quarter she was
working independently, and that's when she ran into trouble.
The results she got were just the opposite of the technicians
and Weigert, but she was confident she was right. Dr. Weigert
went over everything and was sure she was wrong, and they
didn't feel she should continue working on the project. Weigert
told her it had been Collier's decision and there was nothing
he or she could do about it. Later, there were rumors around
that she had made up her results, but she never knew who
instigated them. So she asked Weigert about them. He had

heard them, too, and tried to find out how they got started. Then she had a problem with Sanders. Fortunately, they didn't go into the problem. But Collier had supported Sanders and it cost her a quarter and then some.

That wasn't unusual, as Richardson was discovering. According to Linda, even Walt had had a problem with Sanders and the promotions committee. He'd had to repeat two courses and miss a summer of research work. Richardson always wondered why Walt didn't work for him that summer. Walt was too smart to have fouled up any courses. What had really happened?

He gobbled down a sandwich and then went upstairs to read to Carolyn who was just going to sleep. It had been almost a week since he last found time for this but they picked up right where they'd left off—*The Tin Woodman of Oz,* Chapter 11. "As they followed a path down the blue grass hillside . . ." By the time he finished Chapter 12 his daughter was asleep.

Then, he and Josh played a game of chess and debated the White Sox changes for the 1980 season. Britt Burns looked like he might make it. If Baumgarten, Trout, Dotson, Wortham, and Kravec came through, they might do all right. Even without much of an infield.

Josh won the chess game, making their running total Joshua, 171, Dad, 129.

Once the children were settled, Paul and Bobbie had a cup of coffee and put a movie on the betamax. Woody Allen's *Play It Again, Sam.* It was a time to relax, to wind down.

Who played Sam?

Who the hell played Sam?

What kind of a question was that for him to worry about now? He should be thinking about strychnine, about the five dead patients. Not about Sam.

Humphrey Bogart played Rick. Ingrid Bergman was Ilse. Paul Henreid was her husband. What was his name? Claude Raines was Captain Louis Renault, the prefect of police. He "blew with the wind and the prevailing wind was from Vichy." Peter Lorre played Ugarti. He got killed in the first fifteen minutes. His most famous role and he was on the screen for three minutes at the most. And Sidney Greenstreet owned the Blue Parrot. But who played Sam?

Why strychnine? It's such a lousy poison. It's not potent. You have to use a lot to kill somebody. The murderer must have known something about strychnine. How else would he know enough to use a lethal dose? A physician. Or a medical student. Or a graduate student in pharmacology or physiology.

But who the hell played Sam? It was a better question.

S. K. "Cuddles" Sakall was the maître d'.

Five patients. All five had terminal cancer. Whoever did it must have known enough medicine to pick out the five patients. That leaves out the graduate students. Could it be a nurse?

Victor Laszlow. That was Ilse's husband. The man who had succeeded in impressing half the world. But Sam? God, I must be getting demented to forget such things. I used to remember every line in that movie. Maybe I need to be worked up for my memory loss; I'm as bad as Michaels.

I should have spent more time in the lab. The paper still needs some polishing but it will be okay. I hope. If I spent more time in the lab, maybe the strychnine would still be there. Whoever did it must have known something about strychnine. A physician or a medical student. Two days without a killing. Was that because of security? Or was the killer done? Finished? Ferrari. That was Greenstreet's name. But who played Sam?

CHAPTER 9

F RIDAY was a bleak and windy day, typical for Chicago in late March. Richardson got up quite early and left before Bobbie had a chance to start the coffee. The drive in to the hospital was slow and dreary. The city was enveloped by a dense, drizzly fog, but even on a day like today it was still a great city. It didn't really matter that the low-hanging clouds were as muddy as the steets. It was Chicago, not Cleveland thank God. Chicago, with its beautiful Lakefront, Magnificent Mile, and its ethnic neighborhoods. Every country had its leading city. But Chicago was the only real Second City. No one would call Liverpool the Second City. Or Milan. Or Marseilles. He once proposed a tour of Chicago for a group of visiting European neurologists that would include—among other things—The Art Institute and the University of Chicago with its Henry Moore sculpture on the site of the first sustained atomic reaction. But all they wanted to see were Al Capone's old headquarters in the New Michigan Hotel, the garage where the St. Valentine's Day massacre occurred, the Biograph Theater where Dillinger had been shot, and the Lone Star Saloon on South State Street where Mickey Finn earned immortal fame. Chicago would probably never outgrow this heritage.

Even though he was early, Chris was already at the typewriter and the coffee had been made. Somehow she had managed to finish up the manuscript for the meeting in New

York and gave him the completed paper along with his morning coffee.

"Did you see the message from Hunt?"

"No."

"I left it right on your desk."

"It must be here someplace, but I never saw it."

"The fellowship got turned down."

"You're kidding?"

"No."

"Why the hell—"

"I called Sanders's secretary."

"And . . ." He waited, half knowing the answer.

"Apparently it was Sanders's doing."

"How come?"

"She didn't know . . . or wouldn't say."

"Page Herb for me."

"Herb told me about that business with Mrs. Robin's warts," Chris interjected.

"Trust the old pro."

"What's that 'old pro' bit? You're not that old."

"I'm not?" He pondered for a brief moment and continued. "I don't know. The kids of the players I grew up watching are now in the Big Leagues. Roy Smalley's kid, Ray Boone's, Gus Bell's. Jim Busby's kid got signed by somebody. Hell, Mike Tresh's kid has already retired. That's unreal. Mike Tresh's kid has already come up to the majors, played out his career, and is gone. And with the Yankees, no less. I not only remember when Hank Aaron hit his first homer, I remember the Braves before Hank Aaron, before Milwaukee."

"What's that got to do with being old? You're only forty-four."

"I've been through two generations of ball players and two generations of medical students. At least two generations of medical students. Somehow it seems like a lot more."

He took several sips of coffee and sat down to locate a cigar. "When my Dad went to medical school he grew a moustache so he would look older. When I started med school, I cut off my beard because you just couldn't have a beard in medical school. Now the kids can grow whatever they want."

"And that makes you feel old?"

"No, it's not just that. It's the cultural difference. We think differently. I grew up during World War II. All my thinking is colored by that experience. I remember my Dad going into the Army and our family moving to Texas to be near him. I live with the memories of FDR's death, V-E Day, V-J Day, the discovery of the death camps. Anne Frank was only a few years older. If my grandfather had gone south instead of west, I could have ended up in that house. For these kids those experiences are as remote as the Depression is to me. These kids all grew up in the '60s and '70s. If anything shaped them, it was Viet Nam—not Dachau. We're generations apart and we aren't getting any closer."

"You're not supposed to be getting closer."

"I suppose not."

"I guess I'll page the young Dr. Westphal."

Richardson finally found the cigar he wanted, and after locating some matches, began to read the manuscript while waiting for Herb to answer the page. He only had to wait a few minutes.

"What's up, Chief?"

"We got some bad news this morning."

"About what?"

"The fellowship."

"Oh, that's not news. I knew about that two weeks ago."

"Why didn't you tell me?"

"I guess I just didn't want to think about my not having a job next year."

"I'll get the money somewhere. Don't worry about that, but how did you know?"

"For a genius at observation and deduction, you sure miss some obvious things."

"Like what?"

"You know I've been going with one of Sanders's secretaries, Joanne Edinger, for months. And now we're living together."

Richardson remembered her. He'd just forgotten she worked

in Endocrinology. There didn't seem to be much else to say to Herb about the fellowship.

"Are you going to join us on rounds today?"

"Sure, I'll be there at 9:00."

"Good. We'll go over everyone so you'll be ready to cover for me this weekend."

By 9:10 everyone had filtered in and it was time to start carding rounds.

Linda had just seen Mr. Cohn, who was receiving large doses of steroids. His legs were no weaker and were possibly a bit stronger.

Mr. Wallenberg had finished his twenty-four hours on the cardiac monitor. The results would be back on Monday.

Dr. Sanders was stable. For the first time in almost a week there had been no progression, no worsening.

This encouraged Richardson. "Well, whatever the hell he has seems to have stabilized despite our lack of knowledge and maybe, just maybe, his body may do what we can't do and overcome this damn thing. By the way, what did his EMG show?"

"It hasn't been done yet," Walt responded.

"Why not? We talked about that three days ago."

Herb broke in, "There was a breakdown in communication. I'm not sure whose fault it was. I talked to Adam yesterday, but he was busy going over some charts for you. He said he'd get it done today."

They were still waiting for the thyroid evaluation on Mr. Romberg. The repeat calcium was on the border between low and normal.

"Low or normal? Well, was it low or normal?"

"Low."

"How about the skull films?"

"They're scheduled for today."

"He's still on L-dopa?"

"Yes. Six grams a day."

"Any response?"

"No. He looks just the same."

"Maybe the skull films will help us. Donna, how is Mrs. Turner?"

"She looks great. Awake, breathing on her own. Thanks to Al."

"How did it go last night?"

"We gave her 6 ccs an hour for the first four hours to keep her awake and breathing," Al responded. "Then she needed less and less. Right now she's down to 1 cc an hour. And her pneumonia is better, too."

"So you and Donna saved her life?"

"With some help from you."

Richardson nodded. "Did you ever hear of the Brodman case?"

No one had. "Brodman was a patient in California who tried to commit suicide. He was brought to a hospital emergency room unconscious. To make a long story short, the doctors saved his life. A straight simple case except for one thing. Brodman is now suing the doctors for violating his civil rights! How's everyone else?"

Mr. Dax was unchanged. As was Mrs. Robin.

"How was her brain scan?" Richardson asked.

"Normal."

"I guess we ought to do a CT scan, but it will be normal."

"Why are you so sure, Dr. Richardson?" Sue asked. "You listed a whole bunch of things she could have."

"Could, but doesn't."

"So what's she got?"

"Progressive multifocal leukoencephalopathy, or PML for short. You're all familiar with PML, of course."

The students all shook their heads.

"Herb, tell them about it."

"It's a virus disease of the brain. It happens to people with tumors or other similar disorders and progresses until it kills the patient."

"Always?"

"Unless something else kills him first," Herb answered.

"Like strychnine," Richardson mused, then looked up. "When I was in medical school no one had ever heard of this disease. It didn't exist. Now we see at least one or two cases a year. It's almost an epidemic but, as Dr. Westphal said, it only happens to patients who are already sick in some way. Most of them have cancers of some sort, especially Hodgkin's disease. And most have been on some sort of anticancer medications that suppress their immune responses. Mrs. Robin has been on the same people poisons ever since she received her kidney transplant. That makes her a natural victim for this disease. And if you read the case reports carefully, very carefully, six of the first twelve cases had warts."

"Warts?" Walt echoed.

"Yes, warts. Mrs. Robin has numerous warts on her face and they're new."

"What do warts have to do with PLM?" Linda asked.

"PML."

"PML."

"In one way, nothing, and in another way, everything," Richardson explained. "Warts don't cause PML, but the same abnormalities that make the patient susceptible to warts make the patient susceptible to PML. What causes warts?"

John just shrugged his shoulders, but Al Schilder responded, "Frogs."

Richardson chose to ignore this and turned to the next student. "Walt?"

"A virus."

"Which one? Does anyone know?"

Linda nodded and answered, "Papovavirus."

"And ZuRhein has shown that PML is caused by papovavirus. That's in *Science*, 1965. It's hard to believe that was written fifteen years ago, and now we know that it is caused by a particular papovavirus, called SV 40."

"SV 40?" Linda asked.

"Yes, simian virus 40—a monkey virus. Why was the disease virtually unknown twenty-five years ago and now we see it at least once a year? How could this monkey virus which was once incredibly rare have become much more widespread?"

Everyone was silent. Herb knew and so did Donna, but this was not the time to steal the chief's thunder.

"No one really knows, but one theory is that it was given along with the polio vaccine that was grown on monkey kidneys."

"But I've had polio vaccinations," said Linda. "Does that mean—"

"No, it's just a theory. Although it's the best theory we have. If it's true, it means that in the middle '50s medical science eradicated an epidemic disease of horrible proportions and at the same time, without knowing it, introduced a new disease. A disease that would not appear until the patient got cancer and was put on powerful anticancer medicine. Then when the body's defenses were overcome, the virus could finally grow."

"That's ghastly," said Sue.

"It's worse than that," Walt added. "It's murder."

"Hold on, Walt. It's not murder. First, we don't know for sure that that's what happens. Second, no one could ever have guessed it would happen. We didn't know viruses could do such things. And more important, in Chicago alone, in one summer, more people were saved than all the cases of PML reported so far."

"Then what can we do for Mrs. Robin?" Linda asked.

"I'm not sure. We may be able to do something. I have an idea, but we'll have to see."

As they left the office Chris asked Richardson what time he could meet with Ward and Locke. He told her that 1:00 would be fine. She thought they wanted to see Richardson earlier than that, but she'd check back with them.

The new patient was on 3 West, a surgical floor, so they started there.

"Who saw the new patient?"

"I did," Walt answered.

"What's the problem?"

"It's a young guy. He's twenty-four years old and was admitted for some surgery on a hernia."

"That's not a neurological problem."

"The surgeons," Walt continued, "noticed some abnormal movements and wanted you to see him before they did anything."

"That, in and of itself, is amazing."

"What? That they called you?"

"No. That they noticed something. The movements must be pretty severe. Usually on surgery, the neurological examination is WNL."

"They're not that severe, but apparently they were worse when he came in."

"What are the movements like?"

"They're pretty much limited to his face. He smacks his lips and sticks out his tongue, and his face will pull to one side or the other. But yesterday they saw his arms and legs jerk, too."

"Did you see any arm or leg movements today?"

"No. I didn't see any."

"What do you think he's got?"

"Huntington's chorea?" Walt responded.

"What do you know about Huntington's chorea?"

"It runs in families."

"Correct. What's his family history?"

"Negative. His mother and father are both alive and in good health."

"And without abnormal movements?"

Walt nodded his response.

"That certainly puts the diagnosis in doubt. Sue, what do you know about the heredity of Huntington's chorea?"

"I think it's a dominant trait."

"What's that mean?"

"If either parent has it, half the children will get it."

"That's not quite true. If either parent has it, each child has a 50-50 chance of getting it. That's not quite the same thing. Now, if neither parent has it, what are the chances of someone getting it?"

"Zero."

"I agree with you. But most medical authorities talk about spontaneous appearance of the gene for Huntington's as a new mutation. It's supposed to occur once in a million births. I hate to cast aspersions on anyone, but I tend to be very skeptical since I've been told that the incidence of adultery in this country is higher than that, higher than one in a million. Maybe two or three, perhaps even as high as four, in a million. I, of course, have no personal data in this area. In my clinical experience, however, the patient with so-called spontaneous generation of Huntington's looks like the family's old milkman or the janitor."

Richardson paused for a moment, sat back, dug a cigar out

of his pocket and lit it, and then told them the story of George Huntington and his disease.

"He was a Long Island general practitioner. That's right, a general practitioner. Not only was he not the first physician to observe such patients, he wasn't even the first Huntington to do so. His father and his father's father were both physicians who had been following several families with chorea in East Hampton, Long Island. It was only because of his father's and grandfather's observations that he was able to demonstrate the hereditary nature of the chorea. He had their notes, and because of this he was able to demonstrate the dominant form of inheritance of a disease thirty years before Mendel's observations were published—a triumph of careful clinical observation. How did he describe it? It followed a direct line from parent to offspring, and when this line was broken it failed to reappear in future generations."

Then, after the briefest of pauses, Richardson shifted gears. "You know, Huntington's chorea is a very interesting disease from a historical point of view. It is said that three families with Huntington's chorea were members of a group of some 700 people who left England in 1630 and landed in Salem.

"Salem—a name that conjures up memories of Cotton Mather and witchcraft. It is not known how many unfortunate descendants of these families were accused of witchcraft, but many were, since their abnormal movements were often seen as a grotesque imitation of the suffering of Jesus. One named Elizabeth Knapp was clearly descended from these families and is known as the Groton Witch. The descriptions of her behavior are often more reminiscent of chorea than of Satan worship.

"If any of you wish to pursue this, I would suggest you read the review article 'Even unto the twelfth generation—Huntington's chorea.' It's in the *Journal of the History of Medicine*, in 1961. The author's name was Maltsberger."

Al Schilder's whole face lit up. "You finally did it!"

"Did what?"

"Confused an obscure medical reference with the name of an old White Sox player."

"Huh?"

"Maltsberger, Gordon Maltsberger. He was a pitcher for the White Sox."

"Al, there's more than one Maltsberger. Although I must admit there was only one Gordon Maltsberger. The Maltsberger I'm referring to is J. T. As I recall, he was still a medical student when he wrote this article." Richardson was almost as pleased as Al Schilder was disappointed.

"Back to our patient. Without a positive family history, I am skeptical of the diagnosis. Let's see him."

When they walked into the room, the patient, Andrew Thomas, was seated in his bed, rapidly tapping his fingers like a piano player repeatedly playing the same fractured chord. He looked up when the group entered, stopped strumming, and then began to pick at the top of his pajamas with his right hand while tapping his knee with his left. From time to time he would grimace or protrude his tongue.

As soon as Walt introduced him, Richardson asked his first question. "Speed or coke?"

"What do you mean?"

"You know what I mean. Do you use speed or coke? From what I can see, I'd guess speed—maybe 300 milligrams each day."

"Closer to 350," the patient admitted.

Richardson pursued his point. "Mr. Thomas, how long have you been using such large amounts of the stuff?"

"Six, maybe eight months."

There was little more that Richardson needed to know. After briefly examining the patient he and his crew retired to the hallway.

"The art of observation includes both identifying the individual details and piecing together the entire picture. Walt was so interested in the facial movements, which look like chorea, that he didn't pay any attention to the continuous repetitive finger tapping and button picking. The combination of these stereotyped movements and the facial movements is seen only in two things: amphetamine abuse and cocaine abuse. Since his nose showed no evidence of inflammation, speed was the more likely culprit."

He then asked Al to make sure the appropriate medicines were ordered, and rounds were over.

When Richardson got back to his office it was only 11:30, but Detective Ward was already waiting for him.

"We got a big problem, Doc."

"How so?"

"Well, Willis has everyone watching the private rooms like hawks."

"Everyone?"

"The nurses, mostly," Tom conceded.

"Why?"

"Since everyone who got knocked off was either in a private room or in a room by himself, we figured it would be a good idea to see who goes in and out of the private rooms. He suggested that the nurses help us out by keeping track of all the single rooms."

"And?"

"They found somebody who goes into them at every opportunity."

"Don't tell me. Let me guess."

"Go ahead."

Richardson smiled. It was so obvious and so absolutely unrelated. "Somebody from transport."

"How did you know?"

"It doesn't take a genius to figure it out. They wander around the hospital, have access to every floor, and are poorly paid. So sometimes they look into a private room to see if the patient's out, and if so, they pick up anything that's not nailed down. They even liberate people's false teeth. I don't know what they do with them. But they take 'em. Anything from false teeth to wallets to loose change—it's all petty stuff. It's sort of a fringe benefit. But hell, they're not going around killing patients, except maybe by losing them once in a while."

"This is more serious than that. The kid they got had some cocaine on him."

"So he was pilfering pennies to pay for the coke. It's more expensive than it was when Sherlock Holmes used it. But you can't believe he's guilty."

"You don't even know who we picked up. How can you be sure he didn't do it?"

"None of the transporters are smart enough to have done this. Especially not Steven Johnson."

"How—?" Tom Ward hadn't expected Richardson to know which one they had picked up.

"He's the only one who looks like he's always on coke. But he must have an IQ of 90 and I'm sure he never finished high school."

"Quit after two years."

"Hell, he's got all he can do to read the sports section. He'd never be able to pick out the five patients."

"What if he didn't pick them out?"

"They were picked out. They had to be. They all had terminal cancer. All of them."

"Not all of them." It was nice to be able to correct the professor. Ward went on. "Not all. Just five out of six."

"No, five out of five, plus Collier. That's the only way it makes any sense. And where would he get the strychnine?"

"Are you serious?"

"Yes. We've checked everywhere. The only strychnine that's missing is mine. Transporters may have the run of the hospital but they never get over to the research labs. They'd stick out like sore thumbs over there."

"Doc," the detective explained patiently, "you know a lot about this hospital but not enough about what goes on outside of it. He could have gotten the strychnine the same place he got the coke. Out on the street. It's not hard to come by out there. They use it to cut heroin."

"Tom, do you really think this dumb kid—"

"No, not really. We've booked him for possession of cocaine. Hell, he's been seen in thirty or more private rooms this week, and none of the patients died. Some were a bit poorer after he left, but none of them was murdered. And he's never around here at night."

"What's he do at night?" asked Richardson.

"Don't ask."

"I won't."

"But Dean Willis is fairly sure we've caught the murderer."

"Sure, or hopeful?"

"Both, I guess. He's thinking of relaxing security, and that might be a disaster."

"I'm not so sure that it would be," Richardson said.

"There haven't been any more murders since we've been here, and God knows what would happen without the security."

"Tom, I hate to disappoint you, but the lack of murders may not be due to your being here. Maybe there wouldn't have been any more murders. Even if we had never found out that there had been any murders. Perhaps the murderer was through. It may not have been a lunatic. It may have all been quite calculated from the beginning, and after the—"

Ward interrupted him. "Are you sure, Doc? How do you know that's what happened?"

"I don't. I don't know why the murders seemed to have stopped. But neither do you. You'll have to admit that, Tom."

"I suppose so," Tom agreed and then went on. "Doc, do you want us to leave? Are you that sure?"

"No. Not at all. I'm just considering all the possibilities."

"Willis is fairly sure. No murders in three days. A suspect in custody. He wants us out. Even we can't keep the lid on forever."

"Christ!"

"Can you talk to him?"

"If you leave, would you be off the case?" Paul asked.

"The case would be closed. We'd be all through," Tom Ward replied. "Later, as quietly as possible, we'd charge him with one count of manslaughter."

"We can't let that happen."

"Why not?"

"There are certain things I want you to look into."

Richardson spent the next few minutes going over the results of his chart review with Detective Ward. Ward said that he could make some inquiries in Cleveland if the case remained open. Richardson had Cris call Willis for him. As he waited for Willis to come on the line he shuffled through his mail, scattering letters around his desk. He could picture Willis in his office in a newly starched white coat carefully arranging letters according to some well-defined pattern known only to himself. Willis slowly opening each letter—with a letter opener—removing and reading each letter one at a time. Formalizing each act into a solemn ritual. Richardson knew he should be tactful and start slowly, but it was just not in him today.

"You're not going to crucify that kid for snorting some coke!" exclaimed Richardson.

"What are you talking about?"

"Johnson."

"Johnson?"

"Yes, Steven Johnson. Doesn't the name mean anything to you? He's the kid you're trying to make into a murderer."

"I don't like that accusation."

"Hell, that kid's no murderer. He's too dumb."

"What do you mean, too dumb? Geniuses don't have a monopoly on murder."

"Look, the five patients all had terminal cancer. That can't be coincidence."

"Why not?" Willis asked him.

"We have over 900 patients in this place at one time. How many have terminal cancer?"

"I don't know," the dean admitted.

"I do. Ten to twelve. And in two days five patients get killed and they all have terminal cancer. It can't be a coincidence."

"Maybe he believes in euthanasia."

"Don't give me that. That poor bastard probably thinks euthanasia is a yellow-skinned kid who has slanty eyes. And he wouldn't recognize a cancer if it killed him."

"You may be right."

"You know goddamned well I'm right. Somebody who knows medicine killed those people."

"Maybe."

"No, definitely. A doctor or . . ."

"Not a doctor!" The dean's voice was indignant.

"Most likely a doctor or a student. Maybe a nurse, but I doubt it."

"It couldn't be one of our doctors," the dean insisted.

"Not couldn't. Could, and most likely is." Richardson's hostility was waning. His anger was gone.

"Why are you so sure, Paul?" The dean's voice sounded almost friendly.

"I know where the strychnine came from," Richardson said softly, almost like an apology.

"Where?"

"My lab."

"Oh, no."

"Oh, yes."

Willis made no reply.

Richardson couldn't let it end there. "Look, I don't think anybody from Neurology was involved."

"Can you be 100 percent sure?"

"No, but fairly sure."

"Paul," the dean continued, "you may well be right. Certainly this mess is worse than I thought it was. I'd better have the police stick around . . . and don't you think we ought to have someone keep close tabs on the Neurology residents?"

"No. No way."

"I think we ought to."

"I've got a call from a patient."

"Wait a—"

"I'll call you later," Richardson promised as he hung up the phone. He'd almost forgotten that Tom Ward was still in his office. He stared at the detective, then spoke softly. "I'm not sure that I've been helpful, but at least the case isn't closed. You won't be asked to leave."

"Thanks, Doc. That's what I hoped for."

"What'll happen to Johnson?" Richardson asked.

"It's his first offense. Not much."

"Okay. Tom, if you'll excuse me now, I've got to get some work done. I'm still supposed to be a neurologist."

Richardson put on the FM, got himself some coffee, and lit up a cigar. The paper looked good. He went through the slides for the presentation. They were top-notch. Carl Weigert had done a superb job on them, and Richardson thought that Weigert should probably be listed as first author. The study had been Richardson's idea, but it was mostly Weigert's work. He had Chris retype the first page and list the authors as Weigert, Westphal, and Richardson. That was better. Carl would like that.

As he was about to leave for the airport, Dean Willis called. "How's your patient?"

"What patient?"

"The one who called."

"Mrs. Hammond. She's okay." Paul chuckled. One of the real advantages of having a big practice was that patients were always calling him. Sometimes very conveniently.

"Paul," the dean went on, "stay out of this business."

"Is that an order or a warning?"

"Don't take it that way. Just stay out and let the police work on it."

"If we have to wait for Ward and Locke to solve it, we'll have to wait until next Christmas. They just don't know enough about the hospital."

"Look, Paul. We're all convinced these were murders. You were right. But there have been no more deaths in three days. It may be all over. Hopefully it is all over and that is the most important thing."

"Don't you want this thing solved?"

"Of course I do. We all do. But it's a matter of priorities. You're a diagnostician. You want to make the correct diagnosis. I'm an administrator. I'm more interested in overall management and the problem may have already been managed correctly. So keep your nose clean."

"Don't worry, I will." Richardson hung up abruptly, got his coat, and as he was about to leave for his car, the airport, and then New York, the phone rang again. It was Carol Voss. He hadn't read the protocol yet, so he told Chris to tell her he'd already left. That was the first time he'd done that.

As he drove to the airport he thought about having two days on the town with Bobbie. There might be garbage in the streets, places you couldn't go after sundown, waiters who talked back to you, traffic that never moved, twelve dollar breakfasts with only coffee, orange juice, and a Danish (after all, what do you expect for twelve bucks?), but it was still New York. Just like the song said, "New York, New York, a hell of a town. The people ride in a hole in the ground."

While he waited for Bobbie at the counter, it suddenly struck him: Maybe Collier hadn't been killed because of his expert knowledge. It could be just the opposite: maybe the others were killed to hide Collier's murder and not the other way around. He'd been supposing that the killer got rid of Collier because he didn't want Collier to study the other cases. What if the others were killed to make it look like a maniac was randomly killing people, and all the time Jim Collier was the real target.

That was a pattern that made some sense. It could all have been a smoke screen to cover the murder of Dr. James Collier. But that still left some questions. The other five all had cancer. Was that just a coincidence? Was Cleveland merely a coincidence? Still, if Collier was the only real target there was only one part of the puzzle left to fill in—the killer. Some physician or medical student or . . . Dooley Wilson— that's it! Dooley Wilson played Sam and nobody played "As Time Goes By" like Sam . . . that would explain why there had been no more murders. Maybe he should call Tom Ward and tell him his new theory.

"Hi, lover."

It was Bobbie, and it was time to head for the Big Apple. Willis was right. He'd stay out of it. Until Monday.

CHAPTER 10

SATURDAY was a cold and clear day in New York. Paul and Bobbie got up early. He had to spend the morning at the meeting, so she decided to go shopping and meet him back at the hotel. She'd start at Bloomingdale's and work her way down. When the morning session was over he'd call the hospital, and the rest of the weekend would be theirs.

It was sunny in Los Angeles where John and Renee were looking for an apartment.

In Chicago it was drizzling. Dr. Westphal met the residents and students and saw all the patients. Dr. Westphal. No one would call him Herb today, unless they forgot.

Mr. Cohn had been on steroids for thirty-six hours and was clearly stronger; they no longer considered repeating the myelogram or doing any further surgery.

Linda was quite pleased that Robert Cohn was doing well. Maybe she could get another drink out of it—at least she could hope.

Mr. Wallenberg was getting a little anxious waiting for the results of his monitor, but there was nothing they could do to hurry the computer that read it.

For the second straight day Dr. Sanders was stable. Two days in a row without progression was a good sign. There seemed to be no reason to put him on a respirator to support his respiration. Stokes had done the EMG. It certainly didn't show any evidence of inflammatory neuropathy. It looked a little bit like myasthenia, but he had had two negative myasthenia tests. Overall, Stokes concluded that the problem was in the muscles themselves.

Mr. Romberg was no better and no worse. His skull X-rays were normal. Richardson would be disappointed.

Mrs. Robin was weaker. Her CT was normal. No tumor. No blood clot. No nothing. Richardson was probably right.

Mrs. Turner was awake, off all medications, and doing fine. She wasn't too happy, but people who try to commit suicide often are not too happy.

At 11:00 Chicago time, Richardson called from New York.

"Herb, how's Sanders?"

"Stable."

"No better?"

"No worse."

"Maybe we've turned the corner. What did the EMG show?"

"Muscle disease."

"I've never seen muscle disease do this. Get some muscle enzymes and we ought to get a biopsy on Monday."

"You won one and lost one."

"What did I win?"

"Robin."

"The CT scan was normal?"

" Yes."

"That's too damn bad."

"You said it would be."

"I was hoping I was wrong."

"You weren't. What do you want to do?"

"We'll see on Monday. If that's a win, I'm afraid to ask about the loss."

"Mr. Romberg."

"How so?"

"His skull X-rays were normal."

"That's no loss. It's just a slight delay before the win. Order a CT scan. It will give us the diagnosis."

"A CT scan? In Parkinson's disease they usually don't show much except some atrophy. That won't help us."

"This time the CT scan will help. It won't just show atrophy. It's going to show calcification of the basal ganglia."

"Are you sure?"

"Trust the old pro. How's Mrs. Turner?"

"Fine. She's back to normal. She wants to kill herself."

"Sometimes we save the wrong people," Richardson lamented.

"You win a few, you lose a few."

"We lost a big one today."

"What do you mean?"

"The paper. We weren't in New Haven, but we bombed anyway."

"What happened?"

"Nobody believed our results."

"You're kidding!"

"No. We'll deal with that on Monday. I'm off to *Candide*."

CHAPTER 11

SUNDAY was a very quiet day. Bobbie and Paul took advantage of being away from their children and slept late or, more correctly, stayed in bed late. One problem with having a house full of two kids was that you could sometimes sleep late but you couldn't stay in bed late. They had lunch in the hotel and spent the afternoon at the Museum of Modern Art. The Monets could not compare with those in the Orangerie. Maybe they'd get to Paris next year.

Dr. Westphal made rounds with Al, who was on call. Donna had the day off, and so did the students. Nothing much was happening with the patients; they were all fairly stable. Cohn was a bit better; Robin was a bit worse. Westphal thought that Sanders was stronger. Al disagreed, but that might have been wishful thinking.

As Bobbie and Paul flew home late Sunday night Richardson thought about the murders, the patients, the hospital, his Second City. It had been a good weekend, except for the meeting. Robert Benchley had been right. There were two ways to travel: first class and with children. The weekend had been first class. Still, it would be good to get back home. Maybe the Sox were flying in tonight to start their season. They should have a better opening week than he'd had.

CHAPTER 12

Richardson could smell the coffee as soon as he walked into the office.

"Can I get you a cup?" Chris asked. "You look exhausted."

He nodded his assent to both comments.

"Was your weekend that good? Or that bad?"

Richardson smiled. "A bit of both, I guess."

"I won't ask what was that good, but what was that bad?"

"The paper. Nobody seemed to believe our results."

"Why not?"

"A couple of reasons, I guess. Dan Walker gave the paper just before ours."

"Did he show your slides again?"

"No," Richardson laughed. "Worse than that, he had done almost the same experiment and his results were the opposite of ours."

"And people believed him, and not you!" she exploded. "I can't understand that."

"I can. Dan got there first and he'd done some further work based on his results. It supported his conclusions, not ours."

"Still, I—"

"No. Even I believed his results. Later in the afternoon I met him for a drink."

"Bobbie must have loved that. I thought you two were supposed to spend most of the weekend together."

Even Richardson noted her critical tone. "It didn't take

that long," he smiled apologetically. "Anyway, I had to talk to him and go over all of his data from beginning to end. Besides, Bobbie went to the Met to see that Egyptian Temple of theirs. But I didn't really have any choice. You really can't tell for sure by listening to a ten-minute paper. I went over everything. His data is good."

"Better than yours?"

"I think so. I'll have to go over ours again. What time is Renee supposed to come down this morning?"

Chris checked his appointment book. "Eleven."

"Call her and ask her to bring down her lab books for the last six months. Damn it. We'll have to go over everything from start to finish. What a waste of time! That's the last time we do a completely open study."

"Completely open?"

"That's right. Totally unblinded. Dan's study was blind. The people doing the actual work were blinded. They didn't know which animals had been given what. In our work everybody knew everything beforehand. Renee, Herb, Weigert, even me."

"What difference does that make? You don't think somebody made up results?"

"No, not really. But strange things happen in an open study. Sometimes you see what you want to see."

"That's not a nice thing to say."

"It wasn't nice getting shot down in public, by my own friends, in front of my own friends. Be sure to call Renee and Herb. I'm going to have two sweet rolls and look at my mail. I hope I got some fan letters."

WFMT was playing "Also Sprach Zarathustra," now known as the theme from 2001. What bothered Richardson about that movie was not the inane monkeys or the floating fetus, but the fact that Kubrick had used the wrong recording of "Zarathustra." They should have used the Reiner-Chicago Symphony Orchestra version. Von Karajan's Strauss couldn't hold a candle to Reiner's. Preferably the 1954 recording, but if they needed stereo, the 1962 version would have been okay.

There were no fan letters.

There was a memo from Dean Willis.

March 26, 1980

MEDICAL STUDENTS
HOUSE STAFF
ATTENDING STAFF

The approach of the spring season and the increasing disregard for the accepted standards of dress make it necessary for me to once again remind you that the hospital is not a country club. Attire that may be entirely appropriate in such a leisure setting is not acceptable in the hospital. A shirt and tie are considered standard attire for male house staff. At Austin Flint, the patient comes first, and proper dress indicates a respect for the patient.

Dean Thomas Willis
cc: Office of Student Affairs
TW/mk

He reread the distribution list at the top of the memo:

MEDICAL STUDENTS
HOUSE STAFF
ATTENDING STAFF

In the past, this memo had only gone to the medical students and house staff. Hell, he was the only attending physician who didn't wear a tie, having given them up last year. As if wearing a tie would make him a better neurologist, or make him care more about his patients.

Donna stopped by to welcome him back and ask about his weekend. "Did you have a good time in the big city?"

"Yes."

"We had a nice weekend, too."

"Good."

"Everything went well?" she asked him.

"No. The paper opened to bad reviews. Come to think of it, so did *Candide* the first time, but these were justified."

"What happened?"

"No one threw tomatoes, but almost." Paul repeated the whole story and, as he did, he began to understand things better. "I just screwed up."

"How?"

"I designed the whole thing. It didn't work."

"That doesn't make it your fault."

Richardson wasn't so sure. Chris buzzed him. Dr. Voss was on the phone again, and he hadn't read the protocol. "Tell her I'll call back later."

Herb stopped by to bring him up to date on the patients. Not much had happened on Sunday, and there had been no more murders. Maybe they could go for the record of most consecutive days without any murders. What was that record? Fifty-six. No, that was DiMaggio's hitting streak. There didn't seem to be any reason to beat around the bush, so Richardson gave Herb a full description of the meeting, Walker's paper, their paper, and the apparent conclusion.

"I don't think I screwed up, Boss."

"I don't think so either, but we'll have to go over everything."

"You don't think that—"

"I don't think anything. I'm not accusing anybody. Hell, it's my project. If we screwed up, it's my fault, but we'll have to go over your work and Renee's and Weigert's."

"He'll love that."

"I'll deal with him, but meanwhile, why don't you get your lab notebooks and stop by around noon. You can skip card rounds."

Within ten minutes of Herb's departure, Al, Donna, and the four students had all arrived.

"I have," Richardson began, "devised a surefire one-question test that will invariably identify all true baseball fans."

"That must be just what the world is waiting for," Donna responded sarcastically.

"Certainly. Any ideas as to what the test might be?"

Al pondered this for a moment. "You could have the patients undress and bend over and you could count the splinters."

"I tried that and with some fans it's a worthwhile test. But some fans, real fans, actually use seat cushions, so it's not entirely reliable. Too many false negatives." With that, he turned to Sue. "What are the last two words of the national anthem?"

She paused.

"You had to sing it through. You're not a baseball fan. Al. What are the last two words?" He didn't even have to finish the question.

"Play Ball!" Al shouted.

"Note how he said that. Not 'play ball.' But 'Play Ball!' with guttural excitement. To all true fans that's how the national anthem ends. Once, at opening night at the opera, they played the national anthem, and when it was over I just came out with it. I thought Bobbie was going to kill me."

It was time to get to work.

Mr. Cohn was improving every day. He was now walking with assistance. They were going to start decreasing the steroids.

Dr. Sanders was stable. For the third day he was neither better nor worse. The muscle biopsy would be done late that afternoon and they should have the results late Wednesday or early Thursday.

The report was back on Mr. Wallenberg's cardiac monitor. He had had one short run of arrhythmia.

"What kind?" Richardson asked.

"Atrial fibrillation," Linda replied.

"Does he have any heart disease?"

"No."

"Any murmurs?"

"No."

"Maybe he's hyperthyroid. That can cause atrial fib."

"He doesn't look like he's hyperthyroid," Al commented.

"Still, he could be. Let's make sure he gets worked up for thyroid disease."

Mrs. Turner was out of the ICU and on psychiatry.

Mrs. Robin was stable, and so was Mr. Romberg.

"What about his CT scan, John? Did it get done?"

"Yes."

"Don't tell me. I'll guess the results." Richardson paused. "Bilateral calcification in the region of the basal ganglia."

"How did you know?"

"It had to be there."

"I'm not sure I understand," Sue interjected.

"I've never seen a patient like this myself, but there is one report in the literature of similar cases by somebody named Frame. It's in the *Archives of Internal Medicine*. Sometime in the mid-'60s, I think. He talked about two patients who had Parkinson's disease as a result of bilateral calcification of the basal ganglia. And if I recall correctly, both patients had had thyroid surgery earlier. That gave us the fifth possibility since Mr. Romberg, as you recall, also had thyroid surgery in the past. The key thing is that his parkinsonism never got better. Usually we think of Parkinson's as being due to loss of dopamine. Right, Walt?''

"Yes.''

"So what do we do?''

"We give L-dopa.''

"And what happens?''

"The patients get better.''

"Yes, but why, Al?''

"Because the brain makes dopamine out of L-dopa.''

"And what else, Al?''

When none of the students spoke up, Richardson turned to one of his first year residents. "Donna?''

"I guess L-dopa only works if the brain can respond to the dopamine.''

"Right. But what if the problem is the other way around? What if the dopamine is normal, but the brain can't respond to it? Then the patient would look parkinsonian, but—''

"L-dopa wouldn't work," John broke in.

"Right. Just like Mr. Romberg. And do you know what can cause the brain to fail to respond to L-dopa, John?''

"Bilateral calcification of the basal ganglia, I guess.''

"Precisely. Elementary, but what causes bilateral calcification of the basal ganglia, Linda?''

"I pass.''

"Walt?''

"I pass, too.''

"Al?''

"Three no trump.''

"I'll ignore that. Donna?''

"Usually there is no cause, but let me think. Sometimes it's due to hypoparathyroidism.''

"That's it. Go on.''

"He had his thyroid out fifteen years ago, and the surgery injured his parathyroid glands so that they gave out, and later he developed calcification and parkinsonism."

Richardson nodded. "That's right. Where do we go from here, Al?"

"Prove he has hypoparathyroidism, treat him for it, and he'll get better."

"That's our plan. Let's hope it works."

There were two new patients to be seen, so they made plans to start rounds at 2:00. After the crew left, Richardson called Weigert. He had some good news and some bad news for him. The good news was that Weigert was listed as first author on the paper. The bad news was the paper itself. Dr. Weigert may have been pleased by the good news, but that didn't make up for the bad news. Richardson might not be sure what had gone wrong, but the pathologist was.

"Your people must have screwed up."

"My people?" Richardson was startled by Weigert's attack. How could Weigert be so sure?

"Yes, your people. You give your students and residents too damn much leeway, too much authority. They just can't be trusted that much. Not just your residents, but everybody. Your technician acts like a postdoctoral fellow. You let her get away with murder!"

Richardson tried to ignore the ill-chosen metaphor. Maybe Weigert was right. Maybe he didn't spend enough time in the lab supervising Renee and watching the work being done. But was it just that, or did Weigert know something? "Do you mean Renee Weber?"

"That's the one. She's no better than that friend of hers."

"Who?"

"Linda Sharp."

"What about Linda?"

"When she worked in our department, Jim Collier had to fire her because we couldn't believe her results, and I don't think you can believe what's-her-name's either."

"I'm not sure I agree." Keep calm. Don't get angry. It won't help. Count out the winning streak all the way to fourteen. One, two, three, four, five . . .

"It's staring you in the face," Weigert went on. "Those kids can't be trusted, and Herb Westphal is no better."

"That's bullshit!"

"You're just too close to see it."

"Goddamn it!" Richardson slammed down the phone. "I could kill that son of a bitch." But it was only a research project, and you don't kill somebody over a research project. Damn it. I should have asked him if he wanted to add Collier's name to the paper. Sort of a posthumous thank you. Maybe he'd be remembered better without being on this one.

No sooner had he hung up than Chris buzzed him. Detective Ward was on the phone.

"Congratulations."

"On what?" asked Ward.

"No more murders."

"Thanks, Doc. But are you sure I deserve the congratulations? Last week you had reservations."

"No, I'm not sure, Tom. I wish I were," the doctor reflected. "What can I do for you?"

"Willis has another suspect."

"A real suspect or a sacrificial lamb?"

"Most likely a sacrificial lamb, I'm afraid," the detective answered.

"Who is it this time? The newspaper boy?"

"No. One of the licensed practical nurses."

"Oh Christ! How did he hit on this one?"

"She was in the hospital during all the murders."

"So were lots of other people."

"Not too many. And there's one more thing. Her twin sister just died of cancer, after a hellish course. He thinks it might be euthanasia. At least she might understand what it means."

"How do you feel, Tom?"

"I doubt if she's involved. Too many loose ends."

"Yes, like why did she kill Collier?"

"That's one."

"And how did she get the strychnine?"

"That's another. Not a major one, but another."

Richardson pursued his point more relentlessly than he did with students or residents. But then, this was no game. "And does she know how to use it? Would she know how much she'd have to use to kill somebody? Does she know it would have to be given intravenously? Does she know how fast it works so she'd have time to get away?"

"All your questions are good ones, Doc. There's another thing, too," the detective added.

"What's that?"

"She's a good kid. She's not crazy." The detective paused and then went on. His tone changed from one of concern to one of respect. "But you have to give Willis credit. When he does a job he does it well. He had somebody from administration go over all of the time cards. On a computer yet. I never knew how many people actually worked in a place like this. Between nurses, licensed practical nurses, nurse's aides, and technicians—"

"Get to the point, Tom," said Richardson impatiently.

"Yeah, okay. They did all that and only a dozen or so people were actually here in the building during all of the murders. And she was one of them."

"Why her? There were at least ten others."

"The rest just didn't have access to the rooms."

"Look, Tom, I'll try to help her out." Before Richardson got a chance to say anything else, Tom Ward changed the subject.

"We've got some more information on the murder victims. They were all in Cleveland between 1948 and 1954. Two of them were active in left-wing politics—Todd and Erb. But I don't think Mrs. Schiff was involved in such things, or Prader. He was only a kid then, and Mitchell . . ."

"Hell," Richardson exclaimed. "He never even voted in his life. He thought Lou Boudreau was president. No other ties in Cleveland?"

"None, but we're still checking out their backgrounds. Talk to you later, Doc."

So five out of six had cancer, but six out of six had come from Cleveland. From Cleveland to Chicago. Hell, lots of people come from Cleveland to Chicago. Minnie Minoso, Larry Doby, Tommie Johns. Sometimes somebody even went from Chicago to Cleveland. Barry Latman, for instance. A move from Cleveland to Chicago wasn't unusual. Even Bill Veeck had done it. First he owned the Cleveland Indians, then ten years later, the Chicago White Sox. And both teams won. Before '59, the last time the White Sox had won the pennant was 1919. Bill Veeck had been back for five years but no pennant this time.

Ward was right. You had to give Willis credit. He was thorough. Or was he? The time cards didn't cover everybody, only the hourly employees. Nurses, nurse's aides, LPNs, transporters—all of them were hourly employees. Not doctors. Not the staff. Not the residents. Not the students. Not even his lab technicians. Everybody but the suspects. He'd forgotten to tell Ward his latest theory.

It was 11:00 and Renee was right on time. She had brought all her lab notebooks, though she still wasn't sure why. She brought him up to date on her trip to Los Angeles and also, in passing, gave him a progress report on the lab. And most important, the alpha-bungarotoxin had arrived so they could start the experiments that afternoon. When she finished, Richardson told her about New York, the paper, and the need to check over everything. He didn't tell her what Carl Weigert had said. That bastard. But maybe he was right. Richardson had made mistakes in judgment before. He hoped Renee wouldn't be hurt by his reviewing all of her lab notes. He wasn't accusing her of anything. Or was he, in a way? She showed him the results he was interested in, and he said he'd go over them in detail. She went back to the lab to get ready for the new experiments.

Richardson sat back, lit a cigar, and started reading the tables, the charts, the raw data. At 12:30 Herb Westphal came by to drop off his notebooks.

"Herb?"

"Yes, Dr. Richardson."

"There's one thing I always meant to ask you."

"Yes, sir?"

Sir? Richardson shook his head slowly. "Why did you stop working for Sanders?"

"I'd rather not discuss it."

"I'd rather you did."

"I told you before. I just lost interest. Let's leave it at that, okay?"

"Okay. I didn't mean to butt into your life."

"Yes, you did."

"I guess I did. Uh, the alpha-bungarotoxin has arrived. Renee is anxious to get started this afternoon. Why don't you go over to the lab and help her?"

"Sure, I might as well do something useful. We can keep an eye on each other."

"That's not fair."

"Isn't it?"

"Herb."

"I'll be in the lab, Dr. Richardson."

Maybe Herb was right. Maybe he was picking on them, but he had to be sure. The phone buzzed. It was Dean Willis. He had called to relay the good news.

"I think I know who did it."

"I know. I talked to Detective Ward."

"Don't listen to him. He's not convinced she did it."

"Neither am I. Are you going to continue the security?"

"For the time being."

"That's a good idea. You know, it's possible that Collier was the real target of all this."

"I doubt that. Who'd want to kill him?"

"As far as I can tell, 274 students and 147 residents. And if it's one of the residents, Sanders may be the next one to go."

"I don't believe that for one second."

"You think what you want and I'll think what I want. That's what makes horseracing."

CHAPTER 13

THE two new patients were on 6 West, so the group gathered in the conference room. With Herb back in the lab, the task of coordinating the service fell to Donna. As Richardson entered the room he turned to her.

"Who's on first, Dr. Batten?"

"I don't know."

"Third base!" Al and Richardson replied almost simultaneously.

Donna felt like she had just let herself be hit in the face with a whipped cream pie. She should have seen it coming. But she ignored it. The chief was in a better mood and that's what counted.

Walt had seen the first patient. "Dr. Richardson, you'll love this one."

"Why?"

"He used to be a professional baseball player."

"What's his name?"

"Charles Michaels."

"I don't remember any Charles Michaels. Charles Michaels. Gene Michael was a shortstop for Pittsburgh, LA, and the Yanks. Ralph Michaels briefly played infield for the Cubs in the '20s. And, of course, there was Cass Michaels, who came up with the Sox in '43. He was our regular second baseman for a while, then we traded him to the Senators, got him back from Philadelphia, and then he got beaned. His real name was Casimir Kwietniewski or something like that. But I don't remember Charles Michaels. Did he ever make the Big Leagues?''

"No, he played in the black league," Walt responded.

"It was called the Negro League, not the black league. That was in the good old days before the Big Leagues went Big League. Before Branch Rickey and the Dodgers brought in Jackie Robinson. Before Bill Veeck brought the first blacks into the American League with the Cleveland Indians. Larry Doby and Leroy 'Satchel' Paige.'' For a minute he seemed lost in his own associations.

"What's his history, Walt?"

"He's not much of a historian."

"Nobody ever confused Babe Ruth with Toynbee."

"It's worse than that," Richardson commented. "As far as I can tell from talking to him and his wife, he's had trouble walking and his memory has been getting worse for about two or three years."

"Just his memory?" Richardson asked.

"No. He has trouble concentrating, too," Walt answered.

"Does his memory loss just involve recent memory or everything?"

"I'm not sure what you mean."

"There are at least two different kinds of memory," Dr. Richardson explained. "One is recent memory and that involves learning new things, things that happen to you, and making memory tracings of them. What we call remote memory involves recalling things that were learned in the past, things that happened a long time ago. To test recent memory you take three things and show them to the patient. You make sure you know that he understands what they are and then put them aside. Ten minutes later you ask him what they were and see if he remembers. Did you try that?"

"Yes and no."

"Now I'm the one who doesn't understand."

"I gave him the names of three cities and he repeated them, so he understood. Then I told him I would ask him the three cities later and . . ." Walt paused.

"And?"

"I forgot to ask him."

"It was clear someone had a recent memory loss. In

practice I normally don't resort to such formal testing. I usually just get the patient to talk about something he cares about, like sports or politics. Let's see Mr. Michaels.''

They all gathered around the bedside. Walt introduced Dr. Richardson. Mr. Michaels did recognize Walt, but he didn't remember his name.

''Where were you born, Mr. Michaels?'' Dr. Richardson began.

''Mississippi.''

''Whereabouts?''

''Near Biloxi.''

''When?''

''1910.''

''When did you come to Chicago?''

''Let me think,'' the patient said as he scratched his head. ''Nineteen . . . nineteen twenty-two.''

''What year is it now?''

Mr. Michaels took his time in answering. ''Nineteen hundred and, and sixty-four, as best as I can tell.''

''How old are you?''

''Forty-six.''

''They tell me you were a ball player.''

''Yes sir.''

''What did you play?''

''Shortstop.''

''Who'd you play for?''

''Lots of teams.''

''You remember Josh Gibson?''

''No, not rightly.''

''Satchel Paige?''

''Paige? No.''

''Oh, me. Well, I don't think we have to do any more memory testing. Walt, what were your findings?''

''I, uh . . .''

''I know we don't usually talk in front of patients, but Mr. Michaels won't mind. Do you, sir?''

''Nawsir.''

''Also, he won't remember. Richardson's First Law: If you find yourself talking in front of a patient like we are now, and in a way you usually don't, it probably means that you have unconsciously recognized that the patient is intellectually impaired. He won't comprehend what you're saying or that what you're saying has anything to do with him. So don't worry, Walt. What were your findings?''

"I didn't find too much. Except that his reflexes in his legs—''

"Were absent.''

"Yes.''

"And his position and vibratory senses were gone in both legs?''

"Yes!''

Richardson confirmed these findings, checked the patient's eyes, and they returned to the conference room.

"Jesus, is he wiped out! He doesn't even know who Satchel Paige is.''

"Excuse me, Dr. Richardson,'' Linda interrupted, "but I don't think I know who Satchel Paige is.''

"Yes, but you're not black. You didn't play baseball in the Negro League. He did, and to him and a whole generation of blacks, Satchel Paige was a legend. He was Babe Ruth and Joe DiMaggio and Jackie Robinson all rolled into one and then some. Paige was a pitcher, perhaps the greatest pitcher who ever pitched in the Negro League, and in 1948 Bill Veeck gave him a chance in the Majors with Cleveland. Paige was either forty-two or forty-seven, a rookie at an age when everyone else had already retired, and he was still a winner. He started one game—here in Chicago, in Sox Park. Nobody knows how many people saw that game. They set an official attendance record, but the last 10,000 crashed the gates and never got counted. To see Satchel Paige start a game in the Majors. And he won! In fact, he didn't just win. He pulled out all the stops and pitched a shutout. A one-to-nothing shutout. For almost everyone who was in Comiskey Park that night, that game meant they had arrived. For those who had watched 'the Satch' pitch in that same park against all-black teams for a generation, that was it, That was making it. Not someone like Jackie Robinson, who was All-American in two sports and a college graduate. Satchel Paige was from their ghettos, and he'd made it. If Michaels can't remember him, he has a severe memory problem, to say the least. The cause, of course, is obvious.''

"It is?'' Walt asked. From their expressions it was clear to Paul Richardson that the other students were equally puzzled. But were the residents? Time to move up the ladder. "Al, what's the diagnosis?''

"Syphilis.''

"Right. Why?''

"The combination of mental changes, loss of reflexes in the legs, and loss of position and vibratory sensation in the legs.''

"Good.'' Back to the students: "What do we do to prove a diagnosis of syphilis? John?''

"A spinal tap and a test for syphilis in the spinal fluid, I guess.''

"Very good.''

"When was syphilis first recognized as a disease?'' Richardson surveyed his audience. "Any guesses?''

"Certainly in ancient Rome,'' Walt suggested. "They were so decadent.''

"No. Not ancient Rome. In 1493. At that time syphilis was described as an acute infection. And it first occurred shortly after the return of Christopher Columbus and his crew from the New World. Whether the further spread should be blamed on Christopher Columbus himself or members of his crew is unknown. But that's when the disease first became known to Western Medicine, as a veritable plague that marched across Europe.

"As frequently happens, a military campaign played a major role in disseminating this devastating new disease. In 1494 Charles VIII, king of France, invaded Italy to claim the throne of the Kingdom of Naples. Italy was then made up of a lot of petty city-states and kingdoms, which were constantly at war with one another, so Charles met no real resistance. His army marched right down the peninsula to Naples. Now Charles's army was composed of mercenaries from all parts of western Europe, including French, German, Swiss, English, Hungarian, Polish, Italian, and, of course, Spanish troops. And, as always, the army was accompanied by hordes of camp followers. Of course the term 'camp follower' is merely a euphemism for prostitute. According to most sources, the march to Naples was more a parade of debauchery than a serious military campaign. In late 1494 Charles and his army began their siege of Naples. What happened next is easy to imagine. In army camps at that time, sexual diversions were an expected and welcome change of pace. The women often moved freely from one side to the other, and Spanish mercenaries were present in both Charles's army and among the defenders of Naples. Under circumstances like that the spread of a new venereal disease is easy to understand. By the next spring this new disease accomplished something the Italians could not: Charles's army was devastated, and he was forced to abandon his campaign and retreat. His army disintegrated into undisciplined lawless bands that fled northward and scattered into France, Switzerland, Germany, and their other countries, bringing their new disease with them. At first the new affliction was called Neopolitan disease but soon became known as the French disease. Charles VIII himself died from it in 1498 at the age of twenty-eight. All of Europe knew the ravages of syphilis by 1500.

"When was syphilis of the brain first described?" This was clearly a question for a resident. "Al?"

"Since the usual period between getting syphilis and having your brain fall apart is fifteen to twenty years, I'd guess 1520."

"Not bad. You only missed by 300 years."

"1820?" Al asked. "How could that be?"

"A good question. How could syphilis exist for 300 years before syphilis of the brain, a very characteristic disease, was clinically recognized? And a good question deserves an even better one."

"That was what I was afraid of," Al responded.

"Who was the Viennese psychiatrist who won the first Nobel Prize for psychiatry? Susan?"

"Sigmund Freud."

"Close, but no cigar. Come on, this man's name is a household word. He devised the first effective treatment for syphilis, and he was even on an Austrian bank note and won the Nobel Prize."

No one answered, so Richardson went on.

"Julius Wagner von Jauregg! And what did he do? He invented fever as a form of therapy for neurosyphilis. People with severe syphilis—we used to call it general paresis of the insane—are rare today, but it used to be a common disease. Scott Joplin died of it, and so did Guy de Maupassant. The first great advance in psychotherapy, and today no one knows him. Oh, well. Roger Bannister will probably be the only neurologist the world ever remembers in twenty years."

Sue and Linda couldn't even remember him now.

"Back to our question. Why didn't anyone recognize the mental disease caused by syphilis until Bayle did in 1822? Any guess?"

There were none.

"Fever, recurrent high fever is a treatment for syphilis. Julius Wagner von Jauregg got his Nobel Prize for that. Before 1800 high fevers were common throughout Europe. Malaria was a widespread disease, as were others like relapsing fever, typhus, and many more. Under those circumstances, it would be hard to imagine going twenty years without getting a high fever that would have killed the syphilis bugs in the brain. The major factor may have been smallpox, but by 1800 smallpox was fairly well eliminated by vaccine. As it turns out, there are two possible explanations. Either getting smallpox in some way protects you from getting syphilis of the brain, or the smallpox vaccination itself may somehow make the patient who contracts syphilis more likely to suffer from severe syphilis of the brain."

Al interrupted. "You mean that vaccinating people got rid of smallpox but resulted in an epidemic of syphilis of the central nervous system?"

"That's one explanation."

"Wow! That's like the relationship of PML to polio vaccination."

"I guess it is. They're both just theories, you realize. But I don't know any better explanations."

Richardson decided the discussion had gone on long enough. He had wanted to tell them the full story of Guy de Maupassant's syphilitic madness and Heinrich Heine's syphilis of the spinal cord and then go on to other epidemics of mental illness and how lead poisoning had been the real cause of the fall of Rome. But enough was enough. They made arrangements to do a spinal tap and settled down to start the second case.

Linda went to get the chart, but the patient was down in X-ray. He wouldn't be back for an hour.

"Well, what should we do for an hour? Any ideas, Sue?"

"Can we look at your lab?"

"Sure, Herb and Renee are starting a new experiment today. It might be worthwhile to see what's going on and talk a bit about it."

Richardson's occasional visits to the laboratory were usually at least pleasant. But he knew he'd made a mistake as soon as he walked in and Herb greeted him.

"What brings you up here, Dr. Richardson?"

"Herb, that's not necessary."

Herb made no response and went back to his work. Back to the guinea pigs.

"We had an hour to kill and Sue thought it would be worthwhile to see what's going on here. Why don't you give everybody the fifty-cent tour?"

Herb put down the guinea pig he was about to inject and closed the cage door loudly. Renee stopped her work and the two of them turned away from Richardson and began to explain their experiments. The students and residents all grouped around the cages to listen to Herb and Renee. Richardson walked to the other side of the lab and looked down at the expressway as he listened carefully. There were four cages with six guinea pigs in each cage. Those in the first cage were normal. Those in the second cage had received one dose of alpha-bungarotoxin. They had some difficulty holding up their heads, and their legs dragged a little bit.

"How long did it take for them to get weak after you injected them?" Sue asked.

"A few minutes," Herb explained. "First they began to drop their necks; then their legs got weak. And then we gave them Tensilon."

Richardson looked away from the window as Sue asked another question. "What happened?"

"At the usual dose, nothing. But with a double dose they looked pretty normal."

It was the professor's turn to make a request. "Have you any Tensilon ready, Renee?"

"Yes, sir."

"Why don't you show the students the experiment?"

"You, or the students, Dr. Richardson?" Herb broke in.

"The students, Herb." And me. Especially me.

Herb and Renee prepared the Tensilon while Richardson talked about alpha-bungarotoxin and this study as a possible model of the muscle weakness myasthenia gravis. They hoped it would be just like myasthenia gravis, and Tensilon would make the animals stronger, but their previous efforts had all been failures.

Renee and Herb were ready and gave the injections to the guinea pigs. Within minutes the animals no longer dragged their legs. Then they lifted their heads up and looked just like the normal guinea pigs in the first cage. In two minutes it started to wear off, and ten minutes after the injection they again dropped their heads and dragged their legs.

"Well, what do you think of that, John?"

"It sure worked that time, Dr. Richardson." John smiled at Renee.

"It certainly was impressive, wasn't it? Congratulations, Renee, Herb."

Renee smiled but Herb didn't respond.

"That's what you see in myasthenia gravis when you give Tensilon. Not the ipsi-pipsi improvement that happened when we gave Tensilon to Sanders, but real improvement."

"Dr. Richardson?"

"Yes, Linda."

"How long will the animals be weak?"

"Herb?"

"For at least three months, if not longer."

"Will the Tensilon keep working?" she continued.

Herb shrugged his shoulders and let Paul Richardson answer the question. "That's the big question. The only time we got any response at all, and it was nowhere like this, it only worked for a couple of days. But the guinea pigs were a lot weaker. We'll just have to see."

Herb continued the demonstration. The animals in cage three had received a larger dose of bungarotoxin and were weaker. Tensilon had had no effect before and he and Renee gave another series of injections, but this time there was no response. Dr. Richardson watched this much more closely.

"How much Tensilon did you give that time?" he asked, looking at Herb.

When Herb didn't answer, Renee broke in, "A double dose, just like we gave the other animals."

"Why didn't it work, Dr. Richardson?" John asked.

"That's part of the same question. We'll have to try with higher doses and see if it works. You can't get all the answers in one day." Richardson then nodded to his chief resident. "Let's finish the demonstration, Herb."

The animals in the last cage had received a still larger dose of bungarotoxin. They were much weaker than the other animals and could hardly walk or even support their bodies. Tensilon had had no effect the first time, so Herb and Renee gave each guinea pig an injection of a double dose. They waited and waited but nothing happened.

Richardson looked at his watch. It was time to see the last patient.

"Herb, Renee. Thanks for the show. If you get a chance, Herb, stop by the office before you go home. I'd like to talk to you."

They all walked back to the hospital to see the new patient, but he was still down in X-ray. So they stopped by to see Mr. Romberg.

"I'm . . . no . . . better . . . doctor," Mr. Romberg slurred out.

"I know, but I think we know what's going on."

His eyes lit up a bit.

"When you had your thyroid surgery . . ."

"That . . . was . . . fif . . . fif . . . fifteen . . . years . . . ago."

"Yes, but when they took out your thyroid, the little glands right next to them, the parathyroid glands, also got injured. They're not working anymore, and that's what caused your parkinsonism."

"Can . . . you . . . cure . . . me?"

"I hope we can. We are going to do a few more tests to

prove we're right, and then we'll start some new medicine and see if we can get you better."

"Thank you. I'll do anything you want."

As they left, Richardson remarked, "I hope you all noticed how the hope of a cure improved his speech."

They all nodded.

"Unfortunately, it won't last," Donna reminded him.

"I'm afraid you're right. Al, you look like you have a question."

"I do. Are you sure you should have told him it was due to the surgery?"

"Why not?"

"What if he sues somebody?"

"I never thought of that. But there's no reason to sue the surgeons. They didn't do anything wrong. It's just one of those things that happen. Parathyroid injury is a risk of that kind of surgery. We've known that for a long time. The fact that it could result in parkinsonism wasn't known when he had his operation. You can't blame a surgeon for not knowing a fact that wasn't proven until five years after the operation. That's not part of the rules. As Leroy 'Satchel' Paige said, 'Don't look back; something might be gaining on you.' "

Linda finally got her chance to present the new patient she had worked up.

"Mr. Henry Forel," she began, "is a forty-two-year-old left-handed white male who was admitted to the hospital last night for the first time because of a strange episode of numbness in his neck, which began while he was eating dinner."

Paul Richardson had just begun to sit back, half listening, seemingly paying more attention to Linda's hands and her hair than her words but then his interest picked up. First slowly. Then accelerando.

"He had just finished his meal when he noticed the sudden onset of numbness of the back of the neck. Over the next several minutes the numbness spread down his back and into both arms. Next, he broke out in a diffuse sweat, which was especially severe in his face, and then noticed a tight, uncomfortable feeling in both temples. It felt as if his head might burst at any time. His wife brought him right to the hospital, but by the time they got here he felt absolutely normal. He

denied ever having had a similar experience in the past
and—''

Richardson could no longer restrain himself. He stood up
and interrupted Linda's presentation. ''Let's see the patient.''

''Don't you want to hear the rest of his history, Dr.
Richardson?'' Linda complained. She didn't know whether to
be disappointed or angry.

''No, I don't think so. There's only one significant question you haven't answered, and I hate to say it, but I doubt if
you know the answer.''

''What's that?''

''Did he use chopsticks or just a fork?''

''Huh?''

Linda looked at Dr. Richardson and then at the residents
and other students, but they all seemed to be equally bewildered.

''Let's go.''

Once in the patient's room, Dr. Richardson did not even
wait for the usual introduction.

''Mr. Forel.''

''Yes.''

''You are not, I take it, a true devotee of Chinese food?''

''No. I rarely eat it.''

''But you did last night.''

''Yes. My wife and I went out for our anniversary.''

''You went to Chinatown, I hope?''

Mr. Forel nodded.

''You began with soup, I presume?'' Richardson was at it
again.

''Yes.''

''Wonton soup.''

''Yes, but . . .''

''Was it good?''

''Very. I even had two bowls of it, it was so good.''

''Followed by . . . let me guess.'' Richardson paused briefly.
''Egg foo yong?''

''Yes.''

''Chop suey.''

''Yes.''

''And fried rice.''

''You're absolutely correct!''

"I know. I also know that there is nothing wrong with you."

"Are you sure, Dr. uh . . . Richardson?" On hearing the good news, Mr. Forel's face suddenly had more life in it.

"Absolutely."

"But everyone was worried I might have had a stroke or a heart attack!"

"You had an attack of what is known as 'the Chinese Restaurant Syndrome.' It is probably caused by the monosodium glutamate used so profusely in many Chinese restaurants, especially in the wonton soup." Richardson hesitated just long enough to create an effect, then continued. "I knew you were not a true devotee of Chinese restaurants, since most devotees have all had mild episodes with sweating, et cetera, and you denied ever having had a similar episode in the past. Since the amount of monosodium glutamate is highest in the soup I assumed you began with that. The menu was the typical dinner for two for nondevotees. It's really quite—"

"Elementary!" Al interrupted.

"If I may continue. This is not an unusual problem and, more important, it's not at all serious unless, of course, you are addicted to wonton soup."

"It was good, but I'll skip it next time."

"That's a good idea. Oh, there is one thing. Did anyone ask you what kind of restaurant you were eating at?"

"No."

"I thought not." Richardson chuckled to himself as he left the room.

"Dr. Richardson."

"Yes, Linda."

"You forgot to ask him the one important question."

"The answer was too obvious. They asked for chopsticks, tried them, and then used the knives and forks."

"Oh."

It was time for mortality conference, so Richardson went back to the office while the residents and students headed for the auditorium.

"Any calls I have to deal with?" he asked Chris.

"Two things. Detective Ward wants to see you."

"Set up something."

"I already did; he'll be here at 4:30. And they want the department to formulate a policy on admissions of strokes from the emergency room."

"Put it on the agenda for the next regular monthly meeting."

"You don't have regular monthly meetings," Chris complained. "You've never had regular departmental meetings. You hate them."

"I know."

Chris considered it briefly and then came up with a suggestion. "Should I give it to Dr. Chiari when he gets back?"

"A brilliant idea. Bud has much more patience for such things."

With that he retreated into his office, flipped on the FM, and began rechecking Renee's notebook. He turned off the FM and began calculating. Things looked in order at first glance. He started to analyze each experiment, each result, each statistic. His experience and skill in calculating batting averages, won-lost percentages, and earned run averages, which he had acquired during his misspent youth, still came in handy. As a matter of pride, he refused to use a calculator. He didn't approve of his kids using them in school. He'd been working solidly for an hour when Detective Ward came in.

"I'm not disturbing you, am I?"

"No, come in. I need a break. What's new?"

"Willis wants us to put guards on Sanders twenty-four hours a day. What's up?"

"I told him that it was possible that Dr. Collier was the real target, and if so, maybe someone would want to kill Dr. Sanders."

"Do you really believe that, Doc?"

"I don't know what to believe, Tom. But I doubt if an epidemic of euthanasia has broken out around here. And even if the murderer is a mercy killer, why knock off Collier?"

"No reason that I can think of," the detective responded.

"That's right. No reason. No reason at all. I doubt if it had to do with living in Cleveland, though it could be something that had nothing to do with medicine. Maybe they were all Russian spies. Maybe Mitchell stole the secrets of Bob Feller's fastball for them. Who knows?" The detective didn't laugh, but Richardson wasn't disappointed. It wasn't that funny. Gallows humor. There had to be something connecting the five patients. Maybe Al was right: exposure to some government-made carcinogen. Hell, there's no carcinogen that causes five different kinds of cancer. At least none that he knew of. "We haven't learned anything in our review, Tom. Have you guys?"

"We haven't found anything yet, but we're still working on it."

"So we're left with six deaths in the hospital. Maybe Locke was right. Maybe it's just some crazy jackass."

"The guy must be crazy, Doc."

"Sure, but if he's that crazy, the patients should be just hit or miss—potluck, so to speak. Not five people dying of cancer and an expert on cancer. So maybe it's the other way around. The five murders were just a smoke screen to hide the murder of Collier."

"Why would somebody want to kill Dr. Collier?"

Richardson hesitated and then just shook his head. Too many of his kids had motives. "I don't know. I wish I knew that."

"And why would that involve Sanders?" It was time for Tom Ward to be the hunter.

Richardson answered more slowly than Mr. Romberg. "I don't know." It wasn't as much fun being the prey.

"Level with me, Doc. You're hiding something."

"It's just an idea, a notion, nothing more." Richardson stopped. It was time to find a cigar. That would kill some time. First the cigar. Then the damn matches. He didn't know anything definite. He had nothing to really go on. No hard data. Nothing he could be sure of. "I just have hunches, Tom. It wouldn't be fair to anyone if I—"

"You know Doc, I'm not Dean Willis," Detective Ward broke in.

"I know that."

"You know I'm not going to crucify somebody without evidence."

Evidence—data. It all depended upon your point of view. "I still can't say anything, Tom."

"Have it your own way. But I sure hope nobody else gets killed."

"That's why I talked to Willis. As long as Sanders has personal guards, things will be okay."

"Yeah, we have three officers on eight-hour shifts. Mike Devic, Al Bright, and Frank Balo. They'll sit outside his room."

"In uniform?"

"No, in plain clothes. They'll check everybody who goes into his room."

"Who will they let in?"

"The floor nurses and your people, since you're taking care of him. Who would that be?"

"Everyone on service." He buzzed Chris. "Give Detective Ward a list of everyone on Neurology, including the students."

Ward got up to go. "There's nothing else you want to tell me?"

"Nothing else I can tell you."

"Play it your way. But if you're right, why did the other five all have to have cancer? Was it just coincidence?"

"I'm sorry Tom, I just don't know the answer."

The detective was far from satisfied but since it was obvious that Dr. Richardson was not going to say anything more, he left and Richardson went back to his calculations. He didn't even look up when Chris went home. Each figure became a batting average. It was like being in the bleachers and calculating the batting average of each player each time he came up to bat. It was the same game and maybe just as meaningless. The question wasn't outhitting the Yankees, but beating them. He knew the figures were right, the statistics were right. They had the data. But were the observations right? Would it hold up as evidence? Did each number in the notebook represent a fact? Something that really happened? Evidence in front of a jury of his peers. Or was it just what Renee believed happened, what she wanted to have happen? You never knew. That could happen and it might not even be intentional. There were many ways to be let down. The Sox could lose in so many ways. Maybe Renee just wanted the experiments to work. There was no future in checking any more figures. There was a knock at the door. It was Herb Westphal.

"Herb, what is this 'Dr. Richardson' business?"

"I guess I overreacted a bit."

"A bit! Goddamn it! Cut it out! I don't think you cheated. But maybe there is something wrong with the methods, the way we did the experiments. I have to know. Hell, I got murdered on Saturday. I have to know where we went wrong. It's not you. It's me. I have to know."

"Then why did you have to come up to the lab and check on us today?"

"Believe me, I wasn't checking up on you. The students wanted to see the lab."

"Come on. You don't expect me to believe that!"

"Why not?"

"They know more about the lab than you do."

Richardson looked puzzled.

"You get up there once a month. John is up there all the time. So are Linda and Walt."

"Yes, I guess it was just Sue that asked."

"Nuts! She's even been up there once or twice."

"Look, Herb. I wasn't looking over your shoulder. Forget about it. Wait a minute. If all those students go in and out, one of them could have taken the strychnine."

"You don't think—"

"It had to be somebody with some knowledge of medicine. Let's not even think about it."

The phone rang. It was Al.

"Thank God you're still there!" the first-year resident stated with obvious relief.

"What's up?"

"It's Sanders. He's a lot worse."

"Christ! Where are you?"

"The nursing station."

"Herb and I will be over in a couple of minutes."

Worse was an understatement. Sanders could hardly speak. He had trouble swallowing. His own saliva was collecting in his mouth. He could hardly breathe. He looked frightened.

"Wha's happening?" he slurred out.

"I don't know," Dr. Richardson answered him. "We may have to put you on a respirator. Al, did they do a biopsy?"

"Yes."

"Where? I don't see any bandage."

"Left leg."

"Are the muscle enzyme studies back?"

Al shook his head and then Richardson turned to Sanders. "Bill, we're going to get private duty nurses in here tonight to watch you, and if we have to, we'll put you on a respirator."

As they walked out, Officer Devic introduced himself and checked each doctor's identification, except Richardson's.

"Why didn't you check me?"

"Tom told me that there would be one doctor without a tie, Dr. Richardson. You're easy to spot."

They went back to the office. Al made arrangements for the nurse. He was on duty tonight and would keep a close watch on Sanders. The guinea pigs just didn't seem important anymore.

"What the hell has he got?" Herb asked.

"I suppose he had either muscle inflammation or nerve inflammation," Richardson responded. "Don't you agree?"

"Yes. Should we start him on steroids, Boss?"

"Yes. Large doses. Very large doses."

CHAPTER 14

As usual, his coffee was already poured when he came downstairs, but today there was a difference. Next to his coffee mug was a neatly folded tie. He considered it for a moment. "What's this for?"

"You didn't forget, did you?"

"Forget what?"

"We were supposed to go out to dinner tonight."

"Of course I didn't forget. But why the tie?"

"I'd like you to wear a tie tonight."

Richardson wrinkled his forehead, folded the tie, and started to put it into his jacket pocket.

"Paul, please."

He unfolded the tie and went into the bathroom to put it on. As he did, Bobbie started his English muffin. When he got back he asked, "Where are we going?"

Bobbie turned to him. "I thought we might go to Riccardo's."

"No."

"Why not? You used to like it."

"That was when it was the home of the St. Louis Browns fan club of Chicago. Since they moved out it's not the same."

"Paul!"

"I can't help it; that's the way I am. If it's no longer the last refuge of Ned Garver, Bobo Holloman, or Bow-wow Arft, I'd rather not go there."

"Then where shall we go?"

"Sayat Nova."

Bobbie smiled. They both liked Sayat Nova. It was supposed to be the best Armenian restaurant in the world, and besides, its grotto atmosphere reminded them of Israel, of Jaffa, of Aladdin's Cafe. She would meet him there at 7:30.

He looked out the window. It had begun to snow. Just a light flurry. "I'd better split. Traffic will be slow and I've got a busy day."

"Don't forget to make a reservation."

"I won't." A mere formality. Paul always wanted to make the reservations for dinner but often forgot. Later in the day Bobbie would call Chris and double-check. It wasn't that he didn't care, but there would be other problems to worry about during the day.

Traffic was not bad, considering that it snowed constantly, but the snow wasn't sticking to the ground. It couldn't stick to the ground. The White Sox home opener was in two days. In the good old days, the days of Mayor Daley, he would never have let opening day be snowed out. Rain, maybe. Snow, never.

As soon as he arrived at the hospital, he went straight to Bill Sanders's room. Officer Balo was seated outside the door and stopped him from entering.

"I'm Dr. Richardson."

"Let me see your ID."

"I don't have it with me."

"Then you can go and get it."

"Look, Ward said you guys would let me in. Devic didn't need to . . ." Then he remembered. "Let me take off the tie and then you can let me in."

"No, I'll need your ID, sir."

Fortunately, Herb came by and together they convinced Officer Balo that Richardson wasn't a mad killer. At least they partly convinced him. He let them in but went in with them.

Dr. Sanders was no worse than he had been the night before, but he certainly was no better. He couldn't even swallow his own saliva. He had a temperature. His pneumonia was probably coming back.

Herb walked back to the office with Richardson. "You know Sanders pretty well, don't you, Boss?"

"We interned together here in 1962 and '63. Then we did our residency here at the same time. He did his residency in medicine while I did mine in neurology. I've known him for eighteen years, so I guess I know him fairly well in some ways. Why?"

"What kind of a doctor was he then?"

"That's always hard to tell. I think he was a good doctor. But I think differently than most people."

"How's that?"

"The major difference between good doctors and bad doctors is that good doctors remember every mistake they ever made. We all make mistakes sooner or later, sometimes serious ones. You can't make the kinds of decisions we make day after day, night after night, sometimes all night long, without being wrong sometimes. The good doctors remember, the others don't. Maybe they don't care, maybe they need to forget, maybe they did it too often. But they don't remember. Sanders remembered. In the old days he remembered. Now, I don't know."

Herb went off to check a few more patients, and said he would sit in on the card rounds this morning.

When Richardson got back to the office, the coffee was ready. He hung up his coat.

"You gave in."

"What do you mean?"

"The tie."

"Bobbie made me wear it. We're going out to dinner."

"That's some coincidence," Chris said in a tone that reflected more sarcasm than disbelief. "The memo came yesterday and today a tie."

"Just so they don't send a memo on shining shoes. Will you make a reservation for two at Sayat Nova for 8:00 when you get a chance?" He had remembered.

He looked out the window and couldn't believe it. It was still snowing. It would stop by noon and then it would begin to melt off. At least Holmes had never had to deal with real snow. Fog was bad enough, but snow was worse.

He took a deep breath, went into his office, closed the door, and started looking through Herb's lab book. It was difficult, but he had to do it. After a few minutes he knew he'd get nothing out of it. The methods were fine; so were the results; so were the calculations. But the observations. The same question. Were they real? Is that why Herb had left Sanders? Left or been fired? Why wouldn't Herb talk about it? Why hadn't Collier given him credit for those six months? Sanders must have told Collier something, but what? Herb finally had gotten credit. This was getting him nowhere. The next task was the hardest: to see if Renee's observations were the same as Herb's and to go through everything in both notebooks and compare them step by step. It would take hours. As if that was all he had to do! Nuts!

Chris buzzed him. Everyone had collected for morning rounds. He told her to send them in.

Everyone seemed to have caught Richardson's mood. No one really liked Sanders, but they all cared. He was probably dying and there didn't seem to be anything anyone could do. They started card rounds.

John reported that Dr. Hunt had seen Mr. Romberg again.

"What did he think?"

"He doesn't believe he has parathyroid disease."

"Who cares? He's wrong."

"How can you be so sure?" John asked.

"What else could he have?"

Silence.

"That's right. There may be only two previous cases like his in the history of medicine, but when you've ruled out everything else and all you've got is the improbable, that improbability becomes fact.

"How's Mrs. Robin?"

"Worse. Is there anything we can do?"

"There is one thing; damn it . . ." Not everyone was going to get worse and die. Not if he could help it. There had to be somebody they could help today. He continued, "and it might just work. Listen carefully. We think she's had that virus for fifteen to twenty years, right?"

They all nodded.

"So why is she sick now, Walt?"

"It's the medicines she was given to suppress her own immune responses so that she wouldn't reject the kidney transplant."

"Continue."

"Those medicines depressed her defenses and the virus was no longer controlled."

"Okay, so what can we do?"

John spoke up. "I don't know if it's the right answer, but we could stop the medicine."

"Home run! It's a desperate move, but it might work. If we stop the medicine and her defenses start to work, we might stop the disease. Otherwise she'll die."

"But . . ."

"Yes, Walt."

"If you stop the medicine, she'll reject the kidney."

"True, but she can live on dialysis. If we don't, her brain is going to fall apart day by day before our eyes. I've seen that happen too goddamned often." He sat back. "Let's have some coffee."

He buzzed Chris and asked her to bring in some coffee and some cups and page Mrs. Robin's doctor so he could talk to him.

Linda reported on Mr. Wallenberg. He had thyroid disease and would be started on medicine today. He should be able to go home by the end of the week.

Chris brought in the coffee and everyone took a breather. The phone rang. It was Dr. Hutchinson. Richardson outlined his strategy for Mrs. Robin. Carefully, step by step, he went through the logic. Dr. Hutchinson listened very carefully before he replied, "Paul, are you that sure?"

"Yes."

"Hell, I never even heard of that disease."

"George, that's what she's got, and that's the only way we might save her brain."

"We'd better meet with her and her husband and discuss it with them," the other doctor suggested.

"The sooner the better," Richardson agreed.

"He's here in the afternoon. How about 1:00?"

"Fine."

"I'll pick you up at your office."

Mr. Dax had begun to speak a little better. The results weren't back yet on Michaels's spinal tap, but Richardson was sure that syphilis of the brain was the right diagnosis. They could wait another day before beginning the penicillin.

"How can you be so sure he has syphilis, Dr. Richardson?" asked Linda. "There are so many causes of dementia."

"⁻⁻⁻is eyes." Richardson turned to Walt. "Describe his pupils."

Walt looked at his note card. "Small, equal, not perfectly round. They didn't react to light, but they did accommodate."

"What's that mean?"

"When I shined a light in his eyes the pupils didn't get any smaller, but when he looked at my finger right in front of his nose they got smaller."

"Excellent—a perfect description of an Argyll Robertson pupil, and an AR pupil is virtually diagnostic of syphilis."

Sue shook her head. It was another name to remember. "How can you remember all those names?" she wondered out loud.

Al answered, "That's easy. An Argyll Robertson pupil is just like a prostitute."

Sue looked puzzled. "How's that?"

"I thought you'd never ask," Al beamed. "They accommodate without reacting."

"If I were you," Richardson commented, "I wouldn't publicize your sexual problems."

There was no reason to go over Sanders. Everyone was up to date on his progress, or lack of progress, and they'd see him later.

The new patient was on 7 East, but they decided to start the discussion in Richardson's office.

Al told the story. Mr. Jack Schwann was thirty-one years old, and for the last three years he had spells in which he passed out. That was all he remembered.

"Is that all we know?"

"No. The spells are seizures. People have been with him and they describe real seizures, but there is something I don't understand."

"What's that?"

"At first it only happened when he was watching TV, and only if the picture jumped."

Richardson finally looked interested. At least enough to stop watching the heavy snow falling outside his office window, snow that was beginning to blanket the city.

"You know, that used to be rare, but now it isn't anymore," Richardson began.

"What used to be rare?"

"Seizures triggered by light. For light to do that it has to flash on and off in a regular pattern, and it has to be almost the only light available. Before TV that was rare, but now we see it every year or two. I saw a patient once who had a seizure while driving a car. He was stopped at a railroad crossing. It was a dark night and he started counting the railroad cars as they went by. Then a car came up on the other side of the train and the flashing caused a seizure. He never had another seizure before or since.

"You know," he continued, "almost anything can cause a seizure. Except for flashing lights, other things are very rare, but they do occur. There was one patient whose seizures were only caused by listening to the 'Tennessee Waltz" and only if Patti Page was singing it. Today that would not be much of a problem, but there was a time, believe it or not, when that was a serious disability. Imagine a seizure triggered by the Rolling Stones, Bruce Springsteen, or The Ungrateful Styx or whatever they're called."

"I'm not sure I believe that."

"Why not, Al?"

"It sounds too much like a scene from a bad Abbott and Costello movie, when they were in a cell with a maniac killer whose rages were triggered by a single word. Every time Costello says that word the killer responds: 'Slowly I turn, step by step . . .' and then he chokes Costello. Could that be a seizure?"

"Probably not, but stranger things have happened. Poskanzer has reported a patient whose seizures happened only when he heard the chimes of a certain church."

Al smiled. "A patient for whom the bell tolls."

It was time to get back on track, so Richardson signaled a halt to the digression. "Al, you said 'at first.' "

"Yes, now he has seizures almost every day."

"Is he on seizure medicine?"

"Yes, and he swears he takes it."

"Does he?"

"I think so."

"Any evidence?"

"The blood tests show that he had good levels."

"So his seizures are getting worse despite adequate treatment."

"Yes."

"Any findings on exam?"

"His hands are the same size."

"Good. Anything else?"

"I think he's weak on the right side."

"Time to get to work."

They went on rounds. Richardson's examination of Mr. Schwann added very little. It was obvious that he had a weak right arm. In the conference room Dr. Richardson asked Al what he thought was the problem.

"It's not good. His seizures are getting worse and he's weak on the right side."

"So?"

"So he's got something going on on the left side of his brain."

"Right. But what? Be specific," the senior neurologist insisted.

"A brain tumor is most likely."

"Some weeks are like this. What's been done so far?"

"Nothing."

"Start with a CT scan and skull films. Then we may have to get an angiogram."

They went next to see Dr. Sanders. Officer Al Bright stopped them all and checked their IDs. Richardson still didn't have his, but Balo had warned him that Richardson was wearing a tie today.

Sanders was worse. He virtually could not talk, and his breathing was labored. Richardson told him they were going to put him on a respirator. On their way out they checked

Sanders's chart. The muscle enzymes were normal. The biopsy was still cooking.

Morning rounds were over.

Richardson went back to his office by himself. He sat down to get started on the comparison of Renee's and Herb's results. It lasted about two minutes. He just couldn't do that now.

He got himself some coffee, found a cigar, and went through his mail. There was nothing of note. It was still snowing and WFMT was playing Donizetti. As far as he was concerned, Donizetti had written the same opera twenty-one times and gotten worse with each effort, but maybe that was his own problem. No one else he knew preferred "Bluebeard's Castle" to "Lucia de Lammermoor." In fact, Bobbie liked Lucia. The mad scene. With or without Callas.

He watched the snowflakes which had begun so slowly and gently and were now heavy and relentless. At least three to four inches had collected on the ground and it was still snowing. He'd have to call Bobbie and tell her not to drive in. It wouldn't be worth the effort.

It had to be Collier. That's the only way it made any sense. You killed five to hide the sixth. The other five had terminal carcinoma; maybe the bastard wasn't completely crazy. They were all close to dying, so maybe to a warped mind killing them wasn't so bad. That had to be it, but who did it? Someone on the house staff who was afraid of losing his residency? Someone like Al or Adam Stokes or Herb? They were all moonlighting. If so, Sanders was a more likely victim. He was behind the move to fire some residents. Collier was only supporting him secondarily. No, that couldn't be the motive, or could it? To save a career, a life for a career. No. Maybe.

A student? Lots of students had problems with Collier. Linda. Herb, when he was a student. A student had more to lose. If you lost a residency, you could always get another, but if you flunked out of medical school, what could you do? You might not have to dig ditches or walk the streets, but you really weren't trained for anything else. What kind of a student would do this? Who knows? Somebody who could get into his lab. But then again, anybody could get into his lab.

It came back to that. Somebody who knew enough about neurology. That's what hurt. He never could judge people he liked. Look what had happened with Carol Voss and possibly now with Herb or Renee. No, not Herb. Not Renee. They couldn't have faked any. lab results. He refused to believe that. But still he had to check. Donizetti was replaced by Janáček. The snow continued—soft, clean, quiet, persistent.

At 1:00, Dr. Hutchinson came by and together they talked to Mr. and Mrs. Robin. It wasn't easy, but they crossed the Rubicon and stopped Mrs. Robin's medicines.

It was nearly 2:00 when he got back to the office. There were thirteen patients on his appointment book, but only two showed up. Both new patients had been referred to him for a diagnosis. Linda was seeing one, and he'd see the other one.

As soon as Mr. Henry Berger walked into his office Richardson knew the diagnosis. The patient had an obvious intention tremor, a tremor that appeared when he reached out to do something but disappeared when his hands were at rest. Mr. Berger did not have Parkinson's disease. He had benign tremor. One look at the tremor and Richardson knew that. He always looked forward to seeing new patients partially in the hope that the problem would challenge him, and now that challenge was gone. Fortunately, the second part of the challenge remained. Could he do something to help the patient? He probably could. During his examination his mind began to wander—to Bill Sanders, to Mike Collier. To those damn lab notebooks. He finished his examination, and told Mr. Berger three things: First, he did not have Parkinson's disease, which made him feel better. Second, he had a disease called benign essential tremor which confused him a bit, since he had never heard of it. Third, Dr. Richardson thought he could help him. He wrote a prescription, discussed the drug's side effects, and told Mr. Berger to call him back in two weeks.

As he waited for Linda to complete her examination of the other patient he rummaged through his top drawer. He came across his old appointment cards which read:

PAUL RICHARDSON, M.D.
CONSULTING NEUROLOGIST

Not just NEUROLOGIST, but CONSULTING NEUROLO-
GIST. To see the patients once or twice, make the diagnosis,
and then let their doctors take care of them. A childish
fantasy. To have the fun, the excitement of the chase, the
hunt, the game. To play the game but not get involved in
chronic patient care. It just didn't work; he always got involved.

Linda then presented the last patient of the day, a forty-year-
old woman named O'Brien who complained of pain and
weakness in the palms of both hands. She was otherwise in
pretty good health. Linda thought that she had a bilateral
carpal tunnel syndrome.

"Due to?"

"Pressure on the median nerve in the wrist as it passes
through the carpal tunnel."

"Due to?"

"I don't know."

"What causes bilateral pressure?"

"I don't know."

"You do. You're just not thinking. Anything that makes
the tunnel narrower, like hypothyroidism, or the nerve thicker,
like acromegaly. Let's see the patient."

Richardson examined her, told her she had pressure on the
nerves in her wrist and might need surgery. First, they'd have
to get some blood tests, which he was sure would be normal,
and then Dr. Jackson could do a small, simple operation to
relieve the pressure.

Linda followed Richardson out of the examining room and
back to his office. They both sat quietly for a minute. She lit
a cigarette, and he just stared at the cluttered walls.

"I'm sorry I was abrupt. I didn't mean to be, but things
have been hectic, to say the least."

"It's okay. I'm going to head home if everything's done."

"Wait, I want to show you something—if I can find it."
For a couple of minutes he rummaged through his top drawer
and then, with a glint in his eye, threw a small envelope to
Linda. "Catch. What do you see?"

"An envelope about two inches square, labeled Harlan J.
Berk, Ltd."

"Not on the envelope. Inside it."

"I thought I was supposed to observe everything."

"Touché."

"It's a coin."

"Correct. An ancient coin. A bronze sestertius of Maximinus I, who was emperor from 235 until 238. One of the first soldiers to be proclaimed emperor by the troops. Look at his portrait. What do you see?"

"He's ugly."

"Yes. Historians often compared him to Hercules or Ajax but never to Adonis. What about him is ugly?"

"His chin. It's much too large and sticks way out. And his nose is too big and he has a ridge above his eye."

"Marvelous. What's your diagnosis?"

"Diagnosis?"

"Sure. What causes such prognathism and a prominent supraorbital ridge?"

"Acromegaly."

"Beautiful. I could kiss you." He turned away and then started slowly: "Coin collectors have looked at that coin for at least 100 years since acromegaly was first described by Pierre Marie—a French neurologist, by the way—and as far as I know you are only the second person to make that diagnosis. Acromegaly. It came from two Greek words: *akron,* meaning extremity; and *megale,* meaning large. Largeness of the extremities due to a tumor of the pituitary gland, which makes too much growth hormone. So obvious and yet no one saw it. If you read the ancient historians, they say he was seven feet two inches tall—a true pituitary giant—and that he wore his wife's bracelet as a ring. That's true acromegaly."

"And you were the first to notice it?"

"As far as I know."

"That's brilliant."

"No, it isn't. No slur intended, but a bright medical student could make that diagnosis just like you did. If only we could really observe without prejudice. Oh, well, unfortunately we'll never be able to prove it."

"Prove it?"

"Sure, by getting his skull and finding evidence of a tumor."

"Could that be done?"

"Yes and no. John Hunter, the greatest of all British

surgeons, had a collection of anatomical speciments, including the skeleton of a seven-foot-four-inch Irish giant. When Hunter died in 1793 his collection became the collection of the Royal College of Surgeons. And in 1909 Harvey Cushing, the great neurosurgeon, visited it, examined the skull of Hunter's giant, and found evidence of a tumor of the pituitary. So in reality Hunter's giant is the first proven case of acromegaly. The head of Maximinus unfortunately will never be found. It was severed from his body and thrown into the Tiber. That's enough for today.''

It was almost 4:30 and still snowing. Linda and Chris both left early. Richardson called his wife. It was worse in Highland Park, so she obviously couldn't drive to the city. He wouldn't try to get home until after rush hour. Meanwhile, he'd get started on reviewing those damned notebooks.

CHAPTER 15

THE snow piled up on the expressway almost as quickly as the traffic did. Almost nothing was moving except the large wet flakes. They glittered like the raindrops reflected in the lights of Comiskey Park during a rain delay at a night game. The Sox against the Yanks. The classic struggle of David and Goliath. Pierce against Ford. Billy the Kid against the Philistines. Against the rain and the odds. And David had lost.

It certainly would be useless to attempt to drive to Highland Park in that mess. Maybe after a few hours traffic would be clear and he could start home. It was as good a time as any to start work comparing Renee's results with Herb's.

Richardson poured himself a cup of coffee, put in a saccharine and some Pream, and sat down at his desk. At least it wasn't entirely ersatz. They had used real coffee. Had Sanka helped Mr. Stilling or had he had to give up even Sanka?

He found the two lab notebooks, lit a cigar, turned on the FM, and began to look through them. Renee's notebook went back to July 1979. Herb's went back to March of 1979. He'd have to figure out which experiments were which. Thank God they both numbered and dated each experiment. It wouldn't be so hard to match them up. How to get started?

He walked to Chris's desk, went through her address file, found the number he was looking for, picked up the phone, and dialed the number.

Mrs. Ward answered the phone and then immediately yelled for her husband.

"Hi, Doc."

"How are things going with the surveillance of Sanders's room?"

"You sure confused everybody by wearing a tie," the detective complained halfheartedly.

"I'll try not to let that happen again."

"Otherwise, there are no problems. Only nurses from the floor and people on that list Miss Gowers gave us have gotten into his room."

"Has anyone else even tried?"

"Not that I'm aware of."

"That's good."

"It doesn't mean too much."

"Why?"

"Well, having us there probably would scare the bastard off," Tom explained.

"That's fine. If nobody goes in there who doesn't belong, that means nobody will kill him. So if we can only save his life, he might make it."

"That bad, huh?"

"Yes, but that's our problem, not yours."

"I think I'd rather have my problems. Say, Doc, are you still sure that Dr. Collier was the reason for the other murders?"

"Pretty much so."

"I wish I were so sure."

"It's the only way it makes sense to me, Tom. I can't prove it, but it seems right to me."

"Are you hearing another zebra, Doc?"

"You really have been listening to Willis!"

"Dr. Richardson, I can't stick my neck out like you can. I can't put all my eggs in one basket unless I know it's the right basket."

"I guess not."

"So we'll just have to keep plugging and doing our best to prevent any more problems."

"Make sure your three guys keep up their good work."

"Don't worry; we will. See you tomorrow, Doc."

It was time to get to work. He started with Herb's notebook and found July. July 2nd, Experiment #42. He opened Renee's notebook to the first experiment. July 2nd. Experiment #1. He cleared off his desk so that he could put the two notebooks side by side.

Experiment #42   Experiment #1

Hell, there was no way he could do this. If Weigert thinks these kids did it, let him check their goddamned notebooks. He called Weigert's office, but there was no answer. He looked up Weigert's home number, called, let it ring once, and hung up the phone. He watched the snow for a few minutes.

There have been some rain-delayed games we won. Even some big ones. It wasn't whether you won or lost that counted but how you played the game. Oh, hell. Winning counted, but so did playing by the rules. They had to be followed. So he'd be manager and umpire at the same time.

Experiment #4   Experiment #1

He began to compare them figure by figure. Column by column. Number by number. The same result. One down.

He dialed Bobbie. No, he certainly couldn't leave for another two hours.

Experiment #43   Experiment #2
Experiment #44   Experiment #3
Experiment #45   Experiment #4

It was too late in Boston to call Dan Walker at his lab, and it was silly to call him at home.

Experiment #46   Experiment #5

Five down. No hits. No runs. No errors. Everything matched. The data looked good. Weigert was full of hot air.

Experiment #47   Experiment #6

Richardson got up, stretched, watched the snow for a while, and then went to Chris's desk and looked through her file again. Walker, Dan. They had his home phone number: 9-617-344-2654.

"Dan, this is Paul Richardson."

"Hi, Paul."

"How are things in Boston?"

"A perfect opening day. How about Chicago?"

"Don't ask. It's been snowing all day."

"That's what you have to expect. When you're Midwest, hot air meets cold reality. But you didn't call to talk about the weather."

"No, I wanted to talk about my lab results with you again."

For the next twenty minutes they went over everything from start to finish. There was no question about it. Something had gone wrong in Richardson's experiments. Somebody had screwed up.

Back to work.

Experiment #47   Experiment #6
Experiment #48   Experiment #7

He called Carol Voss. There was no answer.

Seven down. He looked at the two notebooks stretched out before him on his desk and the piles of papers shoved together to make room for the notebooks. It was time to do something with some of those damned reprints. He took a handful and began the work of cross-referencing and filing. There had to be something better to do. Better than watching the snow, or checking experiments. Or filing reprints.

Experiment #49   Experiment #8

He walked into Herb's office. The charts were still piled up all over the place. They had to get to work on them. He knew that Walt had at least started the project. But as far as he could tell, not much progress had been made. Medical records would want the charts back as soon as possible. Maybe sooner. He looked through a number of stacks and located a small pile from the last year of his residency.

J. Bloodworth	227-255
K. Heintzelman	250-409
W. Jones	267-456
R. Meyer	680-308
B. Miller	647-357
R. Roberts	645-302
A. Seminick	288-524
K. Silvestri	250-350

He even remembered some of the cases. He picked up Bloodworth's chart and began to thumb through it. He really didn't care.

He went back to his office. This was useless. It was a waste of time.

Experiment #50   Experiment #9
Experiment #51   Experiment #10

He was on Experiment #61-20 when Linda walked into his office.

"What brings you by?"

"I saw the light."

"Light?"

"Yes, I can see your office light from my apartment." She paused. "Did you get any dinner?"

He wrinkled his forehead. "No, I guess I didn't."

"Why don't you come over? I'll give you something to eat."

He looked down at his desk. Experiment #61. "That's certainly the best offer I've had all day."

They went outside and trudged their way to the hospital apartments. Traffic was still not moving on the expressway. Abandoned cars and trucks were scattered in the lanes. It looked like a long night. After they got to her apartment Linda put some hamburgers into the frying pan and started to make a salad.

"Dr. Richardson."

"Yes."

"Why don't you fix us something to drink and put a record on?"

"What'll you have?"

"Scotch on the rocks."

Linda brought him some ice cubes and he poured the drinks. After he brought one to Linda, Paul began to look through her record collection. All the Bs were there, but so was Bartok. Suddenly his gaze stopped shifting. It was hard to believe, but there it was: the Kubelick recording of the Bloch Concerto Grosso Number One with the Chicago Symphony Orchestra. That recording was one of the great unsung masterpieces of early HiFi. An underground collector's item. Like Horenstein's Mahler and Mengelberg's Strauss. William Kapell.

"Linda, you weren't even born when this was recorded."

"What's that?"

"The Bloch Concerto Grosso. It was recorded in 1952."

"That was the year I was born."

"How did you ever get this record? It's been out of print since you were in braces."

"It took about two years, but if something is really that good then it's worth the effort. The hamburgers are ready."

Paul put three records on the phonograph: the Bloch, Strauss's Four Last Songs, and Villa Lobos.

"Dr. Richardson, can I ask you a question?"

"Anytime."

"It's a personal question."

"Sure, I don't have too much to hide."

Linda smiled. "Do you really care about the White Sox?"

"Is that the personal question?"

"Yes. On rounds you mention baseball and the White Sox so frequently that I just wonder if you really care about them."

Paul Richardson took a deep breath. "Unfortunately, the answer is yes. The White Sox and I have been deeply and irreversibly intertwined since that fateful Sunday in May of 1950." Linda said nothing, so Paul continued, "That Sunday my Dad and I went to a White Sox-St. Louis Browns double-header. Two games between two of the most inept teams in all of baseball. We had box seats. Right next to the Comiskey box. Along about the fifth inning of the game, Mrs. Comiskey . . ." He paused and shook his head almost imperceptibly. "She was the owner of the Sox then. Well, halfway through the second game she called the ball boy over. Boy. He must have been seventy. She told him to give me a baseball. A Big League baseball! One they had actually used in the game! That started it. The 1950 Sox were a bad team. The only thing worth remembering was how forgettable most of the players were. In 1950 I was an ungainly kid who didn't seem to do much of anything very well. So we suffered together. Then came 1951, Minnie Minoso, Nellie Fox, Chico Carrasquel, Billy Pierce, Jim Busby, fourteen straight wins, respectability, and straight As in high school. The pattern was set, and I just never outgrew them. Hell, I got married the year we finally won the pennant!"

Linda laughed. "Was that a good omen?"

"I don't know. We lost the World Series."

Linda hesitated for a long moment before she went on. "Do you care about other sports?"

"Like football and basketball?"

"Yes."

"Not really. I follow them but not because I care about them. Someday you're going to get married."

"Maybe."

"Most likely. And most likely your husband will watch Sunday afternoon football like the rest of us. But not necessarily because he's a fan."

"Then why?"

"Two reasons. The first is to have something to talk about. At the office. At parties. Especially at large parties and other social events. The women tend to collect together and talk about their things: fashions, cooking, kids, and Michelangelo. The men talk about football. So you watch out of self-defense. Some day at dinner I'm going to discuss the Pirenne hypothesis, Hofmannsthal's librettos, Bartok's string quartets, something worthwhile. Someday. The horrifying thought is that I may have already met someone else like that and we both just talked about the old Detroit Lions because it was the thing to do." He stopped.

"You said there were two reasons. I'm almost afraid to ask. What is the other one?"

"Watching the football game is a culturally accepted way of escaping. For three hours you don't have to deal with anything. You can sit there and be with and by yourself."

"I'm not sure I understand."

"It's a way to be by yourself in a busy household. Everybody leaves you alone. You need that sometimes." Then, without a warning, his voice was no longer serious. "And besides, there's nothing more beautiful than a sixty-yard pass to fast flanker against a prevent defense." Richardson paused for a brief moment. "It's my turn to ask you a question."

"Okay. but don't let your hamburger get cold."

"Do you know Walt very well?"

"Fairly well. We went out for a while."

"Is he always that serious? I've rarely seen him smile."

"I'm afraid so. But it's not so hard to understand."

"How so?"

"His dad died when he was ten or eleven. He had been in the hospital for months. Here, in fact. And despite everything that was done, he died. I'm sure that had something to do with his going into medicine. He's really dedicated to it."

"I know he wants to save lives and stamp out disease, but twenty-four hours a day? You can't eat, drink, and live nothing but medicine."

"He has to. He's got to be better than the doctors who took care of his father."

"He's got to save his father's life?"

"I guess so."

The Concerto Grosso was over. George Schick's major recording as piano obbligato.

"There's one lineup I'll bet you know."

"What's that?" Linda seemed dubious.

"Let's take it in order. I'll start."

Linda seemed more than a bit puzzled. She didn't know any baseball players.

"Leadoff man: Theodore Thomas. Number two hitter . . ."

Linda smiled. "Frederick Stock."

"Number three in the batting order, Désirée Defauw. Cleanup hitter . . ."

"Artur Rodzinski." Her reply was faster, louder.

"Rafael Kubelik."

"Fritz Reiner." It was building like a Beethoven fugue.

"Jean Martinon."

"Georg Solti." They both almost shouted and then laughed.

Why did everyone find her cold and distant? Richardson certainly didn't. The enthusiasm and warmth seemed to trouble them both. For a few minutes they listened to Schwarzkopf and then Richardson started talking about the other students. They talked about Sue a bit and then about Renee. Renee and Linda were friends. They had been close friends for a couple of years.

"What's up between Renee and Sanders?" Paul asked.

"Nothing."

"You sure?"

"Yes."

"Then why did she go to see him in the hospital?"

"I don't know."

"Don't know or don't want to tell?"

"I guess it won't hurt. Don't tell anybody, especially not Renee or John."

"I won't. Don't worry."

"There's nothing between Renee and Sanders, but she's afraid there might be or was something . . ." She paused, started, and paused again.

"Yes?"

"Between John and Sanders."

"God, no! You're kidding."

"No. They almost broke up over it. John said nothing really happened. That Sanders just started . . ."

"I don't think I really want to hear all the gory details. Sanders! Jesus! Maybe that's what happened with Herb."

"Herb? You mean Herb Westphal?"

"No, it's nothing. Skip it."

They finished dinner talking about Richard Strauss and the von Bülow letters and Wagner. It was 11:00 and he called Bobbie. There was no way he could get home. He would stay at the office.

It was Linda's turn to ask a key question. "Well, are you or aren't you?"

"Am I or am I not what?"

"Going to stay here, with me?"

He didn't answer for several seconds. How could Robert Morley turn down Dianna Rigg? It would be so easy to say yes. Who'd know? Who'd care? He had to sleep someplace. "No."

Linda closed her eyes tightly for a few seconds, then turned away. She addressed her question half to Richardson and half to the wall. "Why not?"

"Bloch's Concerto Grosso." Why couldn't he just tell her he loved Bobbie and let it go at that? It wasn't that simple.

"I don't understand," she said quietly.

"It just wouldn't be trivial. Nothing ever is for me. And especially with you. It just could not be simple or easy and certainly not trivial. So somebody would get hurt and I'd always remember it."

"I'm still not sure I understand."

"You've been with me on rounds. You've seen how I think, how I remember."

"It must be great to be able to remember so much."

"Sometimes it's easier to forget things."

"What do you mean?"

"As a Sox fan, you have more defeats to remember than victories: I remember them all. But it's the other things I remember that cause the trouble. I remember every patient I ever lost, every mistake I ever made, every woman. Everything. Every hit, every run, and every error. Especially the errors."

"Would I be an error?"

"In the long run, yes."

"Can I . . . ask you a question?"

"Sure."

"It's a personal question again."

"Go ahead."

"Have you ever had an affair?"

The record changed. Bachianas Brasileiras Number 5 began, sung by Victoria de los Angeles and with the composer himself conducting.

"Yes."

"Why?"

"It was better than cocaine."

"That's not true."

"Cocaine's better?"

"No, of course not. But that can't be the reason."

"Why not? Holmes used cocaine."

"And you used women?"

"No, I never used them."

"Then why? Why then, and not now?"

"I'm not sure I know. If I did, I wouldn't be here now or . . ."

"Or?"

"I would have been here last week. Can I ask you a personal question?"

"I guess you have a right to."

"Why me? I'm sixteen years older than you are and I'm not exactly Alan Alda. You don't make a habit of older men."

"No."

"Then why?"

"The same reason, I guess."

"Huh?"

"Bloch's Concerto Grosso."

He smiled. "I think I better go back to the office."

"I do have a couch."

"It would be better if I didn't."

"Why don't you stay with Renee and John?"

"A ménage à trois?"

Linda was not amused. "They live right across the hall. They have a new hide-a-bed. I'm sure they'd be happy to have you stay with them."

"I'm not sure. Renee is pretty annoyed with me."

"Let me call them."

He rummaged through the records again while Linda called Renee. Linda put down the phone. She was right. Renee and John were happy to put him up for the night. They walked across the hall together. Even though it was 11:00 everyone in the medical center was still up. Hundreds of stranded people were wandering around, looking for empty or half-empty beds. Impromptu parties were going on all over the place.

Renee, John, Linda, and Dr. Richardson watched the snow. Renee dug out a set of pictures of John's and Linda's class when they were in their first year of medical school. He remembered lecturing to them. They went over the pictures with him and told him what each of the students was going to do—who was interested in surgery, in family practice, in psychiatry. It was much different from his medical school class when he graduated eighteen years ago. No one in his class planned on going into general practice; everyone had to be a specialist. But a lot of these kids were actually going to go out and take care of sick people. That was a step in the right direction.

It was still snowing when Linda went back to her apartment. It was time to get to sleep. When John went into the bedroom Renee turned to Dr. Richardson. "I'm sorry about yesterday."

"Yesterday?" he asked.

"In the lab."

"Oh, that."

"Herb was very angry and I was, too."

"You shouldn't have been. I had to check everything. You realize that."

"I guess so. But it's like you don't trust us."

"I trust you, Renee. If I didn't, you wouldn't get to do what you do. You almost run that lab. You and Herb. But I'm the one whose reputation is on the line here. I have to know what really happened. I'm sure you didn't do anything, but Christ, things happen sometimes."

John came back and they let the subject drop and said good night.

If he could only be completely sure about the research. It couldn't be Herb or Renee who was wrong. Not again. He couldn't have made that mistake again. Somebody in Weigert's lab must have screwed up. He'd call Weigert tomorrow.

Maybe he wouldn't have to go through all those notebooks. Then he could help Walt get started on those charts. Walt. Was his a good reason to go into medicine? It did result in dedication. Maybe it was the best reason, or maybe the worst. Or both. What difference did it make? Why had he himself gone into medicine? He wasn't sure he remembered anymore. Why had Bill Sanders? Bill Sanders. If some doctor got himself killed around here it should have been Sanders. Maybe we're all killing him by not saving his life.

He watched the snow for another twenty minutes. He'd left his cigars at the office, so he just watched. The promise of spring had been replaced by a blanket of winter. The night seemed absolutely empty. It was easy to feel isolated from the rest of life. Separated from the reality of yesterday and tomorrow. But yesterday with its early scents of spring and tomorrow with its promise that summer would arrive were real.

CHAPTER 16

By the time Richardson woke up at 6:45 the snow had stopped. The sky was cloudless. A clear, bright, sunny April day. The kind of sunny day you prayed for on opening day. Paul Richardson squinted as he looked out the window and listened to the quiet. The silent city was blanketed by well over a foot of snow. It was strange not to hear the noise. So often it seemed to be one of the major products manufactured in Chicago. Without noise, the city seemed transformed, clean, unsoiled. But under the snow it was still the same city with the same problems. And he still had the same problems as well: six murders, those damn lab notebooks, his strychnine.

The official weather report called it fourteen inches. The radio was full of reports of closed highways, closed schools, but not, of course, closed hospitals. From the window he could see that the expressway was still clogged with abandoned vehicles. There was little to watch except the still silence. Only one or two people could be seen straggling into the hospital for the 7:00 shift.

He looked around for something to read. The shelves filled with paperbacks reflected the new heroes: Hunter S. Thompson and Kurt Vonnegut. *Zen and the Art of Motorcycle Maintenance*. John Irving. Where had J. D. Salinger gone? Did Holden Caulfield still live? Carlos Castaneda and Hermann Hesse. Had they really read Hesse and not thought him boring? Or did they just buy Hesse when they were undergraduates in the same way his friends had bought James Joyce?

He had it on good authority that no one had ever read *Finnegan's Wake* from start to finish. He fingered a number of books and finally picked up *Mother Night* and began to reread it. Vonnegut was wrong. You shouldn't make love whenever you can. It wasn't always good for you. The quiet continued until 7:30, when an alarm went off in the other room and John and Renee began to stir.

As they finished breakfast John turned on the TV to see if he could get the news and the weather. Richardson looked up as John flicked back and forth from channel to channel. "Go back to Channel 9, John."

"Why?"

"That was Henry Fonda in *The Male Animal*."

"What's that?" he asked as he flipped back.

"A play by James Thurber and Elliot Nugent. It's based on the Sacco and Vanzetti case." He started to explain but stopped. More than eighteen years separated them. Their education focused on where they were now, not where they had been or how they got there. Maybe they were better off. Maybe they knew more about now or cared more. More of their friends were going to go out and deliver medical care directly to patients. Maybe they'd do more for the country's health than his own class had done; they probably couldn't do much less. He told John to go back to the weather. The reporter seemed to relish the fact that as of 12:01 Tuesday morning it was illegal to have studded snow tires on your car. After all, winter was over.

A little after nine, Linda came by and the four of them tramped over to the office together. Linda made the coffee. By 9:45 Donna Batten had arrived and Chris had called to say she wouldn't be in. Al called. He was snowed in at a suburban hospital where he had worked the night before. Walt and Sue both called. They would be in for rounds. Herb called in. He'd be late, but he'd be in the lab by 1:00, if Richardson wanted him. As far as Richarson could tell, there were only two new consults to be seen. Linda and John each went off to see one of the new patients while Donna made follow-up rounds on the old patients. They would start rounds at 10:45 in Dr. Sanders's room.

That gave Richardson almost an hour to get to work on the

lab notebooks. They were still sitting on his desk, just where he had left them the night before.

Experiment #61   Experiment #20
Experiment #62   Experiment #21

He called Bobbie. The kids were at home. Their schools were closed. Their street had been plowed and there was a guy with a jeep coming down the street cleaning out driveways. If he could get to Highland Park, he could get home. He started again on Experiment #62 and stopped to call Carl Weigert. This was useless. There was no answer. Weigert might not even get in today. For the third time he read through Experiment #62. It was worse than an instant replay of a defeat in slow motion. Experiment #62. He had to do it. He got through experiments #62, 63, and 64.

Experiment #64   Experiment #23

At least there was some variety now. This was the first bungarotoxin experiment. Should he check these, too? He'd better. It was best to be sure. The calculations were different. A little variety helped.

Experiment #65   Experiment #24

The phone rang. Even Mrs. Hammond would be a welcome intrusion.

"Neurology."

"Is Dr. Richardson in?"

"Speaking."

"This is Mrs. Hammond."

"Yes?" Nuts.

"I'm snowed in."

What the hell am I supposed to do about that? he wondered. Maybe I should shovel her out.

"So are lots of people."

"But what if I run out of pills?"

"How many do you have?"

"I'm not sure."

"Well, count your pills and if you have fewer than ten, call your pharmacy."

"But they might be closed."

"Ten pills will last three days, Mrs. Hammond. They'll be open in three days."

"What if I have more than ten?"

"Then don't do anything."

"What if I only have eleven?"

"Take one and call your pharmacy. Goodby, Mrs. Hammond."

That woman. Medicine would be much easier if you didn't have to deal with patients.

Back to work.

Experiment #65   Experiment #24

The phone rang again. It was Donna Batten. They were waiting for him on 6 West. Time to get to work. Dr. Batten was waiting with all four students when he arrived.

"How are things, Donna?"

"Not good."

"Sanders?"

"Yes."

"Damn it!"

"You'd better see for yourself. He's almost completely paralyzed."

As the six of them went into Sanders's room, Officer Balo nodded to Richardson. "I recognize you today, Doc."

"How's that, Frank?"

"No tie."

Richardson felt in his pocket. Where had he put that thing? Bobbie wouldn't like it if he lost a tie. She always picked them out so carefully. Had he left it at John and Renee's, at the office, or at Linda's? "Has anybody tried to get in to see Sanders?"

"Just the nurses and the people on your list."

Richardson was no longer sure that it was important. Sanders might very well die without being murdered.

Donna had not really prepared him for what he found. Sanders was not just worse. The progress had been profound, almost overwhelming, almost complete.

Dr. Sanders was on a respirator. He could not breathe well enough to do without it. He could just barely move his respiratory muscles, just barely enough to trigger the respirator but not enough to survive without it. His life depended on a machine. All somebody had to do was pull his plug. That would be more effective than strychnine. Sanders's eyes were open and he moved his eyes to watch Richardson.

The only sound was that of the respirator pumping air in and out of Dr. William Sanders.

Whoosh . . . . . . whoosh

Whoosh . . . . . . whoosh

Whoosh . . . . . . whoosh

In and out. Richardson finally broke the patterned near-silence. "Good morning, Bill."

Bill Sanders, the patient, blinked to show that he had heard Richardson.

"I have to check a few things. Can you move your head?"

There was no response.

"Bill, I know you can hear me and understand me, so move your eyes up for yes, and side to side for no. Okay?"

Sanders moved his eyes up and down.

"Can you move your head?"

Side to side.

"Can you lift your head at all? Give it a try."

After a pause, Sanders moved his eyes side to side.

Slowly and painstakingly, Richardson tested each of Sanders's muscles. Each time he asked Sanders if he understood the instructions, and each time the eyes went up and down, but each time the muscles moved only feebly or not at all. Sanders could move his fingers and toes weakly. He could move his ankles. But he could not lift his arms or legs.

Next Richardson tested Sanders's ability to feel things—a piece of cotton and a light pinprick. It was clear that there was no sensory loss at all. It was only the muscle system that was involved. At least Sanders's entire nervous system hadn't given out under their watchful eyes. Just one part. And you only needed that part to move, to swallow, to breathe.

Richardson knew that further examination was useless and would add nothing, but it would forestall having to talk to Sanders. God, he'd known him for eighteen years, and maybe in some ways he was an SOB now, but eighteen years ago they had been interns together and friends. They had spent six months out of that year on the same service—alternating night call, taking care of each other's patients, helping each other. Sanders had been a good intern, a damn good one. Overall, Richardson thought, a better intern than he had been himself.

He was a physician who had really cared about his patients. Maybe some things had changed over the years, but you couldn't change that. He thought about the time they had spent on the Intensive Care Unit together, twenty-four hours on and twenty-four hours off. Each morning they had met together at eight o'clock. One exhausted intern and one soon to be exhausted intern. They would go over each patient in a ritual as formalized as the changing of the guard. But with more involvement. Not just the lives of the patients, but also the lives of the doctors. They had their own personal investment in those patients—it was a matter of pride to keep each patient alive until you went home. If the patient was going to die, he should die when the other intern was on duty. They kept a running score. Richardson had won. Sanders had never gotten over that. It may have been more luck than skill, but Richardson had won. Neither of them ever forgot.

Vibration was normal.

Position sense was normal.

The reflexes were decreased but not absent.

There was no reason to go on.

Whoosh . . . . . . whoosh

Whoosh . . . . . . whoosh

Whoosh . . . . . . whoosh

"Bill, listen carefully. We don't know what the hell is going on. It's probably inflammation of the muscles, so we're giving you steroids in high doses. We'll get you through this. Remember the ICU when we were interns?"

Up and down.

"I'm not going to lose this one either, and I'll collect that beer you never bought me."

Up and down.

"We'll be back later. We may set up a twenty-four-hour neurology bedside watch. I don't know. I'll see you before I go home."

They retired to the conference room. No one said anything. They waited for Dr. Richardson to start. The silence was more complete without the pattern of the respirator, but less intense. They all waited for Dr. Richardson.

"He's only two years older than I am. Damn it! We can't . . . Is his biopsy back yet?"

Donna shook her head. "I called this morning. It won't be done until late today."

"Christ! Keep on their asses!"

"What difference will it make? He's already on steroids."

"At least we'll know what we're dealing with. Maybe it won't make any difference, but we might feel less helpless, less stupid, less like helpless idiots. Damn it all! Let's go on to the next case. Who's on first?"

It was not a time for Abbott and Costello. Nor the White Sox. Not with fourteen inches of snow on the ground and an old colleague dying of God only knows what.

John gave a short, precise presentation of a thirty-eight-year-old man named Golgi who was in the hospital because of walking difficulty. As far as John could tell from talking to Mr. Golgi, the problem had started about three or four months ago when the patient started to stub his left foot on curbs. Then he noticed that his left leg seemed to drag, mostly late in the day, and now his left hand seemed a bit clumsy when he tried to play the piano, and maybe his right leg was a bit weak. Since he had to use his right leg more and more because of the trouble with his left leg, the patient wasn't really sure that his right leg was weak.

Next, John reported his findings on neurologic examination. Step by step, with great thoroughness. Richardson was staring out the window at the students' residence hall and pounding his reflex hammer into his palm. Like Commander Queeg fingering ball bearings. The soft rubber made a dull sound as it hit the palm. No one thought Richardson was even listening, but they said nothing. Carefully, quickly, all too quickly, Richardson heard John Adson reduce a man's life to a few paragraphs. To a short story, rapidly told. No triumphs. No agonies. Just a few facts. More like a précis than a short story. A précis that the world would soon forget. John went on. Eyes, normal; sensation, normal. Strength, weak in both arms and both legs, but worse on the left. He had noted twitches in . . .

Richardson broke into John's recitation with a question. It was so unexpected that it caught John off guard. "Twitches?" Such a simple question. "John, did you say twitches?"

"Yes, muscle twitches."

"Where?" he persisted.

"Everywhere."

"Arms?" he pursued.

"Yes."

"Legs?" he pursued.

"Yes."

"Face?"

"Maybe. A few."

"Tongue?"

"I think so."

Whatever spark had appeared in Richardson's voice so briefly had now disappeared. "Six months. He might not even make it to the World Series. Six months. A year at the outside."

This last remark was uttered so softly that John was not sure he had heard it correctly. Richardson knew they would lose this one. John's brief sketch would now be sealed by tapping a few reflexes and observing a few twitches.

"What did you say, Dr. Richardson?"

"Nothing. Let's check those twitches."

They went into Mr. Golgi's room and John went through the usual introduction, but Richardson did not go through his usual routine. Not at all. It was no longer a day for usual routines. He didn't dissect the patient's history with him. He asked no cogent questions. He merely asked Mr. Golgi to take off his pajama top, roll up his pants, lie back in bed. Carefully he looked at each arm. First the right, then the left. Then each leg. Right, then left. The muscles of each limb were jumping. Fine twitches. Not enough to move a finger or a toe. The twitches were more like the gross ripples you see under the skin of horses. He then asked Mr. Golgi to open his mouth. He waited until Donna passed him a small flashlight and then shined the light into Mr. Golgi's mouth. His tongue had the same twitch. He returned the flashlight and left without saying a word. Donna stayed behind and talked to the bewildered patient as Richardson walked back into the conference room.

"John, what's the diagnosis?"

"I'm not sure. I think I know, but I'm not sure. I think he has ALS."

"That's right. Amyotrophic lateral sclerosis. ALS. Lou Gehrig's disease. It killed Lou Gehrig in less than two years. It'll probably do as much for Golgi. If you ever thought God was just, figure out why he invented diseases like this. It slowly destroys all the muscles by killing the nerves that give life to the muscles. The patient gets weaker and weaker. No pain. Just weakness. No loss of brain function. No merciful coma. You just watch your body rot. Then you can't talk, can't swallow, and you're afraid you might suffocate in your own saliva. God in all his infinite mercy. Hell! And there's not going to be a goddamned thing we can do. Except watch. Like reserve infielders on the St. Louis Browns. We watch an exercise in futility."

Donna had caught up with them halfway through Richardson's dirge. Somebody had to say something.

"It's possible it might not be ALS."

"Possible? There are two possibilities that it isn't ALS—remote and none at all. But you're right. We'll have to look. What are those possibilities, John?"

"A poison."

"Such as?"

"A heavy metal—mercury, I think."

"Right. Anything else, John?"

When John didn't answer, he turned to the other students. No one responded. Then to Donna.

"Lead."

"Right. Mercury and lead. What's he do for a living, John?"

"A stockbroker."

"He's probably had as much exposure to mercury as the man in the moon."

"Maybe he lives on swordfish and tuna," Linda suggested.

"It wouldn't make any difference."

"I thought there was a lot of mercury in swordfish," Walt responded.

"There is, but believe me, Walt, it doesn't make any difference."

It just wasn't the time or place to explain to them about how the mercury scare had been one big mistake. One big expensive mistake of nearsighted bureaucrats and consumer protection people who knew less about science than poor Charles Michaels. He'd tell that story another day. Swordfish had the same levels of mercury today that they had had a century ago. It had been so easy to prove. Take a few samples from one-hundred-year-old swordfish—stuffed swordfish from various museums. Measure the mercury levels and you'd learn that they hadn't changed in the last century. In addition, all the swordfish had high levels of other trace metals. There were enough of these other competing elements that the mercury didn't hurt the swordfish. Or the person who ate the swordfish. Even if he ate it three times a day, 365 days a year. Someday he'd tell that story and the one he wanted to tell about King George III's madness—a neurologic disorder that changed the course of the American Revolution. This was not the time, though.

"What else should we do, John?"

"An EMG."

"What will that show us?"

"Well, it will show us that the problem is in the nerves, not the muscles, and that it's ALS."

"Linda, do you agree?"

"I think so."

"You're not sure."

"No."

"Okay. John, tell her what you want to do with your EMG."

"Well, I'll put the needles in muscles all over and prove that the twitches are generalized."

"Good."

"And that the electrical activity of the muscles is the kind seen in ALS and not in muscle disease."

"That's right. You prove that the problem is generalized. We see that at the bedside, of course. But it's nice to confirm it before you tell the patient and his family. Patients, like doctors, have more faith in tests than observations. They're wrong. A good observer makes fewer errors than the best laboratory. You know statistics. On any laboratory test 3 to 5 percent of all normal people will have an abnormal result. No good observer makes that many errors. But the EMG will confirm our clinical impressions that the disease is a disease of the nerves and that it's generalized." He paused. "I haven't seen Sanders's full EMG report. What did Adam Stokes say it showed?"

"Muscle disease," Donna answered.

"But what exactly?"

"I'm not sure."

"Christ! I'll call him later."

The morning was almost gone, but they briefly visited the other patients. Mr. Romberg's parathyroid level was back from the endocrine lab. To the surprise of Ramsey Hunt, but not of anyone on Neurology, the laboratory was unable to find any parathyroid hormone at all in his blood. Donna and Richardson outlined a course of medicine to combat this, and Donna wrote the orders while Richardson explained what they were doing to Mr. Romberg. They hoped he would be able to go home soon, but his response to treatment might take months. They would have to follow him closely as an outpatient; the next three to six months would tell the tale.

Mr. Cohn was improving every day. It was tempting to visit with him longer and bask in his recovery.

Mrs. Robin was the same as before. They had started to lower the medicines that poisoned her ability to fight off the virus destroying her brain. By the end of the week she would be off them altogether.

Mr. Michaels was no better. He couldn't remember Dr. Richardson, and he still couldn't remember Satchel Paige. Such is fame.

Mr. Wallenberg had started his medication and was feeling fine. No more episodes had occurred.

Mr. Schwann's condition hadn't changed, but his CT scan had been done. It looked like he probably did have a brain tumor. However, they couldn't be one hundred percent sure so they would have to do an angiogram. Richardson would let Donna explain the procedure: the needle inserted into his artery going into his head, the injection of dye, the burning sensation, the possible complications. It was time for a break. They'd meet at 3:00 to see the other new patient.

Richardson got back to his office and made some coffee. Would they really be able to help Mr. Romberg? Mrs. Robin? Bill Sanders? Somebody? Mr. Schwann's CT scan sure looked like a malignant brain tumor. The notebooks were waiting on his desk just as he'd left them.

Experiment #65   Experiment #24

He started his routine, but nothing corresponded. The numbers were all wrong. Maybe Carl Weigert was right; they seemed like different experiments. He started again. They were two different experiments. Then he remembered Herb had been on vacation for a week. His #65 wasn't Renee's #24. Westphal must have missed at least four experiments. He glanced through the notebooks. Herb's #65 was Renee's #29.

Experiment #65   Experiment #29

As always, a perfect fit. Maybe too perfect.

Experiment #66   Experiment #30
Experiment #67   Experiment #31

The phone rang. He hesitated. It could be Mrs. Hammond again. She might have lost count. He had to answer.

"Neurology."

"That you, Doc?"

"Yes. What's up, Tom?" In the midst of Sanders's dying of whatever was wiping him out, of Golgi's ALS, of Michaels's syphilis, of Schwann's brain tumor, it was hard to remember last week's strychnine poisonings.

"Not much. I probably won't get in today. This city is so screwed up. It's worse than a snowstorm in Washington, DC. I wondered if anything was going on."

"No. Sanders seems to be going down the tubes without anybody's help. That's probably good for you."

"It doesn't sound so good for you."

"It's not," Richardson sighed. "But at least it's been a week since the last one."

"Eight days, to be exact."

"It seems like years ago." Richardson paused, then continued, "How long are you going to keep up the security?"

"We don't know. Probably the rest of this week."

After discussing the chances of the Sox opening their season this week, Richardson hung up and went back to work.

Experiment #67   Experiment #31

He called Pathology. Dr. Weigert wasn't in yet but would be in later in the afternoon. No, the biopsy on Sanders wasn't completed yet. No, the girl who was Collier's secretary wasn't in today. Three questions. Three strikes.

Experiment #67   Experiment #31

The next experiments were different.

Experiment B-1   Experiment B-1

The first of a new series of experiments with bungarotoxin. Thank God they were numbered differently. At least he didn't have to review those. Not now. Not this season. But he was going to finish this, damn it.

He called the lab—Herb and Renee were both at work. He hoped they wouldn't mind if he stopped by later to see how things went. At least Herb's reply didn't seem hostile.

Experiment #68   Experiment #32
Experiment #69   Experiment #33

There were only eleven more to go and he'd be up to date. He started back to work.

Experiment #70   Experiment #34
Experiment #71   Experiment #35

He called Bobbie. The northbound expressway was still closed.

Experiment #72   Experiment #36

He called Pathology. No Weigert. No biopsy.

Experiment #73   Experiment #37
Experiment #74   Experiment #38

He called Bobbie. The driveway was ploughed out. She and the kids had cleared off the sidewalks. The packing was great. They were going to make a snowman.

Experiment #75   Experiment #39

He started to call Pathology and stopped. He'd finish this job before rounds. Once and for all.

Experiment #76   Experiment #40
Experiment #77   Experiment #41

Experiment #78   Experiment #42
Experiment #79   Experiment #43
Experiment #80   Experiment #44

Done. Finished. Vini, vidi, but he hadn't conquered anything. Yes, he had.

Vini, vidi, vici. Not Gaul. But doubt. The only way it could be his group would be if they were pathological liars who just made up results. You'd have to be crazy to believe that. The problem had to be in Weigert's lab, Weigert's technicians. Not his. Not Renee, not Herb. It was as good as beating the Yankees four straight and then some. Maybe even the World Series.

Weigert wasn't in yet.

Richardson was late for rounds.

All four students and Donna Batten were waiting for him in the conference room. It was Linda's turn. They all noticed that Richardson's spirits had improved. They didn't ask why, probably out of fear that they might rock the boat.

The patient was being seen for evaluation of her migraine headaches.

"You know what Bruyn said about the economics of migraine?"

"Economics?" Linda seemed puzzled.

"He estimates that six percent of the world's population, or 180,000,000 people, suffer from migraine, a number that would allow at least 100,000 physicians to live quite comfortably merely on the proceeds of treating patients with migraine. He also made another cogent observation about migraine. It appears that migraine headaches are more common in women who are blonde, blue-eyed, have beautifully arched eyebrows, and if I may quote exactly, 'well developed mammary protuberances with inverted nipples.' " He paused. "I, of course, have no firsthand information on this issue."

Mrs. Rader had had headaches for almost two-thirds of her twenty-eight years on this earth. Usually she got them once every month or two. They started with a warning—flashing lights. Then ten to fifteen minutes later, a severe throbbing headache started.

"What's that called, Donna?"

"Classic migraine."

"Right. Classic migraine has two phases. During the first the patient has a warning—usually flashing lights—then comes the headache phase. But that's been going on for years. What's she need to see me for?"

"Over the last three weeks she's had constant pounding pain behind her right eye."

The rest of the history added little, and Linda had found nothing on examination. No, she hadn't noted whether Mrs. Rader's nipples were inverted or not.

The visit to Mrs. Rader was spirited. Richardson carefully extracted a history of her previous headaches and the difference between those and her new headaches. He talked to her about the various things that affected her migraine: diet, birth control pills, stress. And then he began his examination. He started with her eyes. The right pupil was larger than the left. He checked it twice and left her sitting in bed. Again Donna stayed behind and talked to the patient.

He didn't even wait to get into the conference room.

"Damn it, we're not going to lose this one. Get Dr. Batten out here."

In a minute she joined them.

"Get the angio done as soon as possible. I don't want her dying on us."

Linda was confused. "Dying? She won't die from a migraine."

"It's not her migraine I'm worried about. Don't you understand what's going on?"

"No. I'm sorry, but I really don't."

Richardson stopped himself. He felt embarrassed. No, worse. He'd made a student feel foolish, stupid. Thank God he hadn't done it in front of a patient. Had he done it to Linda intentionally?

"I'm sorry. It's been a bad day. Forgive me."

"Only if you explain what's going on. I'm lost."

He carefully explained the importance of the change in the headaches and how the present headache suggested that something new was going on behind Mrs. Rader's right eye. The fact that her right pupil was enlarged suggested that the something new was pressing on the nerve to the eye and the most likely thing was a blister or aneurysm from one of the arteries going into the brain. If this blister was there, it could spread at any time, and if it broke or ruptured, the chances were one out of three that she'd die or be left half-paralyzed or totally helpless. If they found the blister and operated on it before it ruptured, they might be able to help her.

It was almost 4:00 and he realized he ought to get to the laboratory and see Herb and Renee. They might have thought it was more of a threat than a promise, but he had to go. Still, there was time for at least one good story. He told them about Lewis Carroll and *Alice in Wonderland*. He explained that almost everything Alice experienced—objects getting bigger, people getting smaller—so many of the things that happened to her senses were really the sort of things experienced by many patients with a certain kind of epilepsy. Had Lewis Carroll had seizures? He left them pondering this issue and headed for the laboratory.

Neither Renee nor Herb seemed overly happy to see him. Before he did anything he picked up the phone and dialed Pathology. Weigert was in.

"Carl, this is Paul Richardson. I've got news for you."

"Yes?" Weigert said slowly.

"My lab results are like Caesar's wife."

"Huh?"

"Above reproach. There's nothing wrong with them."

"Are you certain?"

"Absolutely."

"You must be wrong."

"I'm not. I've rechecked and recalculated everything. If somebody screwed up, it wasn't us. It had to be your people, not mine."

"I don't believe it. I did most of that work myself. I'm not like you. I actually go into my lab and work."

"Don't pull that on me. I'm sure of my facts. I was sure before I checked, but I had to check so I could tell you to lay off Renee and Herb and check your own lab." He slammed the phone down. He'd forgotten to ask about the biopsy. He'd call later.

The atmosphere was warmer. The ice in the lab had melted faster than the snow on the expressway.

"How'd the experiment go?"

Herb and Renee both began to answer and stopped, then Herb took over as they walked over to the cages. The animals in cage one looked much as they had looked on Monday. Their heads were slightly drooped, and their legs dragged a bit. Tensilon had worked again. Renee drew up enough Tensilon to inject three animals. They watched. Once again the Tensilon worked. After two minutes the three injected animals were clearly getting stronger. For a minute or two they looked normal, but after ten minutes it wore off entirely and they again drooped their heads and dragged their legs. It was a repeat of Monday's performance.

"Look at the other cages, Boss."

"Did you inject the animals again?"

"No."

"Jesus, they sure are weaker. That's strange. They received no more bungarotoxin, but they became weaker. Were they worse yesterday than Monday?"

Renee answered, "No, but they were worse this morning when I got here."

"Strange. We'd better recheck that article by Lee on the snake toxins. I wonder if that Lee is related to the Thornton Lee who used to pitch for the White Sox? He won twenty-two games in 1941. I never saw him pitch but we didn't have another twenty-game winner until Billy Pierce won twenty in '56."

Herb smiled. Even Renee enjoyed this non sequitur.

"His kid pitched in the Big Leagues for over a decade. Can you believe that Thornton Lee's kid is already retired?" Richardson shook his head and looked into the cages again. "Did you give them Tensilon again?"

"Yes, and they didn't get any better."

It was time to check Sanders and head home. It was hard to believe, but Sanders was worse. He could barely open his eyes. He couldn't move his fingers or toes. The muscle biopsy was back. The result had found its way to the chart. It was normal.

Normal!

How the hell could it be normal?

It was like doing an autopsy and finding no cause of death. You couldn't exactly put the patient back together just because you didn't know why he died.

NORMAL.

It couldn't be.

His muscles didn't work at all, and the EMG showed he had muscle disease. Where was that EMG report? It hadn't found its way into the chart. He tried calling Adam Stokes at home. No answer.

NORMAL.

He's have to get the full EMG report from Stokes in the morning. He wasn't going to lose this one.

They wouldn't be able to glue Sanders back together again.

He walked back to the office. The mail had finally come. He looked through it briefly. There was a large packet from Pathology, from Jim Collier's office.

Paul Richardson, M.D.
Chairman, Committee on Human Investigation

Dear Dr. Richardson:

Enclosed please find the report Dr. Collier had prepared for the Committee on Human Investigation. I am sorry for the delay, but I could not find the original. Fortunately, I had kept the corrected rough draft. I have retyped it as I did before and am forwarding it to you and other appropriate individuals.

Sincerely,

Ms. Allison Starr

cc: Dr. Hunt, Vice Chairman, Committee on Human Investigation
   Dr. Cannon, Secretary, Committee on Human Investigation
   Dr. Bernard
   Dr. Clarke
   Dr. Krebs
   Dr. Meynert
   Dr. Pick

Dr. Spiller
Dr. Weigert

He looked at Collier's report. It was sixty pages long and included two appendices. It was time to get home. He'd read it tomorrow.

Of all the decisions he had made in the last ten days, this was the only one that cost a life. It would be something else to remember.

CHAPTER 17

IT was good to be back in the old routine. And safe. Richardson stood over the toaster, waiting for his English muffin, and looked out at the backyard. He could smell the freshly brewed coffee as he watched the sunshine bounce off the foot or more of clean snow. If the outfield in Sox Park had as much snow as their backyard, there wouldn't be much chance of the season starting today. No opening day heroics. No repeat of Bob Feller's opening day no-hitter. The Sox were still the only team ever to be held hitless on opening day. No beer and peanuts. You can't tell the players without a scorecard. Bobbie and the kids had made a snowman next to the swing set. They had remembered the tradition he had started and dressed it in his old army hat, boots, and even his captain's bars. On top of that they added his brown tie and belt. The tie must have been Bobbie's doing. He sat down and found the sports section.

The headline answered his question. "Sox Snowed Out." He skimmed the rest of it. Hockey and basketball never really mattered after the first "Play Ball!" of the spring. Bobbie poured him a second cup of coffee. Finally, it was Bobbie who broke the silence.

"Who died?"

"Died?"

"You're only this withdrawn when one of your patients dies."

"Or the Sox lose six straight."

246

"No. You'd like to think the Sox are that important. They're not. I could live through a whole season in which they lost every game—all 154."

"162."

"What?"

"162. They used to play 154, but with expansion they play 162."

"All right, 162. But living with you when one or, God forbid, two of your patients go sour is hell. I'm not sure why you take it so personally. The kids get confused. You act so differently."

"I get paid to save lives."

"It's got nothing to do with getting paid. It was the same in medical school. During your internship it was even worse. It's really never gotten any better."

"It's that bad?"

"It's not a question of good or bad," Bobbie answered. "It's just hard to live with. I'm not sure I'd want you to be any other way. Thank God it doesn't happen as often these days."

"Remember my internship?"

"How could I ever forget that?"

"Remember when I was on the ICU?"

"With Bill Sanders?"

"Yes, with Sanders."

"How is—"

Richardson interrupted his wife's question. "Remember the game we played? Me and Sanders. It was us against the world and death and each other. You couldn't let a patient die while you were on call. No matter what, each and every patient had to live through the twenty-four hours you were on. It was a matter of pride and honor."

"Or maybe just self-defense."

"Self-defense?" Paul wondered aloud. "Okay, maybe it was primarily self-defense. But that doesn't matter. The fact is, it worked. As a pair, we had fewer deaths in our two months than any other pair of interns that year."

"And less sleep."

"So what?"

"Paul, what's that got to do with now?"

"Nothing. Everything. The game goes on, but the positions have changed a bit."

Bobbie looked puzzled but said nothing.

"This time he's the patient and I'm on every twenty-four hours. And he may be dying. Right there in front of me."

"Paul, I'm sorry. I didn't know." Bobbie paused. "Is he really doing that poorly?"

"Yes. He's almost completely paralyzed. He can barely open his eyes. And he can't do anything else."

"My God, what's wrong with him?"

" 'Ay, there's the rub.' I haven't the foggiest notion what he's got. No idea at all."

It was time to leave. All things considered, traffic was not bad. All the lanes were open, and there were only a few snowladen cars scattered along the shoulders. WFMT served its purpose better than it usually did. It was completely diverting. They played five different versions of Visa d'Arte and let the listener guess the soprano. Callas was a giveaway. Tebaldi he knew. He shouldn't have missed Milanov. He had that recording. With Björling and Warren and Leinsdorf conducting. You don't get paid to miss things you should know. He turned off the radio. Thank God he wouldn't have to read those notebooks anymore today. Maybe he'd get started on those charts, and he'd make sure Walt was working on them. It would be better than the lab books—it seemed like he'd reviewed ten thousand experiments. Thank God he didn't have to review the new experiments with bungarotoxin, too. He never could have gotten through another seventeen experiments. Seventeen? Was that all?

He calculated how many guinea pigs they had used. Seventeen experiments and 24 guinea pigs for each experiment came out to 408. Each guinea pig weighed 250 grams or about half a pound. They should have had enough bungarotoxin for another 500 guinea pigs. That stuff was hard to get. Renee and Herb would have to be more careful with it.

Richardson stopped by Sanders's room on the way to the office. He was worse. Other than the whoosh. . . . whoosh of the respirator, there was no sound in the room. Richardson looked at the nursing notes.

Blood pressure—normal.

Pulse rate—normal.

Respiration—fourteen times a minute.

Hell, Sanders wasn't even triggering the respirator anymore. It was going on and off by itself at a predetermined rate.

Whoosh . . . . . . whoosh

Whoosh . . . . . . whoosh

Whoosh . . . . . . whoosh

Fourten times a minute. Each time it forced air in and out of Sanders's lungs. In and out. At least his chest wall wasn't frozen solid by strychnine, so the respirator could work and push the air in and out. Poor Jim Collier. Only a week ago. God. He couldn't get any air in or out and he died. Jim Collier. At least Bill's chest and lungs worked.

Richardson saw a stethoscope hanging from the portable blood pressure apparatus and carefully listened to his old compatriot's chest. He listened as the machine moved the chest wall in and out—moved the air in and out. Still clear. No new pneumonia. Not yet. That was the real threat now. Not strychnine, but pneumococcus. Or worse, some damn hospital-acquired bug that no antibiotic could kill. Richardson looked at the latest lab results.

Liver function—normal.

Kidneys—normal.

Oxygen level—normal.

Muscle biopsy—normal.

NORMAL! Goddamn it! Normal. Did that mean there was nothing wrong? Was this all a charade? He'd have to check all of Sanders's muscles again.

"Bill!" he called out. There was no response. Not even a flicker of the eyelids.

"Bill!" he started to shout, but stopped himself. Sanders wasn't deaf. He could hear. Richardson was sure of that. Sanders could hear, feel, think, understand, even see if you held his eyes open, but he couldn't move. He couldn't even open his eyes anymore. Sanders couldn't move a single muscle anywhere. Richardson would have to make sure everyone realized that this inert mass was alive and understood. Understood everything. They'd have to be careful what they said. You always had that tendency to let your guard down in front of patients on respirators or in coma. But Sanders was awake and alert—or was he? They'd have to prove that. He opened Sanders's eyes. The pupils responded to the light and got smaller. A simple reflex movement. But the eyes didn't move.

Whoosh . . . . . . whoosh.

Whoosh . . . . . . whoosh.

Nothing moved. Nothing but the respirator.

Whoosh . . . . . . whoosh.

Whoosh . . . . . . whoosh.

Richardson had to say something.

Whoosh . . . . . . whoosh.

Whoosh . . . . . . whoosh.

"You missed a big snowstorm. The Sox opener was snowed out."

Sanders wouldn't care. He was an old Yankee fan.

"The steroids should start working soon. I'll be back later. I'm going to order an EEG."

Whoosh . . . . . . whoosh.

Whoosh . . . . . . whoosh.

Somewhere in this favored land, the sun is shining bright. Not here.

Whoosh . . . . . . whoosh.

On his way out he talked to Frank Balo briefly. No one other than those on the neurology service seemed to have any interest in Sanders. No one at all. As he walked back to the office he could still hear the respirator. It haunted him like one of those recurring nightmares of early adolescence. Now, however, it was a nightmare come true.

Chris and fresh coffee were both waiting for him in the office. He had Chris dial the EEG lab.

"This is Dr. Richardson."

"Yes, sir."

"I want a portable EEG this morning."

"We're all booked up, sir."

"I don't care if you have to cancel everything else. I want a portable EEG done this morning." Sometimes he had to pull rank. As head of Neurology, he was able to do this with the EEG lab since they were part of his department.

"Yes, sir. Patient's name?"

"Sanders. Dr. William Sanders. He's on 6 West. Do it this morning and bring me the record."

"Yes, sir." Sometimes it paid to be the chief.

"Early this morning." He slammed the phone down.

"What was that all about?" Chris asked.

"I want to see Sanders's brain waves."

"Do you think he's dead?"

"Just the opposite." Chris was right. They usually did EEGs to prove that the record was flat and that the patient's brain was dead.

"Sanders is alive. I just want to be sure his brain is still normal."

He took his coffee and retreated to his office. Coffee, a cigar, WFMT, and waiting. Waiting for what? He shuffled through some papers. He found an article by Calne on lisuride, a new experimental treatment for Parkinson's disease, and began to read it. He put it down and began looking along his shelves. There was nothing he wanted to read. Not medicine, not history. Not poetry. Not even Conan Doyle.

Two cigars later the entire crew had gathered for card rounds. They were all there. Herb, Al, Donna, and all four students. They exchanged snow stories and then settled down to work. They started card rounds, carefully leaving all mention of Sanders until last.

The angiogram on Ted Schwann had been scheduled. Dr. Vincent would do it later that morning. It was set for 10:30, but if the X-ray schedule followed its usual pattern, 11:00 or 11:30 would be a more realistic expectation.

Mrs. Rader's headache was a bit better. She'd agreed to the angiogram but only after a long discussion. It was hard for her to accept how serious her headaches might be. She'd had headaches all her life. Still, this headache was different. Not much worse, just different.

"Tell me what sorts of things sometimes cause migraine headaches, Walt."

"Foods."

"What kinds of foods?"

"Cheese."

"Do you know what kind?"

Silence.

"Stilton and Camembert. Especially the rind of the Camembert. But do you know why these cheeses cause headaches?" Richardson continued without giving the students or residents a chance to respond, to be right or wrong. "All the authorities say it's because these foods contain something that acts on the blood vessels, a chemical called tyramine. That's what everybody says. But do you know what food contains the highest amount of tyramine?"

Silence. A silence that Richardson finally understood meant Slow down. Teach. Don't lecture. Give them a chance. Do it right.

"Herb?"

"Pickled herring."

"Absolutely correct, and there's never been a case of pickled herring causing a migraine." Take your time and teach. That's what he got paid for. If he couldn't save lives, at least he could teach.

"What else can cause a migraine?"

"Chocolates," Linda suggested.

"In an occasional patient, yes. Anything else, Al?"

"Sex."

"I see you've been reading again." Richardson was pleased. Pleased and proud. Not just because Al knew the right answer, but because he had sought it out on his own. "Paulson and Klawans wrote a paper on that subject. It's in the *Transactions of the American Neurological Association*. A paper on orgasms causing migraine headaches. They described twelve or fifteen patients with orgasmic migraine but without any serious neurologic diseases. An important paper. Do you know why it was an important paper, Al?"

"I think so," his first year resident responded. "The textbooks all teach that any headache caused by intercourse is a bad business. They say it usually is a sign of bleeding in the head, like a ruptured aneurysm."

"Right. But as they pointed out, that's not true. Most headaches caused by sex are just simple migraines. You know, Klawans is not a headache doctor. He doesn't specialize in headaches, so at a meeting once I asked him how come he wrote that paper. He said he only wrote it because he wanted to write a second paper and send it to some prestigious place like the *New England Journal of Medicine*—a follow-up paper dealing with the therapy of such headaches entitled 'The Treatment of Orgasm Related Migraine or What to Do for a F___ing Headache.' I'd like to see the editors turn him down with that one.''

"What do you do for it?" Sue asked.

"Abstain. Of course, some people might think that the cure is worse than the disease." He winced inwardly at his reflex answer. He said it before he had time to think. He always answered that question that way whenever he told this story. But he had forgotten that Sue had migraines. Pay attention. "Really, you treat them like any other form of migraines. Most of the patients do quite well." Enough of this.

Mr. Wallenberg was unchanged. He would go home on Friday.

Mr. Cohn was stronger. He had asked Linda out.

"I guess you really saved his spinal cord."

"What do you mean?"

"In men, impotence is an early sign of serious cord disease." He noticed Linda's face flush. Was she embarrassed or angry? Had he wanted to embarrass her again? "How's Mrs. Robin?"

She was no worse. It was always disheartening to judge a patient's improvement by how quickly she was not getting worse. There wasn't much future in that. At least Mrs. Robin's brain wasn't falling apart before their eyes. At least, not that they could tell.

Mr. Dax was doing well. His speech was improving every day.

"Do you know what the speech area in the brain is called, Sue?"

"Broca's region."

"Right, named after Paul Broca. Do you know who Broca was, John?"

"A neurologist?"

"No, a surgeon and anthropologist. In fact, he was one of the founding members of the Société d'Anthropologie, and it was at a meeting of that society in 1861 that loss of speech was attributed to disease of the left frontal lobe of the brain.

But Broca wasn't the first person to suggest this. He was the first physician to have a patient with loss of speech who died and underwent an autopsy. At that historic meeting Broca displayed the brain of his patient, and in so doing proved the localization of speech. But others knew it before him. Do you know who?''

No response.

"Franz Joseph Gall."

"Who?" asked John.

"Franz Joseph Gall. And do you know how Gall knew? He hadn't carried out any autopsies. How did he know speech was here?" asked Richardson, pointing to the left side of his skull a bit above and a bit in front of his left ear. "How?"

Silence.

"He was a phrenologist."

"You're kidding," Donna responded in disbelief.

"No. He felt bumps on people's heads and he knew," Richardson said. He then explained how after 140 years, science had proven Gall to be correct. The speech area was bigger and could be identified from the outside. Our debt to phrenologists. Or one of them. Gall actually examined the brain of the Marquis de Sade and analyzed it as a phrenologist. Do you know what he found?"

Al's eyes opened widely and he began to answer but Richardson cut him off and continued his monologue. "I'm sorry to disappoint Dr. Schilder, but he did not find any abnormality of the gyrus fornicatus. Gall found that the organs of paternal affection and the love of children were enlarged. So much for phrenology." He hesitated a moment and then continued. "Of course Gall never really defined what he meant by paternal affection and love of children."

It was time to move on. Richardson asked about the other patients.

Mr. Michaels was receiving his penicillin shots. Today he remembered that Satchel Paige was the doctor who saw him the other day and asked him all those questions.

Richardson smiled. He should only be another Satchel Paige. He wished. At least Satchel Paige had had sense enough not to look back.

Mr. Romberg was a bit better. His speech was faster and

clearing. Maybe he would respond. It would take months to tell.

When Sanders's name came up, no one said much. The EMG report was still not back. Richardson called EMG and got Adam Stokes on the phone.

"Where is the EMG report on Sanders?" Richardson asked impatiently.

"I dictated it last week."

"So where is it?"

"Probably lost by the messenger service. How should I know?"

"That's a hell of a way to run a railroad." There were more similarities between the administration of the hospital and that of Amtrak than Richardson cared to think about.

"What did it show?"

"I don't know."

"You did it."

"Yes, but I don't know what it showed."

"Hell, everybody told me you said it showed he had muscle disease."

"I guess it did."

"Quit beating around the bush, Adam. What did it show?"

"As far as I can remember, the function of his nerves was absolutely normal. That's what I spent most of the time on, since I was told you were worried about nerve inflammation. Well, there was no nerve inflammation. I'm sure of that."

"Thank God for small favors. What else did you do?"

"I just did a brief muscle exam, and it didn't show very much. It was hard to say anything for sure. It looked more like myasthenia than muscle disease. But he had two or three negative Tensilon tests."

"Damn it! He doesn't have myasthenia."

"I know. That's what Herb told me, so it must be muscle disease."

"Keep up the good work," Richardson said as he banged the phone down.

No one said much more. There were two new patients to be seen, and the students wanted to watch Dr. Vincent do the angiogram on Schwann. So, instead of waiting for Richardson's order to get going, they just split. Rounds would start at 1:00—radiology time.

He sat back to think about Bill Sanders. Maybe if he went over everything again step by step. Maybe . . . suddenly Tom Ward burst into the office out of breath.

"What's up, Tom?"

"We've had another murder!"

"Oh, Christ!" Richardson exclaimed. Then, as Detective Ward was about to speak again, Richardson asked in a voice that was between a defiant shout and a question, "Not Bill Sanders?"

"No, it wasn't Dr. Sanders. It—"

"Thank God."

"It was a different doctor."

"A doctor?"

"Yes. Dr. Weigert, the pathologist."

Richardson could hardly believe what he had heard. He could understand if Sanders had been killed. "Carl Weigert?" he asked.

"That's right."

"It can't be. Not Carl Weigert."

"Whether it can be or not, Doc, it's true. Dr. Weigert is dead. He was murdered. And it was done the same way as the others."

"With strychnine?"

"I'm afraid so. It looks like you had us watching the wrong doctor."

Richardson began looking for a cigar. Finally, after opening three empty boxes, he found one and lit it. After several minutes of silence, punctuated only by the sounds of a two-car elevated train passing by, Richardson picked up one of the reproduced twelfth-century chess pieces. Were the originals done by the Vikings or the native Angles or Saxons? Would they ever really know? He continued to rub the mounted knight in his left hand and stare at it as if nothing else was of any importance. Then, in a much softer voice than before, he asked, "*My* strychnine?"

"We can't really prove that," Detective Ward answered, "but most likely it was the same stuff—from your lab."

"My strychnine," Richardson repeated.

At what point during the long game had George Bruyn captured the knight? That move was almost as remotely related to today as King Canute himself. "I don't understand. Why Carl Weigert?"

Tom Ward had no answer to this question.

"My strychnine."

It may have been a question or a statement; Tom Ward wasn't sure. But in either case no response was necessary. For once Paul Richardson was not fidgeting. Slowly and deliberately he crushed out his Schimmelpenninck and sat down. He didn't search for another cigar. He didn't look for a match. He sat, almost motionless. As frozen as a patient with parkinsonism. His voice was as soft and halting as Mr. Romberg's.

"Seven. With my strychnine. I still remember ordering that stuff. If only I'd had sense enough to keep it locked up better. My strychnine."

Richardson's words brought no response. There was no need for any reply and no purpose a reply could serve. Tom Ward could feel the pain in each of Paul Richardson's comments. Whatever he could say wouldn't help. Tom knew that the police lab had proved that the murders had been done with Richardson's strychnine.

The analysis on Willie Prader had shown that he was murdered with absolutely pure strychnine. Pure stuff was more likely to come from Richardson's lab than from the street. Ward was sure that the analysis of Weigert's blood would show the same thing.

"Carl Weigert, the poor bastard. Why kill him? He didn't have cancer. He wasn't really an expert on cancer. Not the way Collier was. We must have two or three other pathologists here who know as much about cancer as Carl does. Did. Vic Horsley for sure; maybe even Clarke. Why would someone want to kill Weigert? As far as I know he'd never even been to Cleveland, much less ever lived there."

Again the silence continued until Richardson lit yet another cigar and restarted his monologue. "I didn't even know that he was going into the hospital. He didn't say anything about coming in when he talked to me late yesterday afternoon. I just don't understand."

"What's there to understand? The crazy bastard is on the loose killing people again," Ward asserted.

"Are you sure?" Richardson wondered aloud.

"Sure of what?"

"That he was killed?"

"Yes."

"In the same way?"

"There's no doubt at all about that."

"How come?"

"Bob Locke saw him die."

Richardson said nothing, so Detective Ward went on. "Poor Bob. He may go back to traffic control. He says it was just like those poor guinea pigs of yours. But it was a person, not one of your guinea pigs. Dr. Weigert was looking at him with his face in a hideous grin. His eyes were looking at Bob. His head was thrown back. His arms and legs stuck out, and he stopped breathing. I'm glad I wasn't there. Bob. Poor bastard. He says he'll never forget that grin."

Somehow, Richardson felt sorrier for Weigert than he did for Locke. Bob Locke would survive. "It just doesn't fit."

"Whether it fits or not, he is dead. I thought you'd want to know. Willis won't be able to keep the lid on this any longer."

"Why was Bob Locke in Weigert's room?"

"He wasn't. He was in the Pathology Department."

"I thought you said Weigert was in the hospital."

"No. I didn't say that."

"What really happened?"

"Bob had made arrangements to go through Collier's papers this morning, and when he got there he heard a strange noise in Weigert's office and saw him die. He didn't see anybody coming or going though. Look, Doc, I've got to go."

"Tom, don't take the guards away from Sanders's room yet."

"Don't worry. This place will be crawling with cops if I get my way. And one more thing, Doc."

"What's that?"

"Watch out for yourself."

"Don't worry Tom, I will. Besides, I'm not a patient."

"Neither was Dr. Weigert," Ward reminded him as he left.

Richardson's cigar had gone out. He put down the knight, found another match, and relit his cigar. Where were the rest of the chess pieces? Had George really won the game? Weigert hadn't been a patient. That meant that he didn't have an IV running. Suddenly Richardson's eyes opened wide. He knew what had happened. That was it. It had to be. There was no other explanation. He looked up to tell Detective Ward, but the office was empty. Richardson knew, but he didn't understand. He knew who but not why. Why? Was "why" only a question for philosophers? Why? Why had he done it?

Was that the real reason?

It hadn't been Renee or Herb or any of his kids. He was off the hook.

But why Jim Collier, and why now?

Those were the real whys. No philosophical whys. Real whys.

Why Collier?

Why now?

Why this?

He didn't have much time to think. Dean Willis was on the phone. "Have you heard?"

"Yes. Ward was just here. I don't understand," Richardson began.

"None of us does," the dean interrupted. "Somebody has a vendetta against us. First, the patients. Now the staff. I called to warn you to be careful. This thing is going to hurt us, but—"

It was Richardson's turn to interrupt. "Look. About Carl Weigert. I think I might know why—"

"Not now, Paul. There is no why, no simple explanation. First you thought it would be Sanders. From what I've been told, he seems to be dying all by himself. I don't have time to listen to your zebra theories now. I just wanted each department head to know what was going on. First, the head of Pathology and then the acting head."

"Come on. You don't really think someone is playing *Ten Little Indians* with the department heads. Be reasonable."

"I am being reasonable."

There didn't seem to be much more to say, so Richardson hung up. *Ten Little Indians*. Did Willis know that it had originally been published in England as *Ten Little Niggers*? God how easily the world used to degrade an entire people. How easily we all accepted such things. So some progress had been made. Now it was published as *And Then There Were None*. Would he care? Willis was wrong. There was a 'why.' There had to be. Three of them, in fact.

Where the hell was that goddamned report of Collier's? It was here someplace. Christ. He had to get his office organized. Not just the chess players, but the whole office. Or at least his desk. Could he apply for a grant to have somebody just to keep things in order? A three-year grant was what he needed. The National Institutes of Health had spent money on worse grants. There it was. In the cardboard box covered with tobacco ash.

Paul Richardson, M.D.
Chairman, Committee on Human Investigation

Dear Dr. Richardson:

Enclosed please find the report Dr. Collier had prepared for the Committee on Human Investigation. I am sorry for the delay, but I could not find the original. Fortunately, I had kept the corrected rough draft. I have retyped it as I did before and am forwarding it to you and other appropriate individuals.

Sincerely,

Ms. Allison Starr

cc: Dr. Hunt, Vice Chairman, Committee on Human Investigation
    Dr. Cannon, Secretary, Committee on Human Investigation
    Dr. Bernard
    Dr. Clarke
    Dr. Krebs
    Dr. Meynert
    Dr. Pick
    Dr. Spiller
    Dr. Weigert

He turned the page.

Paul Richardson, M.D.
Chairman, Committee on Human Investigation

Dear Dr. Richardson:

Enclosed please find the report you requested on our standard policy in controlling both human and laboratory investigations. This report should satisfy the National Institutes of Health requirements. I am sorry about the delay in the final submission of this report, but the damaging evidence listed in Appendix II had to be documented. I have discussed this in detail with the individual in question, and he has agreed to resign his staff appointment. I do not think that any other action is necessary.

Sincerely,

James Collier, M.D.

cc: Dr. Hunt, Vice Chairman, Committee on Human Investigation
    Dr. Cannon, Secretary, Committee on Human Investigation
    Dr. Bernard
    Dr. Clarke
    Dr. Krebs
    Dr. Meynert
    Dr. Pick
    Dr. Spiller
    Dr. Weigert

None of them had ever gotten the original. He turned to Appendix II. The typing had been done on another typewriter, by an amateur. Probably Collier himself.

Appendix II—Concerning Erroneous Results Published by This Laboratory in the Last Three Years

"During the course of our review of all research published by faculty members of this medical center, it became apparent that some research was not reproducible and was clearly fraudulent."

He skimmed the rest. No names were mentioned, but it was obvious. If you knew the work of the medical center, it was obvious. Carl Weigert. The late Carl Weigert. That explained so many things. Now it all made sense.

Weigert's insistence that it was Renee and Herb. Richardson should have known it wasn't his kids. And Linda's problem in Collier's lab, working under Weigert. It hadn't been Collier who fired her. It had been Weigert. It was *his* results that were fraudulent. Not hers. Not Linda's. Not Renee's. Not Herb's. But Weigert's. There was only one thing to verify. He told Chris to call Ward and get him to come over as soon as possible. The three questions were answered.

Why Collier? Because he knew.

Why now? To prevent Collier's report from going out.

Why this? Because Weigert hadn't prevented the report from going out.

Poor Carl Weigert. When had it all started? How long had he been making up research results? He gazed at Collier's memo again. At least six years. Six years ago Weigert had applied for an associate professorship with tenure—a lifetime appointment—and had been turned down. He hadn't published enough research. It must have been too tempting. Like the rest of them, he had too many other jobs and there wasn't enough time left over to do the research he could publish. Publish or perish. Four years ago Weigert had gotten his tenured professorship. Why hadn't he stopped? Did he want to get his own department someday, or was it just so damn easy once you started? He'd never know the answers to these questions.

It took only ten minutes for Tom Ward to get back to the neurology office. Richardson sat quietly, puffing a cigar, his face and voice alive with expression and enthusiasm.

"There's one question to answer, and then it'll all be over and you can go home, Tom."

"Sure," Ward responded with more than a trace of sarcasm. "Who did it?"

"I think I know that, Tom, but first tell me about Weigert."

"What's left to tell?" the detective asked.

"Was there a needle mark in his arm?"

"No."

"That's what I thought. You realize the case is over?"

"Over? It's just starting. Seven murders and he says the case is over."

"Not seven, six," Richardson corrected him.

"Weigert makes it seven."

"Weigert was not murdered."

"Are you sure?"

"Yes, he killed himself."

"Why?"

"Jim Collier blew the whistle on him or was about to. You know better than I do that most murderers don't kill people for no reason at all. There is always a reason. Usually a significant one—at least to the murderer. Often it's a problem that's been there a long time and then suddenly something happens and he has to act. That's what happened here. It has to do with research and fraud and academic appointments and reputations. All those things that make up life in a medical school. As far as I can tell, much of Weigert's research was based on fraudulent data. Collier found out and told him, so Weigert agreed to resign. Collier was willing to let it go at that. However, when Collier was scheduled to go into the hospital, Weigert hit on a plan to save his own neck. He destroyed the evidence, or thought he had, and then started killing patients as a smoke screen. With Collier dead and the evidence gone, his career would be safe."

"So Collier was the real target all the time?"

"Yes, and his smoke screen worked pretty damn well. We worried more about the five patients than we did about the one doctor. It was a good trick. You, as cops, would focus on the larger number of victims and we, as physicians, would worry about our patients. We never focused in on Collier's death alone. We scattered our efforts. But it should have been obvious."

"Why?"

"I asked before, 'Why kill patients who were already dying, who were nearly dead?' Answer—because Weigert still had some feelings left. Some vestige of sanity. The victims weren't randomly selected. They were carefully selected. To his warped mind, it wasn't so bad to kill patients who were almost dead."

"So that's why he stopped at six?"

"Yes. He was done."

"Why'd he kill himself now? We weren't on his trail."

Richardson showed him the memos from Collier via Ms. Starr. "He got a copy of this yesterday, just like I did. He read his last night. I didn't. If I had, who knows. Maybe . . ."

"It's better this way."

"Sure. This way Willis can keep it quiet. You want to explain it to him? I'd rather not."

"Okay, Doc. I guess you've explained everything, so I'll get going now." When Ward reached the door, he turned around. "Thanks, Doc."

"Anytime."

"I guess this means we can quit guarding Sanders."

"Yes. He won't get killed."

"Good luck. I hope you save his life."

"Thanks. So do I."

Not having to worry about strychnine was one less worry. It probably didn't make much difference, but it was one less thing to worry about. He still had to worry about Mrs. Rader and Mrs. Robin. And Mr. Romberg. And Bill Sanders. Ward was lucky. He could go home and not worry until the next case started. Detectives were all lucky. Holmes, Poirot, Maigret, Lord Peter Wimsey, Nero Wolfe. All of them. What luxury they had. One case at a time. And they could spend days or weeks on that one case aided by Watson, or Colonel Hastings, or Janvier, or Bunter, or Archie Goodwin. All that time for one case. He, however, still had lots of cases to worry about: Golgi, Cohn, Sanders, Schwann, Romberg, and Rader. No wonder they always solved their cases.

At least no one would come into Bill Sanders's room and quietly put strychnine into his IV and kill him. Strychnine from Paul Richardson's own lab. No more strychnine to worry about. No more lab notebooks to review. No more experiments to go over. Now he could just read the bungaro-toxin experiments and figure out where things stood. Seven-teen experiments. Considering the average lethal dose of alpha-bungarotoxin, they should have had enough of it left to kill at least four hundred guinea pigs—four hundred half-pound guinea pigs or one 200-pound guinea pig. Only there were no 200-pound guinea pigs. Herb and Renee couldn't have wasted that much of the stuff. Maybe they had done more experiments? No. He'd gone through those notebooks thoroughly. There were only seventeen bungarotoxin experi-ments. There should have been enough bungarotoxin left to kill a 200-pound guinea pig. If only he could get down to 200 pounds again. A 200-pound person. Bill Sanders weighed less than 200 pounds. That must be it! Not inflammation of the nerves. Not myasthenia. But bungarotoxin poisoning. The first case on record. Poisoned with pure alpha-bungarotoxin. It was a scientific first, but he'd never write that one up for publication. It did explain everything. The missing bungaro-toxin. Bill Sanders, who looked like he had myasthenia but didn't get better when they gave him his Tensilon. Hell, he was just like one of their guinea pigs. A 200-pound human guinea pig dying of bungarotoxin poisoning, with bungaro-toxin from Richardson's own laboratory.

CHAPTER 18

RICHARDSON sat and thought for a few minutes. He debated having Chris call Ward again. Shouldn't he tell Ward everything he knew? Of course, he didn't really have any proof. He could imagine the entire conversation.

"Tom, somebody is killing Sanders."

"So what's new?"

"No, somebody else. Not Carl Weigert."

"Oh, really? What are they using this time?"

"Alpha- bungarotoxin."

"Alpha what?"

"Alpha-bungarotoxin."

"What's that?"

"A poison from the venom of cobras."

"Where the hell would somebody get that?"

"From my lab."

"Not again. Do you just distribute poison freely or does the murderer have to ask for it first?"

Strike one.

"We don't just give it away."

"Who would take it, then?"

Strike two.

"And, Doc, who would know enough to use that alpha whatever it is?"

Strike three.

He wouldn't call Ward today. This was his baby. It was his poison, but this time it *had* to be somebody from Neurology.

It couldn't be anybody who might just walk into a lab looking for strychnine. Bungarotoxin was different. Strychnine had been around for years. Everybody knows you can kill people with it. But bungarotoxin? A new poison. Damn few people know anything about it or, even more important, that he was beginning to study it. A newly isolated poison used by cobras since the beginning of time to kill their prey. But Bill Sanders had the privilege of being the first person to receive his bungarotoxin from a human snake. It had to be someone familiar with his lab. One of his kids. He'd have to solve this one himself or at least try. He'd give himself time to work it out. Until Monday. That was four days from now. Four days. Then he'd punt. Maybe he should call Tom Ward and ask him to keep Balo, Devic, and Bright on duty for a few more days. How could he explain it to Tom? Hell, the police hadn't done any good, but that had been his fault. He had made sure that they only let doctors or students taking care of Sanders into the room. Only the neurology service was allowed in—only the murderer. Everybody else they kept out. What a great system. And he'd devised it.

Richardson had to find out for himself. He had to. Hell, all that was left for the murderer to do now was pull the damn plug. How could he prevent it? Nurses. If Willis could use them for spying, he could use them for security. Richardson called the chief nurse on 6 West and pulled rank for the second time that day. A new record.

"Sanders can never be in his room by himself."

"He already has private duty nurses, Dr. Richardson."

"On all three shifts?"

"Yes."

"They can't leave the room at any time. Not even to go to the bathroom. That's an order. If anyone leaves the room without another nurse being actually in the room, I'll get them canned."

"Dr. Richardson—"

"That's an absolute order."

"I'll have to ask Dr. Willis."

"I don't care what Willis says. That's my order. Bill Sanders is my patient. What happens in his room is my responsibility. Mine, and mine alone. So listen carefully.

Those nurses are to stay in the room at all times, even if there's a doctor or a student in the room.''

"But the doctors often like—"

"I don't give a damn. That's an order."

"Yes, sir."

His voice was softer now. "And try to make sure he has the best nurses you can find."

"I will, sir."

Now no one could pull the plug. Giving more bungarotoxin probably didn't matter anymore. But the nurses would keep a record of everyone who went in. They always did and of anyone who gave an injection. It was part of their job. It was the damn respirator that counted. That respirator was all that was keeping Bill Sanders alive. How much bungarotoxin did Sanders have in his body?

Next he called Renee and told her not to start any experiments until he got there at 3:00 or so. And then he asked her to set out some new guinea pigs. Next he put in a page for Dr. Westphal. Five minutes later the phone rang.

"Herb, we got a problem."

"What makes today any different from all other days?"

"I want you to meet me in the lab at 3:00 and bring a 20-cc tube of blood."

"Anybody's in particular?"

"Yes, Sanders's."

"Sanders's? You don't think—"

"I do think. Be there."

He buzzed Chris and told her to bring him a copy of the list she had given Ward. The list of those people who had access to Sanders. She brought it in and handed it to him without making any comment. Richardson began to study it.

Paul Richardson
Herb Westphal
Adam Stokes
Al Schilder
Donna Batten
Renee Weber

What the hell was Renee's name on the list for?

John Adson
Sue Evans
Linda Sharp
Walt Simpson

"Chris, what's Renee's name on this list for?"

"Ward wanted a list of everyone in Neurology. I didn't know what it was for."

Was that a fatal error?

Not Renee. She wasn't that jealous. Somebody once said it was easier for a woman to compete with another woman than with a man. Renee had gone to see Sanders in the hospital. This was crazier than thinking she cheated in the laboratory. Nobody was going to kill Sanders over . . . but somebody was trying to kill him for some reason. At least the nurses would be in the room at all times, but was that enough? Maybe he and Herb should stay, too. Herb? What the hell happened between Sanders and Herb? He refused to ask Herb again.

Thank God it was time for rounds. The new patients were on 7 East. Off to the conference room.

The angiogram on Schwann had not been done yet. Things in X-ray were running as usual—like the traffic around O'Hare at 5:00 P.M. on the Friday before a three-day weekend.

Walt presented the first case. Richardson paid as much attention as he could. The patient was named Dawson. A fifty-four-year-old woman. Eight years older than Sanders. Walking difficulty for three years. Getting slowly worse. She never got any better.

He hardly heard the rest of the history. It was 1:30. If it hadn't snowed, they would be throwing out the first ball. "The Star Spangled Banner" and then, "Play Ball!" How many times had he skipped school for opening day? And it had never even been rained out. Snow was inconceivable. He looked around the room. Sue. Was her affair with Sanders really over? Then why would she want to be off the case? It would have been easier to kill Sanders if she stayed on the case. And why not let John take over? John. John and Renee. John and Renee and Sanders. He forced himself to pay attention to Walt Simpson, to the life of Mrs. Dawson. The reflexes in the patient's legs were decreased. There was some sensory loss. He should have listened. What had Walt said about the cerebellar signs? Oh, well, he could just go into the room and wing it.

Walt introduced him to Mrs. Dawson. Richardson talked to her for more than twenty minutes in a disconnected fashion as students and residents stood around and listened, shuffling their feet. Then he asked her to get up and walk without her shoes, please, so he could observe her walking.

Observe.

"Walt, look at her feet. What do you see?"

"Nothing. I don't see anything unusual."

"You see what I see but you don't observe. You don't understand. You don't recognize."

He'd done it in front of a patient. Slowly and carefully now. He really didn't expect them to sniff and feel the ashes of a cigar and then tell him the country of origin of the tobacco or the shop where it was sold. But there were some things . . .

"Mrs. Dawson, I'm sorry if I embarrassed you or anyone else by drawing attention to your feet. But you do have extraordinarily high arches. Does anyone else in your family have such high arches?"

"Yes, doctor. My mother and one brother."

"And your big toes are cocked back."

"Yes, they've been that way for years."

"Were your mother's toes like that?"

"Now that you mention it, yes, I think they were."

"Did your mother have trouble walking?"

"For a number of years before she died, yes."

With that Richardson was satisfied. "I understand you're here to find out why you're having trouble walking?"

"Yes."

"What do you think is wrong?"

She began to cry.

"Are you afraid you have cancer?"

"Yes."

"You don't. You have the same thing your mother had. It's a hereditary problem that runs in your family. There is nothing very much that we can do for your walking problem.

But your mother didn't have that much trouble walking, did she?" Mrs. Dawson nodded her agreement. "And you probably won't have any more trouble walking than she ever had. And," Dr. Richardson emphasized, "you do not have a tumor. You don't have cancer. Dr. Batten will be back later to explain it all to you." With that and a brief smile he left the room. Sometimes you can win one.

The second patient was a young girl with MS. As luck would have it she had been seen by Sue. There was no chance for clever observation or deduction or humor. He hoped the patient would get better this time.

The students went down to X-ray to see if they could finally see the angiogram being done.

Richardson met Herb and Renee in the lab. How could he get rid of Renee without making it obvious? Obvious, and in the long run painful? Shaking his head, he turned to Herb. "Herb, did you get that article by Lee?"

"No," tentatively.

Nodding subtly, "Was it out of the library?"

"Yes," a bit more firmly.

"Hell. We need that article. Renee?"

"Yes."

"Would you mind going downtown to the Crerar Library to get an article for us?" She loved going downtown at his expense.

"No, I'd love to."

He pulled out his library card and ten dollars. "Here's my card and cab fare."

She took both and almost left before Herb gave her the complete reference.

"What's up, Boss?"

Where to start? He told Herb everything. First about Weigert and Collier. Was that only this morning? Then about Sanders. Then, his calculations about the missing bungarotoxin and the obvious conclusion, "It has to be someone from Neurology."

"Why?"

"Two reasons."

"Two?"

"Sanders got worse Monday. By that time the only people

who could get into his room were people from our service and Renee.''

"Renee?"

"Yes, Renee.''

"You don't really suspect her?"

"No, I don't suspect anyone. But somebody did it.''

"Are you sure it was one of us?''

"Yes, especially because of the other reason.''

Herb frowned.

"The new bungarotoxin got here Monday. Somebody had to know that, get into the lab without it seeming unusual, and then get in to see Sanders.''

Herb asked him who was on the list.

"You, me, Al, Donna, Adam, the four students, and Renee.''

"So I'm a suspect again?"

"Not as far as I'm concerned.''

Herb smiled. "Are you sure?"

"Yes. I know something happened between you and Sanders. But I don't want to hear about it. I know you didn't do it.''

"So what do we do?"

Richardson outlined two experiments. The first was designed to see if there was still any extra bungarotoxin circulating in Sanders's blood. It would be much harder to treat him if there were. They would have to get rid of it. Perhaps by an exchange transfusion. Taking out Sanders's blood unit by unit and replacing it with fresh blood. Blood without bungarotoxin. This was where Sanders's blood came in. They took the new guinea pigs and gave them injections of Sanders's blood and waited. Nothing happened. Nothing. A negative experiment, thank God. There wasn't enough bungarotoxin in Dr. William Sanders's blood to poison a single guinea pig. They wouldn't have to do an exchange transfusion.

Now came the hard part: to find out what dose of Tensilon would help the guinea pigs in cage three—those that were weakest and most closely mimicked Bill Sanders. A true animal model. They also had to find out what dose would help the guinea pigs without killing them, and maybe, just maybe, that sort of dose could help Sanders.

They started with twice the usual dose of Tensilon. They injected three guinea pigs and then waited ten minutes.

There was no response. No change. No improvement.

Three times the usual dose.

Another ten minutes went by and again there was no response.

Herb then injected four times the usual dose and the waiting continued.

One minute.

Two minutes.

Three minutes.

A flicker, a little movement for a few seconds, almost a minute. Then severe diarrhea.

Herb shook his head. "Poor guinea pigs."

"Poor guinea pigs, hell! It was either this or cancer research. Let's figure out how much of a longer-acting drug like Mestinon is equivalent to that dose of Tensilon."

After a few minutes the calculations were completed and they gave the equivalent dose of Mestinon.

They waited.

Ten minutes. There was no response. Like Vladimir and Estragon they waited in a bare laboratory only to wait again.

Twenty minutes. No response.

Twenty-five minutes. No response. No, there was a response. Something was happening. A few movements.

Thirty minutes.

A few more movements. One of the guinea pigs even lifted his head up off the floor of the cage.

"Okay. That's the dose range we want. I wish to hell that there was some other treatment we could use. But there isn't. So we'll start with this and pray for time. After all, the guinea pigs will get better in three months. Maybe Bill will, too. Let's go see Sanders. And, Herb, do something with that bungarotoxin. Pour it down the sink or something."

They stopped in the office on the way. Sanders's brain wave test was there. It was normal. Sanders was awake and alert. His brain was normal. He heard and understood everything.

They walked into Bill Sanders's room without first being screened by a police guard. There was Bill Sanders in his

bed, with his private duty nurse and his respirator. In the
half-darkened room with the drapes drawn, only the respirator
gave any sign at all of life.

Whoosh . . . . . . whoosh

Whoosh . . . . . . whoosh

Whoosh . . . . . . whoosh

Whoosh . . . . . . whoosh

Fourteen times each minute.

Whoosh . . . . . . whoosh

Whoosh . . . . . . whoosh

Richardson wondered if Sanders ever got used to that, or
did he just wait to be sure the next whoosh happened? A 1980
version of the Chinese water torture, only worse. If it stopped,
Sanders would be dead.

Whoosh . . . . . . whoosh

Whoosh . . . . . . whoosh

Sanders's eyes were closed.

What could he tell his old colleague? How could he tell
him what was happening to him? "Bill, it's me, Paul Richardson." Of course there was no response. Very gently and
very slowly Paul Richardson reached out with both hands and
opened Bill Sanders's eyes. He stood above him so that Bill
Sanders, who could no longer even move his eyes, could see
his face. Richardson stared into the motionless blue eyes.

"Bill, we finally know what's wrong." But how to explain
it?

Whoosh . . . . . . whoosh

Whoosh . . . . . . whoosh

He started again at the beginning. "We know what's going
on. You have," he paused, "myasthenia. It's very severe.
But it's still some type of myasthenia. And we're going to get
you better. I'm going to collect more than a beer this time."

He and Herb calculated the appropriate dose of Mestinon
and gave Sanders an injection. They waited twenty minutes
and not a damn thing happened. Richardson started to say
something, but he caught himself in time. The built-in safe-
guards worked. Richardson's First Law didn't apply here.
Sanders wasn't in coma. He wasn't unconscious. And he
wasn't demented. Bill Sanders was awake and alert. Paul
motioned to Herb to leave the room with him.

"Can you stay with him tonight, Herb?"

"Yes."

"Are you sure? I thought you usually worked on Thursday nights?"

"I usually do. But Chief, you don't really think I'd walk out of here and leave you alone with all this!"

"No. I was sure you'd stay if I asked you to." Richardson looked at his watch. "This dose of Mestinon should last another four hours. If nothing happens, give him another dose, the same amount in four hours. Then, if that doesn't work, add some Tensilon. That will give us an idea of whether or not more Mestinon will help."

"What about side effects?"

"That's our problem. We can give him something to control the diarrhea, but he may get terrible cramps. We'll have to wing it, I guess."

Herb nodded his head in agreement.

God, it was after 8:00. Time to go home. A forty-minute drive in which the rhythm of the respirator repeated itself in his brain like a terrible lyric from some inane ballad of his high school days.

CHAPTER 19

B Y the time Bobbie came downstairs, Paul had already made the coffee and was toying with his second English muffin. It was hard for her to tell if he even noticed that she had come down. She looked out at the backyard. There was a bit less snow on the ground than there had been yesterday, but only a slight bit less.

"Did you sleep at all last night?" she asked her husband.

"A little bit."

"Do you think Bill will pull through?"

"I don't know."

"It really isn't your fault. Can't you understand that?"

He continued to push the buttered muffin around his plate.

"Why are you so sure that he is being poisoned?"

"It can't be anything else. The nerves can carry the messages to his muscles—the EMG showed that. His muscles are normal—the biopsy showed that. But the message can't get from the nerves to the muscles. That's what bungarotoxin does. It prevents the messages from getting from the nerves to the muscles. It has no effect on the muscles. They're still normal. No effect on the nerves. They're still normal. And that's what wrong with Bill. Nerves—normal. Muscles—normal. Why did it take me so damn long—"

"Couldn't Bill just have myasthenia?"

"No. If he had plain old-fashioned myasthenia, the Tensilon would have worked and so would the Mestinon. It has

276

to be bungarotoxin. My bungarotoxin. It's the only thing that fits.''

"Are you that certain?"

"Hell, yes. I might not be able to prove it in a court of law. But it's true and . . .'' He spun the drying muffin a few more times.

"And?"

"It's my bungarotoxin."

"You're not responsible."

"Just like it was my strychnine."

"Paul, don't."

"Only this time it's worse."

"Why worse?"

"Somebody I know, somebody I like, somebody I trust tried to kill him and may have succeeded."

"Paul, who'd want to do that?"

"It would be easier to ask who wouldn't want to. Hell, everybody has a reason to dislike Sanders. As far as I can tell, the most likely thing is that each person on the service gave him a little bit and the total dose killed him. Like *Murder on the Orient Express*. Everybody in Neurology took part."

"Including you, I suppose."

"Sure. I have a motive. More than one."

"I don't believe that."

"You ought to."

"What motives are you talking about?"

"We could start with jealousy."

"Jealousy?"

"Sure. Remember three or four years ago when you heard about me and Carol Voss?"

"Yes, I remember. Bill Sanders was the one who told me all about it."

"In glowing detail, I'm sure." When Bobbie refused to respond, Paul continued. "And then the two of you started seeing a lot of each other. Meeting for lunch. A few drinks . . ."

"How did you know?"

"I know a lot of things."

"You never said anything to me."

"I know, because there was one thing I didn't know and probably didn't want to know." He got up and poured himself another cup of coffee. He sat back down and looked at the cold English muffin. He took another one and went over to the toaster oven. He might as well find out now.

"Did you have an affair with him?" There it was. Out in the open. He'd never asked. He'd just assumed she had. After all . . .

"Of course not. Did you think I did?"

"Yes . . . or no. I don't know. You would have had every right to have an affair."

"Right? No one has a right to that."

"But after what I had—"

"Paul, that's over and done with. Let's not live with it forever. Why is it easier for me to forget about it than it is for you? You and your perfect memory."

"It's not perfect."

"Damn near and you expect such perfection from yourself."

Paul took the newly burned muffin from the toaster oven, threw it in the garbage, and started another one.

Bobbie changed the tone of the conversation. "Since you have no reason to be jealous I suppose that eliminates you from your list of suspects?"

"Not completely."

"You have other motives? Are you jealous of Bill and someone else?"

"No, but there are other motives than jealousy. Self-protection."

"Self-protection?"

"Yes, self-protection. Bill was going to fire some residents for moonlighting. If he fired Herb, he wouldn't be able to join the staff next year and I need him. And I need Al and Stokes as residents, too."

"That also gives Herb a motive."

"Right. His career would be on the line and so would Al's. And Adam Stokes's."

The muffin was done. He buttered it and sat down to twirl it.

"Especially Al," he added, without breaking the pattern of the muffin's rotation.

"Why especially Al?"

"Everybody knows how much he moonlights. He was the most likely candidate to get axed for moonlighting."

"Would that make him the prime suspect?"

"No. Herb probably has more than one motive."

Bobbie was puzzled.

"There was something between them. I don't know what it was but Sanders knifed Herb's fellowship application."

"That makes Herb the prime suspect."

"Except for one thing: I don't believe he did it."

"That's good enough for me, Paul." Bobbie smiled at him. "But I'm not sure everyone else will be as easily swayed." When her husband made no response, she went on. "Who else wanted to get rid of him?"

He just didn't want to go through the rest of the kids. His kids. They all seemed to have the opportunity and motives. But he needed to talk about it. He had tossed and turned with it all night. It was time to share it with Bobbie. He told her about Donna. About Sue Evans. About Renee, John, Linda, Walt. Everyone.

Then it was time to leave if he wanted to get in early and see Sanders. The drive in was faster than usual. Many cars were still stuck on side streets. They were lucky; their street got plowed out early. The streets around Sox park were clear but the outfield wasn't. It was supposed to get up into the fifties today. Maybe it would melt enough so that they could start the season tomorrow.

He went straight to Sanders's room without changing into his white coat. As he opened the door the familiar dirge hit him. The slow movement of a string quartet: Sanders, Westphal, the respirator, the nurse.

Whoosh . . . . . . whoosh

Whoosh . . . . . . whoosh

"Hi, Herb." He almost whispered as if afraid a loud noise might stop the pattern.

"Hi, Boss," almost as softly.

"How'd it go?"

"Not good. The Mestinon isn't doing very much, if anything. Take a look for yourself." They examined Sanders. He couldn't open his eyes or move them when Herb held them open. They couldn't find any evidence of improvement.

"Did you give him any Tensilon?"

"Yeah, at 4:00. One hour after the three o'clock Mestinon."

"What happened?"

"He could move his eyes and grimaced a little bit."

"That's something. Do you think we can increase the Mestinon?"

"No, he has stomach cramps as it is."

"How do you know?"

"Just put your hand on his stomach."

Paul did just as his senior resident instructed. "You're right. We can't give him any more. When's the next Mestinon due?"

"Nine."

"Good, give him the same dose and then we'll do a Tensilon test at about 10:00."

Richardson began to leave. "You look bushed."

"I am. You look like you didn't have too much sleep either, Paul."

"After the Tensilon test we'll have somebody else babysit for a while and you can get some sleep."

He got to the office in time to join Chris in her first cup of coffee. Then he retired to his office with a cigar. He stared out the window, looking at the snow-clogged streets, and listened to the "L" trains and the FM. It would be almost an hour until everyone showed up for card rounds. Methodically he ran through the names of everyone on the list Chris gave him. Names and motives. Like card rounds. Names and diagnoses. Or, like the opening day lineup:

1. Herb Westphal
2. Al Schilder
3. Donna Batten
4. John Adson
5. Sue Evans
6. Linda Sharp
7. Walter Simpson
8. Renee Weber

Eight possible diagnoses.

There had to be some reason behind it. Some motive. There was always a motive. *One* motive. Anyone who ever read Agatha Christie knew that. Every murderer has a single motive, and the detective has to find what it is. Every time you accused Colonel Mustard of doing it in the kitchen with a lead pipe, you knew he did it for a reason. Somewhere, someone must have had two motives, two different reasons acting simultaneously. Maybe someday, a yet unborn mystery writer will devise a plot in which the murderer has two motives. An original contribution to the field, as original as any Agatha Christie.

Motives:

1. Herb Westphal—Moonlighting; fellowship. What had happened between him and Sanders?

2. Al Schilder—Moonlighting, possibility of being fired. If Sanders was going to find a scapegoat on the house staff to fire, Al was the leading contender.

3. Donna Batten—Had she had an affair with Sanders? She couldn't have. There were some rumors. Did he start them? Could they be true?

4. John Adson—What was going on between John and Sanders? Renee and Sanders?

5. Sue Evans—After what Sanders did to her, it might be justifiable homicide if she killed him.

6. Linda Sharp—Bitterness over losing a quarter seemed an unlikely motive. But what really happened between her and Sanders?

7. Walt Simpson—What had happened between Walt and Sanders? Walt had had to repeat two courses and miss a summer's research. That hadn't helped his chances of getting his residency at Harvard or Johns Hopkins. Hadn't Walt complained once that he was having trouble getting a good letter of recommendation from the dean's office?

8. Renee Weber—See Number 4.

Who else was on that list? The key list. Those who could have seen Sanders on Monday.

9. Adam Stokes

10. Paul Richardson—Nine players and a playing manager. Motives:

    9. Adam Stokes—Moonlighting.

    10. Paul Richardson—No comment.

You needed more than just a motive. You needed motive and opportunity. Colonel Mustard had to get into the kitchen. But who had seen him on Monday? Balo, Bright, and Devic hadn't kept any records. They hadn't been asked to. Another error. He was so damn sure that none of his crew had killed Collier or the five patients. So confident that the only thing that mattered was keeping everyone else out. The cops were told they didn't have to monitor him and his crew, and they had done their job. No outsiders came in to kill Sanders, only insiders.

Only Sanders knew who came in to see him, and he wasn't able to talk. If he lived, they might know someday. The bungarotoxin might take four or five months to wear off. The chances of his getting pneumonia and dying were high unless they could get him stronger.

Chris buzzed him. Everyone was waiting to start card rounds. It was almost time for the Tensilon test. But they had to go over all the patients as carefully as ever.

Mrs. Robin was about halfway off her medication. She was no worse. Maybe that was better. Minimally so.

Mr. Wallenberg was to go home today. Time would tell.

Mr. Romberg was again a little better. His voice was stronger, he spoke a bit faster, and he could get up by himself. He was anxious to get home as soon as he could.

Mr. Michaels was still getting his penicillin and he wanted to know when Dr. Satchel was coming to see him again. It wasn't exactly a remarkable recovery.

"What happened on the angiograms?"

"We're batting .500," Al responded.

"What's that mean? Did we find what we were looking for in one out of two?"

"No, that means X-ray did one out of two."

"Christ, which one?"

"Schwann."

"And?"

"They found his tumor. Jackson put him on the OR schedule for Monday."

"What about Mrs. Rader?"

"They never did it."

"Damn it! When are they going to get it done?"

"Late today."

"What happened yesterday?"

"They didn't finish Schwann until 3:30."

"Don't tell me. It was 3:30, and being radiologists, it was time to go home."

"All right, I won't tell you."

"Is that it?"

"No, they had an emergency to do and she got bumped."

There were two new consults, but they hadn't been seen yet. Thank God. And nobody else had to be seen today.

As he left the office Chris gave him some better news. Arnold Chiari was back in town.

"Good. Call him and tell him to make rounds tomorrow."

"Tell him?"

"No, ask him, but in a way so he can't say no. I need Bud's help."

When he got into Sanders's room Herb was sitting next to the bed, fighting to keep himself awake. Richardson walked in as quietly as he could.

Whoosh . . . . . . whoosh

Whoosh . . . . . . whoosh

He couldn't stand that sound. It was even worse than listening to Minnie Minoso strike out.

Whoosh . . . . . . whoosh

Whoosh . . . . . . whoosh

Whoosh . . . . . . whoosh

What differentiated man from all other species was that man could invent new diseases.

Alcoholism.

Drug addiction.

Industrial toxicity.

Alpha-bungarotoxin poisoning.

Whoosh . . . . . . whoosh

Whoosh . . . . . . whoosh

Whoosh . . . . . . whoosh

"Herb?"

Herb jumped slightly.

"When did he get the Mestinon?"

Herb looked at his watch. "About an hour and ten minutes ago."

"Where's the Tensilon?"

Herb took it out of his pocket.

They went to the bedside and Richardson bent over in front of Bill Sanders's face. He reached down slowly, then carefully pushed Sanders's eyelids back and held his eyes open.

"Bill, we're going to give you some Tensilon. Keep trying to move your eyes."

Herb gave Sanders the Tensilon, then they both stood back to watch the motionless face and closed eyes. As they waited Paul tried not to think of Sanders as if he already were a death mask.

Whoosh . . . . . . whoosh

Whoosh . . . . . . whoosh

Fifteen seconds. Time was such a strange thing. As long as you take it for granted, it means nothing. But then you're suddenly aware of nothing else and it becomes all-important.

Thirty seconds.

Whoosh . . . . . . whoosh

Whoosh . . . . . . whoosh

The respirator continued to play on.

Whoosh . . . . . . whoosh

Whoosh . . . . . . whoosh

One minute. Would Godot ever arrive?

Nothing happened. There was no perceptible change.

Whoosh . . . . . . whoosh

Whoosh . . . . . . whoosh

Whoosh . . . . . . whoosh

A harmony without any rhythmic variations.

Whoosh . . . . . . whoosh

Two minutes. Did Godot ever arrive?

Suddenly the lids moved and the eyes opened. The death mask was alive. Godot had come. Beckett was wrong.

Up.

Down.

Side to side.

"Bill, move your eyes up if you're having stomach cramps."

The eyes went up.

"How bad are they? Hell, you can't answer that."

"Bill, listen. Up for yes, down for no. Are the stomach cramps bad?"

Up.

"Too bad to tolerate?"

No response.

His eyes had moved for only a minute or so and at the cost of severe cramps. But at least they had gotten some response. Walt walked in to see his patient just as they were finishing. They told him what he should watch for and went back to the office, leaving Walt and the nurse to watch the respirator, Bill Sanders, and each other.

"Herb, you were feeling his stomach."

"Yes."

"How bad were the cramps?"

"Bad."

"How often do you think we can give him Tensilon?"

"Every half hour or so, maybe every fifteen minutes. But why? It doesn't help much. He can only move his eyes for a minute or so."

"That may be all we need."

"For what?"

"To find out who's killing him."

CHAPTER 20

H_{ALF} an hour later Herb and Richardson were back in Sanders's room. This time Richardson didn't even hear the respirator.

Again Richardson stood over Sanders's bed. He opened Sanders's eyes and stood in front of him. He felt like shouting. But not to overcome deafness or to be heard over the respirator. Where to start? At the beginning.

"Bill, listen carefully. I'll take it slowly, but listen carefully. You do not have myasthenia. It's not myasthenia. Somebody has been giving you a poison that causes something like myasthenia. The poison is called bungarotoxin. Bungarotoxin is a type of snake venom. It came from my lab. Somebody had to take it from there and give it to you.

"What you have is like myasthenia. The Tensilon should work well enough so that you can move your eyes for at least a minute or two.

"Listen very carefully. After we give you the Tensilon I'm going to ask you some questions. I want you to answer them by moving your eyes.

"Move your eyes up for yes.

"Move your eyes down for no.

"Side to side if you're not sure. That's up for yes, down for no, and side to side for maybe.

"I want to know about Monday. That was the day you got worse. Think about that day. Somebody who saw you that day must have been the one." Herb took out the Tensilon, filled a syringe and injected the Tensilon through the IV. Five days before bungarotoxin had gone through the same IV. Herb stood back and watched the sweep hand of his watch.

They waited.

"One minute," Herb announced.

Both Herb and Richardson watched Sanders's eyes closely, but nothing happened.

Again they waited. Richardson again heard it.

Whoosh . . . . . . whoosh

Whoosh . . . . . . whoosh

"Two minutes." Still no movement. Then the lids flickered and the eyelids moved. The eyes, Sanders's eyes were open. They moved. Up and down.

"Bill, did you understand?"

Up.

"Say yes."

Up.

"Say no."

Down.

"Let's get started. Did Herb see you on Monday?"

Up.

"Al?"

Down.

"Donna?"

Up.

"Stokes?"

Down.

"Any students?"

Up.

"Who? Damn it, you can't answer that. Sue Evans?"

No answer. The Tensilon had already worn off. Their time was up.

"How did the cramps feel, Herb?"

"Pretty strong. They're still going on."

They would have to wait until the cramps cleared. Then they could try again. There was nothing to do but wait.

Five minutes. Herb felt Sanders's abdomen and shook his head.

Ten minutes. Herb again felt Sanders's stomach and again shook his head. The cramps were less severe but not completely gone.

They waited.

Richardson began to hear it again.

Whoosh . . . . . . whoosh

Whoosh . . . . . . whoosh

So far they had eliminated Al and Adam. Or had they? Sometimes it was hard to keep the days straight in the hospital. When you were that sick in a bed. Each day seemed like the one before and the one after. Could Sanders be that sure? Could he believe him? Hell, he had to believe Sanders. It was all he had to go on. Al and Adam were out.

Whoosh . . . . . . whoosh

Whoosh . . . . . . whoosh

Whoosh . . . . . . whoosh

Once again the only sound in the room was the respirator.

Whoosh . . . . . . whoosh

Whoosh . . . . . . whoosh

A sound of emptiness.

Whoosh . . . . . . whoosh

Whoosh . . . . . . whoosh

Fifteen minutes. Herb nodded. The cramps were completely gone.

Herb drew up another syringe full of Tensilon and went over to the IV and waited for Paul's signal.

"Bill, here we go again. I am going to ask you some more about Monday. Just five days ago. You had done fairly well over the weekend. You were stable for the first time. Monday was the day you got worse again. That's the day we have to know about. If the cramps get to be more than you can stand, move your eyes up and down again and we'll stop. But put up with as much as you can. Here we go."

Herb gave the injection through the IV. It took less than two seconds. It would be so easy to look like you were checking the IV and inject something. Strychnine. Bungarotoxin. Anything.

They waited and watched. Herb his second hand, Richardson the closed eyelids.

"I want to know about the students. The students who came to see you on Monday."

"One minute."

Nothing. No eye movements. The room always seemed

quieter while they were waiting. And the respirator seemed louder.

"Two minutes."

The eyelids began to move. First just a little flutter. On the right. Then the left. Then they opened and moved up and down.

"Did Sue Evans come in here?"

Up.

"John Adson?"

Up.

"Linda Sharp?"

A pause and then the eyes moved from side to side.

"Walt Simpson?"

Up.

Who else, he thought. Renee. "Renee Weber?"

Up.

"Can you remember anyone else? It's important."

No response. The fleeting eye movements were replaced by severe stomach cramps.

Time to wait. It was like being in the service again. Hurry up and wait. "They also serve who only stand and wait."

The two doctors stepped away from the bedside and respirator and stood by the window. Richardson stared out at the melting snow. "I've been asking him the wrong question. It had to be injected. Even the ancients—Plutarch, Horace, Galen, Celsus—knew that you have to ask the right question."

Herb Westphal looked at Paul Richardson as the older physician continued. "Snake venom. It always has to be injected to kill. If someone drinks it, it's harmless. The snake has to bite you and put its venom into your bloodstream."

"So?"

"That means whoever gave Sanders the bungarotoxin had to put it into his IV. It's so obvious. If Galen knew it, how could we not know it? Damn it."

Whoosh . . . . . . whoosh

Whoosh . . . . . . whoosh

"Boss, wouldn't it be obvious if somebody came in and did something to the IV?"

"No, that's the beauty of it. That's how Weigert got away with it. If you've got an IV, you're fair game. Anyone who comes into your room has a right to your IV. Not only that, almost every time you walk into a room and the patient has an IV, what do you do?"

"Check it."

"That's right. You check it; everybody does. Whenever you're in a room with a sick patient with an IV, you check it. It's second nature—one of those things you acquire during your internship. You do it by force of habit. The patient learns to expect you to do it and you do it unconsciously. Only somebody did this consciously."

They waited.

After ten minutes Herb checked Sanders's abdomen. He shook his head and they went back to waiting.

"Maybe we shouldn't have known it had to be through the IV. Lancisi and Morgagni weren't so sure."

"Who?" Herb asked.

"Lancisi and Morgagni."

"Who did they play for?"

"They weren't a double-play combo, Herb. Giovanni Battista Morgagni and Giovanni Maria Lancisi were the two greatest Italian physicians of the early eighteenth century."

"Oh sure, I've heard of Morgagni. He was a pathologist, wasn't he?"

"He was both a clinician and a pathologist. Lancisi was a great clinician, the physician of several popes, and even wrote a book on sudden deaths. One of his books had an etching showing Cleopatra dying with a snake wound around her arm, and in the book he raised the question as to whether the snake bit Cleopatra or she just drank the venom.

"Morgagni accepted the challenge, reviewed the ancient sources, and concluded that the snake bit her. Lancisi wasn't so sure. In a series of letters, they quoted everyone—Plutarch, Dio, Seutonius, Horace. Fortunately, they never had any data to refer to."

"Fortunately?"

"Sure, nothing like a little data to end an argument, and it was such an eloquent debate. You can drink all the bungarotoxin you want and it won't give you myasthenia. It has to be injected. I've been asking the wrong damn questions. I should have known better."

Herb looked at his watch, went back to Dr. Sanders's side, next to the respirator, reached below the sheet, palpated the patient's abdomen, and shook his head slowly, quietly.

Whoosh . . . . . . whoosh

Whoosh . . . . . . whoosh

So far they hadn't made much progress. They'd eliminated Al and Adams, maybe Linda. If Sanders was right. Lying in that bed hardly able to move every day. Could he really remember Monday that clearly? Had all those people seen him that day? His room must have been like State and Madison. The Sox should only draw as big a crowd. Why had they all seen him? Because he was so sick and a patient of theirs? And despite everything he did to them they still cared? All but one. But who?

Herb stayed by the bed and every minute he went through the same ritual: palpating the abdomen and shaking his head.

Donna? She was one Richardson could account for. Donna should have seen Sanders on Monday and every other day as well, since she was the resident on the case. She must have seen him every day, checked his IV each and every day, including Monday.

What about the students?

Walt? Okay. He was assigned to follow Sanders. Like Donna, he should have seen Sanders every day. And checked the IV.

Herb reached under the sheet again, and then shook his head. Richardson went over to the bed and put his hand on Sanders's abdomen. The cramps were still quite strong. They would have to wait longer this time.

Whoosh . . . . . . whoosh

Whoosh . . . . . . whoosh

Why had the other students gone to see Sanders?

Sue? Why? She was off the case. She'd asked him to take her off the case because she didn't want to see Dr. Sanders.

John? He didn't have a reason. Or did he? Why had Sue wanted Walt to follow Sanders and not John?

Renee? Why had she gone to see Sanders? And Monday wasn't the only time she had been in Sanders's room. He himself had seen her come out of Sanders's room one day last week.

Five more minutes had elapsed. Herb again shook his head. But this time he also said, "They're beginning to get lighter. We shouldn't have to wait too much longer." It was time to wait again for a few more minutes.

One more check. Herb nodded his head and finally the cramps cleared. He began to draw up the Tensilon, but Richardson told him that they would wait another five minutes. Then, he hoped, they wouldn't have to wait as long after the next one. The respirator seemed to be getting louder again.

Whoosh . . . . . . whoosh

Whoosh . . . . . . whoosh

Richardson went over each one in his head: Donna, Sue, John, Walt, Renee. Not Herb. He never even considered Herb.

It was time to start again. It reminded Richardson of Chicago's most famous murder. The St. Valentine's Day Massacre. When the police got to that garage on Clark Street, one of the victims was still alive. Frank Gusenberg. "Who shot you, Frank?" they asked. "Nobody shot me," he answered. Bill had to be able to tell them more than that. He had to.

Whoosh . . . . . . whoosh

Whoosh . . . . . . whoosh

"We've got to give it one more try, Bill. Same day— Monday. Same cast of characters. Same ground rules. This time we're going to focus on the IV. Think about your IV on Monday."

Herb had already drawn up the Tensilon. It two seconds it went through the IV and into Sanders's bloodstream.

They waited.

"One minute." The eyelids stayed frozen.

"Two minutes." A flicker, a flutter.

"Think about the IV. Did anyone seem to do anything with the IV? Anyone?"

The eyes opened widely. More widely than before. The eyes began to move. Up.

Up and down. Up and down. Up and down.

After a minute the eyes stopped.

They both felt Sanders's stomach. The cramps were severe

and almost constant. The game was over for a while. They stood on either side of the bed, staring at each other. There was nothing else to do. There was no reason for both of them to stay. They'd let Walt watch him for a while. Walt. They'd both almost forgotten he was there. Throughout the whole procedure he had just stood quietly and watched, a silent spectator.

Whoosh . . . . . . whoosh

Whoosh . . . . . . whoosh

Whoosh . . . . . . whoosh

Finally, Richardson nodded his head toward the door.

Whoosh . . . . . . whoosh

Whoosh . . . . . . whoosh

All three of them slowly left the room. Once they were in the hall, Herb and Richardson both took a series of deep breaths.

"Walt, you saw him each day."

"Yes."

"Did you—"

"Yes," Walt interrupted. "I checked his IV every day."

"I wasn't going to ask that. I wanted to know if anyone else came in while you were there and acted strangely."

"No. Not that I can remember."

"Walt, do us a favor. Stay with him for a while."

"Paul?"

"Yes, Herb."

"We better wait a while before we try again. His stomach can't take much more."

"What time is it?"

"A quarter after 11:00."

Richardson thought for a moment, calculated, hedged his bet. "Let's try again at 1:00."

"Okay. If it's all right with you I'm going to go shave and take a shower."

"Go ahead. You need it. Meet me at the office at 1:00. Walt will watch him for us."

Richardson stood in his office, sipping coffee and smoking. He hadn't learned very much. All that and what had he learned? It was more frustrating than reading all these damn experiments. Christ, there must be something to do to kill time until 1:00.

The meningitis charts. The prospect didn't thrill Richardson, but they had to get some work done on that study; they were so far behind. Walt was usually so reliable, yet he hadn't done much of anything since they started the project a month or so earlier. He would talk to him about it when things settled down. When and if.

He walked into Herb's office. The charts looked just as they had last week. They were piled up everywhere. Richardson smiled as he thought about the year when he and Sanders were interns together. He'd look at some of the old charts, which were piled by year: 1958, 1947, 1968, 1962. That was it, 1962. The year of their internship. There might be some cases he'd remember. If he read some of those, he might be able to strengthen their protocol and make it easier to read the case histories of patients neither he nor Walt had ever seen. He looked at the list:

R. Barrett	467-365
W. Bickford	688-327
C. Conaster	277-384
A. Dark	322-433
R. Elliott	283-474
J. Heath	319-582
T. Holmes	325-439
M. McCormick	303-417
N. Potter	615-286
M. Rickert	211-316
C. Ryan	213-238
B. Salkeld	242-411
B. Voiselle	500-363

Obviously he must have seen some of these patients. If they were a baseball team he'd remember them—the names, the batting averages, the slugging percentages, the won-lost records, the earned run averages, whether or not they could hit left-handed pitching. But they weren't a baseball team. They were a lot of patients who had meningitis during the year when he had been an intern. He picked out one name that seemed familiar.

M. McCormick. He began to look through the chart and found the intern's admission note. It was his note, written eighteen years earlier. He read it carefully. In his own handwriting: "Neurologic exam: WNL." He had been like every other intern. His smile broadened as he remembered the patient. It had been a rather straightforward clinic problem. They had diagnosed his meningitis quickly, treated him adequately, and had been lucky. Mr. McCormick had gone home in two weeks in perfect health.

Elliott. Elliott. He seemed to remember that patient, too. He sat down, found one of Herb's cigars, lit it, and started shuffling the chart. As soon as he started reading the records, he remembered. He remembered it all. As clearly as if it were an epic White Sox–Yankee game or Satchel Paige's one start. Elliott had been Sanders's patient when they were on 6 East together. Sanders had admitted him late one Sunday night. One of six or seven sick patients admitted on a busy Sunday night. He had just been discharged two days before after a routine appendectomy. He'd been treated postoperatively with antibiotics for one week and sent home. Two days later he was back in the hospital with a high fever, delirium, and a stiff neck. Severe meningitis, probably hospital acquired. After three days he wasn't getting any better and the penicillin didn't seem to be helping. They had many long discussions on how to get more penicillin into the brain. Then, one night, Sanders hit upon an idea. They would do a spinal tap, but instead of just taking fluid out they would put the penicillin in. Right into the fluid that bathed the brain. The resident agreed and they did it. He remembered it all so clearly. He wondered if Sanders still did. He had been off that night. Nuts, if only he'd been there when they talked about it. He knew that it wouldn't work. As clever an idea as it seemed, it was dangerous. Too damn dangerous. It might even kill the patient. Richardson had read Maynard Cohen's article. Not many people knew that yet. After all, not many people read the *Journal of Neuropathology and Experimental Neurology*—it wasn't exactly *Life* magazine. Richardson never forgot the look on Sanders's face when he showed him the article. Poor Bill. He'd cared. Seeing Mrs. Elliott and those two little kids didn't help. Richardson still remembered the kids. Joan had a little boy, Willie. Had Sanders ever learned what had really happened? He hadn't gone to the brain cutting.

One o'clock arrived and Herb and Richardson were back in Sanders's room. They told Walt that he could take a break and also told the nurse she could take an hour off for lunch. At first she hesitated, but then remembered that it was Richardson who had given the order that the nurses weren't to leave the room. She thanked him and left.

Whoosh . . . . . . whoosh

Whoosh . . . . . . whoosh

It was time to get started again.

Herb drew up the Tensilon and Richardson started again.

"It's us, Bill. The Gold Dust Twins. We're going to take it from the top again. Back to Monday. Monday and the IV."

He nodded to Herb and Herb injected the Tensilon through the same IV. Herb lifted his wrist and focused on the second hand of his watch.

They waited.

"One minute," he announced.

The eyelids had not moved, but no one had expected them to move that soon.

"Two minutes."

The eyelids began to twitch and the eyes opened.

"Are you having cramps?"

Up.

"Should we stop?"

Down.

"Let's go. Did anyone do anything to the IV?"

Side to side.

"You can't remember?"

Down.

"Try, Bill. Try to remember. Did anyone handle the IV?"

Down.

"Shit." He paused very briefly and then continued.

"Bill, I want to know who saw you every day or every other day. Do you understand?"

No response.

"Should we try again, Boss?"

"Yes, as soon as his cramps slow down. Make sure the nurses are scheduled for tonight."

"I won't need any help."

"But I will tonight," Richardson replied.

"You?"

"Sure. You can't stay up two nights in a row, and I probably won't sleep tonight anyway if last night was any judge. Look, make sure they arrange nurses for tonight."

"Both shifts?"

"Yes, and I'll get Walt to stick around, too."

Herb went out to take care of the nursing arrangements, leaving Richardson in the room alone. Alone with Sanders and the respirator. Suddenly it seemed much louder again.

Whoosh . . . . . . whoosh

Whoosh . . . . . . whoosh

"Bill, we're going to have to ask some more questions. It's too hard to remember about the IVs, so I want you to think about who came in here to see you often while you were sick. Whoever is doing this had to see you often to get away with it. Think about it, old buddy."

It was after 1:30 when Westphal got back. His being there made the respirator seem quieter.

Herb checked Sanders's stomach and it was soft. He drew up the Tensilon and, as Richardson nodded, gave it to Sanders. They were off to the races again. Play ball!

"We just gave you another injection, Bill."

They waited.

One minute.

No response. No movement of the eyelids.

Two minutes.

The eyelids moved. The eyes opened.

"Bill, we want to talk about anyone who saw you frequently, right?"

Up.

"Herb Westphal?"

Up. That figures.

"Al Schilder?"

Up. Maybe he wasn't eliminated. Sometimes the guinea pigs got worse on the second and third day. Damn it.

"Donna Batten?"

Up.

"Adam Stokes?"

Down.

"Sue Evans?"

Up.

"John Adson?"

Up. Why? Richardson wondered.

"Linda Sharp?"

Down.

"Walt Simpson?"

Up.

"Renee?"

No response.

But how often did they see him? They'd have to try again.

They waited until 2:00, all the while listening to the respirator. Each one was lost in his own thoughts.

At two, Sanders's abdomen seemed soft enough to try again.

Herb drew up the Tensilon.

"How much of that have we got?"

"Plenty, Boss. I had the pharmacy give me ten vials."

Herb gave the injection.

One minute.

No response.

Two minutes.

The eyelids moved. The eyes opened. The eyes moved.

Up and down, up and down, almost violently.

Richardson shrugged his shoulders. An overdose. Game called. It probably didn't make much difference. They didn't seem to be getting anywhere.

"Herb, you stick around for a while until I get Walt in here. I've got to start rounds. I'll get back around 5:00, I hope."

The students and residents were waiting in the conference room. Richardson spoke privately to Walt Simpson, and Walt left to stay with Sanders. It was 3:00. The private duty nurse should also be there.

They were now four consultations behind. Four new patients to be seen. John had seen the first.

"What's the problem, John?"

"I'm not sure. It's not simple. She has more than one thing wrong. She has episodes when her personality changes and she appears to be crazy. But in between she is normal. Then at times her urine turns dark and now her legs are weak.''

Richardson smiled. Porphyria. The disease of George III. He'd get to tell that story today.

"Let's have the whole story. Start at the beginning.''

Suddenly there was an emergency page over the loud-speaker for Herb Westphal, Al Schilder, and Paul Richardson. The problem was on 3 East.

Dr. Richardson, Al Schilder, and Donna Batten raced out of the room and down the stairs. The students hesitated a second and then followed them.

Down from 6 to 5.

Down from 5 to 4. On the fourth floor landing Richardson suddenly realized he had again been asking the wrong questions. He knew the right one now. He'd ask Sanders at 5:00. God, it was so obvious.

Down from 4 to 3.

Herb Westphal was already there.

"What's up?''

"They got a patient with a seizure who stopped breathing.''

Not again. It couldn't be. Weigert was dead. That was all over. It was a thing of the past. As remote as last year's batting averages. They arrived at the nursing station.

"Where?'' Richardson asked half out of breath.

"Room 301,'' the nurse answered.

They all ran to 301. Herb Westphal got there first.

A young man, in his twenties, was convulsing in the bed. His face was contorted by continuous jerks, and his arms and legs jerked back and forth. His eyes were rolled up.

His eyes were rolled up!

Richardson breathed a sigh of relief.

"What do you think, Herb?''

"A plain old-fashioned fit.''

"Thank God. A plain old-fashioned run-of-the-mill seizure. Just like Hippocrates described. A true convulsion.''

CHAPTER 21

T HEY had been watching the seizure for only a few seconds when the intern caught up with them. He filled them in following the same time-honored formula.

Name—Hortega

Age—twenty-nine

Race—White

Sex—Male

Chief complaint—Uncontrolled seizures

History of present illness—His first seizure had been at age three and he probably didn't take his medications very regularly, if at all. This present burst of seizures began about ten minutes ago and had been seen first by a medicine tech who was passing out the 1:00 P.M. medicines.

Just two hours late, Richardson noted to himself.

The med tech had pushed the panic button because she thought the patient had stopped breathing. Al was resident on call, so they left him in charge and walked back up the stairs.

If only he'd asked the right question the first time, Richardson thought to himself. They'd wasted a whole day, but it probably didn't make much difference. He only had to wait another ninety minutes. Twelve hundred and sixty respirations.

They sat down again in the conference room and John got started. The patient was a thirty-two-year-old female who . . . Suddenly, there was another emergency page over the speaker—for Paul Richardson. He was wanted on the phone. It was Dean Willis.

"I hear we've had another murder."

How did he know about Sanders? And even if he did, it was still just an attempted murder.

"I wouldn't say that, exactly."

"What do you mean, exactly? The nurse on 3 East just called me. The patient had a seizure and quit breathing. I was never convinced that Weigert did it anyway. I'm calling the police in. This has to stop."

"I'm sure it already has."

"What do you mean?"

"I left Al Schilder with the patient five minutes ago, and with any luck at all he should have been able to stop the seizures by now."

"Huh?"

"That's right, the patient is alive. He's a run-of-the-mill fitter, just a plain epileptic. Nothing fancy. Keep your shirt on."

"But the nurse said he stopped breathing."

"Patients in fits often stop breathing for a while. Weigert didn't come back from his grave. I've got to see some sick people." With that he abruptly hung up the phone.

John started again. Richardson half listened. "She was well until age twenty-two, then experienced a two-month period of very peculiar behavior. Then she seemed fine again." Would Sanders ever be fine? In an hour or so they could try the Tensilon again.

Richardson couldn't believe his ears. Another emergency page. For Herb Westphal, Al Schilder, and Paul Richardson. He listened again. This page was for Mrs. Rader's room. That was the last thing he needed today. Why the hell hadn't they done the angio yesterday?

Herb, as always, got there first. Like a good center fielder, Herb Westphal always seemed to be where the action was. Why did things have to happen like this? Whenever you had someone with an expanding aneurysm there was always that possibility that something would go wrong, the threat that the thin-walled blister would suddenly burst just like a dam. Blood under high pressure would pour out uncontrollably at the base of the brain. Such blood could compress the brain and even tear it to pieces. To Richardson, an aneurysm typified the absurdity of life. One minute you could be in perfect health but still have a small, unsuspected blister somewhere in your head. In another minute that blister could kill you. Yet you should be rational in planning your life.

Herb was at the bedside. Mrs. Rader was obviously in pain. She kept her eyes squeezed shut and moaned audibly, almost continuously. Herb bent over her and tried ever so slowly, ever so gently, to bend her head forward. Slowly, gently, with both hands behind her head, he lifted. Her neck would not bend. As he lifted Mrs. Rader's head, her shoulders came off the bed, her moans became quieter. The squeezing of her eyes changed into a grimace. The sounds became silent. A wordless, silent scream. There was no audible sound coming from her lips, but its echo bounced off the walls of the small room.

Donna spoke first. "Did she burst her aneurysm?" It was as much a statement as a question. A fait accompli.

Herb didn't answer. It didn't seem necessary. He just moved his head. It was sort of a nod and a shake and a shrug all at once.

Richardson closed his eyes briefly. That's what was wrong with medicine. So many patients and so many things that could go wrong. In baseball you only had to play one game at a time.

"When did it happen?" Richardson asked.

This time Herb answered. "About an hour ago."

"Oh, hell! How is she?"

"Not bad. She's got a terrible headache and a stiff neck, but she's awake and alert." Herb went on to give the details of his evaluation of Mrs. Rader.

Other than the stiff neck, there was no evidence of any change in her condition. She could move both arms and both legs without any weakness. Her speech was normal, her vision unchanged.

They walked out into the hall. No one felt like saying very much. Again it was Donna Batten who interrupted the silence. "It could be worse."

"That's not much of a consolation, Donna." Richardson slowly and painstakingly explained everything to the four students. No back and forth. No Socratic method. A straight-forward explanation.

If only they had done the angiogram and operated. Maybe they wouldn't have operated until next week anyway. It was yet another question to think about when things got too quiet. If they ever did.

"We'll have to sedate her and lower her blood pressure. She's a young girl. We can't let her die, Herb."

Herb walked toward the nurses' station but stopped when he heard Richardson's voice again. "There's just one more question. One more answer I have to know. How did he manage it? How the hell did Watson manage it? Every time he wanted to drop everything and tag along with Holmes there was someone waiting to take care of his patients. That should only happen to me. Just once. That's all I ask." If it ever did, he'd probably feel superfluous.

It was after 4:30 by the time they had gotten Mrs. Rader stabilized. Her blood pressure was down and she was resting quietly. No more silent screams were piercing the air. But Richardson could still hear the first one, and so could West-phal. If all went well, she would bleed no more and then in a few days they could do the angiogram. If all went well.

Nobody was interested in hearing John's story. He wasn't even interested in starting it. The patient could wait until the next morning and be presented to Dr. Chiari then.

Teaching rounds were over for the day. Richardson started back to his office by himself. Herb went to check on the patient in 301, and the students went home. For them it was an early day. It was for Chris, too. She had already left when Richardson got to the office. There was the usual list of patient messages and phone calls to return: Mrs. Hammond and Mr. Berger, who needed a new prescription. His pharmacy would call. Mr. Stilling called to say that the switch to Sanka had worked. He felt so much better that he wanted to sing about it. Mrs. Hammond had called again. He sat back and listened to the FM. Offenbach. This was not the time for Offenbach. He switched off the FM and stared out the window, watching the elevated train go by every five minutes. Rush hour had begun.

It was 5:00. Time to see Sanders.

Richardson walked back to the hospital and into Sanders's room. There were two people sitting quietly in the half-darkness opposite the respirator. One was the private duty nurse, trying to look like she was doing something other than just listening and waiting. The other was Walt Simpson. He'd been there most of the afternoon.

Whoosh . . . . . . whoosh

Whoosh . . . . . . whoosh

Whoosh . . . . . . whoosh

"Walt, what are you doing tonight?"

"Nothing much."

"Good. I'd like you to stick around here and help me keep an eye on Dr. Sanders. Herb stuck around last night, and he needs some sleep."

"I'll be able to stay. I have nothing else I have to do."

"Good. Maybe we can kill two birds with one stone and work on these charts while we wait here." When Walt made no reply at all, Richardson continued, "There's no reason for both of us to be here at once. You've been here for the last couple of hours. Why don't you take a break for dinner? I'll be here until you get back."

Whoosh . . . . . . whoosh

Whoosh . . . . . . whoosh

Walt again said nothing but started to leave the room. Richardson's voice stopped him. "Walt, we've got to get that work done. Do me a favor. Bring some of the records in here and we'll work on them while we're keeping an eye on Sanders."

Walt just nodded and left. Richardson didn't understand Walt's attitude. There was a time when he had been so hard-driving, even enthusiastic to get work done. To get the research done. To become a doctor. To start a career. To become a perfect doctor. As if there could ever be a perfect doctor. These last few days he had been so different. Maybe it was just the strain they had all been under. Watching someone else die, someone you knew, was never easy. Especially when you were still a student.

With Walt gone there were just the four of them. The nurse, Sanders, Richardson, and the respirator. Four was a crowd. It didn't take much coaxing to convince the nurse to go downstairs for dinner. Even the cafeteria had a better atmosphere than this single half-lighted room.

That left three. Richardson and Sanders and the respirator.

Whoosh . . . . . . whoosh

Whoosh . . . . . whoosh

At times Richardson was tempted to shut that damned machine up.

Did the noise bother Sanders? Or the silence between the noises? With each whoosh Sanders's chest moved up and then down as the air went in and out. In with the good air. Out with the bad air. Up and down. But no other movements. His eyes were closed. Nothing else in the room seemed to move, not even Richardson, who sat quietly. Richardson's eyes moved away from Sanders and began to look around the room. He didn't have to look very hard.

Herb had left bottles of Tensilon all over the room. Richardson got up and picked up a bottle—an unopened bottle. He removed the top, found a syringe, and drew up the Tensilon. Then he walked over to the bed.

"Bill?"

Whoosh . . . . . . whoosh

Whoosh . . . . . whoosh

"Bill, I have to do it once more. There is one more question. Just one more question. It's more important than the others. I know this is no fun for you, but I have to do it. Stick with it." He felt more like Ellery Queen now. Asking for a "dying clue." That was a bad choice of analogies. Maybe it was just an "almost dying clue."

"You're going to have to think back two weeks, before I first saw you in the hospital. To when you were being treated for pneumonia. The poisoning had to start then. I have to know who saw you then. Who from Neurology? Think about that time. You were in the hospital for pneumonia. You were on the infectious disease service. You weren't having any trouble swallowing or speaking, just pneumonia. You probably had lots of visitors, but whoever did this had to see you then and again this week. It had to be someone from Neurology." Someone from my team. My crew. One of my kids with my bungarotoxin. "Bill, let's get started."

Richardson injected the Tensilon. "Here we go."

He waited by himself this time. His eyes moved back and forth from his watch to Sanders's eyes. Back and forth.

Whoosh . . . . . . whoosh

Whoosh . . . . . . whoosh

One minute. One slow agonizing minute. The second hand continued to move. The eyelids didn't.

Whoosh . . . . . . whoosh

Whoosh . . . . . . whoosh

It was almost two minutes. The eyelids began to twitch and flicker and then Sanders opened his eyes. There was no time for the preliminaries. Sanders knew the game. He knew the rules. Maybe he knew the murderer, the would-be murderer. Richardson went down the list.

"Herb?"

Sanders moved his eyes down. Why had he even asked? And wasted precious seconds.

"Stokes?"

Another no. Another suspect eliminated.

"Donna Batten?"

Down. Three members of his team. Members of the first string. Three down. Three noes.

"Al Schilder?"

Up. Goddamn! Up. Why? Why had Al seen him? There was much less enthusiasm in his voice as he continued. "Sue Evans?"

Up. She'd been on Infectious Disease before she started on Neurology. She probably had a reason to see him. A legitimate one?

"John Adson?"

Down. That will make Renee happy.

"Linda Sharp?"

Down. At least the field was not expanding.

"Walt Simpson?"

Up. Very weakly, but definitely up.

That was it. The effect of the Tensilon had worn off. "That's all, Bill. We've narrowed it down. We've got three candidates. Three suspects." He felt Sanders's stomach. There were still some moderately severe cramps, but they were done. The field was down to three: Al Schilder, Sue Evans, and Walt Simpson.

Sue Evans was easy to account for. But did that make any difference? Sure, she had a legitimate reason to see Sanders. But she also had a motive. Was that enough reason to kill somebody? Women get dumped all the time without resorting to this. It didn't seem like much of a motive. Neither did Weigert's motive, if you thought about it. So, Sue had been there at the right time with a motive. MS or no MS, it was a motive. Two others: Walt and Al. Then he remembered that both Sue Evans and Walt Simpson were on Infectious Disease taking care of Sanders before they started on Neurology. That gave Walt a legitimate reason to be there. Right place, right time. And a motive. Walt may have had a motive. That lost summer. Walt was too damn smart to have flunked anything. What kind of trouble had he had with Sanders? The same as Herb? Why did Al Schilder visit Sanders then? Not to wish him well and pass the time of day. Right place. Right time. And Richardson had to admit Al also had a motive. But it couldn't be Al. Al Schilder knew who Luke Appling was and Ted Lyons. . . . So had Al Capone.

Richardson sat back and looked at the closed eyes. He tried not to think.

Whoosh . . . . . . whoosh

Whoosh . . . . . . whoosh

At least everybody else was in the clear. Al hadn't seen him on Monday. That's what Sanders had said, no, signaled, earlier. Down. Al hadn't seen him on Monday. Was Sanders sure? In the hospital the days had no individual identity. Paul Richardson wasn't sure he could remember Monday. Which patients had he seen on Monday? Michaels? Yes, Michaels. Had that only been Monday? Maybe Al had seen Sanders on Monday. Maybe that down was an up. This was getting him nowhere.

Whoosh . . . . . . whoosh

Whoosh . . . . . . whoosh

The rest of the crew was in the clear. Herb, Stokes, Donna, Renee. Richardson jumped up. God bless it, he'd forgotten to ask about Renee. He'd been so upset about Al. Damn it.

"Bill, I forgot one person. I'm sorry. But we have to give it one more try."

More Tensilon. Richardson found the same bottle and the same syringe and started again.

Another injection.

Another wait. He looked back and forth from his watch to Sanders's eyes.

Then, after a minute and a half, a flicker. First one lid and then the other. The eyes opened. Up and down, up and down, in rapid succession.

"Oh hell," Richardson's half shout reverberated off the window. He'd forgotten to check the cramps. He'd given the Tensilon too goddamned soon. "Sorry, Bill." He felt Sanders's abdomen. The cramps were severe. Richardson was sure they were painful. Another quiet pain. Which was worse, Mrs. Rader's empty scream or Sanders's silent whoosh?

For the next half hour Richardson waited and counted the respirations. He tried hard not to think of Sue Evans, of Al Schilder, or of Walt Simpson—but especially not of Al and Sue. At 6:00 the nurse came back. Richardson greeted her as if she had just slugged a grand slam home run in the bottom of the ninth against the New York Yankees. He left her in charge. Dr. Simpson would be in by 7:00. She should stay in the room and help him watch things and Richardson would be back by 9:00 or 10:00 or so. Then he fled.

It felt good to be back in the office alone. He put on some coffee and the FM. Offenbach would not be so bad. WFMT was broadcasting a play. Chekhov. Not at a time like this. His life already had more clouds of gray than an entire anthology of Russian plays. He would have preferred Kaufman and Hart. Even Neil Simon, but not Chekhov. He switched the dial. The Schumann Spring Symphony. *The Pathetique* would be more appropriate. As soon as he sat back it started again.

Al. Why Al? Why did Al visit Sanders? To beg? To plead? To kill? Could a Sox fan kill somebody other than a Yankee or an umpire?

Sue? She certainly had a motive.

Walt? He had opportunity and motive, but he was so dedicated to saving lives. However, all of them were. Walt alone with Sanders? There was nothing to worry about with the nurse in the room.

The Spring Symphony seemed to drag on. It must be a German conductor. Spring. Had the Sox gotten their game in? Probably. He couldn't remember an opening game that he hadn't listened to at least part of. He got up and looked out the window. Much of the snow was gone. They had probably played. If his day was any barometer, they'd undoubtedly lost. He wandered around the office and finally poured himself some coffee. He called Bobbie. He told her he probably wouldn't be home tonight, and she didn't ask why.

He forgot to ask her about the White Sox. He sat and looked at the phone for a while. Why not just call Al? He was the resident on call. Page him and talk to him. It seemed so simple.

His coffee was getting cool when he called the page operator and asked her to page the Neurology resident on call. Was it an emergency page? she asked. No, not an emergency page. Just a routine one. In three minutes the phone rang.

"Dr. Stokes."

"Adam, this is Richardson. I thought Al was on call."

"He was."

"What happened?"

"We switched."

"I can tell you switched. Why?"

There was a pause.

"Why?"

"You better ask Al."

"I'm asking you."

"Al's working in an ER."

"Not again."

"Do you need him?"

"Yes. Do you know which ER?"

"No. But I can call his wife and find out."

"Do that and call me back." Richardson hung up and walked out of his office. He walked through the outer office and looked into Herb's office. It seemed to him that all of the charts were still there. Maybe Richardson would bring some over to Walt, but he really didn't want to read any himself. Not now. The phone rang. Richardson picked it up and got the number from Stokes. He hung the phone up and looked at it and back at the piles and piles of charts.

He went back to the outer office and got some more coffee. At least there were some cookies left. He'd talk to Al later. In the morning. Not tonight.

He looked at the bulletin board. It was almost as cluttered as the bulletin board in his own office. Notices, announcements, edicts. Some useful, most not. There was a list of patients of the neurology service dated January 17. At least it was 1980. Only two and a half months out of date. He took it down and scanned the board to see what else he could weed out.

March 21, 1980

The Neurological Society of Chicago

Monthly Meeting
Tuesday, April 15

SCIENTIFIC PROGRAM

1. A familial nervous disease with cirrhosis of the liver: S. A. K. Wilson

2. On dystonia: H. Oppenheim

3. Twenty years experience with L-dopa: A. Barbeau

4. Brief report: On the fanning of the toes: J. Babinski

Cocktails, 6–7
Dinner, 7–8
Program, 8:00

That sounded like a pretty good meeting. Better than most. He'd take the residents. They'd all go out to dinner someplace else where they could relax together and they would get to the meeting in time for the scientific program. He'd treat all the residents and even the students—all of them that weren't in jail by then.

Then his eye caught a memo Chris had put up specifically for him—one that he had seen before:

March 26, 1980

MEDICAL STUDENTS
HOUSE STAFF
ATTENDING STAFF

The approach of the spring season and the increasing disregard for the accepted standards of dress make it necessary for me to once again remind you that the hospital is not a country club. Attire that may be entirely appropriate in such leisure settings is not acceptable in the hospital. A shirt and tie are considered standard attire for male house staff. At Austin Flint the patient comes first, and proper dress indicates a respect for the patient.

Dean Thomas Willis
cc: Office of Student Affairs
TW/mk

Bobbie probably asked her to put it up. Did Linda have his tie? Maybe he'd go back to wearing ties. Why not? He'd start when he was forty-five.

NEUROLOGY STUDENT SERVICE:

1. John W. Adson	4th year	
2. Susan Deborah Evans	3rd year	
3. Linda Rebecca Sharp	4th year	
4. Walter Elliott Simpson	4th year	

Four future doctors, and maybe one was a murderer. Not John, he was out. Not Linda, she was out. Whoever the killer was, it wasn't Linda Rebecca Sharp. Rebecca Sharp. Becky Sharp. That name seemed to ring a bell, but he couldn't quite place it. Sue. Susan Deborah Evans. She wasn't out. But was she in? Could she really be a murderer, a murderess? Richardson didn't want to believe that. But if it wasn't Sue, who was it? Al? No. Walt? Not Walt; he was so dedicated to saving lives. Saving lives and stamping out diseases. No, not Walt. It wasn't Walter Elliott Simpson. WALTER ELLIOTT SIMPSON! ELLIOTT!

The kid's name hadn't been Willie. It had been Wally! Wally Elliott. Now Walter Elliott Simpson. Walter Simpson, née Elliott. His mother must have remarried.

How could he have missed it? It was right there all the time. Staring him in the face. Where was that chart? With the rest in Herb's office.

He went back to Herb's office. The charts were as he had left them. He found the 1962 pile.

R. Barrett	467-365
V. Bickford	688-327
C. Conaster	277-384
A. Dark	322-433
R. Elliott	283-474

That was the one he wanted. R. Elliott. He skimmed the summary and then he found what he was looking for. The initial admission workup by the intern, Dr. William Sanders.

This was truly looking for a dying clue. A dying clue written eighteen years earlier at 2:00 in the morning by a dead-tired, overworked intern. Thank God that Sanders had also been a compulsive intern. Richardson found Sanders's workup. The same formula: Name, age, race, sex, chief complaint, history of present illness, past history, family. There it was. Children—two:

son, age 8—Wally
daughter, age 5—Joan

Wally Elliott. His father died. His mother must have re-married later and then eight-year-old Wally Elliott became twenty-six-year-old Walter Elliott Simpson. When had Walt started to review the charts? Four, no six weeks earlier. He must have read this and blamed Sanders for his father's death. But Sanders hadn't killed his father, and the penicillin hadn't killed Walt's father. But they didn't know that when he'd died, and you couldn't tell that from reading the chart. Two months later, when the pathologists had finished all their studies and their special stains on the brain tissues, they knew the answer. Mr. Robert Elliott had died of meningitis. Not of the cure. He hadn't lived long enough to die of the cure. The autopsy report, as always, had never gotten into the hospital chart. It was neatly filed away somewhere in Pathology. All this because of a penicillin reaction that hadn't happened. Penicillin. The first miracle drug. A Nobel prize for Fleming. And Chain and Florey. But it didn't always work. Sometimes it failed and patients died.

Harry Lime, the Third Man, had killed people with penicillin. He had diluted the penicillin with dust and people bought it from him. Doctors bought it on the Vienna black market for treating meningitis, but the children either died or ended up in mental wards as vegetables. Harry Lime deserved to die in a Vienna sewer. But not Bill Sanders.

Walter Simpson. He became a doctor to be like the doctors who had tried to save his dad, or better. But now he thought those doctors had killed his dad.

Richardson walked back from his office to Sanders's room. There was no victory in the diagnosis. No win. It was like traveling to Elsinore and getting there during Act 5 to tell Hamlet that Claudius was innocent. King Claudius hadn't killed your father. The ghost had lied. If you'd only seen the final pathology report. As soon as he entered the room, he asked the nurse to leave.

He sat quietly with Walt and listened to the respirator.

Whoosh . . . . . . whoosh

Whoosh . . . . . . whoosh

"Walt."

"Yes, sir?"

"How's Joan?"

"She's fine." He paused. "I didn't know that you knew my sister. I've never mentioned her."

Whoosh . . . . . . whoosh

"I don't know her. I didn't even remember she existed until ten minutes ago, when I read her name in your father's chart."

For a few minutes they both sat in silence and listened.

Whoosh . . . . . . whoosh

Whoosh . . . . . . whoosh

Whoosh . . . . . . whoosh

The respirator sounded like the grim refrain of some old folk ballad. Repetitive and yet so necessary.

Whoosh . . . . . . whoosh

Again it was Dr. Richardson who interrupted the pattern.

"Your father died of his infection."

Walter said nothing.

"I looked at the slides myself once when I was studying Pathology years later. The penicillin didn't kill him. And even if it had been the penicillin, it wouldn't have been Sanders's fault."

"He killed my dad."

"No, he didn't. We thought it was the penicillin at the time, and that's what we wrote in the chart, but it wasn't the penicillin. It was hospital-acquired meningitis. He died of meningitis."

"Don't lie to me. I read that chart. I must have read it a hundred times. At first I couldn't believe it. They killed my dad. The doctors killed him." He stopped and fought back his emotions.

"They didn't kill him."

"I don't believe you. They gave him the penicillin, and two days later he was dead. It had to be the penicillin. And my mother thought you doctors were so wonderful. If only I could be a doctor . . ."

"Look, Walt. That type of reaction takes at least five days—"

"They should have known better," Walt interrupted Richardson. "I'm a student, and I know enough not to do that."

"You know that now; you wouldn't have known it eighteen years ago. Most doctors didn't know it then."

"How can doctors kill patients?"

"You're almost a doctor, aren't you?"

Whoosh . . . . . . whoosh

Whoosh . . . . . . whoosh

"Walt!"

"Yes, sir."

"You're supposed to graduate in eight weeks?"

"Yes."

"And you tried to kill someone?"

Walt didn't answer.

"And you did it intentionally. Not inadvertently. Not because you wanted so desperately to save a life."

Walt said nothing.

Whoosh . . . . . . whoosh

"I'm going to have to tell the police, Walt."

"I know that."

"I hope we can save Sanders. It'll make it easier for you. Attempted murder is a much less serious charge. You might as well go home now. There's no reason for you to stay here any longer."

There was no need for Richardson to stay either. No one was going to try to kill Sanders. No one would pull the plug. Trying to save his life would be much less dramatic. It would take months before he would really begin to regain his strength. Richardson checked the Mestinon orders and went back to his office.

He made two calls from his office. First he called Ward. He told him the whole story from beginning to end. Ward said he'd take care of it from there. That's what he got paid for.

Then Richardson called Bobbie and told her that he'd be home in an hour. She told him the bad news. The season had finally opened and the Sox had lost. One down, 161 to go. Opening day had come and gone. Opening day and the voice of the turtle had been heard across the land.

He had driven over halfway to Highland Park when he finally remembered. Mark Koenig. How could it have taken him two weeks to remember? Mark Koenig. Shortstop. New York Yankees, 1925–1930. Mark Koenig had played shortstop for the '27 Yanks. Maybe he wasn't getting senile after all.

CHAPTER 22

It was Saturday morning again. The snow, which only five days earlier had assumed an air of permanence, had proven to be as ephemeral as the White Sox's pennant hopes. Only occasional collections of soot-stained slush served to remind anyone who noticed them of the pristine white blanket which had silently coated the city. For the second straight week Paul Richardson didn't make rounds. Only one week ago he had been in New York to present the paper. Carl Weigert's last paper. Richardson would have to make some sort of public retraction. That Saturday Herb Westphal had made rounds for him. This Saturday his associate, Bud Chiari, made rounds. Herb Westphal was there, as well as Donna Batten, Al Schilder, Sue Evans, John Adson, and Linda Sharp. But not Walt Simpson. Not Walter Elliott Simpson. No one seemed to pay much attention to his absence. Students at times missed weekend rounds. Maybe Walt was tired. After all, he had put in a great deal of time taking care of Dr. Sanders. Or maybe he just wasn't feeling well.

The entire crew went with Dr. Chiari to see all the patients. Nothing much had changed since Friday. Mrs. Rader was resting quietly, her blood pressure under control. Her headache was much better and there was no evidence of any further bleeding. They would do the angiogram on Monday if all went well. Mr. Romberg seemed a bit better. He would be discharged on Sunday, but it was too early to tell if he would really improve. A longer follow-up was necessary. Maybe in six months they would know. Mr. Hortega, the patient with seizures in 301, had responded quite well to the medications and was in good condition.

Paul Richardson spent his day at home. He had wanted to relax and watch the Sox game, but instead he spent most of the day on the telephone telling his story to Ward and Willis and an assistant district attorney named Anthony Fanconi.

The phone calls went on and on all day long. Richardson felt as if he were a ball being bounced back and forth in an unending rundown on the base paths of some unfamiliar field where the rules were different. From Ward to Fanconi. From Fanconi to Willis. From Willis to Ward and back to Fanconi. Mostly to Fanconi. Over and over again.

Was Richardson sure it was bungarotoxin? Yes. How did he spell that? B-U-N-G-A-R-O-T-O-X-I-N. Was he absolutely sure? No, not of the spelling. Was he sure that Dr. Sanders was being poisoned with whatever it was? The poison was bungarotoxin, and, yes, he was sure that Sanders was being poisoned with it. Could Richardson prove it was bungarotoxin? No. Was he sure? Yes! Absolutely sure? Would he swear to it? Yes. How could he be so definite? Medically he knew that it couldn't be anything else. When you have eliminated all the other possible diagnoses, whatever remains, however improbable, must be true.

In between harassments Richardson called Dan Walker and told him about Weigert's folly, about the fabricated research results. Could he publish some sort of explanation in the transactions of the meeting that Dan was editing? Dan felt he could and should, although it wouldn't help Paul's scientific reputation, since he'd participated in the papers. But it had to be done.

More phone calls:

Willis
Ward
Fanconi
Voss
Ward
Fanconi
Ward
Willis

Fanconi

The questions went on and on. Where did it come from? The venom of the deadliest snake of all India. Was he absolutely sure? That it came from a snake? No. That Sanders was being poisoned with it? Yes. Was he sure that Walter Simpson did it? Yes. Could he prove it? No. Had Simpson admitted that he had done it? Not really. Could he prove Sanders had gotten bungarotoxin? Absolutely prove it? No. Would Sanders die? No. Or maybe. Who knew? Richardson certainly didn't. At first Richardson didn't understand that it was harder to prosecute someone for attempted murder than for murder, and to prosecute someone for attempted murder with a poison that couldn't be proven to be in the victim was even more difficult. Was he sure he couldn't prove it? Wasn't there any test for bungarotoxin poisoning? Hell, as far as he knew no one else had ever been poisoned with it, except by being bitten by a snake. You had to give Walt credit for originality.

By the time he finally got off the phone, the ball game was over. He managed to get the score on the postgame show. The Sox had lost again. You can't win 'em all.

A SIX-MONTH FOLLOW-UP

IT was a clear day in early October. There was an east wind off the lake. Cold and bitter. Paul and Bobbie had just returned from the Fifth International Symposium on Parkinson's Disease in Vienna. Vienna, the city of Beethoven and Mozart. And Schubert. And Mahler. Almost the city of Mahler. But Vienna never really accepted Mahler, nor Schoenberg, nor Berg, nor Freud. Sigmund Freud, who had started as a neurologist and died as an expatriate. The Vienna of Julius Wagner von Jauregg, of Harry Lime. Paul had once worked in Vienna briefly and every person he met told him how he had personally saved three Jews during the war. After all, the Viennese weren't Germans. If that were true, the Viennese Jewish community must have survived intact. But there were no Jews in Vienna. Paul felt uncomfortable in Vienna and had not really wanted to come back, but he had to. The meeting was important and he had to put his reputation back in order.

The paper, based on some new work Renee had completed before she departed, was well received. After Vienna they had gone to Amsterdam. The city of Rembrandt and a fourteen-year-old Jewish girl. On Sunday morning in Amsterdam Paul had walked up Prinsengracht by himself to pay his homage to Anne Frank. She was more meaningful than the six million, for she was not just a number. Had she lived, she would only be a few years older than Paul. She died of typhus when she was not much older than his daughter. Typhus! Nobody died

of typhus. Nazi typhus. A virulent strain, previously unre-
corded.

Her diary was published so the world wouldn't forgive and
forget. Wouldn't it be better sometimes to forget? At least a
few things. Simpson. Sanders. Why hadn't he made the
diagnosis sooner and saved Sanders's life? Did his own feelings toward Sanders . . . ? He'd never know. If he had read
that memo, could he have saved Weigert's life? Maybe it was
better in the long run not to have read it and just let things run
their own course instead. Like all physicians, his life was
geared toward interrupting the natural flow by saying "no"
and trying to change the course of events. Perhaps it was
better sometimes not to say no.

As always, Bobbie had made the coffee and was having
her first cup while Paul was still upstairs. She sat down and
read the paper, putting aside the sports section for Paul.

Herb Westphal was in Italy. He had finished his residency
and was now a member of the staff. He'd never gotten the
fellowship, but somehow Paul Richardson had found the
necessary money to support him. He had gone to Italy to
present a paper for Richardson in Rome. Rome, the city of
Bernini and Mussolini. Its contribution to modern medicine
paralleled that of Dayton, Ohio, but the architecture was
better. The presentation was well received, though Herb wasn't
sure how many people really understood his English. The
exposure would help start Herb on his way as a recognized
scientist. After the meeting he stayed on for an extended
vacation, since Joanne Edinger had been able to go with him.
Paul thought that they made a good couple.

Adam Stokes was now chief resident and was busy keeping
the service organized.

Al Schilder and Donna Batten were now second year residents and thriving.

A new head of Pathology had been appointed to replace
Dr. Collier. There had been two candidates. Richardson had
been on the search committee and his choice, Osmond Sacher,
got the job.

Mr. Cohn was fine. Whatever had been pressing his spinal
cord had never come back.

Mrs. Robin was dead. Even after she was off all the

medicine, the virus kept spreading. By July she was completely paralyzed and having difficulty breathing. Late in July she contracted pneumonia and died.

Mr. Romberg had continued to improve. He went to his daughter's graduation in June, and by August he was back at work half-time.

Much to the relief of Dr. Richardson, Mrs. Irene Hammond had moved to Washington to be near her son. He was in the State Department, or, if Mrs. Hammond was to be believed, he *was* the State Department.

Mr. Dax's speech improved—both his English and his French. His speech didn't get back to normal but he was able to speak to the point where he could lead a fairly normal life.

Mrs. Rader survived her ruptured blood vessel and the subsequent surgery. Mr. Schwann was not so lucky with his brain tumor. He survived his surgery by only three months.

Mr. Michaels completed his course of penicillin and was able to remember that Satchel Paige once pitched for the Kansas City Monarchs but not much more. Limited progress at best.

Mrs. Turner left the psychiatric ward on May 2 and on May 3 she visited a lawyer. By July 7 Paul Richardson knew that he was being sued for depriving her of her right to commit suicide.

Mr. Golgi was still alive, but barely. He was now bedridden and hardly able to speak or swallow.

Dr. William B. Sanders died on April 18, Patriot's Day, of pneumonia.

Linda Sharp was now a senior student and still undecided about where to intern. John Adson was interning in Los Angeles. He and Renee were married in August. Sue Evans was interning at the medical center and would start her residency in Neurology there on July 1, 1981. There was still no evidence that she had MS.

Walter Elliott Simpson was now Dr. Walter Elliott Simpson and an intern in Boston. When Sanders died, no test existed to prove that he had been poisoned by alpha-bungarotoxin. The work of Ringel and others, in which they measured alpha-bungarotoxin in experimental animals, just wasn't specific enough. It measured both alpha-bungarotoxin and whatever substance is produced in the body of patients with myasthenia. All that the experts could tell by examining Sanders's blood was that he had either been poisoned with bungarotoxin or that he had the highest levels of the myasthenia-producing antibody yet recorded. So there was a chance, a possibility—according to the experts—that Bill Sanders had had myasthenia. A slim possibility but a possibility. In the end the experts could not prove beyond the shadow of a doubt that he had been given bungarotoxin. Without that proof there was no crime and no criminal. To Richardson it was a medical certainty. The diagnosis was correct and it was there on the death certificate.

Cause of death: Alpha-bungarotoxin poisoning.

A medical fact, but not a fact of law. It would not stand up in court. The district attorney wouldn't touch the case. Richardson couldn't even get Willis to flunk Simpson out of medical school. Dr. Walter E. Simpson.

Walter Elliott Simpson.

What was it that Holmes had said? Something about doctors being the first among criminals when they go wrong. As always, Holmes was right. That was in "The Adventure of the Speckled Band." Dr. Roylott. In the end justice had triumphed in that tale. It was only in detective stories that the thankless serpent turned its sharp teeth onto its own master. The Austin Flint Medical Center had no swamp adders that could stick their fangs into Walt Simpson. So instead they did the next best thing and gave him his diploma and sent him on his way to Boston for his internship.

The Chicago White Sox, despite their brilliant young pitching staff, had had another bad season. Wait 'til next year. Better yet, wait until '59.

Paul Richardson lingered in bed, listening to WFMT. They were playing the recording of Bloch's Concerto Grosso for String Orchestra with Piano Obbligato (no. 1) with Rafael Kubelik conducting the Chicago Symphony Orchestra and George Schich playing the obbligato piano. It was the reissue electronically reprocessed for stereo. Not quite the original monaural version paired with either Bartok's Music for Stringed

Instruments, Percussion, and Celesta or Hindemith's Symphonic Metamorphoses on Themes of Carl Maria von Weber.

But acceptable.

It was Bloch who had broadened his musical horizon beyond Richard Strauss and Tchaikovsky. He owed him a personal debt. Bloch and so many others he had never met had helped to shape him: T. S. Eliot and Ring Lardner. Lorenz Hart and Joseph Conrad. Anne Frank and Holden Caulfield. Kazantzakis and Hemingway. Basil Rathbone and Jacob Nelson Fox. Especially Rathbone and Fox. One introduced him to Sherlock Holmes. The other set the tone of his life. He, more than anyone else, represented the Chicago White Sox of the '50s, the boys of his summer. His hands weren't good enough for him to be a great fielder, he was too slow to be a great runner, and he was too small to be a great hitter. Despite all this, for more than a decade, he was an All Star who led the Sox. And for one season he was the best ball player in the American League, and they had won the pennant.

Jacob Nelson Fox laying a bunt down the third base line. A thing of beauty. Was it worth less than George Schich's piano obbligato or T. S. Elliot's first poem, a lyric by Lorenz Hart, or Vanzetti's last letter?

When Paul Richardson came downstairs, the sports section was waiting for him.

The headline read:

VEECK SELLS WHITE SOX

Bill Veeck was once again gone from the Big Leagues. Probably forever. Now who would look back for Satchel Paige?

No one.

About the Author

Harold L. Klawans, M.D., is a senior attending physician and professor of Neurology and Pharmacology at Rush Medical College in Chicago. He also holds the distinction of being the only American editor of the *Handbook of Clinical Neurology*, a seventy-volume neurology encyclopedia. Dr. Klawans is the author of over 300 scientific articles and an author/editor of over 30 scientific books. His novel *Informal Consent*, also featuring Dr. Paul Richardson, is available in a Signet edition.